I0635482

Attempted Compromises

A Pride & Prejudice
Variation

TIFFANY THOMAS

COPYRIGHT INFORMATION

This is a work of fiction. Names, characters, organizations, places, events, and incidents are either the products of the author's imagination or are used fictitiously. Any resemblance to actual persons, living or dead, or actual events is purely coincidental.

Copyright © 2024 by Saving Talents. All rights reserved. Except as permitted under the U.S. Copyright Act of 1976, no part of this book may be reproduced, distributed, or transmitted in any form or by any means including, but not limited to electronic, mechanical, photocopying, recording, or otherwise, or stored in a database or retrieval system, without the express written permission of the author.

ISBN: 978-1-956548-18-1

For my dear, loving Grandma Lindsey,
whose strength of spirit and stalwart faith
have made me into who I am today.
Without your wisdom and example
to guide me in the Hargrave line, I would be lost.
Thank you for being one of the most incredible women
I have ever known.

Table of Contents

Prologue

Longbourn, 1797

The nursery was filled with the sounds of laughter and mischief as little Elizabeth Bennet darted around the room, her hair flying in every direction. Her nurse, Mrs. McGinty, sighed in exasperation, clutching a tiny toothbrush and attempting, yet again, to call the lively six-year-old to order.

"Miss Elizabeth! You must come here at once!" Mrs. McGinty ordered, trying to hide her exhaustion behind a stern tone. Elizabeth only giggled, racing around the table as Mrs. McGinty tried in vain to catch her.

"No, I don't want it! It tastes awful!" Elizabeth cried, her small face twisted in defiance. She held her hands over her mouth, shaking her head wildly as she continued to evade the nurse's grasp.

Mrs. McGinty tried to reason with her, switching to a gentler tone. "But teeth must be cleaned every night, my dear. Otherwise, they'll get all sorts of nasties inside them, and then you'll have a dreadful ache."

"No, they won't!" Elizabeth replied, her voice muffled from behind her hands. "My teeth are strong as anything, and they don't need to be cleaned!"

Mrs. McGinty closed her eyes and sighed, finally sitting down in defeat as Elizabeth darted into the corner with triumphant glee. "You are the most stubborn child I've ever known, Miss Elizabeth Bennet," she muttered under her breath.

Two nights later, the house was quiet under a blanket of midnight darkness. All was still, save for the muffled sounds of sobbing coming from the little bed in the nursery.

Elizabeth whimpered as she clutched her aching jaw, tears streaming down her face. She buried her head in the pillow, but the pain only grew sharper, piercing her with every throb. Her mother's gentle snores were coming from down the hall, and after what felt like an eternity, Elizabeth gave up on being brave and started wailing as loudly as her little lungs would allow.

Moments later, Mrs. Bennet rushed into the room, her nightcap askew and her face marked with sleep. She lit a candle and leaned over her daughter's bed, frowning in a mixture of irritation and worry.

"Good heavens, child! What on earth is the matter?" she exclaimed, touching Elizabeth's tear-streaked cheek.

"It hurts, Mama," Elizabeth sobbed, pointing to the swollen side of her jaw. "It hurts so, so badly!"

"Oh, dear." Mrs. Bennet sighed, her patience wearing thin. "I knew this would happen if you kept on refusing to let Nurse clean your teeth! Very well, I shall send for the apothecary."

Within the hour, the apothecary, Mr. Jones, arrived, his face lined with both wisdom and weariness. Mr. Bennet— disturbed from his heavy slumber— ushered him into the nursery, where Elizabeth lay curled up next to her mother, still crying and clutching her cheek.

"Ah, Miss Elizabeth," Mr. Jones said kindly, setting his bag on the table. "Let's have a look at this troublesome tooth, shall we?"

Elizabeth, now exhausted and miserable, opened her mouth just enough for Mr. Jones to peer inside. He held the candle close and examined her little teeth with a practiced eye. After a moment, he nodded gravely and stepped back.

"Just as I thought," he announced. "It's a rotten tooth, caused by a lack of proper cleaning." He glanced over at Mrs. McGinty, who stood with her head bowed, wringing her hands.

Mrs. Bennet sighed heavily, crossing her arms. "I warned her of this very thing," she said, glancing at Mrs. McGinty. "How could you let it get to this point?"

Mrs. McGinty looked up, her face flushed. "Begging your pardon, ma'am, but Miss Elizabeth is… well, she's a handful. She runs wild, and no amount of coaxing or reasoning can make her do what she doesn't want to."

Mr. Jones raised a hand, silencing the exchange. "It's lucky this isn't a permanent tooth, so we can pull it without much trouble. However," he said, turning to Elizabeth, "it will hurt quite a bit, as it's deep in the back and not loose at all."

Elizabeth's eyes widened in fear, and she whimpered, clutching her mother's hand. Mrs. Bennet sighed and stroked her daughter's hair.

"Mr. Jones, do you have something to ease her pain?" Mrs. Bennet asked. "Surely there's something to make it more bearable."

Mr. Jones nodded. "Laudanum, madam. It should help her relax enough to fall asleep, and then I can remove the tooth."

He prepared a cup of weak tea and added a drop of laudanum, handing it to Mrs. Bennet. "Now, Miss Elizabeth," he said, turning his attention to the little girl, "I want you to drink half of this. It'll help you feel very sleepy."

Elizabeth obediently took the cup, sipping the bitter mixture with a grimace. "It tastes terrible," she mumbled, her face twisted in displeasure.

"Yes, yes," her mother said, smoothing Elizabeth's hair. "Just drink up, and soon you won't feel the ache at all."

After Elizabeth finished half the cup, they waited, watching as she lay back against her pillows. But as fifteen minutes passed, it was clear that the laudanum had done nothing to lull her into slumber. Instead, Elizabeth continued to squirm in discomfort, her eyes still wide open.

Mr. Jones frowned, glancing at his pocket watch. "That should have been more than enough to ease her into sleep," he murmured, shaking his head. "Well, best not to take chances. Miss Elizabeth, drink the rest of it, and then try to close your eyes."

Obediently, Elizabeth drank the rest of the tea, pulling a face at the bitter taste. Another fifteen minutes passed, yet she was still wide awake, wriggling on the bed and clutching her cheek as she whimpered in pain.

"Strange," Mr. Jones muttered to himself, scratching his chin. "Well, there's nothing for it. We'll try another drop, though that should be more than enough for a child her age."

He began to pour a fresh cup, but Elizabeth started crying. "No more tea! My belly hurts!"

4

"Just a few more swallows, my dear," Mr. Jones said, putting just a dash of tea into the cup and tipping a drop of laudanum in. "It'll taste quite nasty this time, but there's not much of it. There's a good girl."

Sniffling, Elizabeth obeyed, tipping the small bit of tea back into her mouth. Her face screwed up, and she looked as if she were going to spit it out, but then she swiftly gulped it down. She lay back with her face twisted in pain and exhaustion.

After a few more minutes, the effects of the laudanum began to take hold. Elizabeth's eyelids drooped, but she didn't quite fall asleep. Instead, she started giggling softly, her words slurring as she looked around the room in a dreamy, dazed state.

"Mama... I think I'm flying," she murmured, her small hands reaching out to grab at imaginary shapes in the air.

Mrs. Bennet sighed in relief, brushing a stray hair away from her daughter's face. "Well, at least she's calm," she said, casting an anxious glance at Mr. Jones.

"Indeed," Mr. Jones replied with a nod. "Let's proceed before she becomes fully aware again."

With her hands still reaching and her head swaying, Elizabeth barely noticed as Mr. Jones and Mr. Bennet prepared her for the extraction. Mr. Bennet gently held her shoulders, while Hill, the footman, positioned himself at her side to keep her head steady. Mr. Jones took his pliers in hand and gave a solemn nod to both men.

As the cold metal touched her aching tooth, Elizabeth's eyes shot open, and she let out a piercing scream, thrashing against the hands that held her in place. Her arms flailed wildly, her little fists pounding against her father's chest.

"No! It hurts! Stop, please!" she shrieked, her voice hoarse with pain and fear.

"Hold her steady!" Mr. Jones called, gritting his teeth as he worked to secure his grip. Elizabeth's cries filled the room, echoing through the house as the pliers clamped down firmly on the stubborn tooth.

With a final, wrenching tug, the tooth came free, and Elizabeth let out a whimpering sob, her small body sagging as the pain receded. Mr. Jones quickly stuffed a piece of cotton into the bleeding gap, applying gentle pressure to stem the flow.

"There now, my dear," he murmured softly. "It's all over. The bad tooth is gone."

Elizabeth lay back, exhausted and trembling, her chest rising and falling in shaky breaths. Her cheeks were wet with tears, and her voice was just above a whisper as she spoke.

"It… it still hurts," she said, her face crumpling as fresh tears welled up.

Mr. Jones patted her hand gently. "Yes, my dear, it will hurt a little while longer, but it's much better now. The worst of the pain will fade soon."

Elizabeth nodded, closing her eyes as she tried to calm her breathing. The laudanum, though ineffective in putting her fully to sleep, seemed to soften the edges of the pain enough that she could bear it. She stayed awake for another hour, her small hand clutching her mother's. She whimpered occasionally, but the pain was duller, no longer the sharp ache that had kept her awake.

Mrs. Bennet and Mr. Jones sat beside her until she drifted into a light sleep, her soft breathing filling the room as the night settled around them. As he packed his things to leave, Mr. Jones glanced back at Elizabeth, a look of concern flickering in his eyes.

"A curious child," he murmured to himself as he left. "Very curious indeed."

Longbourn, 1802

A bright, sunny afternoon found the children of Meryton gathered near the great old oak on the edge of the Lucas property. Elizabeth Bennet, now eleven, was in the center of a lively group, her brown curls bouncing as she laughed and chatted. Nearby, Jane stood with Charlotte Lucas and some of the other girls, watching with a mixture of interest and concern as the boys dared one another to climb the enormous tree.

One of the Lucas boys, Thomas, puffed out his chest and pointed up. "I dare you, Ned Goulding, to climb all the way to the top!"

The Goulding boy glanced up at the lofty branches and shook his head, laughing nervously. "No one could climb that high—it's impossible!"

Elizabeth's ears perked up at his remark, and she stepped forward, hands on her hips. "I could climb it!" she declared, her voice brimming with confidence.

"Oh, Lizzy, don't," Jane pleaded, a worried look in her soft blue eyes. "It's dangerous."

Elizabeth scoffed, her chin held high. "It's not dangerous. You'll see!" And with that, she grabbed the lowest branch, determined to prove her bravery.

Jane, standing beside her with a concerned expression, reached out to tug on Elizabeth's sleeve. "Lizzy, don't—please. You don't have to prove anything to anyone."

Elizabeth only grinned, flashing a mischievous look at her companions. "Oh, come now! What's life without a little adventure?" She gave Jane and Charlotte a cheeky wink before adjusting her grip and pulling herself up with ease. The girls on the ground exchanged anxious glances, but Elizabeth paid them no mind as she climbed higher and higher, her limbs agile and quick.

"Elizabeth!" Charlotte called from below, shielding her eyes as she watched her friend ascend. "Come down at once! You'll hurt yourself!"

But Elizabeth was already climbing higher, nimble as a squirrel. The boys watched with awe as she climbed branch after branch. Her skirt caught once on a twig, but she pushed forward, undeterred. Higher and higher she went, until she reached the very top. A triumphant smile spread across her face.

"I told you I could do it!" she crowed. She held on tight as she looked around, surveying the landscape from her newfound perch. She felt invincible, her heart pounding with exhilaration.

"Come down now, Lizzy!" Jane called up, her voice shaking with worry. The other girls echoed Jane's plea, but Elizabeth just laughed, waving a hand at them.

"All of you are just afraid," she teased, glancing around to take in the view. "I can see all of Meryton from up here!"

"Please, Lizzy!" The fear in Jane's voice was persuasive.

But as Elizabeth began her descent, a sudden flurry of wings exploded from a nearby branch. A startled bird took flight, screeching as it fled the disturbance. Elizabeth gasped, losing her balance in her shock, and her hands slipped from the branch. She fell with a sharp scream, tumbling through the branches until she hit the ground with a sickening thud.

The world spun, her vision blurred with pain as she lay on her side, clutching her arm, which throbbed with an agony sharper than anything she had ever felt. Tears streamed down her cheeks as she tried to move, only for the pain to grow even more intense.

A piercing scream tore from her lips as she attempted to rise for a third time, and all the frozen children were suddenly moving at once. The boys exchanged panicked looks, and in an instant, they scattered to get help, dashing back to their homes or toward Lucas Lodge, where the adults could be found.

Jane, pale and trembling, knelt beside her sister, gently brushing back Elizabeth's hair. "Oh, Lizzy," she whispered, her voice breaking as she watched her sister writhe in pain, cradling her arm.

Charlotte Lucas knelt beside Elizabeth, her own face pale with worry. "Hold on, Lizzy. Thomas will fetch Papa—he'll help you."

Within minutes, Sir William Lucas arrived, his face etched with worry as he crouched beside Elizabeth. "Good heavens, child," he murmured, assessing her injury with gentle concern. "We must get you home at once."

Carefully, he lifted her into his arms. The movement caused pain to surge through Elizabeth's arm, but she pressed her lips together, trying to be brave. Sir William carried her back to Longbourn, his strides long and urgent.

Mrs. Bennet and Mr. Bennet were alerted, and Mr. Jones was summoned once more. When her parents arrived, Elizabeth lay on a chaise in the parlor, tears streaming down her cheeks as she clutched her injured arm, every small movement sending waves of pain through her body.

Mr. Bennet's mouth tightened as he looked down at Elizabeth, his hands trembling as he stroked her hair. "It'll be alright, Lizzy," he whispered, though his voice betrayed his anxiety. "We'll have Mr. Jones tend to you, and you'll be good as new."

Mr. Jones was announced and entered the parlor, his face lined with concern as he looked down at Elizabeth. "Well, young Miss Bennet, it seems you've found yourself in a bit of trouble again."

Elizabeth managed a weak smile, her face pale as she nodded. "It… it hurts something awful, Mr. Jones."

Mr. Jones' face grew serious as he inspected Elizabeth's injured arm. He probed the area with gentle, yet practiced, care. "A nasty one, indeed. Now, I'll give you some laudanum to ease the pain before I set the bone. Mrs. Bennet, you should leave now."

Mrs. Bennet let out a small shriek and rushed from the room, calling for her smelling salts.   Sir William put his hand on Mr. Benett's shoulder. "I'll stay, my friend."

Nodding, Mr. Bennet motioned for Dr. Jones to continue. The apothecary reached into his bag and brought out the small bottle of laudanum. "This will help ease her pain, at least enough for me to work," he told the adults in the room.

Elizabeth eyed the bottle warily, remembering her toothache from years before. Mr. Jones poured two drops into a small cup of water, stirring it before handing it to her. "Here you are, Miss Elizabeth. Drink up, and let's wait a bit for it to take effect."

Elizabeth drank the bitter medicine, grimacing at the taste. They waited, watching as the minutes ticked by, but although she grew a bit drowsy, the pain remained just as sharp and unrelenting.

"Mr. Jones, it still hurts," she whispered, her voice quivering.

Mr. Jones frowned, scratching his head. He glanced at the parents, then poured two more drops, handing her another spoonful. "This should be plenty," he murmured, watching as she took the second dose.

Sir William, who had stayed out of concern, raised an eyebrow. "Are you certain that's wise, Mr. Jones? Why, when I had three drops last year after my accident, it knocked me out for the better part of two days— and I'm thrice her size!"

Mr. Jones shook his head, glancing at Elizabeth with curiosity. "Yes, ordinarily, I would think so. But Miss Elizabeth… well, she seems rather resilient to the effects of laudanum. This happened the last time she had laudanum for a rotting tooth, but I had assumed she would have outgrown it by now. Quite unusual, I must say."

The room fell silent as they waited. Elizabeth's eyelids drooped, and she appeared woozy, but the pain was still evident in her face. She whimpered, clutching her arm, the broken bone sending sharp stabs of agony through her every time she moved. "Papa… I think the room is spinning!" she whispered with a small laugh, her head lolling to the side.

Mr. Jones took a deep breath, casting a sympathetic glance at Elizabeth's father. "Very well, let's proceed. I'll need to set the bone quickly. Elizabeth, this will hurt, but only for a moment."

Elizabeth, still in her hazy state, only nodded, her gaze unfocused. As Mr. Jones took hold of her arm and began to pull, a fresh wave of pain coursed through her, piercing the haze of laudanum. She let out a strangled cry, twisting and writhing as the agony surged anew.

Mr. Bennet grabbed a wooden brush from the table nearby and pressed it into her mouth. "Bite down, Lizzy," he whispered, his voice thick with emotion. "I know it hurts, but be brave, my darling."

Elizabeth clamped her teeth onto the brush, biting down with all her might as tears streamed down her cheeks. Mr. Bennet held her, his own eyes glistening as he murmured soothing words, though his heart ached with every sob that escaped her.

"Hold her steady," Mr. Jones instructed, and Mr. Bennet's muscles tensed as Mr. Jones took hold of her broken limb.

As Mr. Jones pulled at her wrist, Elizabeth's entire body went rigid. She let out a muffled scream, biting down so hard on the brush that the wood began to splinter. Tears streamed down her face, and her skin was pale and clammy, the agony overwhelming her senses.

Mr. Bennet's own cheeks grew wet as he held his daughter, his heart breaking at her pain. "It's all right, Lizzy," he whispered, his voice choked. "I'm right here. Just hold on a little longer."

Elizabeth's breathing grew rapid, and for a moment, it seemed as if she might be sick from the pain. Mr. Jones worked swiftly to set the bone and with a final, sharp snap, the arm was set in place.

"It's done," Mr. Jones said, wiping the sweat from his brow.

Elizabeth lay back, her body limp with exhaustion, her face pale and damp with sweat. She looked up at Mr. Bennet, her eyes heavy with pain but filled with relief.

"It's done, Papa," she echoed, her voice barely more than a breath.

"Yes, my brave girl," Mr. Bennet murmured, wiping a tear from his own cheek as he stroked her hair. "It's finished, and you were so very strong."

Elizabeth collapsed against her father, her face ashen and her breathing ragged. Mr. Jones dabbed her forehead with a damp cloth, glancing down at her with a look of concern. "Given her unusual tolerance, I'll administer two more drops to help her rest," he said, though his voice held a note of reluctance.

13

He administered the final dose, watching carefully as Elizabeth's breathing slowed and her eyelids began to droop. The agony in her expression softened, and her body finally relaxed, though she didn't fall fully asleep. Instead, she drifted in and out of a light doze, murmuring as the laudanum took hold.

As he packed up his bag, Mr. Jones shook his head, glancing over at Mr. Bennet. "Your daughter is quite remarkable, sir," he said. "I've never seen such a tolerance for laudanum in someone so young. Quite unusual, indeed."

Mr. Bennet managed a faint smile, still holding Elizabeth's hand as she drifted in her half-conscious state. "Yes, she's a remarkable child," he replied, his voice filled with pride and love. "Stubborn as anything and brave to the bone."

Elizabeth murmured something in her sleep, and Mr. Bennet leaned down to press a gentle kiss to her forehead. For tonight, she was safe, and that was all that mattered.

Chapter 1

Rosings, 1808

The darkened skies hung heavy over Rosings Park as Fitzwilliam Darcy dismounted his horse, the usually composed gentleman now disheveled and mud-streaked, his black mourning attire marked with dirt from the furious ride. The express he'd received that morning from Lady Catherine had been brief but alarming.

Come to Rosings at once. Anne has been attacked.

Darcy pushed past the footmen at the entrance, ignoring the shocked faces of the household staff as he swept through the hallways. His boots thudded urgently on the polished floors. The grief he had borne for the past six months since his father's passing, now intermingled with a sickening dread. How could something like this have happened? Lady Catherine had given no detail in her letter—only the desperate command to hurry.

Darcy's heart pounded as he strode into the drawing room without waiting for the footmen to announce him. His aunt, Lady Catherine de Bourgh, paced in front of the fireplace, her face tense, her usual proud countenance dimmed by something that looked startlingly like fear.

"Fitzwilliam," she said, voice laced with a mixture of relief and agitation. "Thank goodness you're here."

Darcy took a steadying breath, his mind racing with questions. "What has happened?" he demanded. "Where is Anne?"

"She is resting," Lady Catherine said, the words brittle. "She was set upon by a... a scoundrel." Her face twisted with anger and disdain, her hands clenched at her sides. "The brute dared to strike her, all because he wanted... But you will see her soon enough."

Darcy's heart clenched, and a grim resolve formed within him. "Who did this?" he asked, his voice low.

Lady Catherine's face darkened. "George Wickham."

For a moment, Darcy thought he'd misheard her. "Wickham?" His mind flashed to his late father's godson, the man who had plagued him for years with his lies and manipulations. "How did he—?"

Lady Catherine cut him off, her tone trembling with a bitterness that Darcy had rarely heard from her. "He accosted Anne on one of her morning drives." She took a deep, shuddering breath. "Apparently, he has been lurking on the edges of Rosings for weeks, watching, waiting for an opportunity. The coward seized upon her when she was alone, in her phaeton." Looking away, her voice became quieter but no less bitter. "He forced himself upon her, Fitzwilliam. And then he had the audacity to come here, demanding her hand."

Darcy's hands clenched into fists, his mind reeling at the sheer brazenness of it. "Demanding—?" He choked out the words, fury and disbelief battling within him. "He thinks he can simply—"

Lady Catherine's face hardened, her expression fierce. "He claimed that now he has 'rights,' that I must allow him to marry her or he would ruin our name, our family's honor."

Darcy closed his eyes, the rage within him swelling as he imagined Wickham's fury and the depths of his desperation. "But... you told him to leave?" he asked, struggling to piece together the sequence of events.

Lady Catherine's lips curved in a grim smile. "I had him dealt with in the way such scoundrels deserve. Two of my footmen dragged him from my sight and beat him thoroughly. I was about to arrange to have him impressed into the Navy, but the worm escaped along the way to the nearest port." Her voice dropped to a venomous whisper. "But he will not return to Rosings. He knows that if he does, he will face the worst of consequences."

"And Anne?"

"I was sure Anne would be safe once he left, but—"

"But what, Aunt Catherine?" Darcy pressed, his voice low and menacing.

The silence that followed was heavy, punctuated only by the crackling of the fire. Lady Catherine finally looked up, her steely composure broke for a moment. "I did not realize, Fitzwilliam... I did not realize the extent of what he had done to her until it was too late. Wickham... compromised her."

The shock of her words hit Darcy like a physical blow, his body tensing as he absorbed the implications. "Compromised?" he repeated, his voice choked with anger and disbelief.

Lady Catherine nodded slowly, her gaze fixed on the floor. "I did not know at first. She is… changed, Fitzwilliam. Withdrawn, and frightened. I thought that would be the end of it, but then her health began to falter. The doctor has confirmed it." She hesitated, then took a deep breath, steeling herself. Darcy could see the desperation in her eyes. "She is with child, Fitzwilliam. And that child will bear the stigma of Wickham's treachery."

The words struck Darcy like a physical blow. His hands clenched into fists, his mind racing. The very thought of Wickham harming Anne, his own cousin, was enough to make him sick with rage.

"With child," he repeated, the words hollow as they left his mouth.

"Yes." Lady Catherine's voice was filled with a blend of desperation and determination. "Do you understand now why I called you here?" she asked, her tone urgent. "You must marry her. You must preserve the family's dignity. If you marry her, no one need ever know the truth."

Darcy felt the weight of her words settle heavily on his shoulders. He had mourned the loss of his father only months prior, and the responsibilities of Pemberley, his family's legacy, were already daunting enough. But to take on a marriage—especially one born out of such horror—was something he had never anticipated.

"I… I don't know," he replied, struggling to process it all. "I came here for Anne's sake, but marriage… marriage was never something I considered."

Lady Catherine's face hardened, and she moved closer to him, her gaze fierce. "Then consider it now," she snapped. "Do you think

I want this, Fitzwilliam? My daughter's name in tatters, her life destroyed?" Her voice dropped, and she added, "If you refuse, she will be alone and ruined. This is the only way."

"What of Anne?" he asked finally, his voice softer, more resolute. "What does she say to this?"

Before Lady Catherine could respond, he heard a muffled sound coming from down the hall—a voice, soft and tremulous, barely audible.

"Anne..." he whispered. Without waiting for Lady Catherine, he strode quickly down the hall and up the stairs to Anne's chamber, pushing open the door.

Anne sat by the window, her thin frame draped in a dark shawl, her face pale and withdrawn. Her eyes were red-rimmed, her cheeks streaked with silent tears. She did not look up as he entered, but her hands twisted anxiously in her lap.

He took a hesitant step toward her, his heart heavy. "Anne?"

She turned at the sound of his voice, her gaze distant, haunted. She seemed barely to register his presence, her eyes filled with a kind of quiet despair.

After he repeated her name once more, she finally looked up, her expression filled with a quiet despair that struck him to the core. He felt a surge of protectiveness rise within him, mingling with a fierce anger at Wickham for having caused her this pain.

"Anne, I... I am so sorry. I came as soon as I heard."

Anne shook her head, letting out a hollow laugh. "What good does it do?" she murmured, her voice a mere whisper. "My mother sees only the scandal, not the pain." Her voice trembled, and she looked away, her shoulders sagging under the weight of her misery.

A sharp voice interrupted them as Lady Catherine stepped into the room, her face stern. "This is not the time for self-pity, Anne," she said coldly. "You should have fought harder."

Anne dissolved into gut-wrenching sobs. "He had... a knife..." she gasped out.

"Then you should have died. Better dead than stained with sin and dishonor."

Darcy's jaw clenched as he watched his aunt's harsh words pierce Anne, worse than any blade could. Without a second thought, he stepped between them, his gaze hard as he faced Lady Catherine.

"That's enough, Aunt Catherine," he said firmly. "She has been through enough. She does not need your reproach."

Lady Catherine's eyes narrowed, but she held her tongue, sensing the authority in Darcy's tone. He turned back to Anne, his heart breaking for her. "Anne, I cannot change what has happened, but I can... I can offer you protection," he said softly. "If you will allow me, I will marry you. We will face this together."

Anne's eyes filled with fresh tears, her lips trembling as she looked up at him. "You would... marry me?"

He nodded, his resolve hardening. "Yes. I will not allow you to face this alone."

Lady Catherine quickly stepped forward, nodding in approval. "It is the right decision," she declared.

"But only on my conditions," Darcy replied coldly.

"What conditions?" she demanded in return.

"This child will inherit Rosings Park, but it will *never* be allowed to inherit Pemberley. I will not allow the lineage to be so tainted."

Lady Catherine gasped. "But think of the talk! What will people say when your firstborn child isn't your heir?"

"Their talk does not bother me."

"But, you will care for the child, won't you?" Anne broke in.

At her gentle plea, Darcy turned back to his cousin. The fear in her eyes caused his face to soften. "Of course, Anne. The child is guiltless. I simply will not allow anyone save my own blood to inherit a Darcy estate. You are a Fitzwilliam and a de Bourgh, neither of which has claim on Pemberley. But in all other instances, yes, I will treat the child as my own."

"Very well." Lady Catherine's ragged agreement behind him brought a look of relief to Anne's face.

Darcy nodded, though the weight of the situation settled heavily on him. The marriage would secure Rosings, but as the child born from this marriage—Anne's child—would never inherit Pemberley, his family's estate would remain without a direct heir. The future he had imagined, of a marriage born out of choice and love, was an impossible dream now.

He cast those thoughts aside, focusing instead on Anne, who was looking at him with a mixture of gratitude and sorrow. He would do what was necessary. He reached out, taking her hand gently in his, and gave her a reassuring smile. "We will do this together," he promised.

In the days that followed, Darcy arranged to take Anne to London, where they would be married and she could be cared for by skilled doctors and a midwife. She needed more than the familiar walls of Rosings; she needed proper medical attention, and Darcy was determined that she would have it. Lady Catherine had been outraged at first, but Darcy's will held strong.

They traveled in silence. The curtains of the carriage framed Anne's pale face as they left Rosings behind. Darcy's heart ached with the weight of his decision, yet he felt a fierce determination to see it through. This child, whatever its parentage, would bear the name of Darcy, and he would do everything in his power to protect both Anne and her unborn child.

In London, Darcy made arrangements with the best physicians, ensuring that Anne would be comfortable and attended to. He visited her regularly, offering words of encouragement, but he could see the toll that Wickham's cruelty had taken on her. She was a shadow of the cousin he had known, her spirit diminished and her once-gentle demeanor marked by a resigned sadness.

One day, as he sat by her bedside, she looked at him with a faint smile. "Thank you, Fitzwilliam," she murmured. "For everything."

Darcy felt a pang of sorrow as he looked down at her, but he offered her a gentle smile. "You are family, Anne."

Two months later…

The halls of the Darcy townhouse were silent but for the sounds of gasping sobs and anguished cries filtering through the door to Anne's bed chamber. Fitzwilliam Darcy paced the corridor outside the birthing room, his heart twisting with every scream that tore through the walls. Two days. For two days, he had listened, powerless, as Anne fought and struggled within.

His hands clenched at his sides, helplessness washing over him as another scream reached his ears. He had tried to stay calm, had tried to prepare himself for this day, but nothing could have braced him for the unrelenting agony of her suffering. The doctor had assured him it was normal, that first labors often took time, but it was becoming unbearable to wait any longer.

In the quiet moments, when he could drown out the screams and remember the happier sounds of her voice, his mind drifted back to their last few months together. He saw Anne as she had been then, pale but smiling as she sat in her favorite chair by the window, her hands tenderly resting on the swell of her belly. She had radiated a gentle peace that had eased his own troubled mind.

"You know, Fitzwilliam," she had said one evening, looking at him with an almost childlike joy, "I think… I think I am happy." Her hand had smoothed over her stomach as she sang, her voice a quiet lullaby for the unborn child who already seemed to know her love.

Anne had spoken of her hopes and dreams, of the kind of mother she would be, promising to be gentler, kinder than her own had been, to let her child feel cherished, not stifled.

"If I am to be a mother," she had said softly, "I want to be a good one. I want to be like…" she paused, her voice catching. "Like yours was; so kind, so compassionate. The complete opposite of my own."

He felt the ache of those memories in the present, his heart heavy with the contrast of her dreams and the harsh reality she was enduring.

At last, he heard the door creak open, and Dr. Williams emerged, his face grave, worn with a fatigue and worry that Darcy had not seen before.

"Mr. Darcy," he began, his voice low, "I'm afraid there is little we can do. Mrs. Darcy is failing. Her frame… it's too narrow to allow the child to pass. And she is bleeding heavily. She… she will not survive this." He swallowed, and in that moment, Darcy felt his heart begin to break. "If you wish to say your goodbyes, you must come in now."

Darcy was dumbstruck. Never in all of the many plans he had formed had he considered this outcome. Numb with despair, Darcy followed the doctor into the dimly lit room. The air was thick with the scent of sweat and blood, and there, on the bed, lay Anne. Her face was pale, her hair plastered to her forehead, but she managed a faint, weak smile as she saw him.

"Fitzwilliam," she whispered, her voice drowned out by her own labored breathing. "Please… I need you to promise me something."

"Anything," he replied, his voice choked with emotion as he knelt beside her, taking her trembling hand in his.

"Save my baby," she whispered, her eyes filled with a desperate plea. "Please, Fitzwilliam… I know I am dying, but don't… don't let my baby die with me. Let… let my life have meant something."

Darcy felt a lump rise in his throat, his heart breaking. He glanced at the doctor. "Is such a thing even possible?"

The doctor hesitated. "There is… there is one who might help," he admitted reluctantly. "A young student surgeon, a Dr. James Barry. He has some… radical ideas, and he has considered the notion of cutting the womb to save a child. There are records of something similar occurring in ancient times— no one knows if they are real, however. Such a procedure… it will be fatal to the mother, which is why it simply isn't done."

Darcy clenched Anne's hand tightly, his voice thick with grief as he looked down at her. "Anne, I… I can't. I can't let them do that to you."

Anne's eyes filled with a quiet resolve. "Fitzwilliam… I am going to die," she said, her voice calm despite the tears that filled her eyes. "Please. Don't let my death be in vain. Let it… let it be for this child."

Darcy felt his own resolve waver, his heart breaking as he looked into her pleading eyes. Finally, he nodded, his voice trembling as he whispered, "Very well. I… I will do as you ask."

A faint smile crossed her lips, and she squeezed his hand with the last of her strength. "Thank you," she whispered, her voice fading. "And please… find him— or her— a mother. Someone who will love him… the way I could have loved him."

"I promise," he choked out, the words almost inaudible as he felt her hand grow weaker in his grasp. "I will find him someone who will love him as if he were their own."

The doctor gestured for Darcy to leave, but he shook his head, refusing to let go of Anne's hand. He stayed at her side as her wave after wave rolled across her stomach, draining her life with each contraction.

After an hour, a small, bare-faced young man arrived and immediately went to work. "We will give her laudanum," Barry explained in the youthful tone of that seemed more suited to a lad not yet matured. "It will dull the pain, though it cannot erase it."

Darcy nodded, his gaze fixed on Anne's face as they prepared the laudanum and administered it. Her eyes grew heavy, her breathing slow and shallow as the drug took effect. She looked at Darcy, a faint smile on her lips, and he leaned forward, pressing his forehead against hers, murmuring the lullaby she had sung so often to her unborn child.

"Sleep, my little one… rest in love's embrace…" he whispered, his voice breaking as he repeated the words of the lullaby she often sang to her growing womb. He felt her hand grow weaker in his, and his heart shattered with every passing moment.

He kept his eyes on her, his voice soft as he sang to her, willing her to feel his presence, his love, until the end.

The child was delivered at last, its small form blue and still as it entered the world. Darcy dared not look, his focus remaining on Anne, his voice a soft caress against her ear.

"He's not breathing!" came the strained voice of the doctor.

Darcy's gaze shot up, his heart pounding as he saw the child, impossibly small, held in the doctor's bloody hands. The baby's skin was a dusky blue, and it lay still, lifeless.

"He's too small…" the young doctor whispered.

"Well, he was a full month early," Dr. Williams murmured, worry lining his face. He looked to the midwife, his voice steady but urgent. "Here, please, take him and see if…"

The midwife took the baby, her hands deft but gentle as she turned the child over, her fingers rubbing his back in firm strokes. "Come now, little one," she whispered. "Come now, feel the warmth of this world. Breathe."

Darcy felt himself leaning forward, his own breaths shallow as he watched, unable to tear his gaze away. Every second that passed felt like an eternity, the silence growing more unbearable. The midwife adjusted the baby's head, cradling him closer as she gave a small, resolute nod.

"Let me…" she said softly, lifting him slightly. She delivered a sharp, quick tap to the child's back, then rubbed his chest with a firm but tender hand.

And then, there was a sound—a faint, whimpering gasp. Darcy's breath caught as the baby shuddered, his tiny mouth opening as he finally drew in his first, tentative breath. A feeble, fragile cry filled the air, the sound weak but unmistakably alive.

"There we are," the midwife murmured, relief flooding her voice as she wrapped the child in a soft blanket. She looked up, offering the baby to the doctor, her expression both reverent and exhausted. "He's breathing now."

"It's a boy, Mr. Darcy. You have a son," Dr. Williams belatedly informed him.

"At the faint sound of the cry, Anne stirred, her eyelids fluttering as she turned her head towards them. "Please…" she slurred, her voice heavy with exhaustion. "Let me… let me see him."

The midwife brought the swaddled bundle to her, lowering him into her arms. Anne gazed down at her son, her face filled with wonder and love despite the shadows of pain that lingered in her eyes. A tear slipped down her cheek as she looked up at Darcy.

"Remember… remember your promise, Fitzwilliam," she murmured, her words faint but resolute. "Find him… a mother."

Darcy's own voice was choked as he nodded, clutching her hand as he replied, "I promise, Anne. I swear it to you."

With a final, weary smile, she closed her eyes; her grip loosening as she drifted away, the last traces of life slipping from her frail body. Her cheek rested on the head of her baby as the room fell into a hushed reverence.

Darcy stayed by her side, his heart breaking as he watched her last breaths, and the tiny, fragile creature she had left behind became his only anchor in a world that had suddenly grown far colder.

Chapter 2

Ramsgate, 1811

The gentle sea breeze swept across the shore at Ramsgate, filling the air with the tang of salt and a cool freshness that Darcy hoped might bring some ease to his young charge. Little Andrew, only two years old, sat quietly on the sand, his pale face framed by soft wisps of blond hair. He watched the other children with wide eyes as they scampered across the beach, their shouts of laughter and play echoing in the air.

The child's nurse— a kind woman named Rebecca— seated nearby, kept a watchful eye on him, ready to attend to him at a moment's notice. Yet, it was Darcy himself who sat closest to the boy, bending down to brush sand from his small hands and answer a thousand questions that spoke of a bound deeper than what was customary for a father of Darcy's status.

His gaze softened as he watched Andrew, a mixture of affection and worry in his expression. Since birth, the child had struggled with "the asthma," as the doctors called it—a wheezing and difficulty in breathing that seemed to worsen during times of illness or excitement. It pained Darcy to see him so subdued, unable to run and play as the other children did. But he tried his best to offer him a comforting presence, one that would reassure him of his place in the world, despite the trials he faced.

"Do you see the waves, Andrew?" he asked, pointing to the rolling blue water. "They come in and out like this every day. Perhaps, one day, you might run in them yourself."

Andrew nodded slowly, a faint smile flickering on his face as he looked up at Darcy. The sight tugged at Darcy's heart, and he smiled back, reaching out to brush a stray hair from the boy's forehead.

"I don't think he understands you, sir," Rebecca said in her thick brogue.

Smiling ruefully, Darcy nodded in response, his gaze wandering back out to the water. As he sat there, his thoughts drifted back to Town, where he had spent recent weeks struggling through dreary gatherings and shallow conversations.

The past months had been a trial for him since coming out of mourning for his late wife. Lady Catherine had been enraged over her daughter's death, forcing him to banish her to the dower house. Her fury was such that she had become almost manic; ranting and raving to everyone within earshot that Darcy had murdered her daughter in order to gain Rosings Park.

Darcy's uncle, Lord Matlock, had attempted to reason with her, but her mind was too far gone. Darcy was forced to move her to the Dower House in Kent— without a carriage— where she could only spew her vitriol to the servants he paid to keep her contained.

Time was no longer Darcy's ally. Free from two years mourning for his wife, he had been swept into the social demands of his position once again, a responsibility he daily grew to resent. Between the cloying debutantes and their matchmaking mothers, he began to feel that his world truly had become a stage.

This trip to Ramsgate with Andrew was a welcome respite from the monotony of London and its upper class. The excuse was to visit his sister and attempt to improve his son's health with the sea air, but he couldn't deny that the sudden trip was as necessary for him as it was for them.

"Brother!" came a cheerful voice from behind, breaking his somber thoughts.

He turned to see his younger sister, Georgiana, approaching with a small parcel in her hands. There was a spring in her step and her face was alight with excitement. Beside her walked Mrs. Younge, her chaperone, who observed with a mild expression as Georgiana hurried forward.

"Oh, Fitzwilliam, look at the ribbon I bought!" Georgiana exclaimed, holding up a delicate pale-blue ribbon that matched her eyes. "And there were the loveliest bonnets in the shop! I couldn't decide between one with flowers and one with feathers, but Mrs. Younge told me I should wait and think on it a little longer."

Darcy smiled indulgently, though he noted Mrs. Younge's strained expression as she kept her distance, watching them with a polite but detached demeanor. He longed to see Georgiana happy and social, making friends her age rather than clinging to him and her governess for companionship.

"And have you made the acquaintance of anyone else here, Georgiana?" Darcy asked, hoping she might have found some new friends among the other young ladies.

A faint blush crept into her cheeks. She glanced nervously at Mrs. Younge, her gaze dropping as she murmured, "No, Fitzwilliam, not yet."

31

Darcy's brow furrowed, and he cast a quick, appraising glance at Mrs. Younge. It struck him as peculiar that his sister, who was young, shy, and easily influenced, had yet to make any acquaintances. After all, Mrs. Younge's primary responsibility was to guide Georgiana into the company of those her age and social class. Surely, she could have arranged an introduction or two.

Turning to Mrs. Younge, he raised an eyebrow. "I should think that, by now, Miss Darcy would have had the chance to meet a few young ladies of similar standing. Are there no other acquaintances in Ramsgate?"

Mrs. Younge offered a polite smile, inclining her head. "I am afraid, sir, that I am not well-acquainted here myself. I had hoped, now that you are here, you might attend a local assembly this evening. Should you do so, there may be an opportunity to meet some of the local families or other seaside guests. If any of the ladies have younger daughters or sisters, they might provide Miss Darcy with suitable companionship."

Darcy considered her words, his gaze drifting back to Georgiana, whose hopeful expression betrayed her eagerness for approval. He could see that she longed for a wider circle, and he felt a pang of guilt that his preoccupation with Andrew's health had kept him from attending to her needs as he should.

"Yes," he agreed at last with a faint sigh. "I suppose I could attend. Perhaps there will indeed be a few familiar faces, and introductions can be made."

Georgiana's face lit up, her eyes sparkling as she looked up at her brother. "Oh, thank you, Fitzwilliam! I know you don't enjoy assemblies, but I'm ever so grateful."

He offered her a soft smile, reaching out to squeeze her hand. "You deserve friends, Georgiana. And if attending an assembly is what it takes to find you good company, then it shall be done."

Mrs. Younge inclined her head respectfully; a faint, satisfied smile on her lips. "Then it is settled. I shall make all the necessary arrangements to secure the exact details for you, sir. Miss Darcy and I will be eager to hear of your success tomorrow morning."

As they stood there, Darcy felt Andrew tug on his sleeve, his small hand clutching Darcy's coat as he pointed to the shore.

"Look, Papa," the child murmured in his soft voice, pointing to a crab scuttling across the sand. Darcy felt a pang at the title, which came naturally from the boy's lips, though it was not his own child he held.

"Yes, Andrew," he said. He lifted him up and placed him in his lap. "Isn't it remarkable how it moves sideways?"

The child nodded, his tiny hand reaching out toward the little creature, and Darcy held him close, feeling a surge of tenderness as he cradled the boy. He had never intended to take on the role of a father to Anne's child, but the bond he felt with the boy, the affection that had blossomed in his heart, was undeniable.

He sat there quietly, holding Andrew, knowing that for all the struggles and duties, he would continue to do all he could for the boy. And that night, he would also strive to fulfill his responsibilities to Georgiana, for both children deserved every bit of love and protection he could give.

That night, as Fitzwilliam Darcy entered the assembly room, a hush fell over the gathered guests, followed almost instantly by the telltale hum of whispers. His arrival had been duly announced, the master of ceremonies drawing attention to his name and status, and Darcy felt the weight of countless pairs of eyes upon him.

"Mr. Darcy of Pemberley!" He had heard the whispers as soon as he stepped inside. "A wealthy widower, still in want of an heir, they say."

"Have you heard? He's just out of mourning… he's quite eligible now."

"Imagine, a second chance at Pemberley's fortune…"

Darcy clenched his jaw, feeling the familiar sense of irritation rise within him. He knew his return to society would mean increased scrutiny, but to see people openly speculate on his marital status and his need for an heir felt invasive, even vulgar. Yet, he reminded himself of Georgiana, her shy request for friendship lingering in his mind. Tonight was about her, about her chance to find companionship; he would bear this for her sake.

Despite his hopes, however, Darcy realized quickly that he knew no one in attendance. The room was filled with faces unfamiliar and expectant. He scanned the sea of guests, searching for anyone of mutual acquaintance, but his search yielded no familiar connections. Resigned, he made his way toward the master of ceremonies, who received him with a polite bow and immediately set about introducing him to a number of nearby families.

"Mr. Darcy, may I present Miss Clarissa Harford and her mother, Mrs. Harford?" the master of ceremonies intoned, his voice respectful yet formal.

34

Darcy inclined his head politely, his gaze settling on the young woman before him. Miss Harford, a bright-eyed girl with golden curls, dipped a curtsy, her cheeks pink with excitement. Darcy's courtesy was returned with an eager intensity that was unnerving. He had the distinct impression that she was holding her breath in anticipation.

"Mr. Darcy," she greeted, in a breathless voice. "It is a pleasure to make your acquaintance."

"Likewise, Miss Harford," he replied politely, offering her his hand as the music began for a dance. The pair moved to the floor, joining the other couples in a set, but Darcy's enthusiasm was already flagging. As he led her through the turns and steps, Miss Harford's giggling responses to his polite questions felt hollow, insipid, her interest in him clearly overshadowed by her eagerness to make an impression.

After the dance ended, he was immediately introduced to another family, followed by another, and then another; each young woman more eager than the last. Their smiles were wide and fixed, their attempts at conversation faltering as they resorted to trite compliments about his estate, his dancing, his very presence.

After a fourth dance, Darcy withdrew to the edge of the room, stepping behind a pillar to gain a moment of respite. He closed his eyes, grateful for the brief break from the suffocating parade of forced smiles and shallow conversation. The noise of the room buzzed around him, but his attention was caught by a pair of voices nearby, the words unintentionally clear.

"Darling, you simply must find a way to get Mr. Darcy's attention," a woman's voice urged, soft but insistent.

"Mama, I don't think he will notice me," replied a girl's hesitant voice.

"Then make him notice!" the mother insisted. "Why, during your dance, you could… perhaps find a way to stumble. Fall into his arms, let him catch you. No gentleman could refuse a compromise in such a case—he would be honor-bound to offer his protection."

Darcy felt a surge of anger and disgust rise within him, his face hardening at the notion. So this was the scheme? To manufacture a situation that would force him to take responsibility, to entangle him through a false pretense of duty? He clenched his fists, disgusted that even here, his honor was something to be manipulated.

The woman continued, her voice a low murmur, "Imagine, a life with all that wealth and comfort at your disposal, my dear. You simply must try."

Darcy had heard enough. Without a second glance, he straightened and walked toward the exit, his back rigid with determination. He had tolerated this assembly for the sake of Georgiana, hoping for some semblance of decency among the guests, but this was more than he could stomach.

The night air was cool outside, the calm of the open sky a stark contrast to the stifling assembly. He took a deep breath, letting the cold wind fill his lungs, grounding himself after the evening's vexing display. His thoughts turned to Georgiana—perhaps it was naïve of him to hope for her to find suitable friends among such company. He must protect her from this insidious world for as long as he could.

As he walked away from the assembly hall, he resolved to look elsewhere for Georgiana's companions. This experience only confirmed what he had feared: there were those who would stop at nothing to ensnare him, and by extension, his sister. He would not let them succeed.

~

Darcy arrived home earlier than expected, his footsteps echoing on the stone steps of the quiet townhouse. The footman stationed by the door started at his unexpected appearance.

"Mr. Darcy, sir!" the footman stammered, quickly regaining his composure. "I—I wasn't expecting you quite yet."

Darcy raised an eyebrow. "Clearly," he replied, his tone clipped. "Is something amiss?"

The footman hesitated, glancing over his shoulder as though uncertain whether to speak. "There's... a guest, sir."

"A guest?" Darcy's brow furrowed. No guests were anticipated in his absence, and Georgiana was not yet of an age to be entertaining company unsupervised.

Without waiting for further explanation, he strode down the hallway and made his way to the drawing room, his steps quick and purposeful. He reached the drawing room and paused. Peering in through the crack of the partially open door, his heart froze.

There, on the settee, was the one person in the world he actually despised.

George Wickham sat on the settee, his frame too close to Georgiana's slight form. He was leaning in, his head inclined toward her ear, whispering something that made her cheeks flush.

Wickham's hand rested on the back of the settee behind her shoulders, his gaze fixed on her with a look Darcy knew all too well—a perfect predator cornering its prey.

A surge of rage coursed through Darcy's veins. He slammed open the door. Wickham jumped up in alarm.

"Wickham!" Darcy's voice cut through the room like a blade, every syllable laced with fury.

"Ah... Darcy," Wickham said, his false casualness betrayed by the widening of his. He rose from his seat, adjusting his coat as if trying to brush off Darcy's presence.

Darcy's jaw clenched, his hands trembling with rage. "What do you think you are doing here?" he demanded, his voice low and dangerous. "Have you no shame, Wickham? Do you truly think I would permit you near my sister, after everything you have done?"

Wickham, momentarily stunned, quickly regained his composure. He leaned against the arm of the settee with a practiced smirk. "Darcy! I was merely keeping your dear sister company in your absence," he said smoothly. "I thought it would be a kindness to her, as she seemed so... lonely."

Darcy's jaw clenched, his eyes narrowing as he took a menacing step forward. "You have no right to be here, near her, or in this house."

Wickham's face paled, the smirk slipping. He shifted uneasily, glancing toward the door as if calculating his chances of escape. "Now, Darcy," he said, a flicker of fear in his eyes, "there's no need for threats. Surely you would not resort to such... unsavory measures."

"Unsavory measures?" Darcy repeated, his voice dangerously calm. "After all you have done? If it weren't for Georgiana, I would summon the footmen to finish what Lady Catherine began." His voice dropped to a chilling whisper. "Or I would call you out myself and ensure you paid for the ruin you brought to Anne and the stain you nearly cast upon Rosings."

The threat hung heavy in the air, and the color drained from Wickham's face, his usual bravado vanishing entirely. Without another word, he hedged around Darcy toward the door, his gaze darting from Darcy to the hallway. He gave a final glance at Georgiana, whose expression was a mixture of confusion and horror, and then bolted from the room, disappearing before Darcy could grab him.

Georgiana looked up at Darcy, her face a mixture of confusion and shame. Before she could speak, Mrs. Younge appeared in the doorway, a perplexed expression on her face.

"Mr. Darcy?" she asked, looking between him and Georgiana. "Is something the matter?"

Darcy's eyes met hers, and he wasted no time. "Mrs. Younge," he acknowledged her coldly. "Your employment here is terminated. You have failed in your duty to my sister, and I will not tolerate your lack of discretion."

Mrs. Younge's face paled. "Sir—surely there's some mistake—"

"There is no mistake," Darcy interrupted sharply. "You were charged with the care and protection of my sister, and yet you allowed her to be alone with a man I specifically forbade from ever approaching my family. Your negligence is unforgivable."

Mrs. Younge opened her mouth to protest, but Darcy's expression silenced her, and she bowed her head, retreating from the room without another word.

Once she was gone, Darcy turned his attention to Georgiana. His expression softened as he took a seat beside her. She looked up at him with wide, tear-filled eyes, her voice trembling as she asked, "Fitzwilliam, what... what did he mean? Why did you send her away?"

Darcy took a deep breath, gathering his thoughts before speaking. "Georgiana, there is much you do not know... and I fear I must now explain. Wickham—" he paused, struggling with the words, "—Wickham is not the man he appears to be. His presence here, near you, was a violation of trust and decency. He is a man of deceit and cruelty. His actions are the very definition of dishonorable."

Georgiana listened in silence, her gaze fixed on him. He knelt beside her and took her hands in his with a steadying breath. He continued, his voice growing heavier with each word. "Georgiana, I need you to understand something very important." His tone was gentle but firm. "Wickham is not our friend."

Georgiana's eyes widened. Tears gathered as she whispered, "But... why?"

Darcy closed his eyes briefly, steadying himself. This was not a truth he had wanted to share with her, but Wickham's presence in their home had left him no choice. He looked at her with somber eyes, his voice thick with the weight of revelation. "Georgiana, the child... Andrew, whom you know as your nephew—he was not born of love or choice. Wickham forced himself upon Anne, and it was his intention to use her for his own gain. He… he violated her in an attempt to gain wealth and status he did not deserve."

Georgiana gasped, her hand covering her mouth as the color drained from her face. "Oh… oh, Fitzwilliam… I did not know…"

Darcy squeezed her hands, his gaze filled with sorrow and resolve. "You could not have known, and I did not wish you to carry this burden. But you must know now that Wickham cannot be trusted, nor can you ever permit him to approach you or our family."

She nodded, tears slipping down her cheeks, her expression one of devastation and horror. "How could someone do such a thing?" she whispered, her voice trembling. "How could he be so… so cruel?"

"Because of greed. He tried to secure Rosings for himself by… vile means, hoping to gain control of Anne and the estate. There are those in this world, Georgiana, who seek only their own gain, regardless of the cost to others. But you are safe now, and I will protect you, no matter the cost."

Georgiana's cheeks flushed with shame and fear as she looked down, trembling. "Oh, Fitzwilliam… I did not know. I thought… I thought he was kind, that he… cared about me."

"It is not your fault, Georgiana," Darcy said. "Wickham has spent his life deceiving people, preying upon kindness and innocence. He will not trouble you again—I swear it."

She nodded, her face still pale, but there was a faint glimmer of relief in her eyes. "Thank you… for telling me," she whispered, squeezing his hands. "I understand now."

Darcy felt a surge of protectiveness and he placed an arm around her shoulders. "You are safe now, Georgiana. I will see to it that you are protected, always."

As he held her close, he felt the weight of his promise settle within him. Wickham's despicable schemes would find no purchase here. He would ensure that his sister and Andrew were shielded from the darkness Wickham had brought upon them, for they deserved a life free from his treachery and harm.

Chapter 3

Netherfield, 1811

The journey to Netherfield had been long, and the chilly autumn wind whipped at the windows of the carriage as Darcy peered out, his mind uneasy despite Georgiana's quiet companionship. Georgiana sat beside him, her eyes fixed on the passing scenery. Across from them, little Andrew rested against the cushions, bundled in a thick woolen blanket with a contented smile, his breaths shallow but steady.

Darcy cast a concerned glance toward the boy, whose frailty weighed heavily on him. The winter air in Derbyshire had proved too harsh for Andrew's delicate lungs, and though the dirty air of London had helped a little, Darcy had found no satisfactory solution—until he had run into Bingley at White's.

The invitation had been genuine. Bingley's warmth and enthusiasm shone as he insisted that Netherfield would be the ideal retreat for the family, a place where Andrew might breathe a little easier and Georgiana could enjoy a bit of fresh countryside air. Darcy, after careful consideration had agreed, though he had privately vowed not to let Georgiana or Andrew out of his sight.

The carriage slowed as they neared the entrance to Netherfield and Darcy allowed himself a small sigh of relief. The air felt fresher here, crisper, and he dared to hope that Andrew might find some relief in this gentler climate. As they pulled up to the manor, the front doors opened and Bingley stepped out, his face breaking into a welcoming smile.

"Darcy!" he called out cheerfully as the footman opened the carriage door, offering a hand to help Georgiana down. "Welcome to Netherfield! And you, Miss Darcy," he added with a kind smile, bowing politely.

"Thank you, Mr. Bingley," Georgiana replied, returning his smile shyly.

"And you must be Andrew," Bingley continued, crouching down to greet the young boy as Darcy lifted him out of the carriage.

Andrew gazed up at Bingley with wide eyes, and Darcy saw the faintest hint of a smile on his face as Bingley chuckled. "Well, I hope you'll feel right at home here, young sir. We've plenty of cozy rooms and warm fires for you."

"Fank-oo," Andrew murmured softly, clutching Darcy's hand tightly as they made their way inside. The warmth of the hall was a welcome change from the chill outside, and Darcy felt a wave of relief as they settled in, his mind finally beginning to ease.

The afternoon passed with quiet contentment. Andrew spent most of his time by the window, watching the autumn leaves fall with fascination, his breath misting the glass. Georgiana explored the gardens and the estate grounds, the gentle expanse of countryside a refreshing change from London's bustle.

Darcy, meanwhile, spent most of his time close by, dividing his attentions between his sister and Andrew. Wickham's actions that summer lingered constantly at the back of his mind, a reminder of the danger that seemed to shadow his family's peace, and he resolved to let neither of them stray far from his sight.

Later that evening, after Andrew had fallen asleep and Georgiana retired for the evening, Darcy found himself in Bingley's study, seated by the fire. Bingley poured them each a glass of brandy. The warmth of the room, combined with the quiet of the house, gave Darcy a rare sense of calm, and he leaned back in his chair, allowing himself a moment of reflection.

After a quiet moment, he spoke, his voice measured. "Bingley," he began, pausing as he considered how best to frame his thoughts. "I've been considering a change in my life."

"Oh?" Bingley raised an eyebrow, leaning forward with a curious expression. "Are you finally to sell Pemberley so I can purchase it for my sister?"

Darcy gave a bark of laughter. "No, nothing nearly so drastic." He took a steadying breath. "I believe it's time I seriously consider remarrying."

Bingley's eyes widened in surprise, though a grin quickly replaced his initial shock. "Well, that is unexpected. But certainly, it's not a bad idea. Andrew and Georgiana would benefit from having a lady about the house—someone who can help raise the boy and be a companion for your sister." He paused, an amused glint in his eye. "And I suppose you, too, could benefit from a bit of warmth in your life."

Darcy chuckled, but his tone turned serious as he continued. "It's true. Andrew needs stability, and Georgiana would benefit from having a mother figure, but the decision is more complicated than that." He leaned forward, his gaze intense. "If I marry, it must be to a woman who is kind, someone who will care for my family as though they were her own."

Bingley nodded thoughtfully, then leaned back with a teasing grin. "Well, if it's a wife you seek, I do know one lady who would be all too eager to volunteer... my sister, Caroline."

Darcy froze, searching for the right words to let his friend down gently. "Bingley... your sister is... well, she... that is to say..." He paused, floundering for a moment.

Bingley burst into laughter, clapping his hands in delight at Darcy's discomfort. "Oh, Darcy, don't look so horrified! I wouldn't let you marry my harridan of a sister even if you wanted to. Georgiana and Andrew are too delightful to expose to Caroline's vitriol."

Darcy couldn't help but let out a small laugh of relief, shaking his head. "Thank heavens, Bingley. I was struggling to be tactful. I could never... entertain such an idea."

"Believe me, I know her faults all too well," Bingley said with a wry smile. "And rest assured, I shan't be encouraging her ambitions on that score. She'd drive you mad and likely make your sister's life a misery, too. Caroline has her charms, but they are neither maternal nor compassionate."

Darcy took a long sip of his brandy, feeling a weight lift at Bingley's easy dismissal. "Precisely. I need someone with far more depth of character than the usual society miss. She must have a true capacity for compassion, as well as the ability to manage the demands of both Pemberley and Rosings."

Bingley leaned back, swirling his brandy thoughtfully. "Then you'll need someone with a good heart and some experience, I think. But I daresay," he added with a wink, "you may not find her in the circles of London. You're nothing more than the heir to Pemberley there."

Darcy sighed, conceding the truth of Bingley's words. The London social set had shown little interest in his role as a father and guardian. "I had hoped that among the more well-connected families, I might find someone suitable—someone who at least understands the responsibilities of a great estate. But in truth, none I have met seem suited to the demands of Pemberley, let alone to being the acting mistress of Rosings."

Bingley tilted his head, a thoughtful smile on his face. "And what of Meryton?"

"Meryton?" Darcy echoed, scoffing. "Whoever I choose will be mistress of Pemberley, and she must manage both it and Rosings from afar. Some country miss is unlikely to be familiar with such duties."

Bingley raised a hand to stop Darcy's protests. "I know, I know… you're looking for someone exceptional. But," he continued with a light grin, "I wouldn't rule out finding such a lady among the hedgerows and heather. Sometimes, the most extraordinary people come from the most ordinary places."

Darcy scoffed, giving his friend a skeptical look. "You cannot be serious. The mistress of Pemberley, and an acting mistress of Rosings, must have a great deal of experience and refinement. The position requires a specific type of woman—one who has been trained to manage large estates."

Bingley shrugged, an easy smile spreading across his face. "You never know, Darcy. Perhaps someone here in Meryton may surprise you."

Darcy shook his head, still unconvinced. "Here? In this small part of the country, I highly doubt I'll find anyone there suited to the responsibilities I require."

"Well," Bingley replied, undeterred, "it's fortunate that we'll have the opportunity to see, as I accepted an invitation for us to attend an assembly in Meryton tomorrow evening. You must come, too."

Darcy's brow furrowed, a hint of annoyance in his gaze. "An assembly? You know how I detest such gatherings. They are little more than an endless parade of shallow social displays."

Bingley laughed, clapping him on the shoulder. "Perhaps, but you mustn't be so quick to judge. Besides, you might find something of interest—or someone—at this particular gathering."

Darcy's brow furrowed. "And if I do not?"

"Then at least you can be assured of some amusement," Bingley replied with a grin. "But consider this—if you don't attend, my sister Caroline will almost certainly stay behind with you to keep you company."

Darcy winced, the thought of a solitary evening in Caroline's company sending a shiver down his spine. He took a resigned sip of his brandy, setting the glass down with a sigh.

"Very well," he said with a resigned sigh. "I shall attend. But do not expect me to find any revelations there."

Bingley clapped him on the shoulder, his grin unrelenting. "We shall see, my friend. We shall see."

Caroline stepped back from the study door and felt a flush of humiliation. She had never expected to hear herself discussed in such a… dismissive tone. Darcy, the man she had set her sights on since the beginning of the Season, the man whose fortunes, status, and refinement matched her ambitions precisely, had just declared her unsuitable. And Charles had laughed—laughed!

How dare Charles speak so poorly about me to his friend?

Her embarrassment was quickly replaced by a steely determination. The nerve of Darcy—to speak of her as though she were some mere upstart, incapable of fulfilling the role of his wife and mistress of Pemberley. And Charles—her own brother—dismissing her so glibly, calling her a *harridan*. The insult gnawed at her, leaving her seething.

I'll show them! I'll show them all!

As the voices inside quieted, Caroline stepped back, schooling her features into a mask of calm. She had known that winning Darcy would not be easy, and that he would require convincing; after all, his expectations were notorious. But this… this was beyond what she had anticipated.

In her mind, Caroline Bingley could already envision herself at Pemberley, dressed in the finest silks, her name spoken with reverence by those she entertained, her influence stretching across Derbyshire and beyond. Mistress of Pemberley… it was her birthright as much as it was Darcy's; it was simply a matter of time before he realized it. She had all the accomplishments, the breeding, and the elegance to fit the role. Who else could possibly embody the poise and sophistication required for such a position?

The notion that Darcy saw her as unfit—that he wanted someone of *kindness* and *warmth*, someone who could be a devoted mother to his sister and nephew—was laughable.

Kindness and warmth, she thought with a faint sneer. *What does kindness have to do with running a vast estate?*

Darcy was deceiving himself. He needed a woman of control, someone who could maintain the legacy, not a little milkmaid full of tenderness.

Her mind raced. Darcy had spoken of wanting a wife who would "care for his family like her own." Well, Caroline could do that. She would fawn over Georgiana, sing her praises, accompany her at the piano, even listen to her tedious conversations, if need be.

As for that sickly child Matthew, or whatever his name was… surely, with time Darcy would see that the boy's health made him an unfit heir, and he might turn his attentions to a son of his own. Still, she could charm the child if that was what it took. Caroline's mouth pursed at the thought of fawning over Darcy's fragile son, but it was a small price to pay if it softened Darcy's heart. Children were simple creatures; a few sweets, some lavish gifts, and the boy would think of her fondly.

A shadow of a smile touched her lips as she considered her plans. Yes, she would befriend Georgiana and dote upon little what's-his-name, until Darcy could not imagine a more affectionate mother figure. In his eyes, she would be everything he professed to seek.

Yet a quiet, unrelenting voice in the back of her mind lingered on Darcy's words: *"She must be someone loving and kind."* She pushed down her frustration, but a niggling doubt remained. What if Darcy refused her attention outright? What if, despite all her efforts, he still deemed her unfit?

A chill shivered down her spine, and she straightened her back. She would not wait on chance alone. No, if all else failed, she would find a way to ensure her position.

A compromise.

Caroline felt her determination harden, her gaze focusing on a single point in the hallway as her plan solidified. If subtle charms and careful manipulation failed to sway him, there were other, more... *drastic* measures she could take.

Her lips curled into a smile at the thought. A compromise was all it would take to bring about an engagement. A slip of the foot, an innocent mishap... even a brief scene that would arouse suspicion, and Darcy would be honor-bound to protect her reputation. And he was far too upright, too concerned with his family's name, to allow a scandal to touch them.

"Yes," she murmured to herself, her voice low and resolute. "If Darcy cannot be convinced by persuasion, he can be convinced by obligation."

Her plan was settled; its logic as flawless as the lacework on her gown. Darcy may have believed she wasn't suited to his expectations, but she would rewrite those expectations to suit herself. She would ensure her place in his life, one way or another.

With a final glance at the study door, Caroline straightened, a cold glint in her eye. Yes, she would be Mrs. Darcy, and she would enjoy the luxury, status, and power that title afforded her. She would not accept any other outcome. Whatever Darcy might think now, he would soon see that there was no woman better suited to his life and his ambitions than herself.

She, Caroline Bingley, would be the next Mrs. Darcy, and no one—not her brother, not Georgiana, and certainly not Darcy's own misguided ideals—would stand in her way.

Darcy adjusted the cuffs of his coat, straightening the fine fabric one last time before stepping quietly into Andrew's room. A soft glow from the small candle on the nightstand illuminated the child's gentle face, his pale features peaceful in sleep. Darcy leaned down, brushing a tender kiss to his forehead, and felt a surge of gratitude at his son's steady breathing.

Leaning over, he pressed a tender kiss to Andrew's forehead. "Sleep well, little one," he whispered.

The nurse, Rebecca, stood nearby, her eyes watchful yet soft. She offered a reassuring smile as Darcy straightened, casting a last look over Andrew.

"Don't worry, sir," she said softly, her heavy brogue apparent even in a whisper. "I'll keep a careful eye on him. Enjoy your evening."

Darcy nodded appreciatively. "Thank you, Rebecca. His health seems better here, but we can't be too careful."

"Indeed, sir," she replied. "The country air does him good."

Darcy felt a pang of reluctance as he left the room. With one last glance at Andrew, Darcy quietly left the room and made his way down the corridor to Georgiana's chambers. He found his sister seated comfortably by the fire, a book open on her lap. Across from her sat Mrs. Annesley, Georgiana's new companion, whose warmth and intelligence had quickly earned Darcy's trust— along with the credentials he had meticulously verified. She looked up from her knitting as he entered, giving him a polite nod.

"Fitzwilliam!" Georgiana exclaimed. She set aside her book and rose to greet him. "Are you leaving for the assembly now?"

"Indeed," he replied, returning her smile. "I wished to say goodnight. I trust you're enjoying Mrs. Annesley's company?"

Georgiana's eyes brightened as she glanced at her companion. "Very much. Mrs. Annesley is helping me with my studies, and she's promised to read with me."

Darcy gave Mrs. Annesley an approving nod, gratitude in his gaze. "Thank you, Mrs. Annesley."

"It's my pleasure, Mr. Darcy," she replied warmly. "Miss Darcy is a most diligent student."

"Soon you will be accompanying me to these events instead of simply bidding me farewell," he said with a smile.

She shrank back. "Not so very soon?"

"Of course not. You are to stay my baby sister until you are fifty years old," he replied with mock gravity.

Georgiana giggled, and he kissed her on the top of her forehead. Returning to her place by the fire, she gave him a small wave as he exited the room.

Having complete his farewells, Darcy descended to the front hall, arriving promptly at the appointed time. Bingley waited by the door, dressed in evening attire, hands folded behind his back. He paced the hall with a slightly bemused expression. "Ah, Darcy," he greeted him with a chuckle. "Punctual as always."

"Is Miss Bingley not joining us?" Darcy inquired, glancing around.

Bingley rolled his eyes, casting a glance up the grand staircase. "Still dressing, I'm afraid," he muttered, exasperation clear in his voice. "I've already been waiting thirty minutes. You'd think it was her own ball, the way she's carrying on."

They both stood in silence, a faint tension settling as the clock ticked on. Finally, a rustling at the top of the stairs. Darcy looked up, and his eyes widened involuntarily as Caroline appeared, making her grand entrance with a theatrical flair that was impossible to ignore.

Her gown was an overwhelming sight—a garish concoction of deep green silk, draped with lace and studded with clusters of beads that caught the light at every angle. But the pièce de résistance was the cloud of feathers adorned her sleeves and hem, and a particularly large one perched jauntily in her hair, bobbing with every step. The entire effect bordered on the absurd.

Bingley pressed his lips together, clearly struggling to keep a straight face. He cast a sideways glance at Darcy, whose expression remained carefully neutral, though a slight tightening around his eyes betrayed him.

Caroline descended the stairs with her head held high, her gaze fixed on Darcy. "Brother, Mr. Darcy," Caroline greeted them, her voice dripping with affected sweetness. "I hope I haven't kept you waiting too long."

"Not at all." Darcy offered a slight bow. "We have ample time."

She smiled broadly, stepping forward to link her arm through Darcy's with a familiarity that caught him off guard. "You are too kind," she purred. "It's so endearing to see you as a loving father and brother. Family is everything, is it not?"

He looked at her in astonishment but she continued speaking, her voice dripping with admiration. "I saw you pass my room to say goodnight to both Andrew and dear Georgiana. Such devotion. Any woman would be privileged to be a part of your family."

Darcy inclined his head slightly, offering a polite smile while concealing his discomfort at her overly familiar touch on his arm.

Caroline tilted her head with an exaggerated sigh. "I would have said goodnight as well, but it grew so late and I didn't want to disturb their rest." Her tone suggested that, of course, the delay had been entirely out of her control.

Bingley coughed, which Darcy suspected covered a laugh. "Yes, Caroline," he said with forced calm, "we're all keenly aware of your punctuality."

Caroline gave her brother a disdainful glance before turning back to Darcy, her expression flickering back to adoration as she awaited his response.

Darcy inclined his head, extricating his arm under the guise of adjusting his cuff. "Indeed," he agreed. "Family is of utmost importance."

"Perhaps tomorrow evening," she persisted.

Bingley cleared his throat, stepping forward with a conciliatory smile. "Well then, shall we be off? Wouldn't want to miss the opening dance."

"Of course," Caroline replied, casting a lingering glance at Darcy before allowing her brother to lead the way.

Darcy nodded, falling a step or two behind to increase the distance between them, though she seemed determined to remain close as they made their way outside. He glanced at Bingley, who shot him a sympathetic look that was not without amusement.

As they moved toward the door, Darcy couldn't help but reflect on Caroline's sudden display of familial concern. It seemed a transparent attempt to align herself with his values—a notion that left him uneasy. Her usual demeanor lacked the genuine warmth he sought in a companion, and tonight's performance only heightened his reservations.

Stepping into the crisp evening air, he resolved to maintain his composure for the duration of the event. The carriage awaited, and as they settled inside, Caroline positioned herself beside Darcy, her voluminous gown occupying more than her fair share of space.

The journey to the assembly was filled with Caroline's chatter about the local society and her anticipation of the evening ahead. Darcy's responses were politely sparse, his thoughts elsewhere. He gazed out the window at the passing landscape, wondering if perhaps Bingley was right—if somewhere among the attendees tonight, he might find someone who truly embodied the kindness and sincerity he desired.

But as Caroline's feathers brushed against his arm for the third time, he couldn't help but feel a twinge of skepticism. The night promised to be a test of patience, if nothing else.

Chapter 4

Elizabeth Bennet spun lightly as her dance with Mr. Lucas came to an end, laughter bubbling up as she curtsied and thanked him. The Meryton Assembly was in full swing, with lively music, familiar faces, and warm conversation filling the hall. As the final notes of the set died away, Elizabeth moved from the dance floor. Snippets of chatter floated around her, carrying the invariable rumors and gossip.

"Did you hear? The Netherfield party will be arriving shortly."

"Yes! They say Mr. Bingley is quite young and very charming—and rich, too, if the rumors are to be believed."

"Oh, but his friend… the gentleman who came down with him? Mr. Darcy, I think they called him? A man of wealth beyond imagining, and recently widowed, poor fellow. And he has a young son, quite ill from what I've heard."

Elizabeth's interest piqued. She had overheard talk of the Netherfield party earlier in the week, but little had been said of Mr. Darcy, aside from his wealth. She imagined he must be a reserved, solemn man, the kind who would rather avoid society altogether. The thought made her feel a bit sorry for him—he must be bearing a tremendous weight, and the constant attention to his status and fortune could not make it any easier.

How difficult it must be to be alone with a young child, and always under society's scrutiny.

As she sat down, her friend Charlotte Lucas appeared by her side, nudging her playfully. "Lizzy, have you heard the latest? A new family has taken Netherfield, and they're said to be incredibly wealthy."

Elizabeth laughed. "You know I have, between your mother and mine."

"He is supposed to come tonight; at least, that is what he told my father."

"Oh, is he?" Elizabeth replied with a playful smirk. "I wonder if he'll find our little town and its people agreeable or decide we are all frightfully provincial."

Charlotte laughed. "Time will tell. But they're said to be quite distinguished— look, I believe that's them arriving now."

Elizabeth followed Charlotte's gaze to the entrance. The Bingley party had arrived at last, drawing all eyes as they made their way through the hall. Charles Bingley looked every bit the amiable gentleman, his expression open and friendly as he greeted everyone he met. Beside him stood his sisters: Miss Caroline Bingley, whose extravagant gown and feathered hair contrasted starkly with her brother's easy charm, and Mrs. Hurst, who seemed indifferent to the crowd altogether. Both wore expressions that spoke of a certain reluctance, or perhaps even disdain, for their surroundings.

And then, just behind them, came Mr. Darcy.

Elizabeth was surprised. Far from the quiet, diminutive man she had pictured, Mr. Darcy was tall, with a proud, solemn expression and a dark gaze that swept across the room without lingering on any one face. His lips were set in a firm line, and there was something about him that seemed, for lack of a better word, cold.

Sir William Lucas approached the newcomers, and Elizabeth watched as Bingley engaged warmly with him, smiling and greeting the crowd. Darcy remained almost motionless, his dark gaze flicking over the assembled guests with a restrained, indifferent air. Elizabeth felt her initial sympathy waver as he barely acknowledged Sir William's introduction, offering only a curt nod.

She tried to imagine his experience of the evening, enduring the stares and whispers that followed him—no doubt tired of rumors about his wealth and widower status. Still, his demeanor seemed less the sorrow of grief and more a proud detachment, a superiority that bordered on disdain.

Her thoughts were interrupted as Sir William approached her family with Mr. Bingley. She quickly forgot Darcy's distant manner; Bingley's eager, warm smile as he was introduced to Jane was unmistakable. Elizabeth watched, delighting in the immediate kindness he showed her sister, his gaze lingering on Jane with genuine admiration.

She felt a surge of hope for Jane. If the man's fortune is as grand as they say, then this could be quite an evening.

Mrs. Bennet, always one to seize an opportunity, lost no time in hinting that her daughters were accomplished dancers, and to Elizabeth's delight, Jane was soon led onto the dance floor with Mr.

Bingley. His easy conversation and Jane's shy replies blended into the lively music.

Elizabeth began to turn back to Charlotte, but the sight of Mrs. Bennet making her way toward Mr. Darcy stopped her short. Her mother's face was alight with purpose, and Elizabeth felt a faint sense of dread. Mrs. Bennet wasted no time in hinting—far too eagerly—that Mr. Darcy might consider a dance with one of her daughters.

Darcy's response was unmistakably chilly. He inclined his head as he spoke, and though his words were too quiet to carry, the look of dismissal on his face was evident.

Elizabeth's cheeks flushed, her irritation growing as she observed his condescending demeanor throughout the duration of the set. As soon as it finished and Bingley had escorted Jane to Mrs. Bennet, he made his way to his friend. The look on Darcy's face soured even further, and Elizabeth strained to catch their words.

"Come now, Darcy," Bingley said with a grin. "It's a pleasant assembly. Surely you might wish to enjoy yourself and dance with a few of these young ladies?"

Darcy's expression remained impassive. "Bingley, you know that I am not in the habit of dancing with women of no consequence," he replied, his tone clipped.

Elizabeth's pulse quickened as her irritation grew. She turned away when she saw Bingley point in her direction. Darcy's response was easily heard above the noise. "She is tolerable, I suppose, but not handsome enough to tempt me into remarriage."

A rush of heat flooded Elizabeth's face, her breath catching at his unexpected rudeness. She looked away, her stomach twisting at the casual, cutting dismissal of her worth.

Of course, she thought bitterly. Of course he would find the assembly and its guests beneath him. How foolish I was to imagine any other reason for his coldness.

She tried to calm herself, turning away from the crowd before anyone saw her distress. Darcy's expression and tone were clear—he had no interest in polite sociality, least of all with her, and he had left little to misinterpretation. His words stung sharply, but she reminded herself that this was a man who had lost his wife and was raising a child alone. He had every right to be indifferent, even cruel, to protect himself and his son.

Perhaps his late wife had been a great beauty with a good deal of accomplishment, she mused, feeling her earlier curiosity settle into a vague sadness. Perhaps no one can measure up to her memory. He must have loved her very much.

The man, it seemed, had chosen a life of cold solitude rather than face those memories, and she was just another passerby in a room full of strangers.

"Lizzy, are you all right?" Charlotte's voice brought her back to the present, and she nodded, managing a small smile.

"Oh, yes. I... I think I'll just step outside for a moment. A bit of fresh air would be nice."

Charlotte looked concerned but nodded, and Elizabeth slipped through the crowd, heading for the doors that led outside. Slipping onto the terrace where the chill air stung her cheeks and gave her a brief reprieve from the noise and the hurt. There, beneath the stars, a rebellious tear slipped down her cheek, the hurt mingling with disappointment for the man she'd briefly imagined him to be.

She brushed away her tears, squaring her shoulders. She would not let one man's opinion—a man who was likely miserable—ruin her evening. Though Darcy's words echoed in her mind, she pushed them away, reminding herself that his disdain had little to do with her, and everything to do with the grief he must carry.

It took several moments for her to compose herself. She smoothed her gown and patted her errant curls into place. When she returned to the assembly, she would hold her head high, determined not to let anything dampen her spirits. She would dance, laugh, and enjoy herself—she would not let Darcy ruin her evening.

Moving inside with a light step, she joined her family and friends, her spirits lifted once more as she pushed aside her momentary hurt. Darcy might be a man of fortune and status, but his opinion mattered little compared to the genuine warmth and enjoyment she felt among her loved ones.

As soon as the words were out of his mouth, Darcy groaned internally.

What on earth possessed you to say that, you fool?

He'd intended only to avoid yet another dance by deflecting Bingley's enthusiasm, but the curt, dismissive words had slipped out, and they had been far louder than he had intended.

Trying to ease his discomfort, he cast a subtle glance in the girl's direction. Elizabeth Bennet—*if Bingley's memory for names can be trusted*—was moving away, her expression guarded. He couldn't help but wonder if she'd caught his careless remark. The thought gnawed at him. She'd been so animated just moments before, her lively eyes and easy smile brightening the room. She reminded him, oddly enough, of Georgiana—spirited, kind, and quietly resilient. And here he was, perhaps the reason for her leaving the hall with such urgency.

His stomach twisted as he watched her slip out through a side door, her expression unreadable.   *She must have heard.*

A pang of shame coursed through him. Miss Elizabeth Bennet—she'd only stood there politely, no doubt willing to dance if asked, and he'd cast her off as though she were nothing. Now, she was likely outside in tears, her evening ruined by his carelessness.

He drew a deep breath. The crowded room around him was suddenly more stifling. Miss Bingley's perfume hung thick in the air, and the noise of the crowd beat a cadence in his brain.

What a fool you are, he thought again, suppressing the urge to excuse himself from the assembly entirely.

Had he wounded her so deeply that she was outside now, sobbing in solitude? The thought made his heart sink. He could picture Georgiana's delicate frame in Elizabeth's place, eyes cast down in hurt and confusion. The image unsettled him even further.

Beyond his guilt lay another worry, albeit a bit less significant . What if she chose to share his words? If Miss Elizabeth spread the story of his slight to her friends and family, he and Bingley would be pariahs before the week was out. He could already hear the voices of those around him, murmuring about his wealth and widowhood—soon enough, they'd add his rudeness to the litany of gossip. "What an severe brother. What a terrible father."

Confound it, he thought bitterly. He half-expected her to storm back into the room and announce his insult to the entire assembly. It would serve him right, after all, to become the subject of public disdain. He braced himself, half-wishing for a chance to apologize—though how, exactly, he would approach her was another matter. The minutes passed and Miss Elizabeth remained absent. His guilt only grew sharper.

His gaze remained fixed on the door she'd gone through, half-contemplating going after her. But then, to his surprise, Miss Elizabeth returned, her head held high, a bright, almost defiant smile on her face as she moved back into the room. Darcy felt a surge of relief mixed with admiration.

She's stronger than I expected.

Before he could fully consider his next move, Mrs. Hurst drifted over, her gaze sweeping the room with a languid disinterest before settling on Darcy with a faint, practiced sigh.

"I must say, Mr. Darcy," she began, feigning a pained smile, "it seems our present company lacks the refinement of Town."

Darcy inclined his head politely, his patience thinning.

Miss Bingley's perfume curdled the air beside him before she appeared at his elbow. "Indeed, Louisa," she said scathingly. She cast a sidelong glance at Darcy, her tone one of carefully cultivated disdain. "There's no one here I'd wish to dance with outside of our own party."

Darcy suppressed a sigh. He knew where this was going, and he supposed it would be easier to oblige them than to continue lingering near them, feeling their expectant gazes. Summoning what little patience he had left, he extended a hand to Mrs. Hurst. "Shall we?"

Mrs. Hurst's mouth curved into a triumphant smile. "Certainly, Mr. Darcy," she replied, dipping her head as she accepted.

As they moved through the steps, Darcy kept the conversation polite and minimal. Mrs. Hurst, thankfully, made no attempts to probe further into his thoughts. Instead, she rambled about fashion and London, seemingly oblivious to the curtness of Darcy's replies.

Each turn of the dance brought Miss Elizabeth back into his view. Thankfully, she had rejoined her friends and seemed cheerfully engaged despite the recent upset. The realization that he'd caused her even a moment of distress continued to gnaw at him, and he could not shake the desire to somehow make amends.

The dance with Mrs. Hurst concluded, and Darcy gave the obligatory bow before stepping back, nearly stepping into Miss Bingley. If he had been any closer, he might have knocked her to the floor. A fleeting look of disappointment crossed her face before being replaced with a simpering smile. She signed meaningfully. Darcy, resigned, extended his hand once more.

"Miss Bingley," he said, "may I have the pleasure of this dance?"

"Oh, Mr. Darcy," she simpered, as if she hadn't anticipated his request at all. "Of course I'll dance with you!"

With his conscience still prickling, Darcy managed a curt nod, letting Miss Bingley take his arm. Her perfume overwhelmed him again as they made their way to the floor. As the steps of the dance brought them close, she leaned in, speaking with affected sweetness.

"Oh, Mr. Darcy, I cannot tell you how much I admire your devotion to your family," she cooed. "To care for both your son and your sister so well… it truly takes a remarkable man."

Darcy resisted the urge to sigh, knowing all too well where this conversation was headed. "It is simply my duty," he replied shortly, hoping to dissuade her.

"But one must truly love children to take on such responsibility!" Miss Bingley continued, undeterred. "I absolutely adore children. Why, I feel as though I know dear Matthew myself."

Darcy's face hardened as he looked down at her. "His name," he corrected coolly, "is Andrew."

"Oh, of course—Andrew," she amended quickly, a nervous laugh escaping her lips as she stumbled slightly in the dance. "How silly of me."

The steps of the dance took them apart and further conversation dwindled.

Darcy's discomfort rose with every step. The collective eyes of the assembly bore into him. Though his polite smile remained fixed, inwardly the agitation festered. Miss Bingley's attempts to ingratiate herself with him felt more contrived with every word, and he wished fervently for the dance to end.

How can I escape? he thought, his patience thinning.

When the last twirl of the dance ended, Darcy offered her a stiff bow and walked away. Her pretense of modesty was as transparent as her motives.

She returned to her brother's side, leaving Darcy free at last, if only for a few moments. As the final dance of the evening was announced, he made a decision. Gathering his courage, he crossed the room to where Elizabeth stood, engaged in conversation. His heartbeat quickened as he approached, the sting of his earlier words fresh in his mind. Bowing formally, he extended his hand.

As he approached, he saw her eyebrows lift slightly. He felt a pang of embarrassment, knowing he deserved her derision, but he couldn't leave the night unfinished without an attempt at reparation.

"Miss Elizabeth," he began, then started again, his tone softened. "Would it... perhaps be tolerable for you to join me for the final dance?" He smiled his most charming smile. "If you can withstand my poor manners, that is."

Elizabeth's expression was unreadable, but he detected a flicker of amusement in her eyes.   There was a pause as she studied him, her hesitation drawing out every ounce of his regret.

Elizabeth's eyes widened as Mr. Darcy approached, bowing with impeccable formality. For a moment, she was stunned into silence. His tall, imposing figure was difficult to ignore, but it was the earnest look in his eyes that surprised her most.

Was he really asking her to dance? And yet… she realized with a jolt that he was. Of all the women in the room, he had come to her, in a tone much softer than when he had denigrated her looks.

Elizabeth felt her pulse quicken as she processed what he was saying. His words weren't quite an apology, but there was unmistakable remorse. She hadn't expected him to even remember the slight, let alone acknowledge it in a way that was almost… humble. Perhaps Mr. Darcy was not as unfeeling as she had first thought.

Could he truly feel sorry? For all he knows, I didn't even hear him.

Her initial impression of him had been so set, so solidly dismissive that she hadn't considered he might try to make amends. Yet here he was, his expression serious, his posture slightly tense, as though he, too, were unsure of her response. With that, she realized something that surprised her even more—*He's nervous.* Mr. Darcy, the proud, aloof figure who had spent the evening looking down upon them all, was showing a glimpse of something almost vulnerable.

She felt herself softening toward him, the instinct to forgive him rising naturally, but just as quickly, another thought stopped her. She could feel her mother's gaze on her from across the room, burning with anticipation. If she accepted, her mother would interpret the dance as a sign of interest—a sign that could fuel endless speculation and mortifying assumptions. The last thing she wanted was to give Mrs. Bennet reason to believe that Mr. Darcy was pursuing her, or she him.

As she wrestled with her decision, her gaze fell on her sister Mary, seated nearby with her book held protectively in front of her. Her face was pinched with quiet disappointment as she watched the couples on the dance floor, and Elizabeth's heart squeezed at the sight. Though Mary tried to appear content, clutching her book as if it were a shield, Elizabeth could see the faint glimmer of tears in her eyes. She had not been asked to dance even once, and her attempt to appear unaffected made Elizabeth's heart ache for her.

Elizabeth's chest tightened, her admiration for Mary's quiet courage mingling with a pang of guilt. She couldn't bear the thought of enjoying this dance while Mary watched, pretending not to mind that no one had asked her.

Turning back to Darcy, she offered him a small, gracious smile. "Thank you, Mr. Darcy, but I must confess, I am rather worn out." She tried to keep her voice light. Her heart felt the disappointment of the words, but she knew it was the right choice.

His eyes widened, and she laughed slightly to herself. *I wonder if anyone has ever turned him down before.*

"However," she continued, glancing meaningfully toward Mary, "my sister Mary is still quite fresh, as she has not yet stood up to dance this evening." She met his gaze with a significant look, hoping he would understand her intent. "If you would be so kind, I'm sure she would be honored."

She held her breath, silently pleading that he might understand the unspoken request, that his earlier apology was not a mere formality but a sign of true decency. *If he is truly kind*, she thought, *he will know what this means.*

Darcy's eyes followed her gaze toward Mary, lingering on her sister's downcast expression and her attempt to hide her disappointment behind her book. Elizabeth could almost see the moment of recognition in his eyes, his proud expression softening with understanding. He turned back to her and nodded; his face somber yet composed.

"Of course, Miss Elizabeth," he replied quietly. "Thank you for the introduction."

Warm relief washed over her as she watched him extend a hand to Mary, who looked up with surprise, her book slipping slightly in her hands. Elizabeth pressed her fingers to her lips, a quiet sense of satisfaction filling her as Darcy bowed before her sister. For a fleeting moment, Mary's eyes lit with astonished delight, and Elizabeth could hardly contain her joy at seeing her sister's quiet longing fulfilled.

Perhaps, she thought, *Mr. Darcy has more heart than I had given him credit for.*

Though his initial insult had hurt, his willingness to turn it into an act of kindness spoke volumes, revealing a depth she had not expected. As she watched him lead Mary to the floor, Elizabeth allowed herself a small, hopeful smile.

Perhaps he is kinder than he seems, and perhaps more so than even he knows.

And, just for tonight, that was all the apology she needed.

Chapter 5

The morning dawned bright and clear, a sharp contrast to the dimly lit assembly hall of the night before. Elizabeth welcomed the cool air as she stepped outside, drawing a deep breath and letting it fill her lungs. The quiet countryside stretched before her, calm and undisturbed, and as she set off down her favorite path, she let her mind wander over the events of the previous evening.

Her thoughts lingered, of course, on Mr. Darcy. His apology—if indeed that dance invitation had been one—was unexpected, and for a man of his evident pride, rather significant. And yet, beneath that initial impression of haughty indifference, she'd glimpsed a depth that intrigued her. She couldn't help wondering what kind of man he truly was.

Perhaps, she mused, his isolation is not merely a product of arrogance but a kind of self-protection. As a widower and father, he was likely weighed down by responsibilities and memories. Still, his behavior had bordered on insulting. What a curious mix of contradictions.

The morning air felt bracing as she continued along the path, her shoes crunching lightly on the frost-covered ground. Beyond Mr. Darcy's unexpected approach, Elizabeth found herself delighted by Mr. Bingley's clear admiration for Jane. His open, friendly manner had charmed nearly everyone in attendance, but his gaze had seldom strayed far from her sister.

To have danced twice! Elizabeth thought happily. For Jane, who so often carried herself with quiet reserve, Mr. Bingley's attention had been a gift well deserved.

A soft rustling in the nearby trees pulled her from her thoughts, and she glanced up, smiling at the cheerful birds hopping between the branches. Her feet led her instinctively along the winding path, and the familiar route provided her with a chance to reflect more deeply, free from interruptions or curious questions. She could almost hear her mother's excited voice chattering on about Mr. Bingley's fortune and the prospects for Jane, and she smiled to herself, grateful to have this peaceful interlude before the day's inevitable conversations began.

As she turned back toward Longbourn, her thoughts shifted to Mary and the gentle pride she'd felt watching her sister on the dance floor with Mr. Darcy. For Mary, who seldom attracted notice or praise, the experience must have felt like a triumph. Elizabeth hoped that her sister would hold onto that moment, allowing herself a bit of confidence and joy. She herself had seen Mr. Darcy's expression soften, had sensed an unexpected kindness beneath his otherwise inscrutable manner. It left her both intrigued and uncertain. Perhaps there was more to him than met the eye, and she found herself wondering, just for a moment, if she might have misjudged him.

By the time she returned, the household was just beginning to stir. Inside, breakfast was being laid out, and her sisters were sleepily making their way to the table as the morning sunlight began to pour through the windows. The Bennet household hummed with its usual energy as the family settled into their day.

Soon after breakfast, news of visitors arrived, and the housemaid announced that the Lucases had come to call, as was their custom the day after an assembly. The Bennet sisters gathered in the parlor, awaiting their visitors, who soon entered with cheerful greetings.

"Oh, what an evening it was!" Lady Lucas exclaimed as soon as she was seated, her face bright with the memory of the assembly. "I don't believe Meryton has ever had such an exciting gathering. To have Mr. Bingley and his party there—it was simply grand!"

Elizabeth exchanged a small smile with Jane, while Mrs. Bennet, ever eager to discuss the night's events, nodded in agreement. "Oh, indeed, Lady Lucas! Mr. Bingley was so kind, so attentive! And Jane... well, everyone noticed he danced with her twice!"

Elizabeth smiled at their enthusiasm, settling herself next to Charlotte. "It was indeed quite an evening. Mr. Bingley and his sisters made quite an impression."

Lady Lucas leaned forward, her expression enthusiastic. "They certainly did! And what a fine match Mr. Bingley would make for your eldest, wouldn't you say, Mrs. Bennet? I daresay there wasn't a woman in the room who didn't wish to be in Jane's place."

Jane blushed, her gaze dropping shyly to her lap. "I'm sure Mr. Bingley was only being polite," she murmured.

"Nonsense, Jane!" Mrs. Bennet insisted. "It was plain to everyone that he favored you. And why shouldn't he? You are by far the prettiest girl in Meryton."

"Indeed, Jane," Charlotte added with a kind smile. "Mr. Bingley could hardly take his eyes off you all evening."

Elizabeth looked at her sister with fond amusement. She knew Jane would never indulge in such hopes too freely, but it was clear that Mr. Bingley's attentions had left an impression.

Mrs. Bennet, delighted by the turn of conversation, continued eagerly. "But you know, it was not only Mr. Bingley who caused a stir. Mary had the great honor of dancing with Mr. Darcy himself!"

All eyes turned to Mary, who had been sitting quietly in her usual corner. She looked up, startled by the sudden attention, her cheeks flushing as she fiddled with the ribbon on her dress.

"And how did you find him?" Lady Lucas asked curiously. "I do remember thinking him to be quite a proud man, to only dance with his party. That is, of course, until he stood up with you."

Mary glanced at Elizabeth for reassurance before replying. "He was… very civil," she said quietly, her tone hesitant. "He didn't say much, but he was polite."

Maria, the younger Lucas daughter, leaned forward, her eyes wide with curiosity. "What did he say, Mary? He hardly spoke to anyone all evening!"

Mary hesitated; her gaze fixed on her lap. "He… did not say very much," she admitted, glancing up with a shy smile. "But he was kind. I think he must have asked me to dance out of politeness."

Lady Lucas beamed, clearly delighted. "Well, it was a kindness, indeed, for he hardly danced with anyone! And I think it speaks very well of him, that he would notice someone as dignified and accomplished as you, Mary."

The color in Mary's cheeks deepened and she offered a small, grateful smile to Elizabeth. "It was actually Elizabeth's doing. I hadn't been asked to dance, and she... she suggested that Mr. Darcy might ask me."

Elizabeth gave her a reassuring smile. "Mr. Darcy is a man of duty, and I hoped he would take the hint," she said lightly. "And I believe he did. He was very respectful, was he not?"

Mary nodded, a small but genuine smile appearing on her face. "Yes. He was."

Charlotte, observing the exchange with her usual perceptiveness, turned to Elizabeth with a smile. "That was very thoughtful of you, Lizzy."

Elizabeth deflected the praise with a small smile, though she couldn't deny the quiet satisfaction she felt at the memory. Watching Mary's hesitant joy had made the evening all the more special, and if Mr. Darcy's actions reflected even a sliver of true kindness, she would not forget it.

The conversation soon turned back to Mr. Bingley and Jane, with Lady Lucas and Mrs. Bennet eagerly discussing his attentions and his prospects as though an engagement were already imminent. But even as the chatter carried on, Elizabeth noticed Mary holding herself with a newfound sense of pride, as if the dance with Mr. Darcy had given her a measure of confidence she rarely displayed.

As the Lucases eventually took their leave, Charlotte gave Elizabeth's hand a warm squeeze. "It was a lovely evening," she murmured, "and I think you made it brighter for more people than you know."

Elizabeth smiled in return, grateful for Charlotte's words. As she watched her friends depart, Elizabeth felt a pleasant warmth settle over her. Last night's slight may have stung, but seeing Mary's joy—and the unexpected kindness from Mr. Darcy—left her feeling as though perhaps the evening had been more satisfying than she'd realized.

~

A fortnight later.

The drawing room at Lucas Lodge was a warm and lively space, with candles glowing against the evening's chill. Elizabeth had arrived with her family, feeling unusually lighthearted, and she greeted each member of the Lucas family with a bright smile.

Looking around the room to take note of the other guests, she noticed Mr. Darcy seated near the far side near the windows. As she observed him from across the room, she sensed something else—a certain melancholy, perhaps even isolation. He was not in conversation, nor did he appear to take much notice of the joviality around him. He sat stiffly, his hands clenched on the armrest, his expression as unreadable as ever.

It was clear to her that he was uncomfortable in large gatherings, and she decided, on impulse, to draw him into the evening rather than avoid him as she had at the assembly. She hesitated for only a moment before stepping further into the room and deliberately passing by the place where he sat.

He looked up briefly and Elizabeth offered a smile. She took a seat near him, pulling her sister Mary into the circle. Darcy looked slightly taken aback, as though not expecting anyone to initiate conversation with him, but he inclined his head politely.

"Mr. Darcy," she said with a warm smile, "I'm afraid we have kept you sitting here in silence for too long. I hope you will not find me overly forward if I try to engage you in conversation?"

Darcy's expression softened ever so slightly, and he inclined his head. "Not at all, Miss Bennet. I welcome the conversation."

She gave him a bright smile, then gestured to her sister Mary, who stood at her side, looking on quietly. "You might remember my sister, Mary."

Darcy acknowledged Mary with a polite nod, and Mary, encouraged by Elizabeth's presence, managed a small smile in return. Elizabeth continued, searching for a topic he might find agreeable.

"I hear you have a younger sister yourself, Mr. Darcy," she began, keeping her tone light yet interested. "What is she like? I find that siblings often have a way of shaping one another's character."

Darcy seemed surprised at her question. His expression softened, and he replied, "Yes, indeed, Miss Bennet. Georgiana is sixteen. "She is… a talented young lady. She enjoys music, particularly the pianoforte, and is an exceptionally skilled player. She is very reserved, though—she finds comfort among those she knows well and is reluctant to engage with strangers. She is, in many ways, the gentlest of souls."

Elizabeth's face brightened. "Oh, how lovely! In that, she reminds me of my own sister Jane." She gestured toward Jane, who was across the room, listening intently to Mr. Bingley's

78

conversation. "Jane, too, is very gentle and shy around strangers. She feels very deeply and does not often show it, but once you know her, you find she has a depth of feeling that is truly admirable. She has an ability to see the best in everyone, even when others may not be quite so deserving."

Darcy's gaze shifted to Jane, as he considered Elizabeth's words. "Your description of Miss Bennet is… surprising," he murmured thoughtfully. "To see kindness in others, and to show it freely, even when one might be judged for it, is an admirable quality."

"Yes," Elizabeth replied, smiling softly. "Jane finds happiness in others' joys, and even if she feels pain, she does not burden others with it." She glanced at Darcy, noting his rapt expression. "Perhaps your sister is much the same?"

Darcy nodded slowly. "In some ways, yes. Georgiana values her friends and family above all else. She prefers to remain with those she trusts and does not easily seek out new acquaintances."

Mary, who had been listening intently, now ventured to add her own thoughts. "It is a great blessing to have a sister like that, Mr. Darcy. I imagine you must be very proud of her accomplishments."

A faint but genuine smile touched Darcy's lips. "I am. Georgiana is indeed a blessing," he said, his voice laced with an unexpected warmth. He looked at Mary, his expression shifting to one of appreciation for her thoughtful words. "And may I say, Miss Mary, that it is refreshing to meet someone who values the quiet virtues."

Mary blushed slightly, casting a grateful glance at Elizabeth, who gave her an encouraging nod and squeezed her hand. Elizabeth sensed that Darcy's attention was having a positive effect on her sister, who seldom received such recognition. She felt a surge of gratitude for Darcy's kindness and for his acknowledgment of qualities that others often overlooked.

Darcy, noticing the fond exchange between them, relaxed further, his gaze warming as he observed the sisterly bond. He hesitated, as though choosing his words carefully, then added, "Georgiana often speaks of longing for... more freedom, yet she finds herself restrained by her shyness. I have tried to encourage her, but..." He trailed off, looking almost self-conscious. "She is happiest in familiar company."

Mary nodded thoughtfully, considering his words deeply. "I think... many people feel a sense of safety in what they know. Perhaps Georgiana will one day find a friend who will encourage her."

As they continued their conversation, Elizabeth observed Darcy closely, noticing the subtle relaxation in his posture, the slight softening in his expression. She felt a quiet satisfaction in helping him feel more at ease, and an almost instinctive impulse to draw him out further. The aloofness she had associated with him was fading, replaced by something gentler.

Elizabeth found herself wondering yet again if his aloofness was not so much from pride as from a kind of protectiveness, an effort to shield both himself and his sister. She probed further, curious to see if he would open up a little more.

"What a fortunate sister she is, to have such a caring brother," Elizabeth observed. "Do you spend much time with her?"

"Whenever I am able," Darcy replied, a slight smile playing on his lips. "I believe it is my duty to support her, especially as our parents are… no longer present."

Elizabeth's heart softened as she watched him speak, his tone quieter now. For a man reputed to be haughty and cold, there was an unexpected warmth in him when he spoke of family. "I can tell that she must mean a great deal to you," she said gently.

Darcy's eyes met hers, and for a brief moment, the aloofness in his gaze faded entirely. "She does, indeed," he replied simply, with an honesty that Elizabeth found unexpectedly moving.

Just then, Sir William Lucas, with his usual enthusiasm, approached them both, clasping his hands together with a pleased expression.

"Ah, Mr. Darcy! Miss Elizabeth!" he exclaimed, gesturing toward the small space near the piano. "Why not take a turn about the room? Or perhaps even a dance? Miss Mary would be more than happy to provide the music, I am sure."

Elizabeth felt her cheeks warm at the suggestion, and she could sense Darcy's hesitation as well. But she noticed Sir William's earnestness and, feeling herself in a particularly good humor, turned to Darcy with a kind smile, willing to diffuse any awkwardness.

"Thank you, Sir William, but I fear I must decline," she said, glancing at Darcy with a look of genuine politeness. "I am rather worn out from the evening already."

Darcy nodded, seeming both relieved and appreciative of her tactful response. "I understand entirely," he replied, a faint smile touching his lips. "Perhaps on a future occasion."

Sir William looked mildly disappointed but undeterred. "Ah, well, a pity indeed," he said, though he winked at Elizabeth with a conspiratorial grin, clearly still holding out hope. "But another time, I'm sure! It is a rare opportunity to see a gentleman and lady of such presence together."

Elizabeth managed a small laugh, feeling only a faint trace of embarrassment as Sir William moved on to join the others. She glanced at Darcy, expecting to find him discomfited, but to her surprise, he seemed more at ease than before.

"Thank you for sparing me," she said to him quietly, her tone light.

Darcy looked at her, an amused glint in his eyes. "I should be the one thanking you, Miss Elizabeth. It seems you are, indeed, quite generous."

Across the room, Charlotte, ever observant, had been watching the interaction with growing interest. She joined the small group and, when Mary asked Mr. Darcy a question about his sister's favorite composers, took advantage of their distraction to lean down and whisper in her friend's ear. "Lizzy, I do believe Mr. Darcy has taken an interest in either you or Mary. Did you see the way he was listening to you just now?"

Elizabeth stifled a laugh. "Oh, Charlotte, you cannot be serious. He merely found himself in company that did not remind him every moment of his wealth or status."

Charlotte raised an eyebrow, unconvinced. "Perhaps," she said lightly, "but that kind of attention is rare, especially from a man such as Mr. Darcy."

Elizabeth merely smiled, though she felt a small thrill at the idea that Darcy might actually enjoy their conversation. Rather than indulge the thought, however, she focused her attention back on Mary and Darcy, steering the topic back toward interests they could share.

As the evening wore on, the conversation turned to music, and Charlotte, always eager to showcase her friend's talent, suggested that Elizabeth play something for the room. "Lizzy, do play for us. I know we would all enjoy it."

"Oh, Charlotte," Elizabeth began, modestly protesting, but seeing the expectant looks from those around her, she relented. "Very well, but only if everyone promises not to judge too harshly!"

Darcy's eyes met hers, and he nodded. "I am certain we would all be delighted, Miss Bennet."

Elizabeth made her way to the pianoforte, her fingers settling on the keys as she thought of a piece that would lighten the mood in the room. She chose something lively, something full of energy, and as she began to play, the notes filled the air with a joyful cadence. She let herself become absorbed in the music, allowing her emotions to flow freely as her fingers danced across the keys.

Darcy found himself transfixed by her performance. There was a radiance in her expression, an honesty in her movements that captivated him completely. Her playing was more than just skill—it was a glimpse into her character, her spirit, and the joy she found in the moment. He could not look away; drawn into the brightness she exuded with every note.

Miss Bingley, who had been watching Darcy's movements the entire evening, scowled at Darcy's rapt attention with growing annoyance. Her eyes narrowed, and she leaned over to him with a practiced sigh.

"I believe I know what you are thinking," she purred near his ear.

Darcy leaned away from her. "I doubt it."

"You are thinking about how absolutely abhorrent it would be to spend your lifetime in company as tedious as this backwoods gathering."

"You are mistaken," he replied coolly, "as it reminds me very much of those in Derbyshire."

She blanched, and he continued, "I was, in fact, meditating on the pleasure of spending time in good conversation with someone whose eyes are so fine."

"Might one inquire who inspired such reflection?"

"Miss Elizabeth Bennet's."

Miss Bingley's mouth fell open, and she gaped at him for a full thirty seconds before sniffing disdainfully and moving away to whisper furtively with her sister. For his part, Darcy returned his focus to the bewitching sight at the piano.

The piece ended, and the room broke into applause. When she finished, Elizabeth turned back to the room, her cheeks flushed with the energy of the performance. Darcy found himself clapping with genuine appreciation. She offered a graceful nod and returned to her seat beside Mary, who whispered a quiet compliment.

Elizabeth felt a lingering warmth from Darcy's reaction, his attention more intense than she'd expected. For once, she saw him not as a distant acquaintance, but as a man capable of deep feeling and care, even if he kept it carefully guarded. She looked at Charlotte, who raised an eyebrow with a knowing smile.

Later that evening, as everyone bid their farewells, Elizabeth gave him a warm smile. "I hope my company this evening was tolerable, Mr. Darcy," she said, a hint of teasing in her voice.

Darcy met her gaze, and for a moment, he seemed on the verge of saying something more personal. He quickly masked his expression, however, offering a polite nod. "More than tolerable, Miss Elizabeth," he replied softly. "It was… exceptional."

Elizabeth felt her heart flutter at his words, her earlier impressions melting further away. She watched him leave, a faint warmth lingering in her heart. She still did not fully understand him, but the evening had left her with an impression she could not quite shake—that perhaps Mr. Darcy, beneath his reserved exterior, was far more than he appeared.

Chapter 6

One week later…

The morning's calm at Longbourn was shattered when the maid brought in a note addressed to Jane, its elegant seal unmistakably from Netherfield. Mrs. Bennet's eyes lit up as soon as she saw it.

"A note from Netherfield! How delightful," she exclaimed, ripping it from Jane's hand before she had a chance to open it.

"I believe, my dear, that letter is not addressed to you," Mr. Bennet said, raising his eyebrow at his wife's behavior. "Unless, of course, you've been lying to me about your name these last twenty years."

Mrs. Bennet huffed and passed the envelope back to her daughter.

Jane opened the note carefully, her cheeks coloring slightly. "It's an invitation to dine at Netherfield this evening," she said, her soft voice pleased. "Miss Bingley has asked that I join their party, as the gentlemen will be dining with the officers."

Mrs. Bennet's hands flew together in excitement. "Oh, Jane, this is perfect! Such an opportunity— if only the men were there! Of course, you must go—and you must look your very best."

Jane smiled gently, though Elizabeth noted the flicker of unease on her face. "Mama, may I take the carriage? It would be the easiest way to arrive without—"

"Nonsense!" Mrs. Bennet interrupted. "The fresh air will do you good. You shall go on horseback—it will give you such a fine, healthy glow when you arrive."

Elizabeth frowned. "Mama, the clouds—"

"Precisely!" Mrs. Bennet interrupted, waving her hand dismissively. "The carriage? Such a waste when the distance is so short. You shall go on horseback, my dear. The exercise will bring color to your cheeks."

Elizabeth set her embroidery aside. "Mama, surely the carriage would be more sensible, especially as the weather looks uncertain."

Mrs. Bennet waved her hand dismissively, ignoring her. "Oh, there will be no rain until much later, I'm sure of it. And if we are so fortunate as to have a downpour, she will need to stay the night."

Elizabeth sighed, biting back her protest. She watched as Jane prepared herself for the visit, her serene demeanor masking the apprehension Elizabeth suspected she felt.

Heavy, grey clouds were gathering in the distance before Jane even set out. The wind picked up as she rode away, her figure silhouetted against the darkening sky. Elizabeth stood by the window, unease creeping into her heart.

Please, Lord, don't let her get caught in the storm.

The Bennet household had not been wrong in expecting Jane's reception at Netherfield to be warm. Upon her arrival, Caroline Bingley greeted her with the customary airs of politeness, though with an undercurrent of superficial charm.

"Miss Bennet, you look quite chilled!" Caroline Bingley exclaimed, ushering the soaked girl toward the hearth. "Whatever possessed you to ride in such weather?"

Jane allowed herself to be guided and attempted a small smile. "It was just beginning to rain when I left, and I thought it would pass."

Georgiana Darcy offered her chair near the fire to Jane with a shy but kind gesture. "Please, you must warm yourself."

Realizing that introductions had not yet occurred, Miss Bingley quickly performed the service as Jane took the seat. Moving across the room, Georgiana observed Jane with wide eyes. Though not yet formally out in society, she had been included in the evening at her brother's suggestion.

Dinner began with an unusual undercurrent. By the time the first course was served, Jane's complexion had paled, and she pressed a hand lightly to her temple. She excused herself from engaging fully in the conversation, her usually soft voice now tinged with fatigue.

"Are you quite well, Miss Bennet?" Caroline asked, her tone light but with a trace of skepticism.

Jane smiled faintly. "I may have caught a chill on my ride over, but I assure you, it is nothing of concern."

Georgiana's brow furrowed, but she remained silent, unsure if it was her place to speak. Caroline, meanwhile, exchanged a quick glance with Mrs. Hurst, her expression unreadable.

By the time dessert was served, Jane's condition had visibly worsened. She attempted to rally, her politeness compelling her to endure the meal, but it was clear to everyone present that she was feeling ill. Georgiana, always observant, noticed Jane's quiet pallor and leaned over to speak softly. "Perhaps you should rest, Miss Bennet. You look unwell."

"Perhaps we ought to call for your carriage— oh, that is right, you rode over," Caroline said with a titter. "Well, perhaps we should send you home in one of ours."

"But it is pouring rain!" Georgiana cried, looking out the window.

Frowning, Caroline looked outside as well, and she was dismayed to discover that she once again could not argue with the younger girl's observation.

"We should wait until the gentlemen arrive to tell us the state of the roads," Mrs. Hurst said, eyeing her sister uneasily. "In the meantime, Miss Bennet, allow us to have a room made up for you."

"I would not wish to be a burden," Jane whispered.

Caroline feigned concern but seemed more interested in maintaining appearances. "Of course, you must rest, Miss Bennet. The journey was no doubt taxing."

Georgiana, however, rose immediately. "Shall I fetch a servant to help her upstairs?" she asked, her voice earnest.

Caroline waved her hand. "That won't be necessary. I'll ensure she is seen to."

Jane was escorted to a guest room, her fever rising as the evening wore on. Mrs. Hurst suggested calling for the apothecary, but Caroline dismissed the idea, insisting that rest would suffice and that Jane would soon be on her way home.

When Darcy, Bingley, and Mr. Hurst returned from dining with the officers, however, they were greeted by a strained atmosphere. Darcy immediately noticed the tension in the air, his gaze narrowing as he took in Caroline's unusually guarded expression.

"What has happened?" Bingley asked, his tone sharp with concern.

Caroline hesitated, then adopted a tone of mild reassurance. "Miss Bennet fell ill during dinner, Charles."

"She seemed fine at first," Mrs. Hurst added, "but she grew pale during dinner and asked to lie down. She was caught in the rain on her way here."

Bingley's expression darkened. "Caught in the rain? Why was she riding in such weather?"

Darcy echoed his friend's frustration. "She rode here in the rain? Surely, she did not choose to do so willingly."

Caroline gave an exaggerated shrug. "Who can say? She should have known better than to come on horseback with such clouds overhead."

"She said it hadn't begun to rain when she left," Mrs. Hurst explained, "but by the time she arrived, it was pouring."

Bingley's rubbed his forehead with a worried hand. "Why would her family send her on horseback in such weather?"

Darcy's jaw tightened, but he said nothing. Instead, he glanced at Mrs. Hurst, who said, "She is resting upstairs now."

Bingley's face darkened with worry. "Why was I not informed sooner?"

"I didn't want to disturb you," Caroline replied smoothly. "There was nothing to be done; she simply needs rest."

Darcy's expression grew stern. "Has the apothecary been called?"

"There was no need," Caroline said, waving off the suggestion. "I've ensured she is comfortable.   Besides, she should be on her way home before the man could even arrive."

"Not in this weather," Darcy replied grimly. "The creek is over its bank; we scarcely made it home ourselves."

Bingley was already halfway to the stairs. "I must see her."

Caroline called after him. "Charles! You cannot simply barge into a lady's room."

Bingley was undeterred, his concern overriding his sister's reassurances. Darcy followed, his mind racing. Though he had spent the evening in good company, the thought of Jane's delicate state unsettled him. He knew well the dangers of an untreated illness, and his sense of duty to Bingley—and, perhaps, to Miss Bennet—urged him to ensure all was being done for her.

As they reached the guest room, they found Georgiana sitting quietly by the bedside, her hands folded neatly in her lap. She looked up as they stood in the opened doorway, her expression a mix of worry and resolve.

"She is feverish," Georgiana said softly. "But she is resting now."

Bingley's face tightened. "It never occurred to me that she would not take a carriage, or even that Caroline would decline to send one," he murmured. "It was foolish of me. I ought to have ensured her safety."

Darcy placed a hand on his friend's shoulder, his voice calm but firm. "What matters now is ensuring she recovers."

Bingley nodded, glancing back at Jane, who stirred faintly in her sleep. Georgiana rose, moving to stand beside her brother. Darcy smiled his approval. "The servants will take care of her," he said, his tone resolute. "She is in safe hands, and we can summon the apothecary in the morning."

Bingley nodded, though his worry was evident. Darcy admired his friend's devotion and suspected that this situation would only deepen Bingley's feelings for Miss Bennet. As the household settled into an uneasy quiet, Darcy found his thoughts lingering on Jane's quiet strength and Bingley's evident attachment, reflecting on how these moments often revealed the truest nature of one's character.

Elizabeth quietly spread jam on her toast at the breakfast table in Longbourn. Jane hadn't come home the night before, and there had been no word from Netherfield. Just then, the maid entered with a folded note. The sight of it immediately caught her attention, and her unease from the previous day increased.

"This arrived from Netherfield, miss," the maid said, placing it into Elizabeth's hands.

Elizabeth broke the seal quickly, her eyes scanning the familiar handwriting. The letter was from Mr. Bingley, written with all the civility and concern she would expect from him, though its contents filled her with worry.

Jane was unwell. A cold, likely brought on by her exposure to the rain, had left her feverish and confined to bed. Mr. Bingley assured her that Jane was being well cared for, but Elizabeth could hardly sit still long enough to finish reading.

"Jane is ill," Elizabeth said aloud, her voice tight with worry. "She is confined to bed at Netherfield."

Mrs. Bennet looked up sharply. "Ill? Oh, nonsense, Lizzy. She is likely a little chilled, that is all. Mr. Bingley and his sisters will care for her—this is no cause for alarm."

Elizabeth's eyes flashed. "Mama, she was caught in the rain yesterday because you insisted she ride. She should not have been exposed like that."

"Now, now," Mrs. Bennet replied, brushing aside her concerns with a wave of her hand. "It is a slight inconvenience at most. This could work to Jane's advantage. Mr. Bingley will see how delicate she is and feel compelled to dote upon her."

Elizabeth pushed her chair back from the table abruptly, her mind already made up. "Whether it is a slight inconvenience or not, I am going to her."

Mrs. Bennet looked startled. "Go to her? But it's so early, Lizzy! Surely they will send word again if she worsens."

Elizabeth shook her head. "I cannot wait for more news. Jane may need me, and I won't be kept from her."

Mrs. Bennet blinked in surprise. "To Netherfield? But how? The carriage is needed today."

"Then I will walk," Elizabeth said firmly.

"Walk?" Mrs. Bennet looked aghast. "You cannot mean to arrive on foot! It is nearly three miles, Lizzy, and the roads will be wet from yesterday's rain."

"Nevertheless, I will go," Elizabeth replied, her tone leaving no room for argument.

Mrs. Bennet opened her mouth to object but was swiftly silenced by the firm resolve in Elizabeth's eyes. Without another word, Elizabeth left the table to prepare for her journey, wrapping herself in a warm cloak and sturdy boots before setting out.

The walk to Netherfield was brisk, the ground still damp beneath her boots, but the sky above was a soft and cloudless blue. Elizabeth's mind raced as she hurried along the winding country road, her thoughts a jumble of worry for Jane and frustration with her mother's flippant attitude.

The countryside was quiet, save for the occasional rustling of leaves or the call of a bird overhead. Normally, Elizabeth would

94

have found the solitude soothing, but today, her focus was fixed entirely on reaching her sister. She quickened her pace, her skirts brushing against the dewy grass as she cut across a meadow to shorten the journey.

The sun rose higher as she walked, warming her back and lifting some of her tension. As she neared Netherfield, the grand house came into view and her heart quickened. Jane needed her, and she hoped fervently that her sister's condition had not worsened.

How ill is Jane, truly? Is the fever a passing inconvenience, or something more serious?

Her heart ached at the thought of her sister suffering alone in a strange house. Jane was the kindest and most selfless person Elizabeth knew, and the idea of her enduring discomfort without family by her side was unbearable. Elizabeth quickened her pace, her boots crunching on the gravel as she reached Netherfield's long drive.

She hesitated only a moment at the steps of Netherfield to assess the state of her damp boots and muddy hemline, then knocked briskly at the front door. She could feel the flush of exertion on her cheeks, but there was no time to worry about her appearance. She knocked firmly on the grand door.

Whilst Elizabeth was making her way to Netherfield, Caroline Bingley was scheming. Her attempts to entice Darcy by speaking to him about his son and spending time with Georgiana were having no effect on the man. Then an idea struck her at breakfast as she sipped her tea.

If I can show my maternal instincts, Mr. Darcy will see how perfectly suited I am for his family, she thought triumphantly. *Surely it is easy to spend time with one. How much trouble can a two-year-old be?*

Caroline rose gracefully from the table and made her way to the nursery, her skirts swishing with purpose. She had seen little of Andrew thus far, though she had been quick to assure Darcy of her fondness for children. Here, at last, was her chance to demonstrate it.

The nursery door was ajar when she arrived, revealing a small, well-kept room filled with sunlight streaming through tall windows. Andrew sat at a low table, a bowl of porridge in front of him, his dark curls catching the light. The nurse sat with him, helping the boy with his breakfast—a bowl of porridge that he was eating with enthusiasm, albeit messily.

"Miss Bingley," the nurse said with a curtsy, surprised by her presence. "Good morning."

"I thought I might spend a little time with young Master Darcy," Caroline replied with an air of authority. "I so adore children. You may take a short reprieve if you wish."

The nurse hesitated, her expression uncertain. "He is still finishing his breakfast, ma'am. He can be rather… spirited."

Caroline dismissed the concern with a wave of her hand. "Nonsense. Run along; I will manage."

The nurse, Rebecca, reluctantly stepped aside, glancing at Andrew, who looked up from his bowl with wide, curious eyes. "I will be just here, ma'am," the nurse said, moving to the doorway but not actually leaving the room.

Caroline frowned. *But having someone who reports to Mr. Darcy be a witness to my maternal instincts…*

"You may stay," she declared in a condescending voice before approaching Andrew, her smile tight but determined. "Hello there, Andrew," she said in the exaggeratedly bright tone adults often adopt when speaking to children. "What a clever little boy you are, eating all by yourself."

Andrew looked up at her, his large eyes blinking slowly, his spoon momentarily forgotten in his hand. Caroline crouched down, her wide smile revealing perfectly even teeth, though her expression veered into something a bit too sharp, almost predatory. The boy's gaze darted to Rebecca for reassurance, but the nurse had stepped back, hesitant to intervene.

"Do you know who I am, little one?" Caroline asked, leaning closer, her tone sugary. "I'm Miss Bingley. Your papa's dear friend."

Andrew shifted uncomfortably, his small legs swinging beneath the chair. He mumbled something unintelligible, his voice barely above a whisper.

Caroline leaned in further, her face now too close to his. "What was that, darling? You'll have to speak up for Miss Bingley."

Her proximity made Andrew pull back instinctively, his spoon clinking against the side of his bowl. Caroline's wide grin faltered for a moment, replaced by an almost irritated gleam in her eyes. "Now, now," she said, reaching out to brush a nonexistent crumb

97

from his sleeve. "No need to be shy with me. We're friends, aren't we?"

Andrew's small body stiffened, his fingers tightening around the spoon. Caroline's hand lingered on his arm, and her relentless cheerfulness began to feel overwhelming, suffocating even. His lip trembled slightly, though he tried to keep his gaze fixed on his bowl.

"You're such a tidy little eater," Caroline continued, though her tone had lost its earlier warmth. "Your father must be so proud of you."

She reached out again, this time brushing his dark curls in what she imagined to be a comforting gesture. But the suddenness of her movements, coupled with her overly enthusiastic tone, seemed to unsettle Andrew further. He jerked back in his chair, his tiny hand jostling the spoon as he did so.

The spoon tipped precariously, and before Caroline could react, a large dollop of porridge splattered across the front of her gown.

Caroline froze, her expression hardening as she looked down at the pale blob staining her silk bodice. For a moment, the room was silent save for the faint rustling of the curtains in the breeze. She stared at the stain in disbelief, then, her lips tightened and her voice sharpened. "Andrew! How careless of you— Look what you've done!"

The boy's small chest rose and fell rapidly, his breaths shallow, the smile faltering on his face. His lip began to quiver as his earlier unease quickly turned into outright panic. Caroline, oblivious to his mounting fear, stood abruptly, brushing at her gown with a look of pure irritation. "S-sorry," he mumbled, his small frame shrinking under her sudden tone.

Caroline's irritation flared. "Sorry? This is not how a gentleman behaves!"

Andrew's eyes filled with tears, but Caroline paid no heed. "This gown is silk!" she hissed, her tone no longer sweet. "Do you have any idea how difficult it is to clean porridge out of silk?"

Her voice, though not loud, carried a cold edge that made Andrew's eyes fill with tears. Before she could say more, Andrew pushed his chair back with a loud scrape. The boy scrambled down from his chair and bolted from the room, sobbing as he ran out into the hall.

"Andrew!" Rebecca called after him, rushing forward to follow. She paused only briefly to glare at Caroline, her normally composed expression now filled with disapproval. "You frightened him."

"He made a mess, of course," Caroline replied dismissively, brushing at her sleeve as though the smudge were an affront to her very existence. "You should be more attentive. The boy has no sense of discipline."

The nurse frowned but said nothing, quickly leaving to find Andrew. Caroline stood frozen for a moment, then looked down at her dress again with a grimace. "Children," she muttered under her breath. "Such little terrors."

She turned on her heel, muttering under her breath as she exited the nursery, all thoughts of demonstrating her maternal instincts forgotten.

Chapter 7

Elizabeth jumped slightly as the door opened, and she was met by the sound of rushing footsteps. A stressed looking footman stood there, momentarily startled by her unexpected and early arrival. He held the door open for her, but before either of them could speak, a small, sobbing figure barreled past Elizabeth with a wail, his little legs moving as fast as they could carry him.

She barely had time to register the child—a boy of no more than two—before he darted down the steps and into the garden. His legs began to move more clumsily, his cries growing louder with each gasping breath. Without thinking, Elizabeth spun around and followed.

"Andrew!" came a voice from inside, but Elizabeth didn't pause to see who had called out. Her instincts propelled her forward, her skirts gathering mud as she hurried after the child, who had already stumbled down the path and made his way onto the soft, wet ground of the lawn.

He didn't get far. Elizabeth gave chase, but he was already slowing, his sobs turning into horrific ragged gasps that sent panic shooting through Elizabeth. His small body wobbled as he clutched at his chest, his breaths coming in short, desperate wheezes.

She reached him just as his knees buckled, and she dropped to the ground without hesitation, gathering him into her arms. Mud soaked into her skirts, but she paid it no mind as she gathered the boy into her arms.

"Shh, little one," she murmured, cradling him against her chest. His face was streaked with tears, and his lips were tinged with blue, his small frame trembling violently. "It's all right. I've got you now."

The boy clung to her, his tiny fingers gripping her as if she were a lifeline. His breaths were erratic, interrupted by hiccupping sobs, but Elizabeth kept her voice calm and steady.

"You're safe now. I promise, you're safe. Just take deep breaths for me. Slow and steady, like this." She demonstrated, inhaling deeply and exhaling slowly, her calm presence encouraging him to mimic her.

His cries slowed, and he looked up at her with wide, tear-filled eyes.

"Breathe with me," she said again softly, rocking him gently. "In… and out. In… and out. That's it, darling, nice and slow."

It took a few moments, but her soothing voice and rhythmic movements began to work, the boy's breathing gradually evening out. His cries subsided into whimpers as he buried his face in her shoulder. Elizabeth adjusted her grip, tucking his head under her chin as she continued to rock him gently, her hand smoothing his curls.

"That's it. You're so brave," she whispered. "You're doing so well."

She began to rub his back gently, still rocking him. "There we go," she said again, her voice tender. "You're safe now. No one's going to hurt you. Can you tell me what happened?"

The boy lifted his tear-streaked face, his brown eyes wide with fear. "Scary…" he mumbled, his small voice trembling. "Lady…"

Elizabeth's brows knitted together as she tried to piece together his words. "A scary lady?" she asked gently. "Did someone frighten you?"

He nodded, his face buried against her shoulder. "Scary," he repeated, his voice breaking, barely above a whisper.

Elizabeth's heart ached at the fear in his tone. "Oh, sweetheart," she said, her voice filled with quiet reassurance. "No one is going to hurt you. I won't let anyone scare you again. I promise."

The boy's small body trembled as he clutched her tighter, his cries softening into a broken plea. "Papa," he whimpered, the word raw and desperate. "Want Papa…"

Elizabeth hugged him closer, her hand continuing to stroke his back in comforting circles. "I'll help you find your Papa," she promised, her voice resolute. "You're not alone. We'll find him together."

The boy's breathing steadied further, his little body relaxing slightly in her arms as she rocked him on the damp ground. His tears slowed as he leaned into her, exhausted from his outburst. Elizabeth stayed where she was, sitting on the damp ground with the child in her arms, oblivious to the mud staining her cloak and gown. All that mattered was the trembling boy who had found refuge in her embrace.

"Do you feel a bit better now?" she asked after a few moments, tilting her head to look into his eyes. He nodded hesitantly, clutching her collar with one hand as though afraid to let go.

"Good," she said softly, planting a reassuring kiss on his forehead. "We'll get you inside, warm and safe. Then we'll find your Papa, all right?"

Andrew gave another tiny nod, his sobs fading into sniffles as he leaned against her shoulder, his little arms wrapping around her neck.

The sound of hurried footsteps approached from the direction of the house, and Elizabeth looked up, her arms still wrapped protectively around the child. She didn't know who would arrive first—his Papa, or someone to explain what had happened—but one thing was certain: she wasn't letting go until the boy was safe.

"Andrew," a deep voice came from just behind them. She shifted slightly, preparing to rise as the steps grew closer, but for the moment, she stayed rooted to the ground, holding the boy close as he clung to her trustingly. Whatever had frightened him, she vowed, would not trouble him again—not while she was there to protect him.

Darcy had just reached the door to his chambers, the faint smell of leather and polish from his riding boots still clinging to him after the brisk morning ride with Bingley. He glanced down the hall, prepared to enter and enjoy a brief moment of quiet before the household's bustle inevitably intruded.

Before he could open the door, the sound of running footsteps caught his attention. He turned sharply to see Rebecca, Andrew's nurse, rushing past the entrance of the hallway. Her face was pale, her expression frantic as she called out, "Andrew! Andrew, where are you?"

Darcy's stomach twisted. "Rebecca," he called out sharply, his long strides taking him down the hallway of the guest wing to the top of the stairs. "What has happened?"

Rebecca froze mid-step, her wide eyes meeting his as she tried to catch her breath. "Master Andrew, sir," she stammered. "He... he was frightened in the nursery and ran off. I thought he might go to your room, sir, but then I saw him just now as he ran out front door."

Darcy's heart clenched. "The front door?" he repeated, his voice tight.

"Yes, sir," Rebecca said, her voice on the edge of hysteria, the guilt and worry plain in her tone. "I was going to—"

But Darcy didn't wait to hear more. The realization of what the cold air could do to Andrew's already fragile lungs sent him sprinting down the hall and toward the stairs. His boots echoed loudly on the wooden floors as he descended, his mind racing with images of Andrew out in the chill, struggling to breathe. Panic surged through him, a rare but undeniable force that drove him faster than he thought possible.

The moment he burst through the front doors, his eyes darted across the grounds. For one terrifying second, he saw nothing— he saw nothing but the sprawling lawn and the distant line of trees spread out before him. But then a sight stopped him in his tracks.

Elizabeth Bennet.

She was sitting on the muddy ground a short distance from the house, her skirts dark with dirt and her hair slightly disheveled. In her arms was Andrew, his small body curled against her as she held him close. The boy's face was hidden, but his tiny fists clutched her cloak, his sobs faintly audible.

But it wasn't her unexpected presence that struck him most—it was the way she held his son. Andrew was enveloped in her embrace, his face buried against her chest as she rocked him gently, her voice soft and soothing. She was completely unaware of the mud staining her clothes, her entire focus on the small boy trembling in her cradled arms.

Darcy's breath caught, his worry momentarily mingling with astonishment. Elizabeth Bennet—of all people—was the last person he had expected to see at Netherfield, let alone in such a scene. There was something almost otherworldly about her in that moment, her care and tenderness wrapping around his son like a shield.

Shaking himself from his daze, he rushed forward. "Andrew!" he called, his voice filled with both relief and urgency.

Elizabeth's head snapped up at the sound of his voice, her expression startled but calm. Andrew stirred, his small frame still trembling as he turned slightly toward the familiar voice.

"Papa," the boy whimpered, his voice raw and hoarse.

Darcy crossed the distance between them in seconds, dropping to his knees beside Elizabeth and reaching out for his son. "Andrew," he murmured, less panicked than before. "It's all right, my boy. I'm here."

Elizabeth relaxed, allowing Darcy to take the boy into his arms, conscious of the way that Andrew clung to him, his small body still trembling, though his cries had become more hushed. Darcy held him close, his hand smoothing over the child's dark curls. He glanced at Elizabeth, his gratitude evident in his expression.

"He was terrified," Elizabeth said quietly. "He could barely breathe when I found him."

Darcy glanced at her, his gratitude mingling with something deeper—something he couldn't quite name. "Thank you," he said, his voice low. "You've done more than I could have asked."

Elizabeth shook her head firmly. "There's no need, Mr. Darcy. He needed someone, and I was here."

Darcy looked down at his son and saw Elizabeth's hands still hovering protectively. He noticed the way her eyes lingered on Andrew, her worry for the boy clear even now. As his gaze lingered on her, he took in her mud-streaked skirts and the faint flush on her cheeks from the cold.

"Do you know what frightened him?" Darcy asked, his attention momentarily shifting back to his son.

Elizabeth shook her head. "He only said something about a 'scary lady,' but I couldn't understand much more than that. He was too upset to explain."

Darcy's jaw tightened. *Miss Bingley. It had to be.* He had wondered at her sudden exit from breakfast. Rebecca's frustrated glance up the stairs as she raced down the stairs after Andrew, followed by Caroline's cool descent, seemed to confirm his suspicions. He suppressed the sudden surge of rage in his chest. He would address that matter soon enough. For now, his only concern was Andrew's well-being.

"We must get him inside. He lungs cannot handle the cold air for long," Darcy said, standing. Andrew still clung tightly to him. He glanced back at Elizabeth, his tone softening. "And you must come in as well. You look chilled."

Elizabeth hesitated but finally nodded. "Thank you. I originally came to inquire after my sister, but I'd like to be certain that Andrew is well."

Darcy led the way back toward the house, Andrew nestled securely in his arms. His mind swirled with emotions—relief, gratitude, and a growing curiosity about the woman who had so selflessly come to his son's aid. Elizabeth Bennet, it seemed, was far more than she appeared, and he could not shake the image of her on the ground, her arms wrapped protectively around his son.

It was a sight that would stay with him for much longer than he cared to admit.

Elizabeth followed the maid through the grand halls of Netherfield, her mind filled with worry over Jane. The corridors were quiet, except for the faint creak of the floorboards beneath her feet. She clutched her cloak tightly, her boots still damp from her walk. The maid led her to a room at the far end of the corridor, pausing just long enough to knock lightly before opening the door. Elizabeth squared her shoulders, preparing herself for whatever condition she might find her sister in.

The maid motioned for her to enter, and Elizabeth stepped inside. Her breath caught as her gaze fell on Jane, who lay asleep in a large bed, her face pale and her breathing faint. Seated in a chair near the bedside was a young woman with strikingly delicate features. She sat up straight in her chair, her small embroidery hoop clenched in tense fingers. Her blue eyes, the exact shade of Mr. Darcy's, were wide and startled. Her features unmistakably familiar, though soft and feminine where his were strong and masculine.

There was no one else in the room, and Elizabeth hesitated for a moment before stepping forward with a warm smile. "Forgive my intrusion. I am Elizabeth Bennet, Jane's sister. Unless I am very much mistaken, you must be Miss Darcy."

The young woman's eyes widened even more, her shyness palpable. She hesitated, as if uncertain whether to respond. "I—yes, I am," she replied with a voice barely above a whisper. "Georgiana Darcy."

Elizabeth's smile widened. "Then it seems I have guessed correctly. How fortunate that we have been spared the awkwardness of guessing each other's names for too long. I suppose that means we can skip the formalities altogether, don't you think?"

A flicker of a smile appeared on Georgiana's lips, though her shyness was still evident. "It is a pleasure to meet you, Miss Elizabeth," she said, her gaze dropping briefly to her hands.

"The pleasure is mine," Elizabeth replied. "And I must thank you for sitting with my sister. It is a great comfort to know she has been in good company."

Georgiana shook her head quickly. "No, not at all," she said, glancing nervously at Jane. "I was only sitting with Miss Bennet while she rested. She seemed so unwell, and I thought she should not be left alone."

Elizabeth's heart warmed. "That was very kind of you," she said fervently. "Jane is fortunate to have such considerate company."

Georgiana glanced down, her shyness making it difficult to meet Elizabeth's gaze. "I… I only wished to help," she murmured.

Elizabeth decided to change the subject, sensing that the girl might feel more comfortable discussing something less personal. "Do you often sit with unwell guests… or is this a special case?" she asked lightly, her tone teasing.

A small smile flickered across Georgiana's lips. "I think this may be my first time," she admitted, her voice less hesitant.

"Well, I must say, you are doing an excellent job," Elizabeth replied. "Jane looks quite peaceful, and I am sure your presence has been a great comfort to her."

Georgiana's blush deepened, and she glanced toward the door. She stood, smoothing her gown nervously. "I should leave you now. I am sure you would prefer to be alone."

"You are welcome to stay," Elizabeth offered sincerely. "I would not mind your company in the least."

But Georgiana shook her head, her shyness clearly getting the better of her. "Thank you, but I believe she would prefer her sister's company. If you need anything, please let one of the maids know."

Elizabeth didn't press her, recognizing the young woman's shyness and respecting her need for space. "Then I shall see you again soon, Miss Darcy," she said with a small curtsy.

Georgiana hesitated, her lips parting slightly as if to respond, then she simply nodded and slipped quietly from the room.

Once alone, Elizabeth turned her full attention to Jane. She sat at her sister's bedside and reached out to brush her sister's damp curls away from her face. Jane stirred slightly but did not wake. Elizabeth pressed her palm to Jane's forehead— the heat radiating from her skin made Elizabeth's stomach twist with worry.

She's burning up.

"Jane," she murmured softly, but her sister did not stir.

Elizabeth quickly rose and went to the door, calling for the maid. The young woman who had shown her in appeared promptly, curtsying.

"Please ask Mr. Bingley if Mr. Jones might be summoned," Elizabeth said firmly, though her tone remained polite. "My sister's fever seems quite high, and I would feel better if the apothecary could attend her."

The maid curtsied. "Of course, miss. I shall inform Mr. Bingley immediately."

The door closed again, and Elizabeth returned to Jane's side, taking her sister's hand gently in her own. She spoke softly, hoping her voice might reach Jane even in her restless sleep.

"Rest, dearest Jane," she whispered. "Help is on the way."

Elizabeth remained by her sister's side; her worry tempered only slightly by the knowledge that Mr. Jones would soon arrive. For now, she could do little but keep vigil, her hand resting lightly over Jane's as she waited.

～

After what seemed like an eternity, Mr. Jones arrived, his leather bag in hand. His expression calm, yet focused, as he stepped into the room.

"Miss Elizabeth," he said, nodding politely. "I came as quickly as I could. Mr. Bingley informed me of your sister's condition."

"Thank you for coming, Mr. Jones," said Elizabeth, unable to keep the worry from her voice. "Jane has been feverish since last night when she arrived on horseback in the rain, and she seems no better today, according to the maid. Her breathing is shallow, and she hasn't woken since I arrived."

Mr. Jones set his bag on the bedside table and opened it with practiced efficiency. "Let us see what can be done," he said, moving to Jane's side. He placed a hand lightly on her forehead, his expression tightening.

"Her fever is indeed quite high," he said after a moment. "It's fortunate she's been resting, but she'll need close care for the next few days. I'll prepare something to help lower the fever and ease her discomfort."

He retrieved a small vial and a packet of dried herbs from his bag, carefully measuring a dose into a glass of water that a maid had brought at Elizabeth's request. "Has she been drinking anything?"

111

Elizabeth shook her head. "The maid tells me she has been too weak to take more than a few sips of water."

"It's imperative she takes regular fluids," he explained. "She'll need to remain here until she can move about under her own strength—traveling now would only worsen her condition."

Elizabeth's stomach sank at the news, though she nodded in agreement. They roused Jane enough to coax the medicine past her lips. Her eyes fluttered briefly before closing again, but she swallowed the liquid. Elizabeth felt a small measure of relief.

Mr. Jones turned to pack his bag. "I'll return tomorrow to check on her progress," he said. "Keep her warm but not overheated and try to encourage her to take some bone broth when she stirs. With care, I expect the fever to break within a couple of days."

Elizabeth's hands tightened on her sister's, but she nodded. "Thank you," she said softly.

Once the apothecary had departed, Elizabeth returned to her seat by Jane's bedside. The news that they would need to stay at Netherfield for several more days left Elizabeth with mixed feelings. She was deeply grateful for Bingleys' hospitality and Mr. Jones's attentiveness, but the idea of remaining under the same roof as Mr. Darcy gave her pause, for a reason she could not name.

She gazed down at Jane and resolved to set aside her discomfort. Her sister's well-being was paramount, and Elizabeth would endure anything to ensure Jane's recovery. Taking Jane's hand in her own, she whispered, "Rest well, dear Jane. We will weather this together."

And with that, Elizabeth settled into her chair, preparing herself for the days ahead.

Chapter 8

The following morning, Jane's fever had still not broken. Elizabeth sent a note to her mother to request her presence at Netherfield to see Jane, though whether her true motive was to get give Jane the care of her mother, or to force her mother to witness the consequences of her scheming was unknown to even Elizabeth herself.

Thus summoned, Mrs. Bennet descended upon the grand estate like a hurricane, her bonnet slightly askew from the brisk carriage ride and her expression painted with dramatic concern. Mary, Kitty, and Lydia flocked into the house behind her and dutifully followed their mother up the stairs.

"Oh, my poor, dear Jane!" Mrs. Bennet cried at the sight of her daughter. She rushed to her bedside. "Oh, look at you, pale as a ghost! I knew the rain would do you harm, but of course, you insisted on going, didn't you?"

Elizabeth suppressed the urge to remind her mother whose idea it had been for Jane to ride on horseback in the rain. Instead, she stepped forward. "Mama, please keep your voice down. Jane is resting."

Mrs. Bennet ignored her, fussing over Jane with exaggerated gestures. "My poor girl. To think of you here, all alone, without your family! But what wonderful care you must be receiving at Netherfield. Such kind and generous hosts!"

Elizabeth sighed softly. "Jane has been well attended to, Mama. Mr. Jones saw her yesterday and advised that she remain here until she is stronger."

Mrs. Bennet's face immediately brightened. "Oh, yes, of course. She must stay! It would be unthinkable to move her now. How fortunate we are to have such generous hosts as the Bingleys. They must be utterly devoted to ensuring Jane's comfort."

Elizabeth's stomach tightened as Mrs. Bennet's voice grew louder, clearly meant to be overheard by anyone passing in the hall. "Mama, I think we should leave Jane to rest."

After no small amount of urging, Mrs. Bennet eventually left Jane's room and made her way back down the stairs. To Elizabeth's horror, however, instead of going out to the carriage, Mrs. Bennet asked a footman to direct her to Mr. Bingley.

Mrs. Bennet ushered her four daughters into the drawing room and Elizabeth groaned internally. Mr. Bingley was seated near the fireplace, conversing politely with Caroline and Louisa. His good-natured expression shifted slightly when Mrs. Bennet entered the room, her presence filling it immediately with bustling energy.

"Ah, Mr. Bingley!" Mrs. Bennet exclaimed, her voice bright with forced cheerfulness. "How kind it is of you to host my dear Jane during her illness. I must say, it gives me such comfort to know she is under such excellent care."

Mr. Bingley, ever the gentleman, rose to greet her. "It is no trouble at all, Mrs. Bennet. Miss Bennet is a delightful guest, and we are happy to provide whatever she needs to recover fully."

Mrs. Bennet's face lit with satisfaction, and she clasped her hands together as if his words were the highest compliment. "Well, of course, Jane is the sweetest, most obliging creature one could ever meet! Everyone who knows her agrees. And so beautiful, too! Why, I often say that there is no one in all of Hertfordshire who can match her grace and loveliness."

Caroline Bingley, seated primly on a settee, exchanged a significant glance with her sister. Mr. Bingley smiled faintly as Mrs. Bennet continued her effusive praise and answered amicably. "Miss Bennet is certainly a very fine lady."

Lydia and Kitty, tired of their mother's monologue, began to fidget. Lydia, always the boldest, stepped forward. "Mr. Bingley, please tell me you will keep your promise to host a ball here at Netherfield. It would be such fun, don't you think?"

"Yes, a ball!" Kitty chimed in, her eyes bright. "The ballroom must be wonderful. Have you danced here yet, Mr. Bingley?"

Mr. Bingley laughed, though he looked a bit caught off guard. "I have not had the pleasure yet. I confess, I have been rather preoccupied since arriving. However, a gentleman always keeps his word, and as soon as your sister has recovered, I shall allow you to name the day of the ball."

Mrs. Bennet clasped her hands to her bosom, her expression eager. "Oh, what a splendid idea! A ball would be delightful—just the thing to raise everyone's spirits."

Mr. Bingley, now thoroughly flustered, opened his mouth to respond, but Caroline interjected smoothly, her tone icy. "A ball is quite an undertaking, Mrs. Bennet. And with Miss Bennet's health still uncertain, perhaps such plans would be premature."

Mrs. Bennet waved a dismissive hand. "Oh, nonsense, Miss Bingley. Jane will recover quickly, I am sure of it. A young lady in love always does, does she not?"

Elizabeth, who had just entered the room to observe the unfolding scene, felt her cheeks burn. She met Bingley's embarrassed gaze from across the room and offered him a small, apologetic smile.

Mary, sensing the visit would last for some time, found a chair by the window, sighed and opened her book, muttering something about the frivolity of balls. Her voice was lost amid Lydia's continued pleas and Kitty's giggles, already imagining themselves at the center of the festivities.

As Mrs. Bennet carried on, oblivious to the tension she was creating, Elizabeth sank into a chair near the back of the room, wishing, not for the first time, that her family's exuberance could be tempered. Still, she couldn't help but admire Bingley's patience as he navigated the chaos with surprising grace, what with Mrs. Bennet taking every opportunity to further extol Jane's virtues and beauty.

After a tea and half an hour of exclamations and giggles, Mrs. Bennet gathered her daughters to leave. The drawing room seemed to breathe a collective sigh of relief. Elizabeth was only grateful that Miss Darcy and her brother were not present to witness the spectacle.

Elizabeth pressed her fingers to her temple, silently vowing to herself to speak with Jane about their mother's conduct once her sister was well enough to laugh about it. She could only hope that her mother's enthusiasm hadn't entirely worn out the Bingleys' goodwill.

~

The day passed much as it had before, only Georgiana spent a fair amount of time sitting with Jane and Elizabeth. Caroline and Mrs. Hurst visited for a bit as well, causing no small amount of consternation for Elizabeth. Fortunately, they soon became weary of the sickroom and left to discover other sources of entertainment.

As Jane slept, Elizabeth and Georgiana remained by the bedside, falling into silence without the monologues of Caroline and Mrs. Hurst vying for dominance. The two remaining ladies were quiet for a few moments, with Georgiana's hands folded neatly in her lap.

Elizabeth watched her for a moment, taking in the younger woman's quiet demeanor.

"You must find this all terribly dull," Elizabeth said, breaking the silence.

Georgiana looked up, startled by the address. "Oh, no," she said quickly, her cheeks coloring. "I only wish to be of help."

Elizabeth smiled warmly. "You are helping, Miss Darcy. Your presence is most welcome. But surely there are more pleasant ways for you to spend your day?"

Georgiana hesitated, her gaze dropping to her hands. "I do not mind," she said. "Your sister seems… very kind. I imagine she would do the same for me."

Elizabeth's heart softened at the quiet sincerity in Georgiana's voice. "She would," Elizabeth agreed. "Jane is the kindest soul I know. But I suspect you are much the same."

Georgiana's blush deepened. "I—I am not so certain of that."

"Then I shall be certain for you," Elizabeth said, her tone teasing but kind. She leaned forward slightly, lowering her voice as though sharing a great secret. "You are quite unlike your brother, you know."

Georgiana's eyes widened in alarm. "Do you not like him?" she asked, her voice barely above a whisper.

Elizabeth laughed softly, waving a hand to dismiss the worry. "Oh, I like him well enough—though I confess, I did not at first. But he is… formidable, isn't he? You, on the other hand, are much more approachable."

Georgiana's lips curved into a tentative smile. "He is very protective," she said quietly. "Of me, and of Andrew."

"I can see that," Elizabeth replied. "And I imagine it must be a comfort to you, having someone so steadfast."

Georgiana nodded slowly. "It is, Miss Elizabeth," she admitted.

Elizabeth tilted her head, her smile widening. "You must call me Elizabeth. After all, we are practically comrades now, having survived a visit from the Bingley sisters."

A faint laugh escaped Georgiana, though she quickly pressed her lips together, as if afraid she had overstepped.

"Ah, there it is," Elizabeth teased gently. "A smile suits you far better than that serious expression you've been wearing all day."

Georgiana looked down at her hands, her blush deepening. "I suppose I am not used to... to conversing so freely."

Elizabeth leaned back slightly, her tone encouraging. "And why is that, I wonder? Surely you have many acquaintances in London who are eager to engage you in conversation."

Georgiana hesitated, her fingers fidgeting. "I—I am not very good with strangers," she confessed. "I often find it difficult to know what to say."

Elizabeth's heart softened at the girl's vulnerability. "I understand," she said. "But you need not worry about that with me. I promise I won't bite."

This earned another small laugh from Georgiana, and Elizabeth seized the opportunity to shift the conversation to more neutral ground.

"Tell me, what do you enjoy, Miss Darcy? Do you share your brother's love of reading, perhaps?"

Georgiana nodded, her expression brightening slightly. "Oh, yes. I enjoy novels and poetry especially. And music—I adore playing my pianoforte."

Elizabeth's eyes lit up. "Music! That is something we share. Jane is the more accomplished singer, but I do enjoy playing."

Georgiana's gaze lifted slightly, a hint of curiosity in her eyes. "Do you play often?"

"Not as often as I would like," Elizabeth admitted. "Our piano is not the best, and it is difficult to find time with so many distractions at home. But I am certain you must play beautifully, with access to the finest instruments and teachers."

Georgiana's blush returned, but this time there was a spark of pride in her modest response. "I... I do enjoy it very much," she said. "It helps me feel calm."

Elizabeth nodded thoughtfully. "It is a wonderful escape, isn't it? Music has a way of expressing what words cannot."

Georgiana's smile was shy but genuine. "Yes, exactly."

Encouraged, Elizabeth leaned forward slightly. "What about other pursuits? Do you ride or draw, perhaps?"

"I do ride," Georgiana said, her voice gaining confidence. "Though I prefer quiet rides in the countryside. Large gatherings or hunts are not quite to my taste. Sometimes, I wish I could be... stronger on my own. Like you are." Her face flushed a deep red at this admission, and she looked as if she had not quite meant to voice her thoughts aloud.

Elizabeth tilted her head, studying the girl with a mixture of affection and curiosity. "You think me strong?"

"Oh, yes," Georgiana said earnestly. "To care for your sister as you do, and to speak so easily with everyone. My brother told me how popular you were the other night at a neighbor's home. I could never..." She trailed off, her shyness reasserting itself.

Elizabeth reached out, resting a hand on Georgiana's arm. "Strength comes in many forms, Miss Darcy," she encouraged. "I suspect you have more of it than you realize. After all, it takes courage to sit here with a stranger, doesn't it, even when the hostess has left?"

Georgiana looked thoughtful. "I suppose it does," she said at last.

"Indeed, it does," Elizabeth replied with a smile. "And the more you practice, the easier it becomes. Before you know it, you'll be engaging in lively debates and charming everyone you meet."

Georgiana laughed softly, the sound delicate but genuine. "I'm not sure I shall ever manage that," she said, though there was a hint of hope in her voice.

"You will," Elizabeth assured her. "And until then, you have a friend in me. That is, if you'll allow it."

Georgiana's eyes met Elizabeth's, her expression brightening. "I should like that very much," she said softly.

As their conversation continued, Elizabeth found herself charmed by the girl's quiet intelligence and gentle nature. She spoke sparingly, but when she did, her words were thoughtful and earnest. By the time the afternoon light began to wane, Georgiana had even asked Elizabeth a question or two, her curiosity slowly overtaking her shyness.

The dinner bell gonged, and Georgiana rose. "Thank you, Miss Elizabeth," she said quietly as she opened the door to leave. "I... I have enjoyed speaking with you."

Elizabeth smiled warmly. "As have I, Miss Darcy. You are always welcome to join me, whether Jane is awake or not."

Georgiana's lips curved in a small, genuine smile, and she dipped her head in farewell before slipping quietly from the room.

Elizabeth watched her go, her thoughts lingering on the girl's shy but kindhearted demeanor. *So much like Jane,* she mused with a pang of fondness. She hoped Georgiana would continue to open up in the days to come, for there was clearly a bright and thoughtful mind behind her reserved exterior.

The evening at Netherfield unfolded in its usual manner after dinner, the drawing room warm with the glow of the fire and the hum of conversation. Darcy sat at a writing desk, focused intently on a letter. Caroline, having heard that Darcy did not enjoy cards, had rebuffed her brother-in-law's request to play whist or loo. Instead, she hovered nearby, her eyes fixed on Darcy with calculated intent.

"Another letter to dear Colonel Fitzwilliam?" Caroline asked in a cloying manner. "You write to him so often. What must you discuss so regularly, Mr. Darcy?"

Darcy glanced up briefly, his expression impassive. "Family matters, Miss Bingley. And current events."

Caroline leaned forward slightly, her gaze intent. "How thrilling it must be to have a cousin serving in the army. Do you find his letters... enlightening?"

Across the room, Elizabeth, seated beside Jane, caught the exchange and couldn't help but interject. "Colonel Fitzwilliam serves in the Peninsular Campaign, does he not, Mr. Darcy?" she asked, her voice carrying just enough curiosity to draw his attention. "I believe that is what your sister mentioned earlier today."

Darcy looked up, his expression softening slightly as he turned to her. "Indeed, Miss Elizabeth. He is with Wellington's forces."

Elizabeth smiled faintly. "The progress in the campaign has been notable. I read recently of the successful siege of Ciudad Rodrigo and Wellington's clever use of supply lines to outmaneuver the French. Your cousin must be quite proud to serve under such leadership."

Darcy's gaze shifted to Elizabeth, surprise flickering in his eyes. "You are well-versed in military matters, Miss Elizabeth."

Elizabeth smiled. "Only as much as one can be through letters and newspapers, Mr. Darcy. My father often shares accounts of the campaigns, and I find them fascinating. The intricacies of strategy and the courage of the soldiers are remarkable."

Caroline's laughter was sharp and forced. "How... unusual for a lady to take such interest in such matters. I confess, I prefer to leave war and politics to the gentlemen."

Elizabeth turned to Caroline, her smile undimmed. "Perhaps, Miss Bingley. I confess it is unusual, but I also find it broadens the mind more than a fashion magazine would."

Caroline's face turned a brilliant shade of red that clashed with her hair. Darcy returned his attention to his letter, though Elizabeth noticed the faintest upward twitch of his lips.

124

In an effort to redirect the conversations, Mrs. Hurst asked, "Would anyone like music?"

Caroline's expression brightened. "Oh, Georgiana, you must play. Mr. Darcy, you will not object to indulging your sister's talent, I am sure."

The young girl looked towards her brother shyly. Darcy nodded, his expression softening as Georgiana took her place at the piano. The first notes filled the room, her delicate fingers gliding over the keys to produce a lively reel that drew murmurs of approval from the room.

Darcy, seated not far from the piano, rose unexpectedly and approached Elizabeth, who had been quietly enjoying the music from her chair.

"Miss Elizabeth," he said, his voice formal but warm. "Would you honor me with this dance?"

Elizabeth looked up, startled but amused. She tilted her head, studying him with a twinkle in her eye. "A reel, Mr. Darcy? Here in the drawing room?"

"Why not?" he replied, his voice tinged with humor.

Elizabeth laughed, shaking her head. "I see what you're doing, Mr. Darcy. You believe another dance will serve as an apology for the last time. Truly, there is no need. I accepted your apology weeks ago; you need not feel obligated to make amends at every opportunity."

Darcy's eyes glinted. "And yet, I find myself eager to prove I can be tolerable company."

Elizabeth smiled but rose from her seat, shaking her head again. "I fear, sir, that my energy is spent this evening. You shall have to remain content with your other successes, for now."

Darcy inclined his head with a faint smile. "Then I must remain patient—until another time."

As Elizabeth excused herself from the room to check on Jane, Darcy's gaze lingered for a moment. The lively exchange left him with an unfamiliar sense of ease. He turned back toward Georgiana, whose music filled the room with soft, measured notes, his appreciation for her quiet bravery mingling with his thoughts of Elizabeth.

The evening had unfolded in ways he had not anticipated, and as he watched his sister's fingers glide over the keys, Darcy allowed himself a rare moment of satisfaction. For once, the company—and the unexpected conversations—had been more than tolerable; they had been quietly extraordinary.

Chapter 9

The third day of Elizabeth's stay at Netherfield passed much the same as the second, only this time she was encouraged by Jane and Georgiana to go for a walk in the shrubbery.

"You must be greatly missing your daily constitutional, Lizzy," Jane said in a slightly hoarse voice the next morning. "My fever is gone, and I have dear Miss Darcy and a maid here with me. I shall be quite well for half an hour."

"I swear that if anything amiss occurs, I will send a maid for Mrs. Annesley and you immediately," Georgiana promised.

The young girl's companion had visited earlier that morning, and her motherly nature was in stark contrast to Mrs. Bennet's visit. Mrs. Annesley had nursed her late husband through many an illness, she said, and would be happy to be of any assistance if requested.

"Go, Lizzy," Jane urged. "Else you will be much too cross for me to wish to be in your company this afternoon." She softened her teasing with a gentle smile.

Georgiana's eyes widened, but Elizabeth laughed and agreed, collecting her bonnet and cloak before heading down the stairs and outside. The air was unseasonably warm, and the golden sunlight filtering through the trees made her surroundings feel inviting. The shrubbery paths were well-kept and offered an ideal setting for clearing her mind.

Elizabeth turned a corner and caught sight of Andrew Darcy, accompanied by a young woman she surmised to be his nurse holding a small basket. Andrew toddled ahead of her, clutching a toy horse in one hand. His laughter rang out as he bent down to examine a patch of flowers.

"Good morning," Elizabeth greeted with a smile. "It's lovely to see Master Andrew enjoying himself in the warm air."

The girl looked up from her charge, startled, then relaxed when she saw Elizabeth. "Yes, it is, miss."

"My name is Elizabeth Bennet. I don't believe I've had the pleasure?"

Rebecca bobbed a curtsy. "My name is Rebecca; I'm the boy's nanny."

"He seems much happier than the last time we encountered one another," Elizabeth remarked. "He was quite upset when I came across him."

Rebecca shivered slightly. "Yes, that was horrible. Thankfully, young ones recover quickly, and the fine weather has done wonders for him. He's been much less fretful today."

Elizabeth crouched down to Andrew's level, her expression warm. "And how are you, Master Andrew? Do you enjoy being outside?"

Andrew looked up at her, his wide eyes curious. He nodded shyly, holding up his toy horse.

"What a fine horse you have," Elizabeth said with an approving nod. "Does he have a name?"

Andrew considered for a moment before mumbling, "Tom."

"A very good name," Elizabeth said with a laugh, holding out a hand. Slowly, he stepped toward her, placing the horse in her hand.

"Oh, he is quite handsome. Now tell me, does he say, moo?" Elizabeth asked, her face serious.

Andrew shook his head solemnly. "Oh dear," Elizabeth continued. "Perhaps he says, baa?"

A small grin began to form on his lips, and he shook his head again.

"Well, I'm not good at this. Let's see." Elizabeth paused and tapped a finger to her chin. "I've got it," she cried triumphantly. "He says, cluck cluck."

The boy let out a giggle and shook his head fervently.

"Well, then I give up," Elizabeth exclaimed, throwing her hands in the air. "What does he say?"

"Neigh!"

"Oh, that's right." Elizabeth handed the horse back to Andrew and clapped her hands. "What a smart young man you are."

Andrew beamed and neighed again, making the horse gallop through the air. Rebecca's smile was wide as she watched the exchange. "He doesn't warm to many so quickly, Miss Elizabeth. You've a gift with children."

"We're old friends," Elizabeth said reassuringly. "Aren't we Andrew?"

"Of course you are," said Darcy from behind her.

Darcy had walked out to find his son, his concern rising after noticing Andrew's absence from the nursery. Caroline had appeared almost immediately, insisting on accompanying him.

"You really ought to speak with Miss Elizabeth about your son," Caroline said with a feigned air of helpfulness. "She seems to have taken quite the interest in him. Perhaps she hopes for more than mere acquaintance."

Darcy said nothing, his patience wearing thin as Caroline continued.

"She does have remarkable eyes, I'll grant her that," Caroline added with a sly glance. "Though I wonder how her poor connections would look hung on the walls at Pemberley next to your illustrious ancestors. Just imagine, the portraits of a tradesman and a solicitor hanging on the walls next to your uncle the earl and your great-grandfather the duke."

"I believe you give far too much attention to such matters, Miss Bingley," Darcy said, his tone clipped.

Caroline pressed her lips together in mock chastisement but followed him closely as they turned the corner.

Elizabeth straightened at the words from Mr. Darcy, her smile faltering slightly at the sight of Caroline beside him. Before she could greet them, Andrew let out a small gasp and darted behind her skirts, clutching the fabric tightly.

"Andrew?" Darcy's brows knit together in concern as he stepped forward.

Elizabeth instinctively rested a hand on the boy's shoulder, her voice soothing. "It's all right, Master Andrew. No one will hurt you."

Rebecca hurried forward, but the boy shook his head and buried his face further into Elizabeth's gown, his little hands trembling. "Scary," he mumbled, his voice barely audible.

Caroline frowned, then twisted her lips up into what Elizabeth could only assume was an attempt at a smile, though it appeared more like a sinister leer. "Really, Andrew. There's no need to hide like that. Come here, child, and you'll see that I'm not scary."

He let out a whimper. "Scary lady," he said again, his tone more urgent.

What did she do to this poor boy? Elizabeth wondered angrily. Taking a calming breath, she turned to Caroline, her voice respectful but firm. "Miss Bingley, I believe he is frightened. Perhaps it would be best if you allowed him some space."

Caroline's eyes narrowed, her cheeks flushing with indignation. "I have no idea what you mean, Miss Elizabeth. Children do not behave this way around me. They love me. Besides, he's only a child; it's all in his imagination."

Elizabeth's expression remained steady. "Children can feel more than we give them credit for," she replied calmly. "Perhaps it's your tone or your gestures, but he's clearly upset. . Please, give him some space."

Caroline sniffed, her indignation evident. "If you insist." With a dramatic huff, she turned on her heel and stalked back toward the house, muttering about "ungrateful guests" and "spoiled children."

Darcy remained silent, his gaze shifting between Elizabeth and his son. Andrew's grip on her skirts loosened slightly, and Elizabeth crouched down again, speaking softly to him.

"There now," she said gently. "All is well. Your papa is here."

He looked around her anxiously.

"Andrew," Darcy said gently. "It's all right, my boy. I'm here. Come here."

Elizabeth stood up, moving aside as Andrew ran to his father, who knelt and gathered the boy into his arms. Brushing off her skirts, she said with her cheeks faintly pink. "I hope I did not overstep, Mr. Darcy," she said, her tone hesitant. "I only wished to ease his fear."

"You did nothing of the sort," Darcy replied, his voice low but sincere. "Thank you, Miss Elizabeth, for handling it with such care."

Elizabeth nodded, her embarrassment deepening. She turned to Rebecca with a quick smile. "I'll leave you to your afternoon. Thank you for letting me join your game, Master Andrew."

Rebecca watched her retreat, shaking her head slightly. "That is an impressive lady," she said softly, her tone filled with admiration. "I've never met anyone quite like her."

Darcy said nothing, his gaze lingering on Elizabeth's retreating figure, a quiet agreement forming in his mind.

That evening, Jane joined the household in the drawing room for tea after dinner, leaning heavily on the maid's arm. Bingley immediately went to her side, offering his arm with an eager smile that made Jane's cheeks flush with warmth. He guided her to a comfortable chair by the fire, fussing over the arrangement of the cushions and ensuring she had sufficient blankets to be warm.

Jane accepted his attentions with gentle gratitude, her soft smile and quiet replies drawing him into a low-voiced conversation. Their quiet conversation filled the space with a pleasant hum, punctuated occasionally by Bingley's light laughter and Jane's soft, measured responses.

The rest of the household settled into their usual places. Georgiana took a seat near her brother, her embroidery in her lap, while Caroline Bingley and Mrs. Hurst occupied the best spots near the fire, their poses carefully arranged to exude elegance. Mrs. Annesley, who had joined the gathering at Darcy's invitation, sat on the periphery, her calm demeanor contrasting with the sisters' languid air.

"Miss Bingley," Mrs. Annesley began, her tone pleasant and inviting, "I must say, the decor of this room is quite tasteful. Is it the work of a local craftsman, or do you bring such finery from London?"

Caroline barely glanced in her direction, her smile thin and perfunctory. "Oh, I couldn't say," she replied airily. "The house was already well-furnished when Charles leased it."

Mrs. Annesley nodded, undeterred. "It's quite fortunate, then, to find such refinement in a country estate. I imagine it's a pleasure to entertain in such surroundings."

Mrs. Hurst, sipping her tea, raised a brow but said nothing, her silence a clear dismissal. Caroline gave a noncommittal hum, turning her attention back to her embroidery as if the older woman had ceased to exist.

Mrs. Annesley, ever courteous, attempted once more to engage the Bingley sisters in conversation. "Miss Bingley," she said warmly, "your gown this evening is quite elegant. The detailing is exquisite. Is it French lace?"

Caroline glanced up from her embroidery hoop with a faint smile that barely reached her eyes. "It is," she replied curtly, then turned to her sister. "Louisa, did you not say that the latest shipment from Paris will arrive next week?"

Mrs. Hurst nodded, barely acknowledging Mrs. Annesley as she replied to Caroline, leaving the older woman politely sidelined.

Elizabeth, seated on a comfortable chair a short distance away, observed the exchange with increasing irritation. Mrs. Annesley, for all her quiet dignity, had been clearly rebuffed— most likely due to her status as a companion, even though Elizabeth's prior interactions with the woman had demonstrated her to be sharp-witted, well-read, and exceedingly kind.

I must do something. Their pretentious behavior is completely unacceptable.

Rising gracefully, Elizabeth crossed the room and settled beside the older woman. "Mrs. Annesley," she said with a warm smile, "I could not help but notice you were speaking earlier of lace. Are you fond of embroidery yourself, or do you prefer other pursuits?"

Mrs. Annesley turned to Elizabeth, her expression softening with gratitude. "I do dabble in embroidery now and then, Miss Elizabeth," she replied, "but I also play the harp, and I greatly enjoy reading."

"Oh, yes, that's right! I must thank you for your conversation this afternoon about Robinson Crusoe. I had always thought of it as an adventure story, but your perspective gave me much to consider as I sat with Jane."

Mrs. Annesley's face lit with gratitude. "You are too kind, Miss Elizabeth. It is a book that reveals its depths only with reflection, I think."

Elizabeth nodded. "Indeed. I've been mulling over its themes of isolation and resilience. Crusoe's ingenuity in the face of adversity is admirable, but I find myself questioning some of his choices. For instance, his relationship with Friday—do you see it as one of mutual respect or something more... hierarchical?"

The older woman's eyes sparkled with interest. "An excellent question. I suspect Defoe intended it as a reflection of contemporary attitudes, though we as readers are free to interpret it as we will. What is your view?"

"I find his journey fascinating, particularly how necessity drives him to confront his own nature," Elizabeth replied. "It is remarkable how adversity reveals the depths of a person's character."

Mrs. Annesley smiled. "Yes, I agree. I have wondered if Crusoe would have valued human connection as much without his prolonged solitude. Do you think he might represent the resilience of the human spirit, or is he more a cautionary tale about the perils of self-reliance?"

As their conversation deepened, Elizabeth became increasingly animated, her thoughtful remarks and quick wit drawing Mrs. Annesley into a lively exchange. The warmth between them was evident, a sharp contrast to the earlier coolness of the Bingley sisters.

From across the room, Darcy watched the exchange with hidden admiration. Elizabeth's face was animated as she effortlessly engaged Mrs. Annesley in conversation, and the contrast between her lively intellect and the haughty indifference of Caroline and Mrs. Hurst was stark. He found himself silently commending her for behaving as a lady instead of a social-climbing harpy.

She is remarkable. Her kindness, her wit...

His thoughts were interrupted by a soft voice at his side. "It's lovely, isn't it?"

Darcy turned startled eyes to Georgiana, briefly worrying that he had spoken his thoughts aloud. Instead of looking at Elizabeth and Mrs. Annesley, however, Georgiana's gaze was fixed on

Bingley and Jane. Her lips curved in a gentle smile, her shyness momentarily overshadowed by her earnest observation.

"What do you mean?" he asked her.

"Mr. Bingley and Miss Bennet," Georgiana said softly. "It's sweet to see two people so clearly enamored with one another."

Darcy frowned slightly, watching the scene unfold. While it was obvious that Bingley's admiration was sincere, Jane's serene smile seemed unchanged from any other moment he had seen her.

"Bingley is certainly smitten," Darcy murmured, "but Miss Bennet... her demeanor is always so composed. I see no indication that her feelings match his."

Georgiana tilted her head, her eyes narrowing thoughtfully. "Do you think she would be so gentle and attentive if she didn't care for him?"

"She smiles at everyone," Darcy replied. "I fear she is simply... pleasant by nature."

Georgiana's brow furrowed. "If she were fortune hunting, as you seem to suggest, wouldn't she be directing her attentions toward you instead, brother? You are far wealthier."

Darcy turned to her, startled by her frankness. "Georgiana," he said, his voice low, "that is not what I—"

But she interrupted him with a small, knowing smile. "I think she is like me," she said simply. "She isn't effusive by nature, but look at her— she isn't just smiling and nodding. She leans forward when she listens to him, her eyes looking into his as if she's truly interested. And she answers him— not just politely, but with equal intensity, as if their conversation matters as much to her as to him."

Darcy's eyes narrowed as he watched more closely. He had to admit, there was a natural ease between Bingley and Jane, one that hinted at mutual enjoyment rather than mere propriety. His frown deepened as he considered her words. "When did you become so wise?" he asked, a note of surprise in his tone.

She straightened, her cheeks faintly pink. "Perhaps I've always been, Brother. You are only just noticing."

He gave a startled chuckle at her tease. *Where did this new side of my sister come from?*

Oblivious to his thoughts, Georgiana continued, "No, I think it is the new company I have been keeping. Or perhaps," she added with a teasing glance, "I simply learned from your mistakes."

Darcy's lips twitched with a reluctant smile as he returned his gaze to Bingley and Jane. Georgiana's insight gnawed at the edges of his certainty, leaving him with more questions than answers, but only for a few moments.

Involuntarily, his attention returned to the room, his gaze lingering on Elizabeth once more. Her graciousness toward Mrs. Annesley, her lively intelligence, and her ability to navigate the unspoken slights of the evening had not gone unnoticed.

It seemed his sister wasn't the only one full of surprises tonight.

Across the room, Caroline Bingley seethed as she watched Darcy stare at that insipid Eliza Bennet chit. Determined to break his concentration, she said loudly, "Pray, Mr. Darcy, how is your cousin the viscount doing?"

Darcy blinked, startled from his thoughts, but at least his eyes were now focused on her. "I was not aware you were acquainted with Milton."

She felt her face turn red. "Oh, I am not. That is, I just read in the paper that he had taken a fall off a horse while riding down Rotten Row. I do hope he is unharmed."

"I believe it occurred as he was dismounting and suffered no injury. He is walking about just fine."

Darcy then fell silent, his gaze going back to Elizabeth. Desperate for his attention, Caroline said, "Speaking of walking, I believe I shall take a turn about the room. Will you join me, Miss Eliza?"

Elizabeth, who had still been in conversation with Mrs. Annesley, look up with surprise. "Of course, Miss Bingley." She rose to her feet and joined her hostess, and they began to walk in silence.

Halfway through the circuit, Caroline said, "Mr. Darcy, do come and join us. It is quite refreshing."

"I'm sorry, but I believe that would defeat the purpose."

Caroline felt a shiver go up her spine. "The purpose, sir?" she asked in an airy tone.

"Why, yes. There can only be two purposes for your exercise. Either you two are confidantes with secret affairs to discuss, or else you are aware that your figures appear best when walking." Ignoring Georgiana's scandalized gasp at his side, he continued, "My presence would interfere with both objects. From here, I cannot hear you, and I can admire you both much better," he finished with a sly smirk.

Elizabeth let out a shocked giggle, while Georgiana gaped at her brother. "Oh, how dreadful!" Caroline cried, happy to be the recipient of Darcy's teasing. Eager to continue the lighthearted banter, she turned to her companion and ask, "How shall we punish him?"

"Oh, I think Mr. Darcy already has his punishment, as he has quite shocked his sister. Now she knows she can tease him... even laugh at him."

"Tease Mr. Darcy?" Caroline exclaimed shrilly. "That cannot be possible, as he is a man without fault."

Now Elizabeth's amusement displayed itself with a deep laugh, her eyes sparkling with mirth. "A man without fault, is he?" she repeated, turning her gaze toward Darcy. "I daresay, Miss Bingley, that you and I must be speaking of two very different gentlemen. For no man, surely, is without fault."

Darcy raised a brow, his expression poised but amused. "And what faults would you assign me, Miss Elizabeth? I must warn you, this is dangerous territory."

Elizabeth tilted her head, her smile playful. "Oh, I would not presume to list them all, Mr. Darcy. That would take far too long and might damage your delicate sensibilities. But I will say that your tendency toward pride is rather evident."

Georgiana, still recovering from her initial shock, looked between them with wide eyes. Caroline, however, seized the opportunity to defend him.

"Pride!" she exclaimed. "Surely, Miss Eliza, you do not call pride a fault. Pride is what sets a gentleman of Mr. Darcy's station apart from others. Indeed, I think a certain degree of pride is essential."

Elizabeth's gaze remained fixed on Darcy, her tone thoughtful as she responded. "I suppose it depends on the nature of that pride. There is a pride that inspires one to act with integrity, and then there is a pride that blinds one to the worth of others. I wonder which kind you favor, Mr. Darcy?"

Darcy's lips curved slightly, though his tone was measured. "Pride, like all things, must be tempered with reason. I admit I have often been accused of it, but I believe there is a distinction to be made. My pride is rooted not in my station but in my principles. It is a matter of knowing one's own worth and of having the superiority of mind to control your pride, that it does not turn to vanity."

Elizabeth regarded him for a moment, her amusement fading into curiosity. "And do you think it is possible to know one's worth without undervaluing others?"

Darcy's brow furrowed slightly. "I would like to think so. However, I must admit that judgment is not always perfect. We are all susceptible to prejudice, whether we realize it or not."

"Indeed," Elizabeth said, nodding thoughtfully. "Pride and prejudice often walk hand in hand, do they not? And yet, it is the ability to recognize one's own failings that truly sets one apart."

Georgiana, who had been listening quietly, interjected hesitantly. "I think humility must also play a role. Without it, even the most admirable qualities can become faults."

Darcy glanced at his sister, his expression softening. "You are quite right, Georgiana."

Elizabeth smiled warmly at Georgiana. "A wise observation, Miss Darcy. It seems your brother is fortunate to have someone so insightful to guide him."

Georgiana blushed deeply, but her eyes glimmered with gratitude.

Caroline, desperate to redirect the conversation, laughed nervously. "Well, I daresay we have discussed Mr. Darcy's character quite enough for one evening. Shall we return to more agreeable topics? Perhaps some music, Louisa?"

Her voice was high-pitched and strained, betraying her irritation. She shot a pointed look at her sister, clearly expecting support in changing the focus of the room.

Louisa Hurst, ever the compliant ally, set aside her needlework and nodded. "What a wonderful idea, Caroline. Perhaps you might favor us with a song."

Caroline's forced smile tightened as her gaze flicked briefly to Darcy, who had once again turned his attention to Elizabeth. Anger simmered beneath her composed exterior—her carefully constructed scheme to reclaim Darcy's attention had failed spectacularly, and now the entire room had seen her efforts rebuffed.

She took her seat at the piano and played an intricate piece from memory, all the while glaring over the piano in the direction of Darcy, who had resumed staring at Elizabeth.

I will not *be bested by an insignificant country chit! Mr. Darcy will be mine, if it's the last thing I do.*

Chapter 10

Elizabeth was delighted when Jane awoke the next morning feeling almost completely back to her usual self. She went down to breakfast by herself and, at Elizabeth's urging, requested the carriage from Mr. Bingley so they might return home that day.

Mr. Bingley protested immediately, his concern clear. "Miss Bennet, the weather has turned cold again, and you've only just begun to recover. I really must insist that you remain another day. It would be dreadful if you were to suffer a relapse."

Jane, ever the epitome of kindness, smiled gently at his earnestness. "Mr. Bingley, you are too kind. I assure you, I feel much better and would not wish to inconvenience you further."

"Nonsense," he replied with a wave of his hand. "Your health is far too important. You must rest here for at least another day, if not longer."

Miss Bingley, though clearly reluctant, was forced by her brother's insistence to extend their hospitality through the weekend.

Elizabeth and Jane exchanged a glance, and Jane inclined her head in acquiescence. "Very well, Mr. Bingley," she said softly. "We will stay another day, but I must insist on returning home after church tomorrow."

Once all of the arrangements had been settled, Jane returned to her room, tired from the exertions of the morning. Elizabeth helped settle her sister before going in search of something to do.

She was halfway down the hall to the library when the faint strains of music reached her ears. The sound stopped her mid-step, a rich melody floating through the hall with such precision and beauty that it compelled her to follow it. Curious, she moved toward the music room, the notes growing clearer with every step.

When she reached the slightly ajar door, Elizabeth peered inside, expecting to see Caroline or Mrs. Hurst at the piano. Instead, her breath caught. It was Georgiana Darcy, her back to the door, playing with a skill and passion Elizabeth had never before witnessed.

Georgiana's fingers danced over the keys, coaxing a melody so exquisite it seemed to fill every corner of the room with its brilliance. Seated nearby, Mrs. Annesley worked on her knitting, her face serene as she listened to the song that Elizabeth recognized as being from Herr Mozart's *The Magic Flute*.

Ach, ich fühl's, es ist verschwunden,

Ewig hin der Liebe Glück!

Nimmer kommt ihr Wonnestunde

Meinem Herzen mehr zurück!

Sieh', Tamino, diese Tränen,

Fließen, Trauter, dir allein!

Fühlst du nicht der Liebe Sehnen,

So wird Ruh' im Tode sein!

Ah, I can feel it, love's happiness

Is fled forever!

Nevermore, O hours of bliss,

Will you return to my heart!

See, Tamino, these tears

Flow for you alone, beloved.

If you do not feel love's yearning,

I shall find peace in death!

Elizabeth lingered in the doorway, captivated. The room seemed to hum with the beauty of the music, and Elizabeth felt a pang of awe. Georgiana's talent was extraordinary, far beyond what she had imagined for the shy young girl.

Georgiana transitioned seamlessly into another song, this time singing in flawless Italian. Her clear, angelic voice resonated through the room, the foreign lyrics of another Mozart piece flowing with an ease that made Elizabeth's heart ache with admiration.

Bella mia fiamma, addio!

Non piacque al cielo di renderci felici.

Ecco reciso, prima d'esser compito,

quel purissimo nodo, che strinsero

fra lor gl'animi nostri con il solo voler.

Vivi: Cedi al destin, cedi al dovere.

Della giurata fede la mia morte t'assolve.

A più degno consorte ... O pene!

unita vivi più lieta e più felice vita.

Ricordati di me, ma non mai turbi

d'un felice sposo la rara

rimembranza il tuo riposo.

Regina, io vado ad ubbidirti

Ah, tutto finisca il mio furor col morir mio.

Cerere, Alfeo, diletta sposa, addio!

Resta, o cara, acerba morte mi separa

Oh Dio..... da te!

Prendi cura di sua sorte,

consolarla almen procura.

Vado . . . ahi lasso!

Addio, addio per sempre.

Quest'affanno, questo passo

è terribile per me.

Ah! Dov'è il tempio, dov'è l'ara?

Vieni, affretta la vendetta!

Questa vita così amara

più soffribile non è!

Light of my life, farewell!

Heaven did not intend our happiness.

Before the knot was tied,

those pure strands were severed that bound

our spirits in a single will.

Live: Yield to fate and to your duty.

My death absolves you from your promise.

O grief! United to a more worthy consort

you will have a happier, more joyous life.

Remember me, but never let stray

thoughts of an unhappy lover

disturb your rest.

Majesty, I go in obedience to your will...

Ah, let death put an end to my raving.

Ceres, Alpheus, beloved heart, farewell!

Stay, dear heart, cruel death tears me away

O God....from you!

Look after her,

comfort her at last.

I go ... alas!

Farewell, farewell for evermore.

This anguish, this step

is hard for me to bear.

Ah! Where is the temple, where is the altar?

Dear heart, farewell forever!

A life as bitter as this

can be borne no longer!

As the song continued, Mrs. Annesley glanced up and noticed Elizabeth. Her expression shifted to one of surprise before she smiled and held a finger to her lips, signaling for Elizabeth to remain quiet.

Elizabeth nodded, not daring to disturb the spellbinding moment. Georgiana's voice soared, each note carrying emotion so pure it felt almost tangible.

When the song ended, Elizabeth could not contain herself. She clapped her hands, her applause breaking the silence.

Georgiana spun around on the bench, her face pale with shock. "Oh! Miss Elizabeth!" she gasped, her hands flying to her lap. "I didn't know anyone was there," she stammered, her voice tinged with embarrassment.

"I beg your pardon, Miss Darcy," Elizabeth said quickly, stepping into the room. "I could not help myself. That was the most beautiful music I have ever heard."

Georgiana's cheeks turned pink as she averted her gaze. "You... you heard all of it?"

"Indeed, I did," Elizabeth replied with a warm smile. "And I am very glad I did. Your playing and singing are extraordinary. I feel quite privileged to have been an audience, even if it was uninvited."

Georgiana's blush deepened, her shyness rendering her almost speechless. Looking down at her hands, she whispered, "I... I wasn't expecting anyone to hear. I only play for myself, really."

Elizabeth's smile softened. "Well, if it helps, I can assure you that your audience was thoroughly enchanted."

Still, Georgiana fidgeted nervously, clearly uncomfortable with the unexpected praise.

Sensing her unease, Elizabeth decided to lighten the mood. "Perhaps I should play something next," she said brightly. "That way, you'll see how poor my attempts are, and you'll feel much better by comparison."

Georgiana blinked, her mouth dropping open in surprise. "You... you wish to play?"

"Most certainly!" Elizabeth declared. "But be warned, I shall mangle the piano terribly. You might regret this act of kindness. Prepare yourself for something quite dreadful."

Georgiana hesitated, then gestured toward the bench with a small smile. "Please."

Elizabeth sat down and began to play a simple tune, deliberately striking a few wrong notes. She sang along, off-key and with exaggerated expressions, her playful antics drawing a hesitant giggle from Georgiana.

"See?" Elizabeth said, glancing over her shoulder with a mock-serious expression. "Your playing is leagues above mine. Now, will you forgive me for intruding?"

Georgiana burst into laughter, the sound light and genuine. Even Mrs. Annesley chuckled softly.

"Miss Elizabeth," Georgiana said between giggles, "you cannot possibly be this terrible!"

Elizabeth stopped abruptly, pretending to be offended. "I assure you, Miss Darcy, this is the peak of my ability. You mustn't accuse me of lying, else Mrs. Annesley will forbid me from spending any time with you!"

Georgiana's laughter rang out, her face wreathed in a charming smile. "I believe you are far better than you let on."

"Shall we prove it by attempting a duet?" Elizabeth asked.

Georgiana's eyes widened. "A duet?"

"Why not? You lead, and I shall do my best to keep up."

With a shy nod, Georgiana took her place beside Elizabeth. Together, they began to play, their hands moving across the keys in harmony. Laughter bubbled up as they missed notes or misaligned rhythms, but the joy of the moment carried them through.

The room filled with music and mirth, and Elizabeth felt an increased fondness for the timid young woman, whose shyness seemed to melt away with each passing note.

Darcy had been making his way down the corridor when the sound of music and merriment caught his attention. Georgiana's playing was unmistakable, but the laughter… That belonged to Miss Elizabeth Bennet.

Pausing outside the music room, he leaned against the wall and listened. Music poured through the door, interspersed with laughter. Curious, he stepped closer and peered inside.

The sight stopped him.

Elizabeth was seated at the piano beside Georgiana, her fingers moving clumsily over the keys. Georgiana laughed as Elizabeth made a dramatic face, clearly feigning frustration at a missed note. The two of them were engrossed in their duet, their laughter mingling with the music.

Darcy leaned against the door frame, his forehead resting on the cool wood. It was as if all of Georgiana's heartache from that summer had melted away, along with her reticence.

And it was Elizabeth Bennet who had drawn it out of her.

Elizabeth, he thought, the name nearly coming off his lips.

She was unlike anyone he had ever met. Her wit, her warmth, her ability to connect with others—all of it captivated him. Watching her now, so at ease with his sister, filled him with a sense of gratitude and admiration.

Mrs. Annesley noticed him at the doorway and began to rise, but Darcy shook his head slightly, signaling her to remain quiet.

He lingered, watching as Elizabeth and Georgiana navigated their duet with a mix of skill and humor. Elizabeth, ever expressive, pulled faces when she hit a wrong note, prompting more laughter from Georgiana. It was a scene of unguarded delight, and Darcy found himself utterly captivated.

His gaze shifted to Elizabeth, her hair slightly disheveled from her exuberance, her cheeks flushed with warmth. There was a light in her eyes that seemed to illuminate the entire room.

She is extraordinary, he thought, his chest tightening with an unfamiliar sensation.

As the music swelled and Elizabeth burst into laughter once again, Darcy found himself grappling with emotions he could no longer deny.

Elizabeth's kindness and wit had drawn his admiration since they first met, but seeing her here—so effortlessly bringing out the best in his sister—stirred something deeper. She was more than a lively conversationalist or clever mind. She was compassionate, unpretentious, and utterly unique.

Could this be love? Am I falling in love with her?

The question lodged itself in his mind, unsettling and yet oddly comforting. Elizabeth was far removed from the expectations of his station, her family connections unsuitable by societal standards.

Yet none of that seemed to matter.

He remained at the door for a moment longer, reluctant to disturb the scene, his thoughts swirling as he watched the two women share a moment of pure happiness. Elizabeth's laughter echoed in his ears, and he knew, with a clarity he could not ignore, that his feelings for her went far deeper than admiration.

He turned away at last, retreating down the hall, but the image of Elizabeth's smile lingered in his mind. For the first time, he allowed himself to consider the possibility of what it might mean to truly love her—and what he might be willing to do about it.

The household gathered in the expansive foyer of Netherfield, its high ceilings trapping the warmth from the large fireplace but failing to quell the chill of impending goodbyes. Footmen bustled about, ensuring every detail of the departure was attended to. The Bennet sisters' cloaks hung ready, their luggage already loaded into the carriage waiting just beyond the front door.

Jane, her complexion now nearly back to its usual healthy bloom, stood beside Mr. Bingley, who seemed utterly absorbed in her every word. His hand lingered on the back of a nearby chair, his knuckles whitening as though he needed to ground himself against the reality of her imminent departure. Jane, for her part, smiled gently, the very picture of gratitude and decorum, though her eyes betrayed a lingering fatigue.

Elizabeth, meanwhile, stood slightly apart, her gaze alternating between Jane and the room's other occupants. Mr. Darcy and Georgiana stood to one side, the former composed as ever, though his gaze lingered on Elizabeth more often than she noticed. Georgiana, though shy, had ventured a few murmured words of well wishes earlier and now clung to her brother's arm with an air of quiet solemnity.

Miss Bingley hovered nearby, her smile brittle, her words clipped whenever she interjected. Her displeasure at the length of her brother's farewell was evident to anyone paying attention, though no one openly remarked upon it.

As the farewells began in earnest, a maid entered the foyer, curtsied, and approached Darcy. "Mr. Darcy, sir, Rebecca sent me to ask if Master Andrew might come to say goodbye. He has been asking for the 'nice lady,' sir."

Elizabeth blinked, her expression softening at the mention of the little boy. Darcy turned toward her, his gaze searching. "Would that be acceptable to you, Miss Elizabeth?" he asked, his tone low and respectful.

Elizabeth nodded immediately, a warm smile spreading across her face. "Of course, Mr. Darcy. I would be delighted to see him."

Darcy gave a brief nod to the maid, who hurried back up the stairs. The others exchanged curious glances, but no one said a word.

Moments later, the sound of small, excited footsteps echoed down the staircase. Andrew appeared, toddling into the foyer with Rebecca close behind him. His face lit up when he saw Elizabeth, and he let out a delighted squeal.

"Nice lady!" he exclaimed, running toward her with his arms outstretched.

Elizabeth knelt without hesitation, catching him as he flung himself into her embrace. She laughed softly, holding him close as he buried his small face against her shoulder.

Elizabeth knelt to Andrew's level, her warm smile softening as she cradled his small hands in hers. "Andrew, you're such a sweet boy, but I'm not just the 'nice lady.' My name is Miss Elizabeth," she said gently. "Can you say that? Miss Elizabeth."

Andrew's brows furrowed in concentration as he considered her words. "Mizz… Ehz-beh-iz?" he tried, his little voice stumbling adorably over the syllables.

Elizabeth laughed, her heart melting at his earnest attempt. "Close, very close! Let's try again—Miss Eliz-a-beth."

"Miss 'iz-bef!" he exclaimed proudly, looking up at her with wide, excited eyes.

Elizabeth clapped her hands lightly. "Oh, that was very good! One more time—Miss Eliz-a-beth."

Andrew tilted his head and grinned, his attempt this time blending into a charming, "Miss 'iz-bet!"

"That's much better," Elizabeth praised, her eyes sparkling with amusement. "But if it's too hard, you can just call me Miss Lizzy."

Andrew's face brightened, and he nodded eagerly. "Miss Wizzy!" he repeated, the word coming out nearly perfect this time.

She laughed again, wrapping him in a quick hug. "Perfect, young man. I think you've got it!"

Andrew beamed at her triumphantly. Then, as he looked up at her again, his face softened into a look of pure affection. "Miss Lizzy, nice lady," he said, his small voice filled with trust and warmth.

Elizabeth's heart squeezed as she held his gaze. "That's just fine, Master Andrew. I'll always be your nice lady."

"Nice lady, Miss Liz-bet."

"Well, Master Andrew," she said gently, brushing a hand through his dark curls. "It seems I'll have quite the story to tell about the brave young man who bid me farewell."

Andrew lifted his head, his wide eyes brimming with emotion. "Go?" he asked, his little voice quivering plaintively.

Elizabeth's heart ached at the sight of his sorrow. "Yes, Andrew, I must go home with my sister. But I promise I will think of you often."

Andrew frowned, his lower lip trembling. "No go."

Rebecca stepped forward, crouching beside them. "Come now, Master Andrew," she said kindly. "You must say goodbye like a big boy. We'll see Miss Elizabeth again one day."

Andrew sniffled but nodded, his small hand reaching out to clutch Elizabeth's. She smiled at him warmly, her heart swelling with a mixture of affection and sadness.

Darcy, who had been watching the scene silently, stepped closer. His expression, usually so composed, softened as his gaze fell on his son in Elizabeth's arms. "You've made quite an impression on him," he remarked, his voice quieter than usual.

Elizabeth rose, holding Andrew's hand as he clung to her side. She glanced at Darcy, her expression warm. "He's a remarkable child, Mr. Darcy. It has been a pleasure to know him."

Darcy inclined his head, his gratitude evident in the depth of his gaze. "The pleasure was ours, Miss Elizabeth."

Andrew tugged at Elizabeth's hand, drawing her attention back to him. "Bye-bye, nice lady," he said softly, his small voice tinged with sadness.

Elizabeth knelt again, wrapping her arms around him in a final hug. "Goodbye, Andrew. Be good for your papa and Nurse Rebecca."

The little boy nodded solemnly, his eyes glistening with unshed tears. He waved as Elizabeth stood and stepped back, ready to leave.

Bingley, who had been watching the touching exchange with a smile, stepped forward to escort Jane and Elizabeth to the carriage. As the Bennet sisters exited, the warmth of their presence lingered in the room.

Darcy watched the door close behind them, his hand resting lightly on Andrew's shoulder. For a moment, he allowed himself to feel the weight of the departure—not just of Elizabeth's absence but of the space she had begun to fill in his thoughts and his life.

Rebecca's voice broke the silence. "She's quite a remarkable lady, sir," she said softly.

Darcy looked down at his son, who gazed up at him with wide, trusting eyes. A small smile curved his lips as he replied, "Yes, she is."

~

In the carriage, Elizabeth looked back at Netherfield before turning to face her sister.

"Well, Jane? How do you feel?"

"I am doing well, Lizzy. Quite recovered."

"That's not what I meant," Elizabeth replied with a smirk, her teasing tone unmistakable. "Shall I be calling you Mrs. Bingley soon?"

Jane's cheeks turned the faintest shade of pink, and she shook her head. "Lizzy, you must not tease me so."

"Tease you? I?" Elizabeth exclaimed in mock indignation. "Never!"

Jane turned her gaze to the window, though the corners of her mouth twitched upward in a faint smile. "He is very kind, I admit. But you mustn't presume anything, Lizzy. There are no assurances of anything beyond his kindness."

Elizabeth leaned forward, her expression softening. "Jane, you are the very picture of modesty. But I know what I saw, and what I saw was a man entirely smitten. I daresay he'd have proposed already if he'd had the courage."

Jane laughed lightly, though her blush deepened. "You are incorrigible. Mr. Bingley is a friend, nothing more."

Elizabeth leaned back, folding her arms across her chest with an air of mock resignation. "Well, if you insist on denying it, I suppose I'll just have to wait until Mr. Bingley himself tells me he adores you. And when he does, I hope you'll remember I told you first. In the meantime, I shall content myself with imagining you as mistress of Netherfield, while I… well, I shall be quite content as the spinster aunt, making scathing remarks about society from the comfort of your drawing room."

Jane laughed again, the sound clear and unguarded, her earlier shyness momentarily forgotten. "You, Lizzy, a spinster? I think not. You have a charm that cannot help but draw attention—even from Mr. Darcy."

In an effort to mask her discomfort, Elizabeth tossed her head and said in a light tone. "You mean he might be persuaded to give attention to young ladies who are only tolerable?"

"Be serious, Lizzy." Jane gave her sister as stern a look as was possible. "What did you think of Mr. Darcy and his family during our stay?"

Elizabeth hesitated, her brow furrowing slightly. "Mr. Darcy… surprised me," she admitted. "I expected him to be aloof and unpleasant, but he was neither. He was loving towards Andrew, attentive to his sister, and considerate to me."

Jane's smile grew. "You seem to have spent quite a bit of time observing him."

"I couldn't help it," Elizabeth replied, a hint of defensiveness in her tone. "He is... a curious man. Reserved, certainly, but not unfeeling. And he cares for his family deeply—that much is obvious. He is very serious, however."

Jane's expression turned knowing. "Sometimes seriousness can conceal a very warm heart."

Elizabeth considered this, her lips curving slightly. "You may be right. He was not at all disagreeable to me—quite the opposite, in fact. And yet, I cannot imagine him... softening. Not truly. It is as though he is holding something back, even when he is kind."

Jane's smile returned. "It could be that he is waiting for the right person to help him let go of whatever it is."

Elizabeth laughed lightly. "If so, I hope that person arrives soon. It must be exhausting to carry such weight."

"Perchance you might be that person?"

"I highly doubt that, Jane," Elizabeth scoffed. "For all of Mr. Darcy's good qualities, he is much too solemn for me. If I am to be swept off my feet, I'd much prefer someone with a sense of humor."

Jane's smile widened, though she said nothing further.

As the carriage continued its journey, Elizabeth allowed her thoughts to wander. Though she would never admit it aloud, she could not entirely dismiss Mr. Darcy from her mind. His unexpected warmth and quiet attentiveness during their stay at Netherfield had left an impression—one she was not yet ready to examine too closely.

For now, she resolved to focus on her family and her sister's happiness. Whatever lay ahead, she would face it with the same resilience and wit that had always served her so well.

Chapter 11

The Bennet family sat down to breakfast the morning after Jane and Elizabeth's return from Netherfield. The house was unusually quiet—at least by Longbourn standards—as Kitty and Lydia had chosen to sleep later than their wont. That peace, however, was short-lived.

Mrs. Bennet sighed heavily, her spoon clanging against her bowl with exaggerated frustration. "I simply cannot understand, Miss Lizzy, why you insisted on you and your sister returning so soon." She gave her second daughter a baleful glare. "It would have done Jane wonders to remain at Netherfield just a few days longer! How could you be so unfeeling to my poor nerves?"

Jane, ever the peacemaker, spoke before Elizabeth could respond. "Mama, Mr. Bingley was most insistent that we remain until I had fully recovered, but I truly felt well enough to come home. I missed my family, and it would not have been proper to remain in his home once I had recovered sufficiently to travel."

Mrs. Bennet waved off her words with a dismissive gesture. "Nonsense! A lady's comfort is secondary when such opportunities arise! After all, when your father is dead and gone, we will be cast into the hedgerows unless one of you marries well. You have squandered perhaps the only chance you had of catching him."

"Perhaps," Mr. Bennet interjected dryly, peering over his newspaper, "we might leave Mr. Bingley's house to himself and focus instead on preparing for our own imminent guest."

Mrs. Bennet stilled, her fork halfway to her lips. "Guest?" she repeated, her brow furrowing in confusion.

"Yes," Mr. Bennet replied with a measured calm that only seemed to heighten his wife's agitation. "I received a letter several days ago. It seems my esteemed cousin, Mr. Collins, intends to visit. He will arrive this afternoon and stay with us for several days."

Mrs. Bennet's reaction was immediate. She set down her utensil with a clatter and stared at her husband in disbelief. "Mr. Collins?" she repeated dumbly. "Your... cousin? The odious man who is to inherit Longbourn?"

"The very same," Mr. Bennet confirmed, folding his newspaper neatly. "Well, I do believe it is his son, as his letter is much more well-written than his illiterate father's. Here, Lizzy, see what you think of your distinguished relative."

He passed over the missive to his favorite daughter, who took it with an arched eyebrow. She scanned the document, then began to read aloud for the table.

Dear Sir,

The disagreement subsisting between yourself and my late honored father always gave me much uneasiness, and since I have had the misfortune to lose him, I have frequently wished to heal the breach; but for some time I was kept back by my own doubts, fearing lest it might seem disrespectful to his memory for me to be on good terms with any one, with whom it had always pleased him to be at variance.

My mind however is now made up on the subject, for having received ordination at Easter, I have been so fortunate as to be distinguished by the patronage of the Right Honorable Lady Catherine de Bourgh, widow of Sir Lewis de Bourgh, whose bounty and beneficence has proffered to me the valuable rectory of this parish, where it shall be my earnest endeavor to demean myself with grateful respect towards her Ladyship, and be ever ready to perform those rites and ceremonies which are instituted by the Church of England.

As a clergyman, moreover, I feel it my duty to promote and establish the blessings of peace in all families within the reach of my influence; and on these grounds I flatter myself that my present overtures of good-will are highly commendable, and that the circumstance of my being next in the entail of Longbourn estate, will be kindly overlooked on your side, and not lead you to reject the offered olive branch. I cannot be otherwise than concerned at being the means of injuring your amiable daughters, and beg leave to apologize for it, as well as to assure you of my readiness to make them every possible amends,—but of this hereafter.

If you should have no objection to receive me into your house, I propose myself the satisfaction of waiting on you and your family, Monday, November 18th, by four o'clock, and shall probably trespass on your hospitality till the Saturday se'night following, which I can do without any inconvenience, as Lady Catherine is far from objecting to my occasional absence on a Sunday, provided that some other clergyman is engaged to do the duty of the day.

I remain, dear sir, with respectful compliments to your lady and daughters, your well-wisher and friend,

William Collins

"He is arriving at four o'clock today, to stay for nearly a fortnight?" Mrs. Bennet rose from her seat, her voice rising with her. "And you are only telling me this now? How can I possibly prepare the house in time? What will he think if everything is not in perfect order?"

"Why should it matter what he thinks, as he is such an odious man?" Mr. Bennet replied.

"Because he is coming here to offer an olive branch! Do you not understand what this means?" Mrs. Bennet's words were so high-pitched, Elizabeth almost expected the dogs to begin baying in their kennels.

"What do you think it means?" Mr. Bennet's face was positively gleeful at having so thoroughly provoked his wife.

"He is here to marry one of our daughters!"

At that pronouncement, Mrs. Bennet swept from the room, her shrill instructions for Hill echoing so loudly, Elizabeth began to fear for the glass in the windows.

Elizabeth leaned toward her father, a wry smile on her lips. "How long have you known of this visit, Papa?"

Mr. Bennet's eyes twinkled with amusement. "Long enough to ensure that your mother has precisely the amount of time necessary to stir the house into a frenzy but not enough to overdo it."

Elizabeth, who normally would have laughed at her father's antics, winced instead in commiseration for her mother. "You are incorrigible, Papa," she told him.

The morning passed in a flurry of activity. The maids rushed about, dusting and polishing every surface. Mrs. Bennet bustled between rooms, inspecting their progress with wails of ill-use from her husband. The drawing room and guest rooms in particular received special attention, with fresh flowers arranged on each table and the best china set out for tea.

Elizabeth and Jane, seated in the drawing room with their embroidery, watched the commotion with a mixture of amusement and resignation. "I suppose we must be on our best behavior," Elizabeth murmured, threading her needle with care. "It would not do to frighten off Mr. Collins before Mama has had her say."

Jane suppressed a smile. "Lizzy, you must not tease so."

By the time the carriage bringing Mr. Collins pulled into the drive, the Bennet household was as prepared as Mrs. Bennet could manage.

Mrs. Bennet, who had been hovering near the window, let out a delighted squeal. "He is here! Hill, see to the door!"

The family gathered outside of the house to receive him, equal parts curiosity and apprehension. *I can only hope he will be more intelligent than he seems to be in his letter,* Elizabeth thought.

Mr. Collins descended from his gig, his appearance exactly as one might expect from his rambling words. He was a tall, heavyset man with a florid complexion and an air of self-importance that could fill a room as thoroughly as his physical presence. His manners, though scrupulously polite, carried a faint air of condescension that quickly set the tone for his visit.

"Mrs. Bennet!" he exclaimed as he bowed low, his gaze lingering just a bit too long on her bosom before darting back to her face. "How delightful it is to make your acquaintance at last. I must say, you have an air of grace that reflects most favorably upon your household."

Elizabeth raised an eyebrow, but Mrs. Bennet flushed with excitement and exertion. "Mr. Collins! Welcome to Longbourn. We are most pleased to have you here."

Inclining his head in what he clearly thought was a stately manner, he replied, "The honor is mine, madam. To be invited into the home of my esteemed cousin and his delightful family is a privilege indeed."

Mrs. Bennet preened under his flattery, while Mr. Collins's gaze flitted to Jane and Elizabeth. His eyes widened slightly as they settled on Jane, his expression shifting to one of barely contained admiration.

"Please allow me to introduce my daughters: Jane here is my eldest, then Elizabeth, Mary, Catherine, and Lydia."

"Miss Bennet," he said, bowing deeply. "Your reputation for beauty does not do you justice."

Jane blushed and murmured a polite response, but Mr. Collins's attention had already shifted to Elizabeth. His gaze lingered for a moment longer than was strictly proper, and Elizabeth felt a flicker of discomfort as his eyes darted downward briefly before snapping back to her face.

"And Miss Elizabeth," he said, his tone attempting to be gallant but coming off as overeager. "Your presence adds a certain radiance to this gathering. I am most fortunate to be in such company."

Elizabeth's smile was tight, though she replied with practiced politeness. "You are too kind, Mr. Collins."

As Mr. Collins turned his attention towards the other three girls, Elizabeth exchanged a quick look with Jane, who gave her an almost imperceptible shrug.

The newcomer greeted the remainder of the Bennet girls with an eager smile that did little to disguise the way his eyes flickered over each of them in turn. "Ah, such beauty!" he declared, clasping his hands before him. "Truly, Mrs. Bennet, you are blessed beyond measure to have such charming daughters."

Mr. Bennet, who had observed the entire exchange with an expression of wry amusement, stepped forward. "Mr. Collins, I trust your journey was uneventful?"

"Indeed, sir," Mr. Collins replied, clasping his hands behind his back. "The roads were agreeable, and the carriage most comfortable. I must say, I was quite impressed by the efficiency with which my luggage was handled upon arrival. Your staff is to be commended, Mr. Bennet."

"Your praise will no doubt be appreciated," Mr. Bennet said with a faint smile. "And now, if you will excuse me, I must see to a few matters before dinner. But please, come into the house and allow my wife and daughters to entertain you."

As Mr. Bennet made his escape, Mrs. Bennet, clearly enamored with their guest's effusive praise, began to lead him into the drawing room, all the while exclaiming over his "gracious manners" and "elegant speech."

Once seated, Mr. Collins turned his attention back to the ladies, his demeanor eager and expectant. "Mrs. Bennet," he began, "I must say how grateful I am for your hospitality. It is my hope that during my stay, I may come to better understand the many virtues of your household and, perhaps, strengthen the ties between our families."

Mrs. Bennet, sensing a potential opportunity, beamed at him. "Of course, Mr. Collins! We are delighted to have you with us."

As the conversation continued, Elizabeth could not help but notice Mr. Collins's gaze wandering once again, this time toward Mary, whose modest dress and studious demeanor seemed to pique his curiosity. When she looked up from her book and caught him staring, she adjusted her spectacles and promptly returned to her reading, her cheeks pink.

Elizabeth suppressed a sigh. It was going to be an interesting visit.

The following morning dawned bright and brisk, perfect for a walk to Meryton. Elizabeth, Jane, and their younger sisters decided to take advantage of the fine weather. Mrs. Bennet, ever eager to showcase her daughters, was delighted by the plan and insisted they take Mr. Collins along.

"Lizzy," she said with a meaningful glance, "do make sure Mr. Collins has every opportunity to enjoy your company. It is only proper to show him the best of Longbourn's hospitality."

Elizabeth suppressed the sigh rising within her and replied, "Of course, Mama. I am sure Mr. Collins will find the walk most agreeable."

Jane, who had fully recovered, gave Elizabeth a sympathetic smile as the party gathered to set out. Lydia and Kitty skipped ahead, giggling and chattering, while Mary strolled at a slower pace with her ever-present book. Elizabeth and Jane fell in step together, but Mr. Collins wasted no time inserting himself between them.

"Miss Elizabeth," he began with an eager smile, "it is a delight to have this opportunity to converse with you. Walking is such a healthful activity, and the company of such amiable young ladies makes it doubly so."

Elizabeth nodded politely, though her thoughts wandered as Mr. Collins prattled on about the virtues of Lady Catherine de Bourgh, her "gracious" habits, and his good fortune in securing the living at Hunsford.

By the time they reached Meryton, Elizabeth's patience was wearing thin, but her spirits were lifted by the familiar sight of the bustling market street. Mr. Denny, a young officer of the militia and a favorite of Lydia and Kitty, approached the group with a warm smile.

"Miss Bennet, Miss Elizabeth, and ladies," he greeted with a bow. "What a pleasure to see you this fine morning."

Lydia and Kitty, already flushed with excitement, pressed closer to him. "Mr. Denny," Lydia said, her voice bright, "you must introduce us to your new friend!"

Elizabeth's lips tightened at the somewhat forward behavior of her younger sisters, but she knew that to offer any correction would only serve to increase attention.

"Of course," Mr. Denny replied, gesturing to the man at his side. "This is Mr. Wickham, a recent addition to our regiment."

A man stepped forward, dressed smartly in the red coat of the militia. His dark hair and easy smile made an immediate impression, and he bowed with practiced grace. "Ladies," he said, his voice warm and smooth. "It is a pleasure to make your acquaintance."

Elizabeth's first impression was of a man with easy manners and a ready charm. His features were striking, and his uniform seemed to suit him almost too well.

Lydia, ever bold, spoke first. "Mr. Wickham, are you new to the regiment?"

"I am," he replied. "I joined only recently."

"And where are you from?" Kitty asked eagerly.

"From the north," Wickham said casually. "Somewhere between Staffordshire and Derbyshire."

Elizabeth laughed lightly. "Then you will fit right in. It seems we are overrun with northerners of late."

"Yes, like Mr. Bingley and his awful sister," giggled Lydia, eager to be part of the conversation.

"And Mr. Darcy," chimed in Kitty.

"Girls," Elizabeth warned, but Wickham tilted his head, intrigued.

"Indeed?" he asked.

"Why, yes," Elizabeth said, her tone playful. "Our friends, Mr. Darcy and Mr. Bingley both come from up north. Perhaps you know them?"

At the mention of Darcy's name, Wickham's expression faltered ever so slightly. A faint pallor touched his face, and his easy smile became just a touch strained. "Darcy?" he repeated, as if testing the name. "No, I do not believe I have had the pleasure."

Elizabeth, though quick to notice such subtleties, said nothing; she merely arched a brow in quiet curiosity.

"I do have to ask, Miss Lydia, as to how you feel about all northerners," Wickham ducked his head. "I know I probably should not give in to the gossip, but I am eager to hear all the details and ensure that those from my part of the country are comporting themselves well."

"Well, Mr. Darcy and Mr. Bingley are not so very bad," Lydia said, "but Miss Bingley thinks she's better than everyone—even Jane."

"Oh, look!" Kitty exclaimed before anyone could respond, pointing down the road. "There they are now!"

All heads turned to see Darcy and Bingley riding toward them alongside a carriage. Wickham's posture stiffened, and he quickly said, "If you will excuse me, ladies, I must attend to a matter with my commanding officer. A pleasure meeting you all."

His departure was so smooth and unhurried that none of the younger Bennet sisters gave it a second thought. Elizabeth, however, felt a flicker of suspicion. His reaction to Darcy's name and the sudden excuse to leave struck her as odd, but she pushed it from her mind as the Bingley carriage passed them. Darcy and Bingley came to a stop alongside the party from Longbourn. They dismounted, and Bingley beamed at Jane. "We were just on our way to Longbourn to see how you were doing. I trust you are fully recovered?"

Jane offered him a serene smile. "Thank you, sir. I am completely recovered."

"I am relieved to hear it," Bingley replied, his enthusiasm undiminished.

As the two engaged in quiet conversation, Darcy inclined his head at Elizabeth. "It is a pleasure to see you again, Miss Elizabeth."

Elizabeth met his gaze with a warm smile. "Mr. Darcy, hello. Are enjoying your morning ride?"

"I am, thank you." His tone was polite, yet reserved.

"And how is your son? I trust little Andrew is well."

Darcy's expression softened, and his usual gravity lifted for a moment. "Quite well, thank you. Although he has been asking for the nice lady."

"Please give him my regards. He is a charming young lad."

His gaze lingered on her for a moment, his eyes searching hers, before Mr. Collins pushed forward, his excitement barely contained. "Mr. Darcy!" he exclaimed, his voice nearly trembling. "What an honor to meet you at last, sir! I am William Collins, the rector of Hunsford. I must express my deepest gratitude for the living you have graciously bestowed upon me."

Darcy's brow furrowed slightly in confusion, though he replied with measured courtesy. "I am pleased to make your acquaintance, Mr. Collins, though I believe the living at Hunsford was granted by my aunt while she was still managing the estate; I myself had little to do with it."

Mr. Collins' chest swelled visibly. "I consider it my sacred duty to uphold the high standards set by Lady Catherine. And, of course, I am deeply honored to serve under the patronage of such an illustrious family."

Blinking, Darcy took a step backwards from the man, overwhelmed by his effusiveness. "I trust you are settling in well?" he asked neutrally, though Elizabeth thought she detected a flicker of impatience.

"Indeed, sir!" Mr. Collins replied , bowing deeply again with effusive enthusiasm. "I am most humbled to serve under the auspices of such a noble family. Your reputation, sir, is unparalleled, and I am delighted to assure you of my utmost dedication. Your aunt has…"

Mr. Collins, oblivious, continued to expound upon his gratitude for the living and his admiration for Darcy's management of Rosings Park. Lydia and Kitty, meanwhile, grew restless.

"Oh, let us not stand here all day!" Lydia cried. "I must have some new ribbons, and Kitty says she's seen the prettiest bonnets."

Elizabeth sighed, but before she could respond, Bingley turned to Jane. "I hope you will allow me the pleasure of seeing you again soon," he said earnestly. "Perhaps at Mrs. Phillips's card party tomorrow evening?"

Jane inclined her head. "That would be lovely."

Elizabeth's gaze shifted to Darcy. "And will your sister be joining you, Mr. Darcy?"

Darcy hesitated, his expression tightening slightly. "Georgiana has not yet been introduced to society."

Elizabeth nodded, her tone gentle. "I understand. But I assure you, Mrs. Phillips's gatherings are small and intimate—more of a family affair than a grand social event. I believe Miss Darcy might enjoy the company."

Darcy studied her for a moment, his eyes searching hers as though weighing her sincerity. At last, he inclined his head. "If she wishes to attend, I will permit it."

With the plan settled, the group began to disperse. As Elizabeth turned toward the shops with her sisters, she found herself smiling. All thoughts of the odd interaction with the new officer had vanished from her mind when she saw Darcy riding towards them. There had been something undeniably striking in his bearing, something that made her heart leap unexpectedly.

Could I be developing feelings for him? she wondered. Her rapid pulse refused to be ignored, a sensation that was equal parts

176

unsettling and exhilarating. *Is this... could this be the beginnings of love?*

She glanced back as he and Mr. Bingley mounted their horses once more, their figures framed against the autumn sky. Darcy's expression remained composed, but there was a gentleness in his gaze when it flickered toward her. A small smile played at her lips as she followed her sisters into the shop, tuning out Mr. Collins's chatter.

Chapter 12

Caroline Bingley sat in the carriage, seething with rage. *How dare they!* She nearly screeched aloud, watching the exchange with her brother, Darcy, and the Bennet chits. How could everything go so wrong?

The morning had begun with so much promise. She had been attempting to write a letter— something she never did— in an attempt to impress Darcy whilst in the the library. Instead, all she managed to do was ruin the sleeve of her dress.

She stared down at her arm in fury, scowling at the black mark on her favorite dress, a divine burnt-orange creation. The delicate French lace that had cost a fortune in London was complete ruined.

If only my maid weren't such a stupid creature.

Caroline had attempted to send the girl into Meryton to fetch some lace to make repairs, but the simple-minded girl didn't know the difference between tangerine and apricot. Thus Caroline had resigned herself to journeying into the backwater hamlet to personally oversee the purchase.

Bingley and Darcy had offered to escort her, which thrilled her until she realized their intent was to leave her in Meryton and continue on to Longbourn to inquire after the insipid eldest Bennet girl. Once in the village, however, she was quickly abandoned as the very girls she had hoped to avoid were directly in the road.

One of the officers standing with the Bennets had stared at her brother and Darcy, turned pale, and then hastily left the group. "Interesting," Miss Bingley mused aloud as she watched the scene play out before her.

She watched helplessly as she saw Darcy's eyes fix on Miss Elizabeth. He dismounted and engaged the impertinent chit in conversation, causing Caroline to nearly tear out her hair in frustration. By the time she had composed herself, the party had disbanded, and Darcy and her brother were nowhere in sight.

Descending from her coach and entering the shop, Caroline sniffed disdain. *This is a far cry from the high standards of London.*

She made her purchase and left the shop, nearly crashing head-first into the same officer who had practically run from Darcy and Bingley. "Oh!" she exclaimed, dropping her parcel as she stepped back to avoid a near collision.

"My apologies!" The handsome soldier in regimentals dipped a low bow with a flourish, his eyes raking down her body as his head descended. She would have been offended, were she not so flattered. He spied the dropped bundle and smoothly picked it up, handing it to her.

"Thank you, Mr...." Miss Bingley's voice trailed off.

"Wickham. Lieutenant George Wickham, at your service."

"Thank you, Mr. Wickham."

"And you are?"

"Miss Caroline Bingley," she said, inclining her head regally.

"Ah, yes, the mistress of Netherfield," he said with a charming grin.

"Why, yes. Do you know the estate?"

"Not exactly; I am only familiar with your brother's name. He is the good friend of Mr. Darcy, I believe."

"Yes, our families are very close," she said proudly, lifting her nose in the air slightly. "Are you acquainted with Mr. Darcy?"

He hesitated, then said, "I am, yes, but…" He paused and looked furtively around, then whispered, "You seem like an intelligent woman. Can I trust you?"

Finally, someone sees it! She thought triumphantly. Preening, she said, "Of course you can."

He hesitated. "It's not something I can discuss here in public. Might we, perhaps, meet somewhere more private?"

Her brown furrowed. "What could be so secret that we cannot discuss it here?"

He hung his head. "I promise, I will reveal all in good time. It is a matter of life and death, and everything hangs in the balance. I know no one in this town, and the few people I have met seem to be superficial. I need someone with a keen mind and sharp insight, and I think that you are the person I have been praying for. Only you can help me."

As he peered at her beneath long lashes, she felt her heart begin to race. "Fine," she said. "You are right to distrust the people of this backwater village. Even the landed gentry are little more than peasants. Very well ."

"When can we meet?" he asked eagerly.

She paused, thinking. "My brother and Mr. Darcy will be out tomorrow evening. I'm certain I can manage to slip away into the gardens for a walk. Meet me at Netherfield Park."

"I will. Thank you, Miss Bingley. Until we meet again, and please, keep this just between us."

Her breath caught in her throat as he reached for her hand, lifted her fingers to his lips, and placed a lingering kiss on her gloved hand. His eyes burned into hers as he whispered. "Farewell, my dear Miss Bingley."

Caroline could scarcely wait until the following evening. She fidgeted anxiously as she watched her brother, Darcy, and Georgiana put on their wraps and coats. The Hursts were already in the carriage; Mr. Hurst was anxious to enjoy some of Mrs. Philips' fine wine.

"Are you certain you do not wish to join us?" Bingley asked as they headed for the door.

"Quite certain, Charles. I have little desire to spend the evening with such rustics."

"Very well." He gave her a concerned look, then left the house, closing the door behind him.

The idea that she would be leaving the gentlemen to the attentions of the Bennet chits was insupportable, but she had no other option. The prospect of hearing Mr. Wickham's secret was more than her curiosity could ignore. He had been charming, enigmatic even, during their brief introduction, and the hint of tension at the mention of Darcy was too tantalizing to ignore.

The sound of the carriage fading into the distance spurred her into action. She adjusted her shawl, ensuring she looked her best even for the short journey to the garden. It would not do for Mr. Wickham to see her anything less than perfectly composed. Caroline swept through the halls, her heels clicking softly against the polished wood floors, until she reached the back door leading to the terrace.

The evening air was crisp, with a faint scent of autumn leaves and damp earth. Caroline hesitated briefly, glancing over her shoulder to ensure none of the servants were about. Satisfied she was alone, she descended the stone steps and followed the gravel path toward the garden. Lanterns hanging along the path cast a warm glow, their light dancing across the carefully curated shrubberies.

Her heart fluttered slightly as she approached the arranged meeting spot. The prospect of a clandestine meeting thrilled her in a way she would never admit. For all her criticisms of rusticity, there was something invigorating about the rawness of the night air and the daring nature of this rendezvous.

As she rounded a corner, her gaze landed on a figure standing near the fountain, his silhouette illuminated by the soft glow of the lanterns. Mr. Wickham.

He turned at the sound of her approach, his lips curving into a smile as he took a step closer. "Miss Bingley," he said, his voice smooth and inviting. "You are even more radiant than I remembered."

Caroline's lips curved in response, the flattery soothing her earlier irritation. "Mr. Wickham," she replied, her tone light and teasing. "I see you have not lost your charm."

He gestured to the bench near the fountain. "Shall we sit? I believe we have much to discuss."

She inclined her head gracefully and moved toward the bench, her mind racing with questions about Darcy, Georgiana, and whatever secrets Wickham might hold. The possibilities were endless, and Caroline intended to exploit every one of them to her advantage.

She sat down and smoothed her skirts. "So you are acquainted with Mr. Darcy, sir?" she asked him as soon as she had sat down and smoothed her skirts.

"You will never meet anyone more acquainted with him than I, having been acquainted with him since my infancy. How do you find him?"

"He is the perfect houseguest," Caroline gushed with a coy look. "Polite and attentive at all times."

"I am glad to hear it," Wickham replied, his tone measured, though his gaze flickered with something unreadable. "Mr. Darcy can please where he chooses. He does not lack the ability to be an amiable companion when he deems it worth his while. Among those who are his equals in consequence, he is a very different man from what he is to the less prosperous. His pride never deserts him; but with the rich, he is liberal-minded, sincere, rational, and honorable—and perhaps even agreeable, allowing for fortune and figure."

Caroline preened at this subtle evidence of Darcy's regard for herself, interpreting Wickham's words as confirmation that Darcy's treatment of her had always been exemplary. "This does not describe yourself?" she ventured, her voice soft with interest.

Wickham chuckled lightly, though there was a tinge of sadness in his expression. "We were born in the same parish, within the same park. The greatest part of our youth was spent together—inmates of the same house, sharing the same amusements and objects of parental care. My father began life in the law but gave up everything to devote his time to the care of the Pemberley property and the late Mr. Darcy."

He hesitated, then leaned slightly closer, his voice dropping to a more intimate tone. "Forgive me, Miss Bingley. I fear I have been too candid. I have a warm, unguarded temper, which led me to be the favorite of the late Mr. Darcy. It caused his son no small amount of jealousy. He had not the temper to bear the sort of competition in which we stood—the sort of preference often shown to me."

Wickham drew in a breath, his eyes glistening with unshed tears. "The fact is, we are very different sorts of men, and he hates me for it. But," he added, his voice breaking slightly, "until I can forget his father, I cannot wish for anything but the best for my oldest friend."

Caroline felt a warmth rising in her chest. Though she prided herself on her composure, Wickham's vulnerability tugged at her. "I am very sorry to hear it," she murmured, her tone uncharacteristically gentle. "To me, Mr. Darcy has always been the best of men. In fact..." She hesitated, her cheeks flushing slightly

184

before she added, "I daresay I am one of the few who can claim his good opinion. The longer we reside under the same roof, the more certain I am of it. Perhaps," she said with a small, significant smile, "I might even do something to assist you."

Wickham's smile widened, and he stepped closer, his gaze softening as he regarded her. "Do you mean to say, Miss Bingley, that Mr. Darcy may be on the verge of making you an offer of marriage?"

Caroline flushed with pride, tilting her chin up slightly. "I have no reason to suspect otherwise," she said with a satisfied smile.

Wickham's expression turned warm and admiring. "Then I am very happy to hear that my old friend is capable of winning someone as worthy and beautiful as yourself."

Caroline basked in his compliment for a moment, her heart fluttering at his flattering words. The moment was short-lived, however, as her thoughts quickly turned to the vexing presence of Miss Elizabeth Bennet over the past few days. Her satisfaction dimmed, and she leaned in slightly, her voice dropping to a conspiratorial whisper. "There is one thing that causes me concern, however."

"What could trouble someone as capable as you, Miss Bingley?" Wickham asked, stepping even closer, his tone gentle and conspiratorial.

"I fear he may be in danger of a fortune-hunter," she confided with an air of gravity. "One of the local ladies, a certain Miss Elizabeth Bennet, has been using her arts and allurements—along with her sister—to entrap both my brother and Mr. Darcy."

Wickham's brow furrowed as he feigned shock, though his eyes betrayed a spark of interest. "A fortune-hunter, you say? But surely Darcy would not be able to tear himself away from someone as exceptional as yourself."

"I would like to agree," Caroline said with a haughty sniff, "but this girl seems to have ensnared my poor Mr. Darcy. Her impertinence, her lively eyes…" She trailed off, her tone dripping with disdain. "He may not see her for what she truly is."

Wickham's expression hardened, though his voice remained gentle. "Miss Bingley, Mr. Darcy is indeed fortunate to have someone as perceptive and caring as you in his circle. Together, perhaps we can ensure that he avoids such a regrettable mistake."

Caroline straightened, her chin lifting. "I should hope so. I will not stand by and watch that upstart ruin all that is good and noble about him."

Wickham inclined his head, his smile sly. "Then, Miss Bingley, it seems we have a common goal."

Caroline opened her mouth to say more, but the faint sound of footsteps approaching from the direction of the terrace stilled her. Her head snapped toward the noise, her heart leaping into her throat. Wickham's expression shifted in an instant, his easy charm giving way to an alert wariness.

"Someone's coming," he murmured, his voice low.

Caroline's pulse quickened, torn between the thrill of secrecy and the fear of discovery. Before she could decide on a course of action, Wickham stepped closer, his eyes locking onto hers. "We mustn't be seen together. Mr. Darcy… well, he may not take kindly to it."

Her breath hitched slightly as he lifted her hand, his touch warm and deliberate. "Forgive me, Miss Bingley," he said, pressing his lips to her gloved fingers in a gesture both gallant and intimate. "Until we meet again."

Before she could respond, he released her hand and turned, disappearing into the hedgerows with practiced ease. Caroline stared after him, her heart racing as the footsteps grew louder.

She barely had time to compose herself when a gardener rounded the corner. He startled upon seeing her, then tipped his hat and gave a bow. "Sorry to bother you, miss. Just on my way home for the night. Can I help you with something?"

Caroline straightened her shoulders, smoothing her skirts with one hand as she waved him away with another. He bowed again and retreated, leaving Caroline alone once more.

She glanced toward the hedgerows where Wickham had vanished, her thoughts swirling with the memory of his parting gesture. Her lips curved into a small, satisfied smile, certain now that she had found an ally in her quest to protect Darcy—and, perhaps, to secure her own place at his side.

The parlor at the Philips' house buzzed with lively conversation and bursts of laughter, the air filled with the faint scent of tea and candle wax. Elizabeth stood near her aunt, chatting idly with Charlotte Lucas and a few neighbors. Across the room, Lydia and

Kitty were the center of a small group of officers, their flirtatious giggles carrying over the hum of voices.

Elizabeth's gaze flickered toward her younger sisters, shaking her head in mild amusement at their antics. "Kitty and Lydia appear to be enjoying themselves," she said to Charlotte.

"Indeed," Charlotte replied, her tone dry. "Though I doubt they'll leave without monopolizing every officer present."

Elizabeth laughed lightly but couldn't help noticing the absence of the handsome officer they had met the day before. Her thoughts lingered briefly—his easy charm, the way he had paled at the mention of Darcy—before the sound of the door opening drew her attention.

The Netherfield party had arrived.

Mr. Bingley entered first, his warm smile and genial air instantly drawing the attention of the room. Mr. Darcy followed, his tall, composed figure cutting a striking presence. Elizabeth's gaze, however, landed on the younger figure at his side, her arm resting on his.

A grin crossed Elizabeth's face. *She came after all!*

Georgiana Darcy, with her wide blue eyes and shy demeanor, looked hesitant as she scanned the unfamiliar faces. Elizabeth could see her clenching and releasing the hand that hung at her side, and a protective instinct stirred within her.

Excusing herself from Charlotte, Elizabeth made her way over to the newcomers, curtsying as she greeted them. "Mr. Darcy, Mr. Bingley, Miss Darcy," she said warmly. "How wonderful to see you all this evening. Miss Darcy, I trust the drive over from Netherfield was pleasant?"

Georgiana offered a tentative smile, her gaze darting briefly to her brother. "Yes, thank you, Miss Elizabeth. It was quite... pleasant."

"I am delighted you've joined us," Elizabeth said. "Such gatherings can be daunting, but I assure you this company is as welcoming as it is lively."

Georgiana managed a small smile, but her fingers fidgeted with the edge of her sleeve. Sensing her discomfort, Elizabeth turned to Mr. Darcy. "I must thank you for bringing her. It's a pleasure to have her here."

Darcy inclined his head slightly, a flicker of relief in his eyes at her words. Turning back to Georgiana, Elizabeth gestured towards Charlotte and Maria Lucas. "May I introduce you to some friends?"

Georgiana once again looked hesitantly at her brother, awaiting his approval. He nodded, prompting Georgiana to say in a quiet voice, "I... I would like that very much."

As Elizabeth led the younger girl across the room, she whispered in her ear, "Maria is rather shy, like Jane is, and Charlotte is one of my dearest friends. I think you will feel comfortable with them."

They reached the two Lucas sisters, and Georgiana curtsied as introductions were made. "It is a pleasure to meet you both."

Elizabeth motioned to another figure who stood nearby. "This is my sister Mary. Like you, she is very fond of music."

Mary inclined her head politely, her tone measured. "I do enjoy music, very much indeed. Do you prefer playing or listening, Miss Darcy?"

"I enjoy both," Georgiana said shyly, "but I find great comfort in playing."

"You and Mary will have much to discuss," Elizabeth in a playful whisper to Georgiana. "As for my younger sisters, Kitty and Lydia, they are currently quite occupied with the officers. I think it best to introduce you to them another time when their attention is not so… divided."

Georgiana let out a soft giggle, her posture relaxing further. Maria Lucas, emboldened by the levity, confided with a blush, "They are quite handsome in their red coats, are they not? Most of the girls in Meryton are wild about the officers."

"Yes, it seems to be the fashion of the season," Elizabeth said with a smirk.

The group shared a quiet laugh, and Elizabeth felt a warm sense of satisfaction as Georgiana seemed to settle into the conversation.

Shortly afterward, Mr. Philips began arranging tables for cards, and the room filled with cheerful movement as chairs were gathered and partners chosen. Elizabeth found herself partnered with Mr. Darcy, a pairing that sent a subtle thrill through her, though she strove to appear unaffected. Georgiana partnered with Mary, completing their table.

However, just as Darcy was about to deal the cards, a loud voice broke through the gentle murmur of the room.

"Cousin Elizabeth!" Mr. Collins exclaimed, bustling over with an air of exaggerated importance. "Your excellent mother had promised me that you would be my partner for the evening."

Elizabeth's cheeks flushed as several heads turned their way. Darcy, opposite the table from her to be her partner, stilled, his face growing stern as his gaze shifted to Mr. Collins.

"I am very sorry, Mr. Collins," she began in a quiet voice. "I was unaware of my mother's desires, and I have already committed myself to being Mr. Darcy's partner."

Mr. Collins's eyes widened in exaggerated affront. "Miss Elizabeth, it is hardly becoming for a young lady of your station to impose upon a gentleman such as Mr. Darcy! I must apologize on your behalf, sir, for any presumption my cousin may have shown. She is, of course, well-meaning, but sometimes lacks the refinement to—"

"Mr. Collins," Elizabeth began, her voice steady but tinged with discomfort, "I assure you, Mr. Darcy has made the request himself. I am merely—"

"Nonsense, cousin!" Mr. Collins interrupted, his tone bordering on condescension. "It is not fitting for you to monopolize the attention of a man so above your station. I insist you join me at another table."

Elizabeth looked around helplessly for Jane, but her sister was deep in conversation with Mr. Bingley across the room. Her eyes darted to Charlotte Lucas, who appeared at Elizabeth's side with a serene expression and her firm voice.

"Mr. Collins," the elder girl said smoothly, "I was hoping you might join us at our table. My father has been eager to hear all about Rosings Park and Lady Catherine. He believes he may have crossed paths with her at St. James's court, and no one could enlighten us better than yourself."

Mr. Collins blinked, momentarily thrown off course. "Lady Catherine, you say?" His chest puffed out with pride. "Why, of course, I would be delighted to oblige Sir William and share my humble insights."

Charlotte looped her arm through his and steered him toward another table, throwing Elizabeth a quick wink over her shoulder. Elizabeth mouthed her gratitude, her tension easing as Mr. Collins's booming voice receded into the background.

Mr. Darcy rapped the cards against the table. "Shall we continue, Miss Elizabeth?" he asked with amusement.

Elizabeth nodded, her lips curving into a smile. "By all means, Mr. Darcy. I believe we have all waited long enough."

As the games commenced, Elizabeth found herself increasingly aware of Darcy's presence across from her. He was attentive, his reserved manner softening slightly in the intimate setting. Their hands brushed once as they reached for the same card, and Elizabeth felt her cheeks warm at the brief contact.

Georgiana and Mary also appeared to be enjoying their game, exchanging occasional smiles and murmured words. Elizabeth's heart warmed at the sight of Georgiana beginning to come out of her shell.

The evening passed in a haze of easy conversation and gentle laughter. Elizabeth, to her surprise, found herself increasingly at ease in Mr. Darcy's company. His wit, though subtle, revealed itself in unexpected moments, and his occasional smiles felt like small victories.

As the final hand was played and the tables began to disperse, Elizabeth turned to him with a bright smile. "Thank you, Mr. Darcy. You make an excellent partner."

He inclined his head, his expression warm. "The pleasure was mine, Miss Elizabeth."

Her heart fluttered at the sincerity in his tone, and as the evening drew to a close, she felt a quiet contentment settle over her. The warmth of their brief exchange lingered with her long after she retired to bed that evening. As her eyes closed, she fell asleep to the image of Darcy's eyes gazing deeply into her own.

Chapter 13

The following morning dawned crisp and clear, and the Bennet household bustled with its usual morning routines. Jane and Elizabeth, seated together in the drawing room, occupied themselves with needlework while their mother busied herself with instructions for Hill. The hum of conversation carried faintly through the house, punctuated by Lydia and Kitty's occasional laughter as they flitted from room to room.

The sound of a carriage pulling up outside drew everyone's attention. Elizabeth glanced toward Jane with a questioning look, but Jane merely shrugged. The window revealed a familiar sight—the Netherfield carriage coming to a stop at the gate.

Before long, the family assembled to greet their visitors. Mr. Bingley entered the drawing room first, his ever-pleasant smile lighting up the room. Mr. Darcy followed, with his tall and commanding presence drawing notice. Behind them came Miss Darcy, her shy gaze flickering about the room, and Caroline and Mrs. Hurst, both as impeccably dressed as ever.

"What a pleasure to see you all," Mrs. Bennet cooed. "And how kind of you to call on us!"

Bingley stepped forward, a wide smile on his face. "We come with an invitation. We are hosting a ball at Netherfield on Tuesday next, and we would be honored if you all would attend."

"A ball!" Lydia and Kitty exclaimed in unison, clapping their hands with delight.

Mrs. Bennet beamed. "Of course, we will be delighted to join you. Such a thoughtful gesture, Mr. Bingley!"

Caroline, standing slightly to the side, fixed her gaze on Elizabeth, her smile tight. "We, of course, hope to see all your lovely daughters in attendance. And, naturally, any houseguests."

Elizabeth stiffened slightly, her eyes darting to Mr. Collins, who was seated a little apart from the group. His attention snapped to Caroline, and his chest puffed with self-importance.

"Oh, yes," Mrs. Bennet gushed, "we do have my husband's cousin visiting. He is a member of the clergy, you know."

Elizabeth cleared her throat, attempting to steer the conversation delicately. "I am certain Mr. Collins will appreciate the invitation, though perhaps—given his position—he might prefer not to engage in such frivolities."

"Certainly not, Cousin Elizabeth!" Mr. Collins interrupted, his voice rising. "It would be most unbecoming to refuse such a gracious offer." He turned to Caroline with a broad smile. "I shall be delighted to attend, Miss Bingley."

Before Elizabeth could respond, Mr. Collins turned back to her, his expression suddenly shifting to one of determined purpose. "And

Miss Elizabeth, may I have the honor of reserving the first two dances with you?"

The room stilled, all eyes turning to Elizabeth. Her mouth opened, but no words came. Instead, her gaze flickered to Darcy instinctively.

Darcy stepped forward smoothly, his tone calm but firm. "I must apologize, Mr. Collins, but I have already secured Miss Elizabeth's first two dances."

Elizabeth's heart leapt into her throat. Mrs. Bennet and Mr. Collins both stared at Darcy in shock. "When did this happen?" Mrs. Bennet demanded, her gaze bouncing between Elizabeth and Darcy.

Darcy, unflappable, replied, "I was already aware of the ball and made my request at the Philips's card party yesterday evening."

Elizabeth barely managed to suppress her astonishment, while Mr. Collins spluttered indignantly. "This is most irregular—most improper! Cousin Elizabeth—"

"Mr. Collins," Mrs. Bennet interjected suddenly, her tone surprisingly shrewd. "If Mr. Darcy has already asked Elizabeth, you must ask another. What about Mary? She is quite accomplished and would be an excellent partner for you."

"I could not possibly overlook the eldest," Mr. Collins blustered, his indignation growing.

At that, Mr. Bingley, who had been standing quietly, stepped forward with a smile. "Ah, but I asked Miss Bennet for the first two dances myself, sir."

"You did?" Mr. Collins looked at Jane suspiciously.

Jane's eyes widened, and a faint line appeared between her brows. Elizabeth, sensing her sister's hesitation, gently pinched her arm. "Oh, yes," Jane said, her voice soft but steady. "Mr. Bingley asked me last night as well."

Mr. Collins's expression faltered, but Darcy's cool gaze was enough to silence further protest. "Then it is settled," Darcy said firmly. "I believe you will find Miss Mary an agreeable partner, Mr. Collins."

Mrs. Bennet beamed at Darcy's tone, practically vibrating with excitement. Mr. Collins, though somewhat deflated, turned to Mary, who inclined her head politely but looked distinctly unenthused.

Eager to change the topic and ease the tension in the room, Elizabeth turned towards the most timid member of the Netherfield party.

"Will you be dancing as well, Miss Darcy?" Elizabeth asked her young friend encouragingly.

Beaming, Georgiana nodded her head. "My brother has given me permission to attend until the supper dance. I may only dance with him, Mr. Bingley, and Mr. Hurst, however."

"Quite understandable," Elizabeth replied. "I'm sure you will still enjoy the evening, and you needn't worry about unfamiliar partners boring you with dreadful topics, like horse racing."

"Why can't you dance?" Lydia demanded, bounding to that side of the room, Kitty close behind.

"Miss Darcy is only fifteen years old, and she is therefore not yet out," Elizabeth replied calmly.

"Well, if that isn't the silliest thing I have ever heard," snorted Lydia. "I am only fifteen as well, and I have been out these six months at least!"

Kitty giggled beside her, clearly finding Lydia's outburst amusing. Georgiana, however, flushed deeply and cast a nervous glance at her brother.

Darcy's voice cut through the room, calm but firm. "In higher social circles in London, particularly where my sister will eventually find herself, young ladies are not presented until they are at least seventeen or eighteen. It ensures they are fully prepared for the demands of society."

His tone, though measured, carried enough authority to silence Lydia momentarily. Mrs. Bennett, however, was undeterred. "Seventeen or eighteen, Mr. Darcy?" she asked, her voice laden with curiosity. "Why, that seems so... late. Why would one wait so long?"

Darcy inclined his head slightly, his expression polite. "In part, it allows young ladies to develop the poise and confidence necessary for society's demands. It also ensures they are better equipped to navigate its intricacies."

Elizabeth suppressed a smile at the subtle dig, though Mrs. Bennet was oblivious to any possible slight. "Well," Mrs. Bennet began, puffing up with self-satisfaction, "our Lydia is already quite accomplished. There was no sense in delaying her debut."

Darcy's lips twitched as though he were restraining a comment. Elizabeth—sensing the need to redirect the conversation—quickly addressed Georgiana again. "Miss Darcy, I am certain that when you do make your debut, you will be the toast of the season. For now, I hope you will enjoy the ball. And if I may, I would be honored to sit with you for a moment to hear your impressions."

Georgiana's cheeks turned pink, but her smile brightened. "Thank you, Miss Elizabeth. I would like that very much."

Mrs. Bennet, meanwhile, seemed deep in thought, her eyes darting between Darcy and Georgiana. Elizabeth could almost see the wheels turning in her mother's mind as she no doubt imagined the possibilities of such connections.

Lydia, recovering quickly from her earlier indignation, turned to Kitty and whispered something that made them both giggle. Elizabeth ignored them and instead focused on Georgiana, who seemed reassured by the attention and kindness.

"Well," Bingley said brightly, breaking the moment, "we still have many invitations to deliver, so we must take our leave."

As the Netherfield party made their farewells and exited, Elizabeth felt a curious mixture of relief and confusion. Darcy's intervention had been entirely unexpected, and as she watched the carriage pull away, she couldn't shake the lingering warmth that his words had stirred within her.

Caroline Bingley sat rigidly in the carriage as it rattled down the uneven road, her gloved hands curled so tightly into fists that her knuckles ached.

How dare *he?* she seethed.

The audacity of Mr. Darcy to request the first two dances at the ball from that insipid Eliza Bennet was beyond belief. Of all the women in Hertfordshire—indeed, of all the women present in the drawing room—why on earth would he stoop to ask *her*?

She's not even that pretty! Her teeth are the only tolerable thing about her.

As the hostess, *she* should have been the natural choice. After all, Darcy was the man of highest rank. Propriety demanded he honor her with the first dance. It would have been the perfect display of his regard for her, a subtle announcement of their shared understanding. Instead, he had humiliated her in front of the entire household.

She could still see Mrs. Bennet's gloating expression, could hear Lydia's irritating giggles. Worse yet, she had watched as Darcy's gaze lingered far too long on that Eliza Bennet, as though she were worthy of admiration. Caroline's stomach churned with anger, and she drew in a sharp breath, her nostrils flaring.

No, this cannot be true. Mr. Darcy's attentions to that little chit are nothing more than a whim, a temporary lapse of judgment.

He was a man of impeccable taste, far above such rustic charms.

But…

But what if it *wasn't* just a lapse? What if he genuinely admired her? The thought made Caroline's blood boil. She would not allow it. She could not allow it.

"Caroline, are you quite well?" Louisa asked, raising a perfectly arched brow as she glanced at her sister.

"I am completely fine," Caroline snapped, though her tone betrayed her irritation. "Merely fatigued from the day's calls."

Louisa said nothing further, though the slight upward curve of her lips hinted at her amusement. Caroline turned her attention back to the window, where the landscape blurred into a haze of trees and fields. She replayed the scene in her mind: Darcy's calm and deliberate declaration that he had already secured Elizabeth Bennet's first two dances.

Not hers. Not the woman who had tirelessly entertained him and his sister with her wit and refinement. No, he had chosen that rustic, country trollop with her sharp tongue and unremarkable connections.

It was unthinkable.

Her lips pressed into a thin line as her gaze flicked to Darcy, who sat opposite her in the carriage. He seemed utterly unaffected, staring out the window with his usual stoicism, as if he hadn't just turned her entire day into a disaster. Beside him, Georgiana sat quietly, the very picture of composure, though Caroline noted the girl's faint smile.

Even his mute sister approves of this nonsense!

Caroline's indignation burned hotter.

Mrs. Hurst attempted to break the tense silence with idle chatter about the upcoming ball, but Caroline barely heard her. She would not allow this affront to go unanswered. Darcy's actions must be the result of some temporary lapse in judgment, and she would see to it that he was reminded of his proper place—at her side.

When the carriage turned down the road leading to the officers' encampment, Caroline welcomed the distraction. The invitation from Colonel Forster and his regiment   provided the perfect opportunity to bolster her spirits. Captain Forster and his men would be invited to the ball, and if her demeanor was cool enough, perhaps she could demonstrate to Darcy the marked difference between the ladies of refinement and the wild Bennet girls.

After all, the two hoydens will most likely make fools of themselves with the soldiers.   Perhaps I could add something to their wine…?

As the carriage stopped, the gentlemen disembarked first. Darcy strode ahead with Bingley, and Caroline followed with Louisa. The crisp autumn air bit at her cheeks, and she pulled her wrap tighter around her shoulders.

The officers greeted them warmly. Captain Forster accepted the invitation on behalf of the entire regiment.

Caroline made polite conversation, her practiced charm on full display, but her focus wavered when her eyes caught sight of a familiar figure near the edge of the encampment.

George Wickham.

He was speaking to another officer, though his body was angled away from the group, as though deliberately avoiding notice. As Darcy turned slightly, Caroline saw Wickham stiffen, his posture shifting as he subtly moved further into the shadows.

Her eyes narrowed.

As they moved on to speak with another group of officers, Caroline took advantage of a moment when Darcy and Bingley were engaged in conversation. She slowed her pace, her skirts swishing against the gravel, and moved closer to where Wickham now lingered near the edge of a tent. He glanced up, and their eyes met. A flicker of recognition passed across his face, followed quickly by wariness.

"We need to speak," she hissed under her breath. "Soon."

Wickham's expression shifted to one of practiced nonchalance, though she could see the unease in his eyes. He gave a slight nod, then turned away as though their exchange had not occurred.

"Caroline, do keep up," Bingley called cheerfully.

Darcy, she noticed sourly, didn't even glance behind him at her.

I will *be his wife— make no mistake about that!*

George Wickham scowled as he waited in the early afternoon sun at the edge of Netherfield Park for Caroline Bingley to come to meet him. Flipping open the ornate pocket watch he'd won at dice the night before, he groaned. He would need to leave soon in order to return before dinner.

Stupid woman is ten minutes late. Does she want *us to get caught?*

He'd left a note with a young maid at Netherfield to put on Caroline's pillow, informing her of the time for their rendezvous.

The girl had agreed with a giggle, and he'd sent her on her way with a wink and pat on the bottom.

I'll have to come around more often if all the maids at this house look like that.

After waiting another five minutes, Wickham had almost given up. With a sigh of resignation, he turned away and began to the mile walk back towards the barracks.

"Wait!"

The hushed cry and patter of footsteps behind him caused him to tense, then relax as he recognized the voice as belonging to the mistress of the estate.

"About time," he snarled at her, turning around to face her.

Taken aback at his harsh tone, Caroline stopped short, her eyes wide. Forcing himself to paste a pleasant expression on his face, he said in a softer tone, "My apologies, madam. I was merely concerned someone might see us. I allowed my worry to get the better of me."

She straightened her gloves with a sniff. "It took some time to escape my sister's endless chatter about the ball."

"Ah, yes— the ball. I know my fellow officers are quite eager to attend. I imagine you are as well? Surely my old friend would have asked you for the first set by now."

Her face darkened in anger, and he nearly laughed aloud. The entire town was buzzing with the gossip that the Bennet girls had caught the most eligible bachelors in town; Mrs. Bennet had been crowing all morning to her visitors how her three eldest daughters already had partners for the first set.

"He has been… distracted by that wretched Bennet girl," she said, pursing her lips. "I know he loves me, but I do worry he will fall prey to her little games to secure him."

Ha! I bet he does, Wickham thought sarcastically. Aloud, he bowed slightly and said, "It is the lot of all rich men, I'm afraid, to be intrigued by those who are… beneath them. But rest assured, such infatuations rarely last."

Her lip curled in disdain. "If he dances with her first at the ball, all of my chances with him are gone. He means too much to me to allow him to throw away our future together."

Looking at him from under her batting eyelashes, she cooed, "He is your friend, is he not? Please say you will help me."

"How can I help you? He despises me, remember?" He infused his words with faux regret, adopting the wounded air of a misunderstood soul. *Two can play this game*, he thought with derision.

Caroline hesitated, then leaned in conspiratorially. "I think we need to… arrange a situation that will force his hand. I need your assistance to compromise him."

Wickham blinked, momentarily stunned. *Did she just suggest what I think she did?*

Caroline bit her lip, her nerves evident as she awaited his response.

"How… exactly do you plan to accomplish that?" he asked carefully.

Her voice grew more confident as she explained. "I will serve a special tea tomorrow evening after dinner for everyone. I have a unique blend from London—it's truly unremarkable tea, but with the addition of this vial"— she shook a small bottle in front of him— "and a few herbs to mask the bitterness, it will taste exotic. I'll add just enough of the drug to ensure that everyone falls asleep within a quarter of an hour. Once they are unconscious, I will signal you from the window before drinking some myself. You will come in and… arrange matters."

"Arrange matters?" Wickham echoed cautiously, raising a skeptical eyebrow.

"Yes, this is where I cannot do it myself." Caroline's spoke briskly as she outlined the rest of her plan. "You will quickly move Mr. Darcy and myself to his chambers, remove our clothing—" here she blushed before continuing resolutely— "then lay me down next to him, ensuring that we appear… compromised. When he wakes, it will be evident to everyone that he has no choice but to propose."

Wickham's mind raced. "And what of the servants? Surely, they'll notice something amiss."

"I will give them the afternoon off, except for a single maid to serve the tea," Caroline replied with a dismissive wave of her hand. "If questioned, I will simply blame the tea's supplier."

He chuckled darkly. "And you believe Darcy will simply accept such a story? He could hush up the entire matter, especially with no witnesses."

Caroline frowned, her brow furrowing in thought, then she grinned triumphantly. "I will invite the two eldest Bennet girls to join the tea. I'll tell them I need their help with the ball's arrangements. They'll be there to witness everything, and I will take great pleasure in seeing Elizabeth Bennet's face when she realizes she has lost."

Wickham stared at her, impressed despite himself. "A bold plan," he said after a moment. "Though I must say, you've given this more thought than I expected."

Caroline straightened, her expression smug. "I will not leave my future to chance, Mr. Wickham. Darcy and I belong together, and I will not allow some country nobody to ruin my plans."

As she looked at him with satisfaction, Wickham found his gaze wandering over her figure. She was undeniably attractive, but her demanding nature made her an impossible prospect for a man like him. Still, he couldn't help but admire the cunning mind behind her refined exterior.

Too bad she is such a demanding creature, Wickham thought to himself, *else I would try for her dowry myself. But the idea of Darcy being tied to such a shrew for the rest of his life is too good an opportunity to pass up.*

"Very well," he said at last. "I'll do my part. But we must be careful. Timing is everything."

"I quite agree," Caroline said firmly. "Thank you, Mr. Wickham, for your service to my future husband. I won't forget your help once I am Mrs. Darcy."

"You truly are a remarkable woman, Miss Bingley," he said with a charming smile. "My old friend will be very fortunate to have you for a wife. I am in awe of your dedication to your union, and I hope to one day have a woman love me just as much as you do him."

She preened under the compliment, and Wickham allowed himself a small, private laugh. *If only Darcy knew what he was in for. The perfect revenge—and no one will suspect a thing.*

With a final conspiratorial nod, Caroline turned and disappeared back toward the house. Wickham adjusted his coat and set off at a brisk pace, eager to return to the barracks before his absence raised questions. His steps quickened, his mind already savoring the chaos that would follow.

Chapter 14

Elizabeth stepped out of Longbourn's front door, pulling her shawl tightly around her shoulders. The sun was just beginning to rise above the hills, casting a golden glow over the fields and hedgerows that bordered the estate. After the events of the day before, she needed time to think, and Oakham Mount was the perfect place for it.

Fortunately, there was no one around to stop her. Her family was still stirring in their rooms, the household not yet fully awake. Only the faint clatter of Hill preparing breakfast reached her ears. The solitude was welcome. For once, there were no cries of "Mama!" from Lydia, no dramatic exclamations from Mrs. Bennet, and no sharp remarks from Mary about the importance of rising early.

Elizabeth tied her bonnet securely under her chin, then pulled her shawl tightly around her shoulders. The air was cold, but the promise of sunshine brightened the horizon as she made her way toward Oakham Mount. She followed her usual trail, winding through the fields and hedgerows that separated Longbourn from the surrounding countryside. She relished the solitude, the soft crunch of leaves beneath her boots, and the stillness of the world before most of the neighborhood had stirred.

Oakham Mount had always been her favorite retreat, a place where she could think without interruption. Reaching the summit, she paused to take in the view. The valley spread out below her, the roofs of Longbourn visible in the distance, with the chimneys of Netherfield rising just beyond. The sight always brought her a sense of peace, but today her thoughts were anything but serene.

The rocky path to the top of the large hill was overgrown beneath her boots. Few could manage the climb, but to her it was familiar and comforting. Elizabeth had walked it countless times, but today her steps felt lighter, her heart unusually buoyant. She tried to suppress the fluttering sensation that had taken up residence in her chest since the night before, but it was a losing battle. Every time she recalled Darcy's deep voice asking for her hand for the first two dances at the Netherfield ball, her pulse quickened.

She sat on a flat rock and pulled her shawl closer, staring out over the landscape. Her mind was filled with memories of the previous evening and, most especially, the moment Darcy had asked her for the first two dances at the ball.

Why did he do it? Why did he ask me?

Elizabeth had turned the question over in her mind again and again during the restless hours of the night. On one hand, it could mean nothing—he likely noticed her mother's unsubtle matchmaking and felt a polite sense of obligation.

On the other hand, it wasn't as though Darcy were known for his gallantry and charm. Her initial impression of him had been that he was cold and aloof, a man more interested in his own pride than in the feelings of others. Yet, over the past weeks, she had glimpsed another side of him—a man capable of warmth, generosity, and quiet affection.

She pressed her hands to her cheeks, which had grown warm despite the chill. It was impossible not to hope. The memory of his deep, steady voice asking for her hand filled her with a fluttering sensation she could not suppress. But was she reading too much into it? Was she allowing herself to be swept up in the moment without considering the reality of their acquaintance?

He is very handsome, she admitted to herself, *and kind. The way he cares for his son and sister—it is remarkable. But does that mean he feels anything for me?*

It was easy to imagine Darcy at Netherfield now, seated at the breakfast table with his son and sister. The image brought a faint smile to her lips. She could almost hear his low, measured voice as he inquired about Andrew's sleep or Georgiana's plans for the day.

Dear, sweet Andrew.

Her thoughts drifted to the little boy who had so quickly found a place in her heart. His charming smile and earnest nature had endeared him to her from the start. She remembered the way he had clung to her skirts, seeking comfort from a frightening encounter with Caroline Bingley. The memory filled her with a surge of protectiveness, as though she could shield him from all the world's unkindness.

She could almost feel his small hand in hers, see his bright smile when she comforted him. Darcy had seemed so grateful to her for that moment, and she could not deny how it had warmed her heart.

And then there was Georgiana, shy and reserved but with a quiet gentleness that reminded Elizabeth of Jane. She was a young girl yearning for acceptance and understanding, trying to find her place in the world.

And he does an admirable job of lifting her up.

Darcy's attentiveness to his sister spoke volumes about his character, and she admired him for it deeply. He was a man who bore his responsibilities with grace, a man who clearly loved his family.

But is that enough?

Elizabeth sighed, brushing a strand of hair back beneath her bonnet. This was all so new to her. She had never been courted before, never had the experience of a young man declaring his admiration or love. Oh, there had been moments—glances and smiles from neighborhood boys like the Lucases or the Gouldings. But none had ever truly captured her heart, and none had pursued her seriously.

Even in London, during her visits to the Gardiners, she had met gentlemen she liked well enough, but no one who moved her as Darcy did. She danced and even flirted a bit, but she never spent time dwelling on their dispositions or imagining a future with them.

So what makes Darcy so different?

Was it simply his position, his wealth, or the undeniable presence he carried into every room? Was it that he was older, more mature? Was it because he was a father, with a depth of experience she had never encountered in others?

Or was it something deeper—something about the man himself that drew her in? She could not deny that she found him handsome. His dark eyes held a quiet intensity, and his features were strong and well-formed. Yet her attraction went beyond mere appearance.

Yet how well do I truly know him? she wondered. *A month's acquaintance, a few meaningful conversations… is that enough to build a foundation for love? Or am I simply infatuated with the idea of him?*

There was something about the way he carried himself—the way he spoke to Andrew with patience and affection, the way he looked after Georgiana with gentle protectiveness. It spoke of a man who cared deeply for those he loved, a man of integrity and honor.

A man who would be a good husband.

Would he even want to marry again? she asked herself. *He had loved his first wife, didn't he? Or at least, he must have cared for her. And then there is Andrew. Would he welcome a stepmother into his son's life, or does he prefer things as they are?*

Elizabeth sighed, shaking her head at her own foolishness. She was allowing herself to hope, to dream of something that might never come to pass. It was dangerous, this growing attachment, and she knew she must guard her heart carefully.

Still, the thoughts wouldn't stop coming. *Could he feel anything for… me?*

Elizabeth drew her knees up to her chest, resting her chin on them as she considered the possibility that Darcy's kindness toward her was nothing more than politeness. Could it be that he only valued her for her treatment of his family? That his attentions were born of gratitude rather than affection?

The idea stung, and she tried to push it away.

But what if he does feel something for me? Would I be ready to accept it?

The thought sent a thrill through her, but it also filled her with uncertainty. She had never been in love before, had never known what it was to give her heart to another. How could she be sure that what she felt for Darcy was true?

She could not deny her attraction to him—his dark eyes, his strong features, the quiet intensity of his presence. And yet, love was more than admiration. Love required trust, understanding, and a depth of connection that could not be forged in a matter of weeks.

Elizabeth let out a slow breath, her gaze sweeping over the full expanse of the valley stretched out before her. The view was breathtaking from this height. Longbourn looked small and distant, its familiar gables and chimneys just visible through the trees. Netherfield, too, lay below, its grandeur unmistakable even from so far away.

In the distance, she could see dark rainclouds beginning to gather and move closer. Knowing it would mostly likely begin raining in an hour, she was determined to make the most of her time alone in her favorite place.

Her gaze lingered on Netherfield, and she tried to imagine what life would be like within its walls, or the walls of a similar estate— Darcy's estate. Could she see herself in a place like that, walking its halls, playing with Andrew in the nursery, sharing quiet evenings with Darcy in the drawing room? The thought was both thrilling and terrifying.

This is ridiculous. I do not even know if he has any true regard for me, and here I am already imagining things.

She could not— would not— allow herself to get carried away. Whatever her feelings for Darcy might be, she would tread carefully. She would observe, listen, and guard her heart until she was certain of his intentions—and her own.

Her thoughts drifted back to the previous day. His quiet compliments in the Philips' parlor had surprised her, as did those the day before when he asked her to dance. It was not his words alone but the way he spoke them—his sincerity and the warmth in his voice, the way his dark eyes bored deeply into hers.

The fluttering sensation returned. Elizabeth shook her head, fighting the faint smile that had formed on her lips at the memory. *That is enough, you!* she scolded her heart.

Still, she could not ignore the way her stomach had leapt when she saw him ride up with Bingley. Nor could she forget how carefully he had looked after Georgiana during their time at Netherfield or the tenderness with which he had cradled Andrew.

Perhaps it is foolish to hope, but I cannot deny that I feel something. Something I have never felt before.

Elizabeth stood, brushing the dirt from her skirts. The walk down would be easier than the climb, but it would not feel nearly as satisfying. As she made her way back toward Longbourn, her thoughts remained firmly on the man she had come to know over the past month.

Only time would tell if her feelings were true and if Darcy might share them. But for now, Elizabeth allowed herself a small spark of hope, a feeling that perhaps, for the first time, love was not so far out of reach.

Elizabeth's pace quickened as she made her way down the path from Oakham Mount. The grey clouds that had been gathering all morning were finally making good on their threat, and she felt the first drops of rain spatter her bonnet just as Longbourn came into view. The damp chill in the air caused her to pull her shawl tighter around her shoulders, and by the time she reached the front steps, the rain had begun to fall in earnest.

She barely managed to open the door before the downpour began in full force. Her boots, caked in mud from the walk back, left damp prints on the floor as she entered the house. Shivering slightly, she reached down to untie the laces just as Mrs. Hill appeared, tsking at the state of her hem and offering to bring a fresh pair of stockings.

"Thank you, Hill," Elizabeth said with a warm smile, pulling off her boots just as Jane appeared in the hallway.

"Oh, Lizzy," Jane said with concern, "you must be chilled to the bone!"

"Only a little damp," Elizabeth replied, brushing her wet skirts and shaking out her shawl. "But it seems I made it back just in time—listen to that rain."

The two sisters stood for a moment, watching the rain pour down outside the window, the drops pelting the glass in a steady rhythm.

The wind howled as the storm took hold, and Elizabeth felt grateful for the warmth of home.

"I do hope Mr. Collins made it to the posting inn before the rain began," Jane remarked.

"Oh, was he leaving today?" Elizabeth asked in surprise.

"Yes, I believe he said something about the importance of returning to his duties at Hunsford. Apparently Mr. Darcy made a strong case for his return."

Elizabeth laughed. "Well, that certainly was kind of him, was it not? We must hope Mr. Collins remains in Kent for quite some time."

She left Jane and went up the stairs to her room, eager to don a warmer chemise. After changing out of her walking clothes, Elizabeth joined her family at the breakfast table. The warmth of the fire and the hearty spread of tea and toast worked quickly to banish the chill from her bones.

"What positively dreadful weather," Mrs. Bennet declared, looking forlornly out the window. "How are we to receive visitors or make any calls with such a rain? And I had so wanted to go into Meryton today for shoe roses and ribbons for the ball!"

Elizabeth exchanged a look with Jane, trying to suppress a smile at their mother's dramatics.

"Surely the weather will clear by Monday morning, Mama," Jane offered gently, buttering a slice of toast. "That will give us plenty of time before the ball on Tuesday."

"That is hardly the point," Mrs. Bennet replied with a huff. "We have so much to prepare! I must speak to the milliner about my new lace, and there is still the matter of Kitty and Lydia's bonnets. Oh, and your sister Mary requires a proper ribbon for her gown—it is entirely too plain without one."

"I am certain we can make do for today," Elizabeth said calmly. "Perhaps we might spend the afternoon in more industrious pursuits indoors."

Mrs. Bennet let out a theatrical sigh, clearly unimpressed by Elizabeth's suggestion, but said no more. The remainder of breakfast was completed in relative silence, the steady patter against the windows providing a soothing backdrop to the meal.

After breakfast, the Bennet women retired to the parlor, each finding a way to occupy themselves. Elizabeth curled up in her favorite chair with a book, the pages a welcome escape from the dreary weather. Jane worked on a piece of embroidery, her needle gliding deftly through the fabric. Mary sat at the pianoforte, practicing scales, while Kitty and Lydia flitted between projects, making over bonnets and discussing which officers might attend the upcoming ball.

The quiet rhythm of the afternoon was interrupted only by the occasional crackle of the fire or the soft rustle of fabric as Mrs. Bennet inspected Jane's embroidery with a critical eye.

"Lizzy, you do not think this too plain, do you?" Jane asked, holding up her work for Elizabeth's opinion.

Elizabeth set her book aside and leaned forward to inspect it. "Not at all. I think it is quite elegant—simple, but tasteful."

Mrs. Bennet, overhearing the exchange, let out another sigh. "It is well enough, but I do wish we had gone to Meryton today. A bit of new lace would have improved it immeasurably."

Elizabeth and Jane exchanged a small smile before returning to their respective tasks.

It was nearing tea time when the sound of a horse pulling up to the front of the house broke the peaceful quiet. A few minutes later, Mrs. Hill appeared in the doorway, holding an envelope.

"A note from Netherfield, miss," she announced, handing it to Jane.

Mrs. Bennet's eyes lit up as she snatched up the letter, her earlier gloom forgotten. "From Netherfield! I do hope it is an invitation."

She tore open the envelope and began to read aloud, her voice growing more excited with each sentence:

Tuesday Afternoon

Dear Miss Bennet and Miss Elizabeth,

It is with great pleasure that I extend an invitation to you both for tea tomorrow evening. I have recently received a most delightful blend from London, the likes of which I am certain you have never tasted before. I cannot bear to keep such a treasure to myself and insist that you join us to partake in it.

I am certain you will find it as remarkable as I do. I will brook no refusals, as it would simply break my heart were you to disappoint me. In anticipation of your answer to the affirmative, I will make arrangements to send our carriage for you, as I shan't allow anything to stand in our way.

I should also mention that my brother and Mr. Darcy will be in attendance, so it will be a delightful opportunity for further conversation.

Yours most sincerely,

Caroline Bingley

"Is it not the most wonderful thing?" Mrs. Bennet exclaimed, practically dancing in her seat. "Oh, my dears, you must go! And to think—Mr. Darcy and Mr. Bingley will both be there!"

Elizabeth stood and took the note from her mother's hand, her brow furrowing slightly as she read the lines. Caroline's tone was overly familiar, her insistence bordering on condescension, and the mention of Darcy set Elizabeth's heart fluttering uncomfortably.

"I suppose we cannot refuse," Jane said softly, glancing at Elizabeth.

"No," Elizabeth agreed with a faint smile, folding the note. "I suppose we cannot. Although I wonder why on earth she invited us."

"Clearly she wishes to further a friendship with us," Jane said, her eyes shining. "I believe she is more amiable than you give her credit for."

Elizabeth thought back to the harsh looks and snide remarks she had received from Miss Bingley during their time spent at Netherfield while Jane was recovering her health. "Perhaps," was all she replied. "Very well, then. We shall go to tea tomorrow evening at Netherfield."

Mrs. Bennet beamed, her earlier woes about the rain forgotten. "It is settled, then! Oh, what a fine time you shall have. Oh, Jane, you must wear your best silk gown—it will complement your complexion perfectly."

Elizabeth sighed, folded the note and set it aside. "Mama, the invitation is for tea, not a ball. I am sure simple evening attire will suffice."

"Nonsense!" Mrs. Bennet exclaimed. "Every moment in the company of such gentlemen is an opportunity not to be wasted. And Lizzy, do not forget to fix your hair properly this time."

Elizabeth bit back a retort, instead rising from her mother's side to return to her book on her chair. As much as she dreaded enduring Caroline's airs, the thought of seeing Darcy again—despite her best efforts to dismiss it—filled her with quiet anticipation.

She could not help but wonder at Miss Bingley's sudden eagerness to host them. *I do hope it is nothing* too *nefarious that calls us there.*

Laughing at herself, she dismissed the idea with a toss of her head. The rain continued to patter against the windows, but Elizabeth's attempts to read were frequently interrupted by thoughts of the enigmatic gentleman who had so affected her heart and mind.

Chapter 15

The morning of the Netherfield tea dawned with a wintry chill that clung to the air despite the pale sunlight filtering through the clouds. Elizabeth woke to the sound of raindrops pattering faintly against the windowpane and sighed as she gazed at the sky, which threatened to unleash a heavier storm later in the day.

The Bingley carriage arrived promptly at Longbourn that afternoon, gleaming in defiance of the muddy roads from the morning's rain and the cloudy threats of more. Jane and Elizabeth stood in the hall as Hill helped them into their cloaks, their mother bustling about with last-minute instructions and reminders.

"Now, Jane," Mrs. Bennet said, adjusting her eldest daughter's bonnet, "do not let that odious Miss Bingley overshadow you. Remember to sit where Mr. Bingley can see you clearly. And Lizzy," she added, turning to her second daughter, "try not to antagonize anyone. Not everyone appreciates your sharp tongue."

Elizabeth gave her mother a tight smile, holding back the retort that rose to her lips. She was used to these admonishments, but today, her thoughts were elsewhere. As Hill opened the door and the chill of the afternoon breeze swept inside, Elizabeth glanced at Jane, who was already stepping forward with her usual serene grace.

They climbed into the carriage, and as soon as the door was shut and the wheels began to turn, Elizabeth allowed herself to sink into the seat with a sigh. The countryside rolled by, its muted colors softened by the gray skies above. She tried to focus on the familiar sights, but her mind kept drifting back to Netherfield.

Caroline Bingley. Elizabeth couldn't decide which was worse—the idea of enduring Caroline's sly remarks and thinly veiled insults, or the possibility that Caroline would simply ignore her altogether. Either way, she knew the evening would be fraught with tension. The presence of Mrs. Hurst, who so often mirrored her sister's disdain, would do little to improve matters.

And yet... a flicker of excitement sparked within her, unbidden. Darcy. The name alone sent a ripple through her chest, a curious mixture of anticipation and uncertainty. Elizabeth had been replaying their conversations over the past weeks in her mind, each one revealing more of the man beneath the aloof exterior. She found herself eager to see him again, though she quickly reminded herself not to dwell on it too much. It was merely the prospect of engaging in stimulating conversation, she told herself, nothing more.

"You seem lost in thought, Lizzy," Jane said, her voice gentle and teasing. "What occupies your mind so thoroughly?"

Elizabeth turned to her sister with a wry smile. "I was merely considering how best to endure an evening with Miss Bingley. Her charm, after all, is matched only by her graciousness."

Jane laughed softly. "Perhaps you might be surprised. Miss Bingley may not be the easiest of companions, but she does make an effort to host us."

223

Elizabeth arched an eyebrow but refrained from commenting further. Jane's determination to see the best in everyone was both her greatest strength and her greatest flaw. Elizabeth had long since learned to let it go, knowing her sister's outlook brought her peace.

By the time the carriage arrived at Netherfield, the sun had briefly emerged, casting a golden light over the estate. Elizabeth stepped out onto the gravel drive and was greeted by the smiling figure of Mr. Bingley, who had come to the door himself to receive them.

"Miss Bennet, Miss Elizabeth! Welcome, welcome!" He approached with a wide grin, his gaze immediately finding Jane's. "It is always such a pleasure to have you here."

Elizabeth raised an eyebrow as he stepped forward to help Jane descend. "You are opening your own door, Mr. Bingley? What of the footmen?"

Bingley chuckled, glancing back toward the house. "Caroline insisted on giving the staff the afternoon off. She thought a more intimate gathering might be... charming. They'll be back in an hour or so, I believe."

Elizabeth exchanged a glance with Jane. Giving the entire staff even a few hours off was highly irregular. "Quite charming indeed," she murmured under her breath as she stepped inside, the grandeur of Netherfield's foyer uncharacteristically still without the usual bustle of servants.

"I quite like the idea of giving the staff a surprise," Bingley said, grinning at Jane.

Jane returned his smile with one of her own, the flush in her cheeks unmistakable. Elizabeth couldn't help but giggle slightly at her sister's obvious happiness, though her expression turned wary when Caroline Bingley appeared behind her brother, her lips stretched into a tight, overly bright smile.

"Miss Bennet, Miss Elizabeth, how delightful to see you," Caroline said, her tone laced with false sweetness. "We have prepared a most splendid tea for the occasion. I daresay it will be quite unlike anything you have encountered in Meryton."

Elizabeth inclined her head politely, though her instincts told her that something was amiss. Caroline's smile was entirely too... genuine. Her suspicions only deepened when Caroline led them into the drawing room, where the Netherfield party was already assembled. Mr. Hurst lounged carelessly on a small sofa, and Mrs. Hurst greeted them with her usual languid indifference.

Darcy stood by the window, his tall frame silhouetted against the pale light as he gazed out with his usual quiet intensity. He turned towards the door when the Bennet sisters entered, bowing in greeting. Georgiana sat primly on a chair near the fireplace, her delicate features lit with a mixture of shyness and curiosity as she greeted the newcomers with a tentative smile.

"Miss Darcy," Elizabeth said warmly, stepping forward to address the young woman as Bingley guided Jane to a sofa near the fire. "How wonderful to see you again. I trust you have been well?"

Georgiana nodded, her cheeks pink. "Yes, thank you, Miss Elizabeth. It is a pleasure to see you too."

Elizabeth returned her smile, then allowed Caroline to guide her to a settee near the center of the room. Jane and Bingley had already taken their places side by side, their quiet conversation punctuated by the occasional laugh.

"I must tell you all," Caroline announced with a dramatic flourish, "that I have procured the finest tea blend from London. It is a rare and exotic variety, said to be the pinnacle of refinement. I simply could not resist sharing it with such esteemed company."

Bingley raised an eyebrow. "I was under the impression you were rather attached to your usual tea, Caroline. Something about its unassailable refinement?"

Caroline flushed slightly but recovered with a tinkling laugh. "Oh, Charles, you do love to tease. Surely even I can appreciate novelty when it is of sufficient quality."

Elizabeth's lips twitched in amusement at the forced enthusiasm in Caroline's voice, and she caught Darcy's faint smirk as he continued to stare out the window. His apparent disinterest in the proceedings only heightened Elizabeth's foreboding about the evening, though she quickly brushed the thought aside.

With a flourish, Caroline rang the bell, and moments later, a maid entered with a silver tea tray. The arrangement was impeccable—delicate china cups, a porcelain teapot, and a plate of small, intricately decorated biscuits. Elizabeth's brow furrowed at the fact that not all members of the staff were enjoying a respite.

With great ceremony, Caroline began pouring the tea herself. She gave the first cup to Darcy, completely ignoring protocol to serve her guests first. When the last cup was placed in her hands, Elizabeth took a tentative sip, only to wince at the bitter taste that lingered on her tongue despite the generous amount of sugar and honey.

At first, Elizabeth thought it was a cruel prank Miss Bingley had played on her to show her superiority. A quick glance around the room confirmed that she was not alone in her reaction; the others were doing their best to mask their expressions of distaste. Caroline, however, sipped her tea with exaggerated delight, her smile strained as she urged her guests to drink more.

"Come now, drink up," she trilled as a slight sheen of sweat began to appear on her brow. "This really is a most exquisite blend. I went to great lengths to procure it, so I shall be quite offended if you do not partake fully. It has been designed to invigorate the senses and soothe the soul, and is quite all the rage in London."

"It's… unique," Elizabeth ventured, choosing her words carefully. She took another sip, hoping the taste might improve. It did not.

Miss Bingley, clearly unwilling to admit defeat, lifted her own cup with a strained smile. "Oh, I quite adore it. Such a complex flavor, wouldn't you agree?" She took a delicate sip, her expression tightening ever so slightly as she swallowed.

Elizabeth exchanged a wry look with Jane, who had managed only a small sip of her tea. Darcy, too, seemed hesitant, taking a single sip before placing his cup on the table. Bingley, ever the polite host, managed two gulps before coughing softly into his hand. Mrs. Hurst looked dubious, though she drained her cup quickly, likely to avoid Caroline's scrutiny, and encouraged her husband to do the same.

"Come now, do finish," Caroline urged, her voice higher than usual. "I went to such trouble to acquire this treat for us all to enjoy."

She herself grimaced as she took a large swallow, then forced a pained smile as if to provide evidence of her enjoyment.

Despite their reservations, they all dutifully drained their cups, the awkward silence in the room broken only by the occasional clink of porcelain and the rustle of clothing as they shifted uncomfortably in their seats.

Elizabeth reached for her biscuit, eager to cleanse her palate, but as she chewed, she noticed an odd sensation creeping over her. It was faint—a lightheadedness, as though the room had grown just a touch warmer. She shook her head slightly, attributing the feeling to her earlier walk in the brisk air.

It was then that Elizabeth noticed Darcy glancing in her direction, his gaze lingering for a moment before returning to the window. The intensity of his expression made her heart flutter, and she found herself wondering what thoughts occupied his mind. The memory of their recent conversations—the unexpected warmth and understanding that had passed between them—came rushing back, and she quickly looked away, focusing instead on the intricacies of the teacup in her hands.

As she looked around the room in an attempt to distract herself, Elizabeth absentmindedly tapped her fingers on the armrest of her chair, playing a simple melody she knew by heart.

"Fur Elise?" Georgiana's question was soft and weak. Elizabeth frowned as she looked at the girl's pale face.

"Miss Darcy?" Elizabeth leaned forward, her voice tinged with concern. "Are you feeling unwell?"

Before Georgiana could respond, she was interrupted by a small shout from across the room. "Miss Bennet!"

Elizabeth looked up to see Bingley's horrified face staring down at Jane in surprise. To Elizabeth's astonishment, her sister lay unmoving across Bingley's lap. His arms were around the elder Bennet girl, whose head lolled to one side.

"Jane!" she cried, rushing to her sister's side. She felt a strong, steady arm grasp her elbow, steadying her as she swayed. Turning, she saw Darcy looking down at her, his expression sharp with concern.

"Are you well, Miss Bennet?" he asked, his voice firm despite the slight slur creeping into his words.

Elizabeth blinked, her vision momentarily blurring. "I... I believe so," she replied, though her heart raced with unease. "But Jane—something is wrong!"

As she turned her focus back to her sister, she realized Darcy's grip on her arm had slackened. Glancing back, she was horrified to see him collapse onto the floor, his tall frame crumpling like a marionette with its strings cut.

"Mr. Darcy!" Elizabeth dropped to her knees beside him, her hand hovering over his shoulder. His breathing was slow but steady, his face unnaturally pale.

The room descended into chaos. Bingley had slumped forward, his head resting against Jane's shoulder, while Mrs. Hurst and Miss Bingley lay sprawled in their chairs, their tea cups shattered on the floor. Hurst, who had been half-asleep when they arrived, was now fully unconscious, his snores rattling through the silence.

There are no servants.

Elizabeth's mind raced. *Have we been poisoned? Are they all…
dead?*

The thought was terrifying, yet the symptoms seemed more like
an unnatural sleep than anything lethal. Her own slight dizziness had
all but faded, leaving her alert but shaken. Rising unsteadily to her
feet, she scanned the room for help. The bell—she needed to
summon a servant.

At that horrifying thought, Elizabeth turned around again to try
to revive someone—anyone.

Just then, a door creaked open behind her.

Elizabeth spun around, her heart leaping with hope. Instead of
livery, however, the figure standing in the doorway was dressed in
the red coat of an officer, the coloring striking against the subdued
tones of the room.

She recognized him as the handsome officer she had met in the
street the day they had taken Mr. Collins to Meryton. He had called
once or twice at Longbourn as well, but she was not all that
acquainted with him.

What was his name again? She fought against the light fog that
seemed to cover her mind, and it finally came to her.

"Mr. Wickham!" Elizabeth exclaimed, her relief momentarily
overpowering her confusion. "Thank heavens you're here!"

George Wickham smirked to himself as he stepped into the stillness of Netherfield's drawing room. His satisfaction with Caroline Bingley's foolhardy scheme had grown with every step he'd taken toward the house, though he had to admit that working with such an overly dramatic accomplice could be tiresome. Yet, as his eyes adjusted to the dim light of the room, he paused. Something was amiss.

Elizabeth Bennet stood at the center of the chaos, her small figure framed by the elegance of the room, her expression frantic. Around her, bodies lay slumped in various positions—Darcy on the floor, Bingley draped awkwardly over his beloved Miss Bennet, and the Netherfield ladies sprawled in unbecoming heaps.

Her voice pulled him from his observations. "I have never been so relieved to see anyone in my life!" she cried, her voice trembling with desperation. "Something dreadful has happened."

He cursed. Why the devil is she not asleep?

For all his planning, he hadn't expected anyone to be standing upright, let alone coherent. He took in her pale face, relief etched into her features, and then back to the scattered bodies of the unconscious party. Miss Bingley had assured him this would be simple, an easy charade, but now…

"I should say something has," he remarked, his gaze sweeping the room. "But tell me, Miss Elizabeth—" He turned his piercing eyes back to her, his tone hardening. "Did you not drink the tea?"

Her response was immediate, though hesitant. She gasped softly, shrinking back from the sharp edge in his voice. "Th-th-the tea?" she stammered, her brows furrowing in confusion.

He took another step closer, his eyes narrowing. "Yes, the tea. Miss Bingley laced it heavily with laudanum. Did you drink it?"

Her expression twisted into shock, her mouth opening and closing soundlessly as if she couldn't comprehend the question. Wickham's patience, always thin, began to fray.

"Well?" he demanded, anger beginning to creep through his voice.

Elizabeth's voice trembled as she finally answered. "I—well, yes, I did. But why would that—" Her words faltered, confusion and a growing sense of dread coloring her tone.

"Because," Wickham interrupted sharply, his irritation bubbling to the surface, "your hostess intended to ensure everyone was unconscious for the little compromise she planned to arrange. How on earth are you still standing?"

Her hand went to her temple; the very act of thinking through the fog required great effort. "Laudanum has... never worked properly on me," she said. "Even when I broke my arm as a child, the apothecary—"

He cut her off with an impatient wave of his hand. "Never worked? Never?" His mind whirred. What an inconvenient, irritating detail to have overlooked. Of all the ridiculous twists.

"No," Elizabeth said, her voice growing firmer despite her confusion. "It takes an unusual amount to have any effect."

Wickham stared at her, his disbelief quickly morphing into irritation. He exhaled sharply, raking a hand through his hair. "Well, that certainly complicates matters," he muttered, more to himself than to her.

Elizabeth's brow furrowed further. "How do you mean?" she asked cautiously, her voice tinged with alarm.

Wickham turned his gaze back to her, and his usual charming mask slipped away, replaced by something colder, harder. With a great sigh, he spread his hands in a theatrical gesture. "Miss Elizabeth, let me be plain. Miss Bingley is desperate to marry my dear old friend Darcy. So desperate, in fact, that she's enlisted my help to engineer a little scandal. The plan was simple enough—put everyone to sleep with the tea, then create the appearance that Darcy and Miss Bingley spent the afternoon together in a most... compromising position."

Elizabeth's eyes widened as realization began to dawn. Wickham smirked, enjoying the flicker of horror in her expression. "Of course," he continued, "Darcy's nature is such that he would never recover from the disgrace. Miss Bingley would ensure the matter came to light just enough to force his hand. And once they're married..." He gave a theatrical shrug. "She's promised me half her pin money as compensation."

Elizabeth's shock turned to indignation. "You would ruin Mr. Darcy's life for money? Why? You don't even know him!"

Wickham barked a laugh, loud and scornful. "Oh, you poor, naive girl," he sneered. "Of course I know him. Very well."

Her eyes flashed with anger, but Wickham stepped closer, his grin fading as a darker expression took its place. "You want to know the truth?" he hissed, his voice low and venomous. "I despise Darcy. His father may have loved me like a son, but Darcy never saw me as anything more than a rival to be crushed. He's taken everything I ever wanted— everything that should have been mine by right. Do you truly believe I would not seize an opportunity to destroy him in turn?"

Elizabeth flinched at the intensity of his words, but he wasn't finished. "Nothing can stop me, Miss Bennet," he declared, his voice brimming with malice. "Certainly not you. So now we find ourselves at an impasse. You, unfortunately, are still awake. Conscious. A witness."

Her breathing quickened, and for the first time, Wickham saw fear flicker in her eyes. "What do you mean?" she whispered, her voice barely audible.

He leaned in, his voice dropping to a conspiratorial murmur. "I mean, my dear Miss Bennet, that we cannot have you ruining this little arrangement. You're awake when you shouldn't be, and that presents a problem. A problem I intend to solve."

Elizabeth's breathing quickened, her mind racing. "I—I won't say anything," she stammered. "I swear it."

"Oh, I'm afraid that won't do," Wickham said softly, his grin widening. "You see, Miss Bennet, this plan is far too delicate to risk even the slightest whisper of interference. And you—you, my dear—are far too clever for your own good."

Elizabeth's eyes widened in alarm, and she instinctively took a step back. Wickham advanced slowly, a predatory gleam in his eyes, his grin widening into something cruel and wolfish.

"Now," he said, his tone almost playful, "let's see what we can do about that troublesome little habit of yours—staying awake. I can't have you ruining everything."

Wickham savored the moment, each tremor of fear rippling through Elizabeth Bennet only heightening his sense of control. He stepped forward again, his shadow looming over her as he relished the way her eyes darted toward the door, calculating her chances of escape.

Poor little fool. She has no idea who she is dealing with.

He took another step closer to her, then another, his excitement rising with each frightened pant.

Chapter 16

Elizabeth's heart clenched with fear as George Wickham stalked a step toward her, his grin growing sharper, more menacing with each passing second. The faint candlelight flickered, casting shadows across his face and highlighting the malice in his eyes.

Her heart pounded so loudly in her ears that she could barely hear her own thoughts. He advanced towards her, his steps slow and deliberate, like a predator savoring the hunt. Like a waltz. She stepped back as he stepped forward, moving in rhythm with her heartbeat.

"Come now, Miss Elizabeth," he coaxed, his tone mockingly soft. "Don't fight me, and I promise to make this quick and painless."

A cold chill ran down her spine, and she knew instinctively that his promise was a lie. The gleam in his eyes betrayed his words; he intended anything but kindness. When he reached out, his fingers curling toward her arm, she acted on pure instinct.

The years she had spent roaming Hertfordshire with the Lucas and Goulding boys had taught her precisely where to aim. With all the force she could muster, she kicked forward, her foot connecting solidly with the most vulnerable part of his anatomy.

Wickham let out a guttural curse as he collapsed to his knees, his hands clutching his injured anatomy. "You little—" His face twisted in rage, but Elizabeth didn't wait for him to finish.

She ran.

The drawing room door swung open as she dashed into the hallway, her skirts bunching in her fists as she pumped her legs with all her might. The house was eerily silent, and the absence of servants filled her with a sinking dread. Surely someone should have been there—anyone—but the corridors were empty, as if the entire household had vanished.

Her breathing came in ragged gasps, her chest burning as she pushed herself to go faster. Reaching the front door, Elizabeth yanked it open and stumbled outside into the night. The chilling air hit her face as she flung herself through. She could hear Wickham's footsteps pounding behind her, accompanied by his furious curses.

"I swear, you stupid chit, you'll pay for this!" he roared, his voice growing louder with every step.

Elizabeth stumbled down the front steps, her breath coming in frantic gasps. The world outside was cloaked in darkness, lit only by the occasional flash of lightning illuminating the grounds. Thunder rumbled in the distance, the sound vibrating in her chest. The scent of rain lingered in the air, but for now, the sky held back its deluge.

Her mind raced as she scanned her surroundings. The open path to the stables was too exposed, and the road leading away from the house would leave her vulnerable. To her left, the dense hedgerows offered the only possible refuge: the Netherfield maze.

If only Mama knew. Her wild, humorous thought was at severe odds with the terror in her mind, but it somehow lessened her panic.

Making a split-second decision, Elizabeth veered to the left and plunged into the winding, overgrown paths that she hadn't explored in years. She sprinted as fast as she could, her skirts twisting around her legs, hampering her progress, her sense of direction completely abandoned in favor of survival. Every turn felt like a gamble, each twist another potential trap.

She could hear Wickham crashing through the hedges behind her, his curses growing louder. "Do you think I can't follow you in here? I'll find you, you little chit!"

The darkness around her was broken only by the occasional flash of lightning, illuminating her path just long enough to give her fleeting glimpses of the wild, dense path. Her lungs burned with effort, but she didn't dare slow down— Wickham's furious shouts were echoing behind her, driving her forward like the crack of a whip.

Panic surged through her veins as she turned another corner, only to come face-to-face with a solid wall of hedges: a dead end. Wickham's footsteps grew louder, and she knew she had mere moments before he would catch up.

She spun around, her eyes wild with desperation, and spotted a thin gap in the branches to her left. Without thinking, she threw herself into the thicket, the sharp twigs scraping her skin as she forced her way through to the other side.

The passage she emerged into was narrower, the walls of greenery looming high above her. She hesitated, her chest heaving as she realized she had no idea where she was. The maze's twists and turns had disoriented her completely, and the sound of Wickham's pursuit seemed to echo from all directions.

Frantically, she scanned her surroundings, her gaze landing on a hedge that looked slightly thinner than the rest. It was low enough to crawl beneath, and the gap between the branches was just wide enough for her to squeeze into. Without a moment's hesitation, Elizabeth dropped to her knees and scrambled into the small hollow, her breath coming in ragged gasps as she pressed herself against the cool earth.

The branches clawed at her dress and hair, tearing fabric and pulling at her curls, but she didn't stop until she was fully concealed among the leaves. She crouched low, her hands trembling as she rearranged the foliage to shield her further from view.

She crouched low, her bosom heaving as she fought to control her breathing. The sound of Wickham's boots crunching on the gravel grew closer, and she pressed her hand tightly over her mouth, stifling the urge to gasp for air. Her lungs burned, and her entire body trembled with fear, but she didn't dare make a sound.

The thunder above grew louder, a sharp crack lighting up the maze for a split second, and she held her breath, praying he wouldn't find her.

Her heart thundered in her ears as she listened, trying to find the danger. Wickham's voice, sharp and furious, pierced the air. "Come out, you little fool! There's no point in hiding. I'll find you— you can't hide forever!"

Elizabeth pressed her lips together, forcing herself to take shallow, silent breaths. The ache in her chest from holding her breath grew unbearable, but she refused to give herself away. Her muscles locked in place as his shadow passed dangerously close to her shelter.

Wickham's footsteps slowed, his boots grinding against the gravel as he searched the area. She could hear the frustration in his voice as he muttered curses under his breath. Through the gaps in the leaves, she could see his face twisted in anger, his eyes scanning the grounds for any sign of movement. He shouted her name again, the sound reverberating through the still night.

The footsteps retreated slightly, then paused. Elizabeth's heart stopped as she heard him double back, moving closer to her hiding spot. She clenched her fists, willing herself to stay still as the branches above her shifted slightly in the breeze.

Another flash of lightning illuminated the landscape, and for one terrifying moment, she saw Wickham's silhouette mere feet from her hiding place. She bit her lip, tasting blood, as her hands pressed hard against her knees to keep herself from trembling.

Please, God, don't let him find me.

After what felt like an eternity, Wickham let out a string of curses and turned toward the stables, his heavy steps fading into the distance. She dared to lift her head just enough to peer through the leaves. Her breath caught as she saw him stomping down the path toward the stables, his figure fading into the shadows.

Relief washed over her, but she didn't dare move. Her muscles began to burn and cramp from being held so tightly, but she remained frozen in place. Minutes passed, and the only noise was the distant rumble of thunder. Slowly, cautiously, Elizabeth began to shift, her limbs stiff from remaining in one position for so long.

Just as she was about to step out of the hedgerow, the sound of a carriage approaching reached her ears. She froze, her eyes darting toward the drive. The faint glow of lanterns appeared, and her breath caught in her throat as she saw Wickham driving her father's carriage up to the front door. He was alone, his movements frantic and hurried as he pulled the vehicle to a stop.

What is he doing? she thought, panic flooding her veins.

To her horror, Wickham leapt from the driver's seat and ran back into the house. Elizabeth's mind raced. What was he doing? Should she risk running to the carriage to seek help, or stay hidden?

Before she could decide, Wickham reemerged, carrying the limp figure of Miss Bingley in his arms, her body hanging like a ragdoll with her head lolling to the side. Elizabeth clamped her hand over her mouth to stifle a cry, tears streaming down her face as she watched Wickham roughly shove the unconscious woman into the carriage before running back to the house.

Should I help her?

Indecision warred with fear inside her, but before she could make a decision, he returned, now wearing a dark coat she recognized as Darcy's. In his arms, he carried a sack overflowing with silverware, jewels, and a coin purse, which he tossed onto Miss Bingley's prone form.

Wickham paused, glancing around before pulling a white cloth from his pocket. He tied Miss Bingley's hands together, his movements quick and efficient, then climbed into the driver's seat. With a flick of the reins, the carriage jolted forward, disappearing down the road and into the night.

Elizabeth remained frozen, staring at the now-empty drive, her mind unable to process what she had just witnessed. She bit down on her lip until it bled even more fiercely, the salty fluid mingling with the tears streaming down her face. Miss Bingley—whatever her faults—was being taken somewhere against her will, and Elizabeth could do nothing to stop it.

The first drops of rain began to fall, cold and sharp against her skin, but she didn't move. It wasn't until the drizzle turned into a steady downpour, soaking her gown and chilling her to the bone, that she finally broke from her daze.

She stumbled back toward the house, her steps unsteady as the rain plastered her hair to her face. Her shoes squelched with every step, but she hardly noticed. Her only thought was to find help.

The front door banged open as she entered, and her voice echoed through the silent halls. "Hello? Is anyone here? Please, help me!"

The house was eerily quiet, save for the sound of her footsteps and the pounding rain outside. She ran toward the drawing room, her heart sinking as she saw the unconscious figures still sprawled where they had fallen. Darcy, Bingley, Jane—all unmoving, their faces pale.

Elizabeth's gaze landed on Darcy, noting his missing coat and cravat. She realized with a sinking feeling that Wickham must have used them to bind Miss Bingley. Swallowing hard, she tore her eyes away and continued down the hall.

I must find help.

"Hello? Is anyone here?" she called again, her voice breaking. "Please, somebody help me!"

The silence was deafening, broken only by the sound of her footsteps and the pounding of the rain outside. She reached the servants' staircase and descended quickly, nearly tripping in her haste. At the bottom, she burst into the housekeeper's office, her face pale and desperate.

"Miss Elizabeth?" Mrs. Nicholls gasped, her eyes widening at the sight of the drenched and disheveled young woman. "What on earth has happened?"

"Please," Elizabeth panted, clutching the doorframe for support. "You must help me. He's drugged them all—and kidnapped Miss Bingley!"

Mrs. Nicholls could only gape at the bedraggled, bleeding figure in front of her. She could hardly recognize the usually poised young lady from Netherfield where her sister-in-law, Matilda Hill, was a lady's maid. She and Matilda had been steadfast figures in Meryton for longer than most could remember, though her own journey was quite different than her sister's-by-marriage.

Claire Nicholls had come to Netherfield as a wide-eyed housemaid at the tender age of twelve, scrubbing floors and polishing brass under the watchful eye of the former housekeeper. Over the decades, her hard work and quiet dignity had seen her rise steadily through the ranks until she earned her current position, a role she served with no small measure of pride.

In her years of service, Mrs. Nicholls had witnessed all manner of tenants pass through Netherfield Park. From pompous tradesmen flaunting their newfound wealth to flighty heiresses with a penchant for melodrama, the estate had hosted its fair share of colorful characters. None, however, had been quite so difficult as Miss Caroline Bingley. The young woman's whims were as fickle as an April breeze, and her imperious nature made her a trial even to the most seasoned staff.

When Miss Bingley had unceremoniously declared a holiday for the majority of the household staff, keeping only Mrs. Nicholls, the butler, and a single maid and footman to oversee the running of the house, Mrs. Nicholls had accepted the decree with quiet resignation. After all, her fellow servants worked tirelessly to endure their mistress's inconsistent demands. A day of respite for them was hardly something to bemoan. And while Mrs. Nicholls herself remained behind to ensure the household stayed in order, she did so with little complaint. Years of service had taught her to appreciate small mercies where she could find them.

But nothing in her decades of experience had prepared her for the sight that greeted her when Elizabeth Bennet burst into her office, soaked to the skin and trembling like a leaf in the wind. The young woman's dress clung to her frame, dripping water onto the polished floor, and her face was a ghostly shade of pale. Her wide, frightened eyes held a plea for help that sent a chill through Mrs. Nicholls's bones, nearly undoing the housekeeper for the first time in her life.

"Miss Elizabeth?" Mrs. Nicholls exclaimed, rising from her chair in alarm. "What on earth has happened?"

Elizabeth clung to the doorframe as if it were the only thing holding her upright. Her voice was hoarse with urgency as she stammered, "Please—you must help me. He's drugged them all—and kidnapped Miss Bingley!"

For a moment, Mrs. Nicholls could only gape at the girl, the words refusing to settle in her mind. Her head was reeling; she had dealt with many crises in her years of service—fires, unruly guests, broken china—but never anything like this.

Elizabeth Bennet, a young gentlewoman from the neighborhood, had appeared in the her office like a wild animal, with her disheveled hair plastered to her pale face, and her skirts nearly completely torn from her body, clinging to her as the dripped muddy water onto the floor.

As the full weight of Elizabeth's statement sank in, a jolt of adrenaline coursed through Mrs. Nicholls, and she sprang into action. The housekeeper's voice, long unused to such volume, thundered through the room as she bellowed, "John! Get in here at once!"

The butler, startled by the uncharacteristic shouting of his first name, appeared in the doorway, his wide eyes darting between the drenched young lady and his normally unflappable counterpart. "Have a stableboy fetch Mr. Jones immediately!" Mrs. Nicholls commanded, pointing a trembling finger toward the door. "Tell him it's an emergency and he's needed at once!"

John's eyes took in the scene, and he hesitated only a second before bolting down the hall, his boots clattering against the floorboards as he ran.

Turning sharply toward the maid, who had appeared in the doorway with a teapot in hand, Mrs. Nicholls barked, "Forget the tea, Sally! I want you to go to the kitchen and set a large pot of water on the stove to start boiling. Quickly, girl—no dawdling!"

The maid's eyes widened in alarm, but she hurried to obey, disappearing back into the kitchen with the urgency of a soldier responding to orders.

Mrs. Nicholls turned her attention back to Elizabeth, her voice softening as she placed a steadying hand on the girl's arm. "Now, Miss Elizabeth, tell me everything. Who has been drugged? And who has taken Miss Bingley?"

Elizabeth shook her head, her wet curls clinging to her face as fresh tears spilled over her cheeks. "It—it was Mr. Wickham. The officer from the regiment," she choked out. "He… he laced the tea with laudanum. Everyone drank it—Mr. Darcy, Mr. Bingley, Jane—" Her voice cracked, and she pressed a hand to her trembling lips. "They're all unconscious in the drawing room."

"Good Lord," Mrs. Nicholls whispered, her heart sinking as she imagined the scene upstairs. But she pushed her own alarm aside, her years of experience in crisis management taking hold. "And you say he's taken Miss Bingley?"

Elizabeth nodded, her body shaking with the effort to remain composed. "He—he's gone now," she stammered. "He took her in my father's carriage. I wanted to stop him, but…" She trailed off, her voice breaking as she stared off into space, falling silent.

Mrs. Nicholls felt a jolt of alarm, but years of experience quelled her panic. "Come now, child," she said firmly, stepping forward and reaching for Elizabeth's arm. "You're in no state to be running about like this. Sit down in the kitchen and let me fetch you something warm. You need to collect yourself."

Her intent was to guide Elizabeth toward a chair by the desk, but as soon as her hand touched Elizabeth's arm, the younger woman stiffened. Her wide eyes darted to Mrs. Nicholls, and with a sudden cry, she wrenched herself free.

"No!" Elizabeth shouted, her voice rising with desperation. "I have to see Jane! I have to—" She spun away, her breath coming in sharp gasps as she stumbled toward the door.

"Miss Elizabeth!" Mrs. Nicholls called after her, her own voice laced with concern. "Please, wait! You're in no condition—"

But Elizabeth was already running, her steps echoing down the corridor as she made for the drawing room. Mrs. Nicholls followed as quickly as her legs would allow, her heart pounding with a mix of worry and frustration.

Whatever had happened, she knew things had changed forever. This was no ordinary scandal; this was something far darker—and it had invaded the very heart of Netherfield Park.

Chapter 17

Elizabeth stood frozen in the chaos of the servants' quarters, the distant commands of Mrs. Nicholls barely registering in her mind. The housekeeper's firm, authoritative tone echoed in the background as she directed the butler and maid, but Elizabeth felt as though she were underwater, unable to fully grasp the situation. It wasn't until the older woman laid a hand on her arm to draw her away that she came to her senses.

"Come now, child," the housekeeper said firmly, stepping forward and reaching for Elizabeth's arm. "You're in no state to be running about like this. Sit down in the kitchen and let me fetch you something warm. You need to collect yourself."

The warmth of Mrs. Nicholls's touch— which had clearly meant to offer comfort— jolted Elizabeth back into awareness. Shaking her head violently, she pulled herself free of the woman's grasp. Her voice broke as she cried out, "No, I have to see Jane! I have to—!"

"Miss Elizabeth, please!" Mrs. Nicholls called frantically after her, but Elizabeth was already dashing back up the stairs, her skirts dragging heavily with the weight of water and grime.

She could barely feel her legs as she ran, her thoughts focused on reaching her sister. The only thought in her mind was her sister, her beloved Jane, lying unconscious and vulnerable, and the housekeeper's calls to slow down barely registered in her ears.

Her breath hitched as another image intruded—a tall, dark-haired man lying crumpled on the floor of the drawing room.

Darcy.

Her heart clenched painfully at the thought of his still form. She had hidden her growing feelings for him behind layers of denial and propriety, but in this moment, the fear of losing him surged forward, raw and undeniable.

Elizabeth reached the drawing room and flung the door open, skidding to a halt beside the settee where her sister lay with her face down in Bingley's lap. Dropping to her knees, heedless of the puddles forming from her soaked clothes, Elizabeth grasped Jane's limp hand. Her sister's face was serene, her lashes resting gently against her cheeks as though she were simply asleep. But the unnatural stillness of her chest sent a wave of terror through Elizabeth.

"Jane," Elizabeth whispered, then louder, "Jane! Wake up, please!" Her voice cracked, and tears began to blur her vision. "You have to wake up! Please, Jane!"

Behind her, the sound of hurried footsteps announced Mrs. Nicholls's arrival. "Miss Elizabeth!" the housekeeper exclaimed, her breath coming in short gasps. "You mustn't—"

Elizabeth barely registered the words. She shook Jane's shoulder gently at first, then with increasing desperation. "Jane, please, open your eyes!" she begged. But her sister remained still, unresponsive to her touch.

Strong hands grasped Elizabeth's shoulders, trying to pull her back, but she fought against the grip with everything she had. "No!" she cried, her voice rising in anguish. "Let me go! I have to help her!"

"Miss Elizabeth," Mrs. Nicholls said firmly, her voice calm but resolute. "You'll do her no good like this. Come away before you harm yourself or her any further."

"I can't leave her like this!"

"You must," Mrs. Nicholls insisted, her voice steady. "You're exhausted and most likely becoming ill. You'll do neither her nor yourself any good in this state."

Elizabeth struggled for a moment longer before her strength gave out. She collapsed against Mrs. Nicholls, her tears soaking the woman's apron as sobs wracked her body. "She has to wake up," Elizabeth whispered, her voice muffled by the fabric. "She has to."

Mrs. Nicholls held her tightly, her arms strong and steady despite her age. "We'll do everything we can for her, child," she said gently. "But you must let us help."

Elizabeth felt the warmth of Mrs. Nicholls's strong arms wrapping around her, the grip firm but comforting as the older woman whispered words of reassurance into Elizabeth's ear. Over the woman's shoulders, however, Elizabeth could see the prone forms of the other members of their tea party. One face, in particular, sharpened into focus: Darcy's.

A wave of dread filled her. *What if he doesn't awaken? What if he's dead? What will happen to poor Andrew? To Georgiana?*

A lump formed in her throat as she wondered if he was in pain, if he dreamed of Georgiana, if he would ever wake. She attempted to rise to her feet. "Please," Elizabeth whispered, her voice trembling. "I need to see Mr. Darcy. I need to know he's—"

But her pleas went unheeded as Mrs. Nicholls's arms tightened. "Wait until Mr. Jones comes, miss."

A sharp knock at the door announced the arrival of the apothecary, whose weathered face paled as his eyes swept over the scene. "Good God in heaven!" he exclaimed, stepping further into the room. "What in the name of all things holy is going on?"

His voice drew Elizabeth's attention, and she wrenched herself free from Mrs. Nicholls's embrace, her tear-streaked face turning toward the apothecary.

"Mr. Jones," she began, her voice trembling, "you must help them. Please—Jane, Mr. Darcy, all of them—they've been drugged!"

Behind Mr. Jones, several servants crowded in the doorway, their hushed murmurs growing louder as they took in the scattered bodies. Elizabeth followed their gazes and felt her stomach drop as she realized where they were looking—at Jane and Mr. Bingley, still entangled on the settee in a compromising position.

"Oh, Lord," Elizabeth groaned, a fresh wave of mortification washing over her. "The gossip!"

Driven by instinct, she scrambled to separate the unconscious couple, but her arms gave out after only a few attempts. Seeing her struggle, Mrs. Nicholls barked at two manservants lingering near the door.

"Don't just stand there! Get in here and help set this right!" she ordered.

"Just not too much," Mr. Jones warned. "We have no way of knowing exactly what has happened."

The men moved quickly, their faces pale but determined. They lifted Jane slightly so her head rested on Bingley's shoulder, but no more. Mr. Jones turned his full attention to Elizabeth, his frown deepening as he fully took in her state.

"Miss Elizabeth, I insist you sit down immediately," he said in a firm voice, his professional concern overriding any gentleness he would have used in another situation. "You're in no condition to remain standing."

Elizabeth blinked at him, confused, until she caught sight of her disheveled appearance in the reflection of a window, the dark sky causing the glass to act like a mirror. Her dress was torn and stained with dirt, her arms were streaked with blood from deep scratches, and her hair hung in a wild tangle of sticks and leaves. Finally, she allowed herself to be guided to a chair, the weight of the night's events finally pressing down on her. She stared blankly ahead as Mr. Jones crouched beside her, his hand pressing against her forehead.

"You're feverish," he said grimly, turning to Mrs. Nicholls. "She needs dry clothes, a fire, willow bark tea, and rest. At once."

The housekeeper nodded, taking Elizabeth's arm with the intent of leading her out of the room. Before they could leave, however, a low groan came from behind them. All eyes turned toward the source as Mr. Darcy stirred, his movements slow and unsteady as he pushed himself up from the floor.

"What the devil?" he rasped, his voice hoarse as he looked around in confusion. His bleary gaze settled on Elizabeth, and his expression shifted from confusion to alarm as he registered her state.

"Elizabeth! What happened? You are injured!" Darcy took an unsteady step toward her, but his legs wobbled, nearly toppling him over.

Elizabeth opened her mouth to reply, but Mr. Jones stepped forward, his hand on Darcy's arm to steady him. "Mr. Darcy, you've all been drugged with laudanum," the apothecary explained. "Please, sit down before you collapse."

Darcy's eyes darted around the room, his concern deepening as he took in the scattered bodies of his companions. When his gaze landed on Georgiana, a strangled cry escaping his lips. He attempted to crawl toward his young sister, but Mr. Jones tightened his grip, his voice firm.

"Mrs. Nicholls," Mr. Jones said sharply, "take Miss Elizabeth out of here at once. Her fever will worsen if she remains."

Elizabeth tried to resist, but Mrs. Nicholls's grip was firm as she gently but insistently led her toward the door. "Come along, dear," she urged. "You must rest."

"Go, Elizabeth." Darcy's voice was hoarse as he added his voice to theirs.

Only then did Elizabeth allow herself to be led away, but as she stepped into the corridor, she glanced back at the room. Darcy was sitting now, his shoulders hunched as though weighed down by the chaos around him. Her heart twisted at the sight.

For a fleeting moment, she wished she could stay—stay and ensure that Jane was safe, that Darcy recovered, that Georgiana would not wake to a world forever changed. But her body betrayed her, trembling with exhaustion, and she knew she could do no more.

As the door closed behind her, Elizabeth let out a shaky breath, her thoughts racing. She prayed for Jane, for Darcy, for Georgiana. And though she left the chaos of the drawing room behind her, her heart remained heavy with the weight of everything that had happened—and the fear of what was yet to come.

Darcy's vision blurred as he tried to make sense of the chaos unfolding around him. His head throbbed, his limbs felt like lead, and a bitter taste lingered in his mouth. Despite the haze clouding his thoughts, one thing stood out starkly in his mind: Elizabeth.

He watched her retreating form as Mrs. Nicholls gently but firmly guided her out of the room. Her gown was torn and filthy, her arms scratched and bleeding, her hair tumbling in wild disarray. She had looked so fragile, yet her determination to care for Jane had been unshakable, a testament to her strength.

A surge of protectiveness swelled in his chest, followed quickly by a sharp pang of guilt. *How did this happen? Why is Elizabeth injured while the rest of us lay unconscious?*

The questions swirled unanswered as the door clicked shut behind her. He wanted to go to her, to offer some form of comfort or reassurance, but his body refused to cooperate. Instead, he turned his attention to Georgiana, attempting once more to crawl to his sister.

"Miss Elizabeth will be all right," Mr. Jones said firmly, his voice pulling Darcy back to the present. "She's a strong one. Mrs. Nicholls will see to her, and I will check on her as soon as I finish here. For now, sir, you need to focus on your own recovery."

"See to my sister. I am fine."

The apothecary ignored him, keeping his fingers at Darcy's wrist and neck. At last he sat back and said, "Your heart rate is steadier now, but I strongly advise you to rest. Whatever you drank has affected you, and the effects may linger."

Darcy gave a distracted nod, his attention drawn back to his sister. Following his gaze, Mr. Jones said, "I will see to her next, but only if you promise to remain sitting down on this chair."

Snapping his fingers at two footmen who were at the front of the crowded doorway, Mr. Jones barked. "Help Mr. Darcy to his feet so he can rest here."

The young men sprang into action, relieved at having an assignment. They each put one of Darcy's arms around their shoulders and half-carried, half-dragged him up into the seat.

"How is Georgiana?" Darcy asked hoarsely.

"She will be just fine," Mr. Jones replied. "Her heart is a bit slow, but I imagine the drug's effects are stronger on her, being so slight a creature."

Across the room, Bingley began to stir, his groggy movements attracting the attention of the maids clustered in the doorway. The faint murmur of their gossip reached Darcy's ears, irritating him further.

"Bingley," Darcy rasped, his voice hoarse. "Wake up."

Bingley groaned, blinking sluggishly as he raised his head. A dreamy smile spread across his face as his gaze landed on Jane, still cradled in his lap. "Jane," he murmured softly, his tone filled with affection.

Darcy stiffened, his instincts as a gentleman and a friend roaring to life. The scene was scandalous, even if unintentional. The maids tittered behind their hands, their wide eyes fixed on the pair.

Bingley seemed to realize his position at the same moment. He straightened abruptly, causing Jane to slump forward. Jane gasped and woke with a start, her face flushing a deep crimson as she took in her surroundings.

"Oh my goodness!" she cried, sitting upright and pressing her hands to her flaming cheeks. "I—Mr. Bingley—I—" Her words dissolved into a stammered apology as tears welled in her eyes.

"It's all right, Miss Bennet," Mr. Jones interjected, placing a calming hand on her shoulder. "The tea you all drank was drugged. None of you are to blame for your actions."

Darcy's heart clenched as he observed Jane's mortification. She reminded him so much of Georgiana—gentle, kind, and deeply sensitive. *God, please let her live.*

He exhaled shakily, then his eyes narrowed. "Where is Miss Bingley?" He looked around the room. "Who could have done this? And why?" His tone was sharp, cutting through the murmurings of the gathered servants.

The question hung in the air like a lead weight. The maids exchanged uneasy glances, and one of them hesitated before stepping forward. "I—I heard Miss Elizabeth say something about Miss Bingley," she stammered, wringing her hands. "She said she was kidnapped."

The room erupted into whispers and exclamations, but Darcy remained frozen, the word *kidnapped* echoing in his mind. "Who could have done this?" he demanded, his voice low but fierce.

Mr. Jones looked grim. "All I know is that the tea was laced with laudanum," he said. "Beyond that, I cannot say. Miss Elizabeth and Mrs. Nicholls may know more."

A sudden thought struck Darcy. "Where is my son? Please tell me that Andrew is unharmed!"

The question silenced the room. Darcy's voice, usually measured and calm, now carried a raw edge of desperation that made everyone pause. His chest tightened, his breath coming shallow and quick as the implications hit him. Andrew. His son. How could he not have thought of him sooner?

The maids exchanged glances, their earlier nervousness now replaced with a touch of fear. Finally, one of the younger ones stepped forward, her eyes wide and brimming with tears. "I... I haven't seen him since this morning, sir," she stammered. "He was with Rebecca, playing in the nursery."

Darcy's chest tightened as the maid stammered her uncertainty about Andrew's whereabouts. His son—the thought that anything might have happened to him made his vision blur with panic. He shot to his feet, intending to run to the nursery, but as soon as he stood, the room spun violently. He staggered, clutching the back of the chair for support.

"Sir, please sit," Mr. Jones said sharply, steadying him. "You're still under the effects of the laudanum. Moving too quickly will only worsen things."

Darcy clenched his jaw, his heart racing, but reluctantly sank back into the chair. "Then someone—someone must check on Andrew!" His voice cracked with urgency.

Mrs. Nicholls immediately turned to one of the maids, her voice calm but firm. "Emma, go to the nursery. Check on Mr. Andrew and Rebecca. Do not alarm them unless absolutely necessary, but bring me news immediately."

The young maid, her face pale with fear, curtsied and bolted from the room. Darcy's fingers gripped the chair so tightly his knuckles turned white. Every second stretched into an eternity as he counted each breath, his thoughts consumed by visions of his son— helpless, alone, or worse.

"I need to know he's safe," Darcy muttered, his voice almost a prayer.

In the background, Mr. Jones continued his work. He had moved on to Mrs. Hurst, who lay slumped on the settee. The apothecary bent over her, feeling her pulse and checking her breathing.

"She's fine," Mr. Jones announced after a moment, but Darcy scarcely registered the words. His focus remained fixed on the open door, his body tense as he willed the maid to return with news.

Finally, the hurried sound of footsteps echoed in the hallway. Emma appeared in the doorway, slightly out of breath but smiling. "Mr. Darcy," she said, her voice soothing, "Andrew is unharmed. He's fast asleep in the nursery. Rebecca is with him, tidying up. She was completely unaware of what's happened downstairs."

Darcy exhaled sharply, his head dropping into his hands as a wave of relief crashed over him. The tension in his chest loosened, and for the first time since waking, he allowed himself to breathe deeply. "Thank God," he whispered. "Thank God."

Mrs. Nicholls patted his shoulder reassuringly. "Rebecca will keep him safe, sir," she said. "You can rest easy on that account."

Darcy nodded but found little solace in her words. Relief for his son's safety was overshadowed by the chaos surrounding him. He lifted his head, his gaze shifting to Mr. Jones, who had moved to the still figure of Mr. Hurst.

"What of Hurst?" Darcy asked, his voice steady but laced with dread.

Mr. Jones knelt beside Hurst, his expression grave. He checked for a pulse, moving his fingers to different spots on the man's neck and wrist. Time seemed to slow as Darcy watched him work, each second dragging like an eternity.

Finally, Mr. Jones sat back on his heels, his face etched with exhaustion and sadness. "Mr. Hurst is dead," he said quietly.

A collective gasp rippled through the room. Darcy closed his eyes, the words ringing in his ears. His relief for Andrew was now replaced by a heavier burden—the realization that this day's events had claimed a life.

"How?" Darcy asked hoarsely, his throat tight.

Mr. Jones shook his head. "The laudanum was too much for his system," he explained. "Given his apparent fondness for spirits, his body likely couldn't handle the combination. He would have gone quickly, at least."

The weight of the announcement hung in the air like a storm cloud, and Darcy closed his eyes, the enormity of the situation pressing down on him. One life lost, another potentially endangered, and countless questions unanswered.

And Elizabeth—what horrors had she endured to make it back to them? Darcy's jaw tightened as resolve hardened within him. Whoever had orchestrated this would pay, but first, he had to uncover the truth.

Chapter 18

Elizabeth sat in a room she barely recognized, her body limp and unresisting as Mrs. Nicholls and two maids worked around her. The fire in the hearth crackled loudly, its warmth reaching her chilled limbs. Despite the heat, however, she shivered uncontrollably, her teeth chattering, her limbs trembling as if the chill in her bones could not be chased away.

A steaming bath stood near the fire, hastily filled with the boiling water brought up from the kitchen that Mrs. Nicholls had the foresight to order when she first saw Elizabeth. Beside it lay a warm woolen dressing gown with a matching robe, liberated from Mrs. Hurst's closet, as she was the only woman in residence who did not stand a full head higher than Elizabeth.

The room was alive with the sounds of bustling maids, hurried footsteps, and whispered exclamations, but it all felt distant to Elizabeth, as though she were trapped behind a thick pane of glass. Mrs. Nicholls led Elizabeth over to the fireplace and sat her down on a plain wooden chair.

"Come now, Miss Elizabeth," Mrs. Nicholls murmured, her voice steady but tinged with worry. "Let's get you out of these wet clothes. We need to warm you up, my dear. You're chilled to the bone."

The housekeeper's hands worked deftly to unfasten her boots and the buttons on the back of Elizabeth's sodden gown. The fabric of her dress clung to her bruised skin, peeling away with an unsettling sound that made her flinch, though she remained silent.

"Miss Elizabeth," Mrs. Nicholls said gently, drawing her back to the present, "can you lift your arms for me, dear?"

Elizabeth obeyed without thinking, her movements mechanical. She felt the maids slip her tattered gown from her shoulders, their hands careful but firm. The cold air hit her skin, sending another shiver down her spine.

The maids hovered nearby, their faces pale, their eyes darting nervously over the torn fabric and Elizabeth's battered frame. The rustle of fabric and the occasional whispered gasp were the only sounds in the room.

"She's shaking so much," one of the maids whispered, her voice thick with worry. "Is she ill, Mrs. Nicholls?"

"She's in shock," Mrs. Nicholls replied grimly. "Stoke the fire, Alice."

"Oh, look at that bruise," another one of the maids breathed, her voice quavering. She pointed to a deep purple mark on Elizabeth's arm, visible now that the sleeve had been peeled away. "That must hurt something awful."

Elizabeth didn't react. She felt as though she were floating outside her own body, watching as the maids uncovered scratch after scratch, bruise after bruise. The cuts on her arms were long and jagged, angry red lines crisscrossing her skin from her frantic flight through the hedgerows. A deep scratch on her cheek still oozed blood, and the maids clucked with concern as they dabbed at it with a cloth.

The stalwart housekeeper's hands trembled slightly as she worked, her jaw tight with suppressed emotion. "Miss Elizabeth doesn't need your fretting. Go fetch some ointment from the still room. Now."

The younger maid darted from the room, her footsteps echoing down the hall. Elizabeth sat numbly as Mrs. Nicholls began to unlace her stays, her fingers moving with practiced efficiency. As the fabric fell away, revealing bruises forming along Elizabeth's ribs, the older woman let out a tsk of dismay.

"You poor child," Mrs. Nicholls murmured, her voice uncharacteristically gentle. "What have you been through?"

Elizabeth said nothing. The words were trapped somewhere deep inside her, buried beneath layers of shock and exhaustion. She let herself be guided into the bath, the warm water stinging as it met her raw skin. She flinched slightly as the heat touched her battered skin but made no other protest. Her limbs felt heavy, her mind sluggish, and she moved only when prompted by Mrs. Nicholls or the maid, like a puppet being maneuvered on unseen strings.

The water quickly turned murky as the maids gently washed away the dirt, blood, and grime from her ordeal. The dried blood on her chin, where she had bitten her lip to stifle her cries, came away with soft scrubbing. One of the maids wrung out a cloth, her hands trembling. "It's like she's been through a war," she whispered to her companion.

"Hush," Mrs. Nicholls said firmly, though there was a tremor in her own voice. She took the cloth and dabbed at a particularly tender-looking bruise on Elizabeth's temple. "There now, Miss Elizabeth. This ointment will help. Just a bit of sting, but it'll ease the pain."

Elizabeth barely registered the words, her thoughts swirling in a chaotic storm, her mind as numb as her frozen limbs. She felt detached from her body, as though she were watching the scene unfold from a great distance.

As the warmth of the bath began to seep into her, the haze of shock slowly lifted, and emotions she'd held at bay began to rise.

The events of the day played in disjointed fragments— Wickham's sneering face, the maze's twisting passages, the terror that had gripped her chest as she crouched in the hedge, listening to his shouts. She had run, hidden, and fought to survive, but now, in the relative safety of Netherfield, the enormity of it all began to settle upon her.

I was so close to...

She couldn't finish the thought. Her breath hitched, and she squeezed her eyes shut, willing the memories to dissipate. Yet they remained, lurking just beneath the surface, waiting to pounce.

The maids worked in silence now, their movements gentle as they washed away the dirt and blood. Elizabeth felt their hands on her arms, her shoulders, her hair, but her thoughts were elsewhere. At first, fear dominated—sharp, visceral fear.

What if Wickham had caught me? What if I hadn't been able to run? The thought made her chest tighten, her breath coming in shallow gasps until she thought she would drown.

But as the minutes passed, fear gave way to something else: anger. It started as a faint flicker, like the embers of the fire beside her, which grew with each passing moment. How dare they? How dare Wickham and Caroline conspire to harm everyone she loved? To use her family and friends as pawns in their twisted game?

Her hands curled into fists beneath the water, her nails digging into her palms. The heat of the bath seemed to fuel her fury, melting away the numbness that had paralyzed her. She had been terrified, yes—more terrified than she had ever been in her life, but she had faced that fear and lived. She had outsmarted Wickham, escaped his clutches, and survived to tell the tale.

Running didn't make me weak, she thought fiercely. *It made me brave. I lived to expose the truth.*

The maids' whispers pulled her from her thoughts. "Her lip's split," one of them murmured, her voice filled with concern. "Must've bitten it in fright."

"Hold still, Miss Elizabeth," Mrs. Nicholls said as she dabbed a clean cloth over Elizabeth's chin, wiping away the dried blood. "There now. We'll have you patched up soon enough."

Elizabeth obeyed, her body yielding to their ministrations, but her mind continued to churn. The shock was wearing off, replaced by a steely determination that hardened her resolve. She thought of Jane, lying unconscious downstairs, her serene face marred by the knowledge of how close she had come to ruin. She thought of Darcy, his strong frame crumpled on the floor, vulnerable in a way she had never imagined. And she thought of Wickham, his cruel smile etched into her memory like a brand.

I will not let them win, she vowed silently. *I will not let them destroy what matters most.*

"Miss Elizabeth?" Mrs. Nicholls's voice broke through her thoughts, and Elizabeth blinked, realizing the housekeeper was holding out a towel.

She nodded, and the maids lifted her from the bath, wrapping her in soft towels warmed by the fire. They rubbed ointment into her cuts and bruises, their hands careful but efficient. The dressing gown and robe were brought forward, their fabric rich and soft against her battered skin. Elizabeth allowed herself to be dressed, the warmth of the layers cocooning her like a shield against the cold.

Her gaze drifted to the fire, its flames crackling and dancing with a kind of wild energy. She saw herself in those flames—burning, unyielding, determined. She would not let fear silence her. She would speak the truth, no matter the cost.

By the time the maids had finished dressing her, Elizabeth's shivering had lessened, though her teeth still chattered faintly. They wrapped her in warm blankets and placed hot bricks at her feet, their hands quick and efficient.

"She's still trembling," one of the maids whispered, her brow furrowed.

"She'll be all right," Mrs. Nicholls said firmly, though her eyes lingered on Elizabeth with concern. "The worst is over now."

But for Elizabeth, the worst was not over. The fight was just beginning. She would face the others downstairs—Darcy, Jane, the apothecary—and she would tell them everything. She would expose Wickham and Caroline for the villains they were.

Mrs. Nicholls knelt before her, adjusting the folds of the blankets wrapped around Elizabeth's legs. "There now," she said with a small nod of satisfaction. "You'll warm up soon enough. The shivering is just the shock wearing off."

Elizabeth met the housekeeper's gaze, her own eyes clear and determined. "Thank you, Mrs. Nicholls," she said quietly, her voice steady despite the turmoil within. "But I am not done yet."

"You're a strong one, Miss Elizabeth," Mrs. Nicholls said softly, a note of admiration in her voice as she tied the robe's sash. "Stronger than most."

A knock at the door interrupted the moment, and the butler's voice called from the hallway. "Mrs. Nicholls? Miss Elizabeth? The young lady's presence is requested downstairs."

Mrs. Nicholls glanced at Elizabeth, her brow furrowed in concern. "Are you certain you're ready, child? You've been through so much—"

"I am ready," Elizabeth said firmly, standing without hesitation. Her legs trembled slightly beneath her, but she held her head high. "I must tell them what happened."

Mrs. Nicholls studied her for a moment before nodding. "Very well, then. But lean on me if you feel unsteady."

Elizabeth didn't need the offer. With each step toward the door, her resolve solidified. The fear that had gripped her earlier was gone, replaced by a fierce determination. She had endured more than she thought possible, but she had survived. And now, she would speak the truth.

Nothing would stop her.

~

Making her way down the stairs, she was led by the butler to the music room, relieved that the parlor had been abandoned in favor of a more comfortable environment. A footman pulled the door open, giving her a look that seemed to be a mix of pity and horror.

She closed her eyes and took a steadying breath. *You survived, Elizabeth. You escaped, and now you must tell the truth.* With that thought as her anchor, she straightened her back and walked through the door, her head held high.

The gentlemen stood as she entered the room. She paused in the doorway, conscious of the worried eyes upon her. The maids had done an admirable job making her presentable, but no amount of warm baths or woolen dressing gowns could chase away the weariness that clung to her like a second skin.

Darcy sat stiffly near the fire, his posture as rigid as the stone mantle behind him. Bingley hovered protectively beside Jane. Her pale face was framed by wisps of hair that had escaped her hastily arranged coiffure, her large eyes filled with lingering confusion.

Sir William Lucas, who served as the magistrate, occupied a commanding position near the fireplace, his expression one of grave concern. Mr. Jones stood beside him, his weathered face solemn. Near the window sat Mr. Bennet, his usual air of sardonic detachment replaced with a grim determination that set Elizabeth on edge. Reclining on a settee was Mrs. Hurst, her face pale.

The air was thick with tension, broken only by the soft clink of cups as the servants circulated with trays of coffee, chocolate, and lemonade. Another tray of tea and sandwiches was offered, which no-one touched. Elizabeth hesitated in the doorway, unsure if she had the strength to endure what was coming.

"Miss Elizabeth," Sir William called gently, breaking the silence. "Please, join us."

She stepped forward, the weight of their gazes pressing down on her like a physical force. Every step felt heavier than the last as she crossed the room and took the empty seat Sir William had indicated.

"Where is Miss Darcy?" she asked urgently.

"My sister is resting in her rooms," Darcy answered, his face softening. "Other than being quite fatigued, she is well."

"And Andrew?" She held her breath.

"Perfectly safe and unharmed," Darcy assured her. "He and his nurse had retired for the evening, and they had absolutely no idea of what was occurring."

She exhaled and looked around the room. "But where is Mr. Hurst?"

Elizabeth's question hung in the air, the tension in the room thickening as she scanned the faces of those gathered. A shadow passed over Mrs. Hurst's features, and she lowered her gaze to her lap, where her hands rested protectively over the small yet noticeable bulge at her midline.

Mr. Jones cleared his throat, stepping forward. "Miss Elizabeth," he began delicately, his tone measured, "I am afraid Mr. Hurst... did not survive the events of the afternoon."

Elizabeth's breath caught. Her eyes widened as the weight of the words settled over her. "What—what do you mean?" she stammered, her voice barely above a whisper.

Darcy, seated a few feet away, shifted uncomfortably, his brows drawing together in a tight line. "Mr. Jones believes that the laudanum in the tea, combined with the alcohol Mr. Hurst consumed earlier, proved fatal," he said, his voice low and controlled, though his hands were clenched tightly on the arms of his chair.

Elizabeth turned to Mrs. Hurst, whose pale face betrayed her grief despite the stoic mask she tried to maintain. "I... I am so sorry," Elizabeth whispered, her voice trembling. "I did not realize..."

Mrs. Hurst looked up briefly, her eyes glistening with unshed tears. "Thank you, Miss Elizabeth," she said quietly, her voice raspy, "but I would rather not dwell on it any longer."

At this point, Sir William cleared his throat. "Miss Elizabeth, there is some confusion over what occurred this evening, and you are the only one with answers. Can you explain what happened? Mr. Jones has informed us that you said Mr. Wickham was involved and Miss Bingley is missing."

Elizabeth nodded, swallowing hard. She clasped her hands tightly in her lap to stop them from trembling. "Yes," she said, her voice hoarse but steady. "I will tell you everything."

She began her account slowly, carefully choosing her words. She described the tea, the strange, bitter flavor, and the moments when everything had begun to unravel. As she recounted Wickham's pursuit and her frantic escape through the hedgerows, her voice faltered, but she pressed on.

When she reached the part where Wickham had carried an unconscious Miss Bingley to the carriage, binding her wrists before fleeing, a collective gasp swept through the room.

"We must recover her at once!" Bingley cried, leaping to his feet. His eyes darted to Darcy, pleading for direction.

Before Darcy could respond, a venomous voice cut through the room. "Must we?" Mrs. Hurst sneered from her corner, her hand resting protectively over her slightly swollen belly.

Normally so poised and unflappable, the new widow was now a shadow of her former self, her eyes red-rimmed and weary. She had been largely silent since awakening to the news of her husband's death, but now her voice carried a steely edge. "I say, she has made her bed. Let her lie in it."

Jane let out a soft gasp, her hand flying to her mouth. "Surely there's been some kind of misunderstanding," she said faintly, her voice trembling.

Elizabeth pressed her lips into a thin line and shook her head. "No, Jane," she said firmly. "There is no misunderstanding. Miss Bingley and Mr. Wickham entered into this scheme knowingly. They are directly responsible for the chaos here tonight, including the death of Mr. Hurst."

A murmur of agreement rippled through the room.

"He wasn't always like this," Mrs. Hurst spat, her voice trembling with suppressed emotion. "He only drank because of Caroline. She drove him mad. He would say it was the only way to endure her company. And now, she has taken him from me entirely."

Bingley went pale, his face a mask of disbelief. "Will they be arrested for murder?"

Sir William cleared his throat awkwardly, the weight of authority settling uncomfortably on his shoulders. "Intent is a significant factor in such matters. They will need to be questioned thoroughly before we proceed with any charges."

"That may be," Darcy said, his voice cutting through the room, "but Wickham should certainly be arrested for kidnapping. Regardless of intent, he forcibly took an unconscious woman against her will." His jaw tightened, his eyes blazing. "They're likely halfway to Gretna Green by now. Marriage would ensure Wickham's access to her dowry and protect him from immediate consequences."

"Do you truly think he'd marry her?" Bingley asked incredulously.

"Yes," Darcy said flatly. "This is not the first time he has attempted such a scheme with a wealthy young woman. When his plans with… a wealthy young woman of my acquaintance failed, he likely saw Miss Bingley as a new opportunity."

Elizabeth shot him a sharp look. *Does he mean….No, surely not! The poor girl; no wonder she is so timid.*

Bingley slumped back into his chair, shaking his head. "If that is the case," he said, "there is no use chasing them now. They have hours on us. And given what the servants have seen…"

The words hung in the air, unfinished but understood by all. The damage to Caroline's reputation—and by extension, the Bingley name—was irreversible.

Mr. Bennet cleared his throat, drawing all eyes to him. "And it is precisely that damage which brings me here tonight," he said gravely.

Elizabeth tensed, her hands gripping the arms of her chair. "What do you mean, Papa?" she asked warily.

He looked at her, his expression softening for a moment before hardening again. "The rumors are already spreading through Meryton," he said. "Your Aunt Philips arrived at Longbourn with tales of a sordid tea party mere minutes after I received Mr. Bingley's note."

Elizabeth groaned softly, dread pooling in her stomach. "Dare I ask what she said?"

Mr. Bennet's lips pressed into a thin line. "The story is that Mr. Bingley seduced Jane on the settee," he said bluntly. "And when you tried to intervene, Mr. Darcy assaulted you, causing your injuries." He paused, his gaze resting on Darcy. "The loss of your jacket, sir, has only added fuel to the fire."

Elizabeth felt as though the ground had dropped out from beneath her. "No," she whispered. "Surely not—"

"I'm afraid it's true," Mr. Bennet said, his voice heavy with regret. "You and Jane are both ruined."

Jane burst into tears, burying her face in her hands. Elizabeth reached for her, wrapping an arm around her trembling shoulders. "What happens now?" she whispered, her voice barely audible.

"That," Mr. Bennet said heavily, "depends entirely on Mr. Darcy and Mr. Bingley."

All eyes turned to the two men. Darcy's expression was unreadable, his features carved in stone, but Bingley's face lit up with determination. He rose to his feet and turned to Jane. "Miss Bennet," he said, his voice trembling with emotion, "while this is not how I envisioned things, I must confess that I find you to be the most angelic, kind, and extraordinary woman I have ever known. Will you do me the honor of becoming my wife?"

Jane looked up, her tear-streaked face filled with shock and uncertainty. She glanced at Elizabeth, who gave her a small, encouraging nod. "Yes," Jane whispered. "Yes, Mr. Bingley, I will marry you."

The room erupted in murmurs, but Elizabeth's attention was fixed on her father, who had turned his gaze to Darcy.

"And you, Mr. Darcy?" Mr. Bennet said, his voice steady but unyielding.

Darcy stiffened, his dark eyes narrowing. "What are you asking of me, sir?"

Mr. Bennet met his gaze without flinching. "I am asking you to marry my daughter, Elizabeth."

Elizabeth's heart stopped. The room seemed to fall away, the voices around her fading into silence. She turned to Darcy, her wide eyes locking with his.

For a moment, it was as though time itself had ceased to exist.

Chapter 19

Darcy sat in stunned silence, Mr. Bennet's words reverberating in his mind. *You are asking me to marry Miss Elizabeth?* The weight of the situation bore down on him, tightening his chest. His jaw clenched as emotions he could barely name surged to the surface.

His initial reaction was one of intense anger, sharp and hot. *Once again, Wickham's actions dictate my life.*

Memories of Anne, his first wife, surged unbidden. Her pale, trembling face as she whispered her pleas, her hollow eyes filled with the grief of her own shattered innocence. Anne's life—and death—had been marred by Wickham's malice. Now, here he was again, the shadow of that vile man twisting his path once more.

Darcy's fists clenched against his knees. *Haven't I suffered enough under Wickham's machinations? It's always him— always taking, always destroying. Must I be forced into another union because of his self-serving actions?* His heart rebelled at the thought. *Marriage should be a choice, not a penance inflicted by someone else's cruelty.*

And yet… his gaze flickered to Elizabeth, and everything stilled.

She sat tall, her chin lifted in quiet defiance despite the pallor of her face. Her borrowed robe, though clean and warm, could not disguise her exhaustion. And yet, her eyes—those fierce, expressive eyes—burned with a *joie de vivre* that was undiminished by the day's events. They spoke of strength, resilience, and a determination he had come to admire; she was a woman who had faced terror and refused to crumble.

Unbidden, memories of the past weeks rushed in, vivid and insistent.

He saw her cradling Andrew in the cold, her voice soothing, her touch tender as she rocked his son in her arms. That moment had been a revelation, though he hadn't recognized it at the time. A glimpse of Elizabeth's strength, her capacity for love, her ability to nurture even when faced with chaos.

He saw her at the piano with Georgiana, coaxing his shy sister out of her shell with laughter and encouragement. Their shared joy had filled the room, easing tensions Darcy hadn't even realized he carried. She had drawn Georgiana out in a way he had never been able to, her natural warmth breaking through years of guarded reserve.

He saw her in conversation with him—challenging him, teasing him, sharing her thoughts with such clarity and wit that it left him breathless. Elizabeth had a way of looking at the world, at him, that made him question everything he thought he knew. She was unlike any woman he had ever known—strong, intelligent, and utterly captivating.

A realization struck him, sharp and undeniable: *I love her.*

His breath caught as the truth settled within him. The anger he had felt moments before ebbed away, replaced by something deeper,

277

something that made his chest tighten and his pulse quicken. This wasn't like his marriage to Anne—this was different.

This was *Elizabeth*.

How had he not seen it before? The way his heart raced at her presence, the way her laughter stayed with him long after she had left the room. She was in his thoughts constantly, her voice echoing in his mind, her spirit woven into his days.

Darcy's throat tightened as he wrestled with the weight of the moment. Could he truly ask her to marry him under these circumstances? Could he bear to bind her to a man like himself, scarred by duty, loss, and mistakes? Yet, the idea of not asking her, of walking away now, felt equally unbearable.

For a moment, the world narrowed to the woman in front of him: Elizabeth Bennet. The woman he had come to admire, to respect, to cherish. And now, the woman he was being asked to marry.

A throat cleared, jolting him from his thoughts. Darcy blinked, realizing that the room had fallen silent. Every pair of eyes was fixed on him, their expressions ranging from expectation to concern. Mr. Bennet was watching him intently, his brow furrowed, while Elizabeth sat poised, her hands clasped tightly in her lap. She was waiting. They were all waiting.

Darcy inhaled deeply, forcing himself to stand. His movements were deliberate, his posture straight, though his heart thundered in his chest. He turned to Elizabeth, meeting her gaze fully for the first time since the question had been posed.

Her eyes searched his face, and for a fleeting moment, he thought he saw a flicker of fear. But it was gone as quickly as it came, replaced by a quiet resolve that made his chest ache.

He stepped closer, his voice low and steady despite the emotions churning within him. "Miss Elizabeth," he began, his tone formal, "would you do me the great honor of becoming my wife?"

The words hung in the air, heavy with significance. Darcy held his breath, his heart pounding as he awaited her reply, his future poised on the edge of her answer. For the first time in years, he felt the sting of vulnerability—raw, unguarded, and utterly at her mercy.

Elizabeth sat frozen in her chair, her hands clasped tightly in her lap, her heart pounding so loudly she was certain the others must hear it. Every second stretched unbearably as she watched Darcy's face. His expression was unreadable at first, his features a mask of calm neutrality that betrayed nothing of his thoughts.

Then, a flicker of something crossed his face—a tightening of his jaw, a darkening of his eyes.

Anger.

It was unmistakable, and her stomach twisted painfully. He was furious, of course. Furious at being cornered into this position, at having his life upended by Wickham.

Elizabeth dropped her gaze to her lap, unable to bear the weight of his pain. Of course he's angry, she thought bitterly. *What man wouldn't be? He's being forced into marriage with me—a woman beneath his station, who has been ruined by Wickham's actions.*

279

When she dared to glance up again, Darcy's expression had shifted. His features were no longer tight with anger but were now set in a stoic mask of resolve. His back was rigid, his posture impeccable, and his face was devoid of emotion, as though he had donned armor against the weight of what he was about to do.

Elizabeth's heart sank further. *He doesn't want this,* she realized. *He sees it as an obligation, a duty he cannot escape.*

The thought made her chest ache, a sharp stabbing directly into her heart. She had dared to dream, for the briefest of moments, that he might harbor some affection for her, that perhaps his attention over the past weeks had meant something more. But now, that hope felt foolish and naive.

When Darcy finally rose from his seat, her breath caught in her throat. His movements were slow and deliberate, each step precise and measured as he crossed the room. He stopped before her, his tall frame towering above her, and for a moment, she thought she saw something flicker in his eyes—something tender, something vulnerable. But it was gone in an instant, replaced by his familiar unyielding mask.

She wanted to tell him to sit back down, to stop before the words could leave his lips, but she was frozen, caught in the maelstrom of her own emotions. Her breath came shallow and quick, her hands gripping the folds of her dress until her knuckles turned white.

"Miss Elizabeth," he said, his tone cool and distant, "would you do me the great honor of becoming my wife?"

The words echoed in her ears, heavy with formality and duty. *The honor?* The phrase felt hollow, almost mocking, when she could see plainly that he was doing this out of necessity, not desire. Her chest tightened further, and she pressed her hands together in her lap to keep them from trembling. She searched his face desperately for any sign of warmth or affection, but found only the same impassive resolve.

The urge to refuse him surged within her. She didn't want to trap him in a union he would resent. She couldn't bear to tie herself to a man who would look at her every day with the same grim sense of duty she saw now. Yet as her gaze swept the room, her resolve faltered.

Her father's stern expression left no room for argument. Jane, pale but hopeful, watched her with wide eyes, silently pleading for her to do what was necessary. The servants, lingering discreetly in the background, had already been whispering. She could hear their voices in her mind, the gossip that would spread through Meryton if she did not accept.

Ruined. Disgraced. Unmarriageable.

Elizabeth's throat tightened and tears pricked the corners of her eyes. The reality of her situation settled heavily on her shoulders. There was no other choice. If she refused him, her life would be over. She would be an outcast, shunned by society, her family's reputation in tatters. And yet, to accept his proposal knowing he did not truly want her—it felt like a betrayal of her own heart.

She looked at Darcy, her vision blurring slightly as she blinked back the tears threatening to fall. His face was solemn, his gaze steady. Taking a deep, shuddering breath, she met Darcy's eyes. She looked down and relaxed her face, trying to appear calm, though her heart felt as though it might shatter within her chest.

She gave a tiny nod.

"Yes," she whispered, her hands trembling despite her best efforts to keep them still. "I will marry you, Mr. Darcy."

There was a collective exhale at her words, but Elizabeth felt no relief. She locked eyes with Darcy again, her stomach clenching painfully as she searched his gaze for a flicker of understanding, of shared emotion.

But his expression remained unreadable, and she felt more alone than ever.

I will not let them see how much this hurts, she vowed silently. I will not let them see my heart break.

For a moment, Darcy did not move, his expression unchanged. Then he inclined his head slightly, his voice low as he replied, "Thank you, Miss Elizabeth."

The formality of his words only deepened the ache in her chest. As they turned to face the others in the room, Elizabeth kept her gaze forward, refusing to let herself dwell on what she had just agreed to. Her decision was made, her path set. Yet, in that moment, as the weight of her acceptance settled upon her, Elizabeth's heart ached with the bittersweet realization that she might have just sealed her own unhappiness.

Elizabeth took a deep breath as she descended from the carriage Bingley had loaned them to return to Longbourn, as the Bennet carriage had been absconded with by Wickham. It was now quite late in the evening, and Mr. Bennet had ridden ahead to inform his family of the new developments.

The journey had been quiet, both sisters lost in their thoughts. Jane was pale and subdued, her usual serenity shadowed with worry. Elizabeth's body ached with every jolt of the wheels. Despite the soothing ointments, sharp stings and dull throbs remained constant reminders of the harrowing events of the day.

The door opened, and Hill greeted them with a lantern, her eyes widening as she took in Elizabeth's bruised and scratched face. "Oh, Miss Elizabeth!" she exclaimed softly. "Are you—"

"I'm quite all right, Hill," Elizabeth replied, unable to keep the tremble from her voice. "Please, let us inside. It has been a… a difficult day."

The familiar warmth of Longbourn's entry hall greeted them, but it offered little comfort. The moment they stepped inside, Mrs. Bennet's shrill voice assaulted their ears and echoed through the house.

"My Jane! My Lizzy! There you are at last!" She bustled forward, her lace cap askew as she clapped her hands together with glee. "Oh, Jane, I knew Mr. Bingley would come to his senses! And Lizzy—how very clever of you to secure Mr. Darcy at last! Two betrothals, and all in the same week! I am the happiest woman in England; nothing shall ever vex me again."

Elizabeth stiffened, her nails digging into the palms of her hands. "Mama," she said through clenched teeth, her voice low, "this is hardly a cause for celebration."

"Nonsense!" Mrs. Bennet said brightly, entirely oblivious to her daughter's tone. "A wedding is always a cause for celebration, my dear. And two—why, it will set all of Meryton talking! Oh, the carriages, the gowns—how grand it will all be! Why, I must begin

283

planning at once. I was thinking late spring, or perhaps early summer—"

"Mama, stop!" Elizabeth's voice cut through the room like a whip, startling her mother into silence. Her eyes burned with anger. "Do you even see me? Look at me, Mama! Look at my face! Look at my arms!"

"Oh, just a few scratches, which is nothing compared to the triumph—"

"Triumph?" Mr. Bennet's sharp voice cut through the room as he appeared in the doorway. His expression was thunderous, and his gaze locked onto his wife with uncharacteristic fury. "I hardly think triumph is the appropriate word, Mrs. Bennet, given the circumstances."

Mrs. Bennet faltered, her smile slipping. "But, Mr. Bennet, surely you must see—"

"Enough!" he thundered, his voice unyielding. "Do you have any idea what your daughters have endured today? Look at Elizabeth, woman! Look at her injuries!"

Mrs. Bennet's eyes widened as she turned to her second daughter and saw her clearly for the first time since this arrival. The matron's hand flew to her mouth as she gasped. "Lizzy, what on earth happened to you?"

Elizabeth exhaled slowly. "I was chased, Mama. Chased through a maze like an animal by Mr. Wickham, who was trying to kill me. I fought to escape, to save my life and to check on Jane, who I thought had been poisoned and was lying dead in the parlor, as dead as Mr. Hurst. We could have— we all could have—" She broke off, choking on the unspoken words. "And all you care about is a wedding?"

Mrs. Bennet's face paled, and for once, she had no immediate response. Before she could muster a reply, Mr. Bennet spoke up. "That is enough, Elizabeth," he said firmly, yet gently. He turned to his wife, his tone sharp. "And you, Madam, ought to be ashamed."

Mrs. Bennet flinched as though struck. "I—I didn't know," she whispered, wringing her hands. Her gaze darted between her husband and Elizabeth, her composure unraveling. "Lizzy, I didn't understand—"

"Understand? Of course you didn't understand," Mr. Bennet interrupted coldly. "Your frivolity blinds you to everything that matters. If you cannot conduct yourself with the appropriate respect for what your daughters have suffered, then you had best keep silent. Do I make myself clear?"

Mrs. Bennet nodded meekly, her hands twisting together. "Y-yes, Mr. Bennet."

"Good."

Mrs. Bennet's lower lip trembled, and she fell into a chair, dabbing at her eyes with a lace handkerchief. "Oh, Lizzy," she murmured, her voice faint. "What have I done? I am so sorry. I had no idea."

Elizabeth's anger cooled as she watched her mother's face crumble into genuine remorse. "Thank you, Mama," she said quietly. "That means a great deal to me."

Mrs. Bennet sniffled, her hands twisting in her lap. "I could not bear it if you were truly harmed," she whispered. "You say Mr. Hurst is dead? Truly? Oh, my poor, dear girls." She reached out for each of her daughters, squeezing their hands when her words failed her.

Mr. Bennet nodded his approval. "Your young men will call at first light to take their leave before they go to London. There is much to arrange before the wedding. Three days is not a long time."

"Three days?" Lydia's voice rang out from the stairs as she bounded into the room, Kitty trailing behind her. "But that's the day of the Netherfield ball! Oh, I cannot wait to see the gowns and the carriages as everyone comes that evening to celebrate! Mr. Bingley must surely be inviting all his rich friends to come."

"There will be no ball," Mr. Bennet barked, causing Lydia to stop short. "It has been canceled."

"What?" Lydia wailed, her face contorting in dismay. "Canceled? But why? That is most unfair!"

"It is *not* unfair," Elizabeth snapped, her voice cutting through Lydia's protest. She stepped forward, cradling her injured arm. "Do you think this is a game, Lydia? Do you think this is about gowns and dances?"

Her voice rose with anger. "Look at me, Lydia! Look at what Lieutenant Wickham did! He chased me, threatened me, would have killed me if I hadn't escaped. He killed Mr. Hurst, kidnapped Miss Bingley, and tried to kill me. And yet you can only speak of dancing? You had best learn to deal with disappointment, because I will not hesitate to cut you as Mrs. Darcy if you continue to behave in such a wild, selfish manner."

Lydia's eyes widened, and she burst into tears, burying her face in her hands. "You're so mean, Lizzy! How can you say such awful things? I'm not selfish, you're just—"

"Enough, Lydia!" Mrs. Bennet's voice was sharp for once, and she rounded on her youngest daughter with uncharacteristic severity. "You will apologize to your sister this instant. Do you not see what she has endured? Have you no shame?"

Lydia stared at her mother, shock drying her tears . "B-but—"

"No buts!" Mrs. Bennet's voice cracked, and tears filled her eyes as she looked at Elizabeth. She rose from her chair, a rare determination in her expression as she pointed toward the stairs. "Go to your room, Lydia. And do not come down until you can speak with proper respect."

Lydia gaped at her mother. "But Mama—"

"Go!" Mrs. Bennet shouted. Lydia fled up the stairs, sobbing loudly. Kitty hesitated for a moment, then followed her sister with a furtive glance.

The room fell silent, and Mrs. Bennet sank back into her chair, dabbing at her eyes again. She looked at Elizabeth, her gaze filled with regret. "I am sorry, my dears. I don't know what has come over her, but I promise I will not allow it."

Elizabeth offered her mother a small, weary smile. "Thank you, Mama."

She excused herself shortly afterward, her body heavy with exhaustion. Once in the privacy of her room, she sat at her writing desk and stared at the blank sheet of paper before her. Taking a deep breath, she dipped her pen into the inkwell. She must explain her hasty marriage to her Aunt Gardiner. The words felt heavy as she wrote.

Perhaps Mr. Darcy will carry it with him to London for one of his servant's there to deliver for me.

The ink dried on the page, and she folded the letter with care, sealing it with quivering fingers. The weight of the day pressed down on her as she leaned back in her chair, her thoughts racing. Tomorrow would bring another step toward a future she had never imagined. Her world was changing faster than she could comprehend, and though she was determined to face it with courage, a small part of her longed for the simplicity of days gone by.

Chapter 20

The sound of horses' hooves echoed against the cobblestones as Darcy's carriage came to a halt. He stepped out and slowly surveyed the tree lined street. The houses were tidy with modest, well-kept gardens. Cheapside was hardly the most fashionable quarter of London, but it wasn't Jacob's Island, either, and the location caused him to wonder what Elizabeth's uncle's occupation might be.

Darcy had left Bingley at Darcy House, where they would both be staying. Bingley needed to meet with not only his own solicitors, but also those of the late Mr. Hurst. Not only were there marriage articles between himself and Jane to arrange, but there were also many questions regarding the disposal of Mr. Hurst's property and Miss Bingley's dowry that needed to be answered.

Suppressing his trepidation, Darcy straightened his coat and approached the door. He knocked and gave his card to the servant who opened the door. "Mr. Fitzwilliam Darcy of Pemberley and Darcy House to see Mr. and Mrs. Gardiner," he said succinctly, his tone betraying none of the unease swirling within him.

Her eyes widened as she curtsied and ushered him inside. "Please wait here, sir," she said before disappearing into the house, leaving Darcy in the entry hall.

He tugged nervously on the edges of his cuffs. While he had agreed to deliver Elizabeth's note, but the prospect of meeting her relatives—a family he had previously dismissed as vulgar—left him wary. He had envisioned individuals like Mrs. Bennet, all flutter and chatter, and yet here he was, standing before a residence that exuded quiet refinement.

Elizabeth had made it clear she did not expect him to deliver the letter personally, but the dull look on her face as she had spoken to him earlier that morning urged him to do the gentlemanly thing. *Anything to bring the light back into her eyes.*

After only waiting for a few moments, the servant girl returned. "Mrs. Gardiner will see you, sir. Just this way."

Darcy followed the neat-looking maid down the hall and into a charmingly decorated living room. His sharp gaze swept over polished wood floors, modest but tasteful furnishings, and even an arrangement of fresh flowers on a side table. Everything was clean and orderly, with a quiet elegance that spoke of genteel sensibilities.

It was not what he had anticipated.

A poised woman in fashionable attire sat on a small sofa near the fire. Her hair was pinned back neatly, with an expression of curiosity and politeness on her face. She was not beautiful in the way of Elizabeth or Jane, but her features were pleasing, and her presence radiated calm intelligence.

He inclined his head. "Mrs. Gardiner, thank you for seeing me," he said. "Your niece, Miss Elizabeth, requested that I deliver this to you." He withdrew the letter from his pocket and offered it to her.

Mrs. Gardiner took Elizabeth's note and opened it, her eyebrows raising high on her forehead as she read it, her expression shifting through a myriad of emotions. Upon completion, a faint crease appeared between her brows as she folded it neatly and set it aside. "I hope you will forgive me, Mr. Darcy, but I must send for my husband at once. He is overseeing matters at his warehouse, and I feel this matter requires his immediate attention."

She signaled for the servant and dispatched the note with quiet efficiency before turning her attention back to Darcy. "Would you care to wait, or do you have other matters to which you must attend?"

Impressed by her poise and eager to see if Mr. Gardiner was more like his wife or his sister, Darcy accepted the invitation to remain, taking a seat on the other side of the room.

Mrs. Gardiner motioned to a chair opposite her. "While we await my husband," she said, "perhaps you might indulge my curiosity. Are you by chance related to the Darcys of Pemberley?"

Darcy's lips twitched slightly, and he braced himself for what he knew must be coming next. "I am," he replied shortly. "Pemberley is my estate."

To his surprise, her expression shifted to one of fond nostalgia rather than awe. "How extraordinary," she said with a smile. "I grew up in Lambton, you see, the daughter of the rector. Pemberley plays a large part of my earliest memories. It is truly a remarkable place."

Darcy's brows lifted, caught off guard by her genuine, understated reaction. "Indeed?" he said. "Lambton is but a few miles from the estate. You must have known it well."

"I did," she replied. "Though it has been many years since I last visited. My family left when I was quite young." There was a wistfulness to her tone, but she quickly turned the conversation back to him. "My niece writes highly of you, sir. It seems you have done much to assist her in a most trying time. Please accept my felicitations on your engagement."

Darcy cleared his throat, uncomfortable with the praise. "I have only done what was necessary," he said. "Miss Elizabeth's well-being is paramount."

Mrs. Gardiner studied him for a moment, her expression unreadable, before she nodded. "Elizabeth is very dear to us. My husband and I regard her almost as one of our own."

The warmth in her words struck him. He had not anticipated such a strong bond between Elizabeth and her aunt. Before Darcy could respond, the sound of hurried footsteps drew their attention. A solidly built man entered, walking with an air of calm authority. His clothing was well-tailored but practical, and his expression was amiable as he approached. "Madeline, my dear, I came as soon as I read Lizzy's note."

"Edward," Mrs. Gardiner said, rising to greet him. "This is Mr. Darcy, Elizabeth's betrothed. He brought her letter personally."

"Mr. Darcy," Mr. Gardiner extended his hand. "I apologize for keeping you waiting after you have traveled for such a considerable distance. It is very good of you to bring our niece's note personally when you must have much to attend to."

Darcy rose to his feet and shook Mr. Gardiner's proffered hand. "Not at all, sir," he replied. "It is I who am imposing upon you. Miss

Elizabeth has been through quite the ordeal, and it will give her comfort to know that you have received her note."

Mr. Gardiner looked at him thoughtfully. "Of course," he said. "I understand congratulations are in order?"

"Yes, they are," Darcy paused, then hesitantly added, "I am not certain what Miss Elizabeth wrote in her letter, but we are to be married as quickly as possible."

"She said that she had been attacked by a member of the militia while at the estate where you were visiting your friend." At Darcy's nod of confirmation, Mr. Gardiner continued, "Apparently, there are rumors that you are the culprit of the attack, but she assures us that is not the case."

"Absolutely not," Darcy said fervently. "Indeed, my sister, my son, and my servants can all attest to the fact that I have never laid a hand on another person in my life."

"I am glad to hear it," Mrs. Gardiner interjected. "It is very good of you to marry my niece when you have done nothing."

He shifted uncomfortably. "Miss Elizabeth is an estimable woman; I feel fortunate in my future wife. Indeed, I have come to London with Mr. Bingley— the gentleman to whom your other niece will be wed— in order to draw up the marriage articles and secure common licenses. The nature of the rumors is such that haste is imperative."

"That is very good of you," Mrs. Gardiner repeated.

"I do nothing more than my duty," Darcy demurred. "I should, however, be on my way. There is still much to do."

Nodding in understanding, Mrs. Gardiner nodded to a maid to collect Darcy's hat and coat. As he began to walk away from the surprisingly poised couple to follow the servant, Darcy turned back to them and impulsively said, "Mr. Gardiner, I will be meeting with my solicitors tomorrow morning. Would you care to accompany me? I would appreciate your opinion on the settlements and other details, if you are available."

"It will be my pleasure," Mr. Gardiner replied, the surprise he felt evident upon his face.

"That is very generous," Mrs. Gardiner added. "I, for one, am very grateful that you are taking our niece's well-being so seriously, given the circumstances. It greatly relieves my mind. I am only sorry that we will not be able to attend the wedding. Elizabeth means the world to us, and I never thought I would miss it."

Darcy hesitated, sensing an unspoken worry beneath her words. "You are always welcome at Pemberley," he said quietly. "Or at Darcy House, should you wish to visit her in London."

Mrs. Gardiner's relief was palpable. "Thank you, sir," she said, her voice trembling slightly. "That means more to us than I can express."

The depth of their love for Elizabeth was evident, as well as their fear that her marriage might take her away from them. It struck him then just how much Elizabeth was risking by marrying him. She was placing herself entirely in his power, trusting him to honor her and her family despite their differences in station.

As he took his leave, Darcy resolved anew to make that trust worthwhile. Whatever Elizabeth's feelings for him might be, he would ensure her happiness to the best of his ability. It was the least she deserved.

Elizabeth is placing her life in my hands, he thought. *I will do all in my power to ensure her happiness.*

With that vow echoing in his heart, Darcy stepped into the waiting carriage, his purpose clearer than ever.

The morning sunlight filtered through the tall windows of Lord Matlock's London townhouse, illuminating the elegant furnishings and casting long shadows across the patterned carpet. Darcy stood in the center of the drawing room, his hands clasped behind his back, his posture rigid with tension.

Lord Matlock, the Earl of ---shire, sat in a high-backed chair, his eyebrows raised as he regarded his nephew. "A common license, Darcy?" His voice rose in disbelief. "And in such haste? Surely, you must see how this appears."

Darcy's expression did not waver. "The haste is necessary, Uncle. The situation demands it."

"And why is that?" Lord Matlock's asked in a chilly tone.

Darcy hesitated, his gaze dropping momentarily to the carpet. "There were… unforeseen circumstances. An incident involving George Wickham and Miss Elizabeth has necessitated a swift union."

The earl's eyes narrowed, his keen mind piecing together the unspoken details. "Another compromise," he said flatly. "First

Anne, and now this? Fitzwilliam, must you always marry under duress, especially when caused by Wickham? For all you know, this girl was part of the situation."

Darcy stiffened. "This is not like before. Anne was a marriage of duty, an arrangement between families. Elizabeth is—" He faltered, his throat tightening. "She is entirely different."

Lord Matlock raised a brow, unconvinced. "Different or not, have you considered your options? A family of their standing would be easily satisfied with a financial arrangement. It would preserve their reputation without entangling the Darcys in such a union. What is reputation when you have wealth?"

Darcy rose abruptly, pacing the room with restless energy. "You do not understand," he said sharply. "Elizabeth is not someone to be bought off. She is principled, intelligent, courageous—far beyond any woman I have ever known."

"Principled?" the earl drawled, his tone skeptical. "And yet it is her family embroiled in scandal."

"It is not her fault!" Darcy snapped, his voice echoing in the room. "Elizabeth is unlike anyone I have ever known. She has faced more in the last few days than many men could endure in a lifetime, and she did so with dignity and grace."

Lord Matlock arched a skeptical brow. "Grace, you say? A country miss, raised in Cheapside with merchants for relations?"

"She was the one who risked herself to stop Wickham, to protect those she loves!" Darcy bellowed. "I was drugged, unconscious on the floor, in a ridiculous scheme by Miss Bingley and Wickham, in order to force a compromise. Elizabeth risked her life to stop them. She has shown strength and fortitude that would shame most men."

The door opened suddenly, and Colonel Fitzwilliam strode in, his brows raised in curiosity. "I heard shouting," he said casually, his gaze darting between his father and cousin. "What's this? Fitzy is losing his temper? I must hear more."

Darcy turned to his cousin, his eyes blazing. "Richard, this is no time for levity."

"Your cousin," Lord Matlock interjected dryly, "has decided to marry a country miss of questionable connections and bring scandal upon our heads."

Fitzwilliam leaned against the mantel, a grin spreading across his face. "Well, well. I've never seen you so passionate about anything, Cousin. Tell me, who is this remarkable woman who has managed to upend your famed stoicism?"

"Some low-born chit who got caught up in another of Wickham's messes," said Lord Matlock.

Darcy's voice turned steely. "She is the daughter of a gentleman, and her compassion and wit would put many women of the ton to shame. I will not have her dismissed because of her connections."

The earl frowned but said nothing, watching his nephew intently. Darcy's face was flushed with passion, his usual composure stripped away.

"I have seen her kindness in the way she treats her sisters, her courage when she faced dangers most would have fled from, and her loyalty to those she loves," Darcy continued, his voice firm. "She is not just the woman I am *forced* to marry; she is the woman I *want* to marry."

The two men stared as Darcy began to pace. When he spoke again, his voice was softer. "Miss Elizabeth Bennet is clever and kind, with a quick wit that leaves me in awe. She challenges me in ways no one ever has. She has brought light to a life I did not realize was so dark."

Fitzwilliam's grin widened, and he crossed his arms. "A paragon indeed. I must meet her. Anyone who can inspire such sentiment from you must be extraordinary."

Darcy shrugged. "She is no paragon, Richard. She is… simply Elizabeth."

The colonel crossed his arms with a boyish grin. "And there it is. You've fallen in love, haven't you?"

The words hung in the air, and for a moment, Darcy said nothing. Then he nodded, his voice quiet but resolute. "I have."

Lord Matlock remained unconvinced. "Love," he said, his voice tinged with skepticism. "A noble sentiment, but marriage is not built on love alone. Are you certain this young woman feels the same?"

Darcy's breath caught, the question striking a nerve he had not yet dared confront. "She has agreed to marry me," he said carefully. "Her circumstances are… difficult."

The earl's gaze sharpened. "And yet, accepting a proposal is not the same as love, as many Englishmen can attest."

Darcy said nothing, his jaw tightening.

"I wish you well," Lord Matlock said after a long pause. "But tread carefully, Fitzwilliam. Love cannot be one-sided."

Colonel Fitzwilliam clapped him on the shoulder. "Well, cousin, it seems you've got yourself a task ahead. I look forward to meeting this extraordinary Miss Bennet."

Darcy managed a faint smile, but as Fitzwilliam left the room, he turned to stare out the window, his uncle's words echoing in his mind.

Does she feel the same for you?

The question lingered, unresolved, causing the ache in his chest to increase. But whatever doubts lingered, whatever obstacles remained, he vowed to himself that he would prove worthy of her trust and affection.

For both their sakes, he had to.

The polished brass plate of Fenton & Harriman gleamed in the late afternoon sunlight as Darcy and Mr. Gardiner stepped inside. The solicitor's office exuded quiet sophistication—high ceilings, dark wood paneling, and the faint scent of aged parchment mingling with freshly inked paper.

"This firm has quite the reputation, Mr. Darcy," Gardiner remarked as they waited in the front entryway.

"It has served my family for generations," Darcy replied, his tone clipped but polite. "They are thorough, and thoroughness is precisely what we require."

A clerk hurried over and greeted them with a polite bow. "Mr. Darcy, Mr. Gardiner, this way, please. Mr. Fenton is expecting you."

Darcy and Mr. Gardiner exchanged a brief glance before following the young man through a corridor lined with portraits of stern-faced barristers. They entered a spacious conference room where Mr. Fenton, a stately man in his sixties, rose from his chair to greet them.

"Mr. Darcy, Mr. Gardiner," he said, extending his hand to each in turn. "Please, be seated. We've prepared the initial drafts of the marriage articles as per your instructions."

They took their seats at the table, and Darcy folded his gloved hands before him, his posture impeccably straight. Mr. Gardiner, though composed, shifted slightly in his chair, his keen eyes scanning the room before settling on the neat stack of documents before Mr. Fenton.

The solicitor adjusted his spectacles and began. "The provisions you requested have been outlined in detail, Mr. Darcy. To summarize, Miss Elizabeth Bennet will have a jointure of £30,000, and a further sum of £10,000 will be settled for each child born of the marriage. In addition, should anything untoward occur, provisions have been made for Miss Bennet's financial independence. The eldest male child shall inherit Pemberley, with other inheritances to be distributed as outlined below."

Darcy nodded tersely, his expression unreadable. "Go on."

Mr. Fenton continued, outlining the specifics of trusteeship, inheritance rights, and contingency plans. Mr. Gardiner remained silent, though his gaze flicked toward Darcy more than once, his expression betraying a mixture of surprise and quiet approval.

When Mr. Fenton finished, he looked between the two men. "Do these arrangements meet with your approval, Mr. Darcy, Mr. Gardiner?"

Mr. Gardiner cleared his throat. "They are... exceedingly generous," he said slowly, glancing at Darcy with an expression akin to relief. "I confess, Mr. Darcy, I had not anticipated such provisions. Elizabeth will be well-secured."

"They are similar to the ones my father used when he married my mother. Miss Bennet deserves nothing less," Darcy said, his voice firm but calm. "She is an extraordinary woman."

"That she is," Mr. Gardiner agreed.

"We will have three copies drafted and completed by tomorrow morning, Mr. Darcy," the solicitor assured him. "You may collect them before you leave for Hertfordshire."

"Very good," Darcy said. He stood and extended his hand. "I appreciate your efficiency, Mr. Fenton."

The men exchanged handshakes, but as Gardiner turned to leave, he hesitated, his expression thoughtful. "Mr. Darcy," he said softly, "you have done more than most men of your station might. Your actions today speak of both honor and regard. Elizabeth is fortunate."

Darcy's jaw tightened slightly, though he inclined his head. "Thank you, Mr. Gardiner. I assure you, my primary concern is Miss Bennet's well-being."

As they stepped out into the fading light of the London streets, Darcy turned to Gardiner. "I will call at Longbourn tomorrow evening with the finalized documents."

Gardiner nodded, his expression thoughtful. "I believe this union will prove to be a providential one, Mr. Darcy."

Darcy said nothing, but as they went their separate ways, he couldn't help but wonder: Would Elizabeth ever see him as more than the man she was forced to marry?

Chapter 21

The soft winter morning dawned crisp and clear, the sun casting its golden rays over the frosted landscape. Elizabeth stood before her small mirror in her bedroom at Longbourn, smoothing her hands over the delicate fabric of her new gown. The dress, a gift from her aunt Gardiner, was a pale blue muslin with intricate white embroidery along the hem and bodice. The elegant simplicity of it made her feel both beautiful and out of place.

Jane stood beside her, a vision in soft peach, her serene smile steadying Elizabeth's fluttering nerves. "You look lovely, Lizzy," Jane said gently. "Aunt Gardiner chose perfectly."

Elizabeth forced a smile, willing herself to believe it. "If Aunt Gardiner hadn't sent these, I shudder to think what we might have worn."

"It was kind of Mr. Darcy to bring them back from London," Jane replied. "I do hope our aunt isn't disappointed about not gifting them to us herself at Christmas."

A knock sounded on the door, and Mrs. Bennet burst in, beaming with excitement. "Oh, my dears, how radiant you both look! And to think—two daughters married in one day! Mr. Bennet, we are so blessed!" Her chatter was incessant, oblivious to the tension in

Elizabeth's shoulders. "Now, Lizzy, do try to look cheerful. We don't want Mr. Darcy to see you frowning on your wedding day."

Elizabeth nodded, letting her mother fuss with her hair before she finally swept from the room again, leaving the sisters in relative peace before they all bundled into the carriage and made the short journey to the church.

The chapel was modestly adorned with evergreen garlands and white ribbons, a reflection of the hurried nature of the event. The attendees were few: Mr. Bennet, Mrs. Bennet, Mary, Kitty, Lydia, Mr. and Mrs. Philips, the Lucases, and Georgiana Darcy, whose youthful excitement was a sharp contrast to the somber atmosphere of Bingley's mourning.

Darcy stood at the front of the church, his tall frame rigid, his face impassive but his eyes betraying his tension. He was dressed sharply in a dark coat, his cravat tied to perfection, and his expression unreadable as he looked straight ahead. As Elizabeth approached, she felt his gaze shift to her, and the weight of it settled heavily on her shoulders.

For the briefest of moments, she thought she caught a flicker of something in his eyes—admiration? Tenderness? But it vanished as quickly as it came, replaced by his usual stoicism. Her heart sank.

The ceremony began, its solemnity underscored by the rector's low, measured tones. She glanced sideways at Jane, who radiated quiet serenity, her hand brushing against Mr. Bingley's as they waited for the rector to begin. Elizabeth envied her sister's peace of mind. For Jane, this was a love match—Bingley's open adoration left no room for doubt. For Elizabeth... her thoughts stalled as her gaze flickered toward Darcy on her left.

The words of the ceremony washed over her in a haze. She tried to focus on them, but her mind whirled with uncertainty and doubt. Darcy's presence beside her was overpowering, a tangible force that filled the entire church like a storm cloud, ready to unleash; formidable, but somehow life-giving, too. She was keenly aware of every movement he made—the faint twitch of his hand, the steady rise and fall of his chest, the occasional glance he cast in her direction.

When the moment came for her to speak, her throat felt dry, and her pulse hammered in her ears. She hesitated, just for a breath, before forcing herself to say the words. "I do."

The pause was so slight she doubted anyone else noticed it, but Darcy's head turned fractionally toward her, his brow furrowing ever so slightly. Elizabeth's chest tightened. Did he think her unwilling? Did he know how torn she felt, how desperate she was to reconcile the conflicting emotions that had plagued her since he proposed?

And then it was his turn. His response came swiftly, firmly: "I do." There was no hesitation, no doubt. His tone carried a weight of conviction that surprised her, and she found herself glancing at him in surprise. He met her gaze briefly, his expression unreadable, before turning back to the rector.

The ceremony concluded, and the finality of the moment settled heavily over her. They were married. No longer Elizabeth Bennet, but Mrs. Darcy. The thought sent a shiver through her, equal parts exhilaration and dread.

As they exited the church, Georgiana hurried to her brother's side, her delight barely contained. "Oh, William, it was beautiful!"

she exclaimed, her cheeks flushed. "Elizabeth… I mean, Mrs. Darcy," she corrected herself shyly, "you looked so lovely."

Elizabeth smiled faintly. "Thank you, Georgiana. You are too kind."

She received other similar congratulations as if in a dream. *But I am wide awake, and a dream would mean this were a love match.*

The small party returned to Longbourn for a wedding breakfast. The event was kept modest, out of respect for Mr. Hurst's recent passing, but Mrs. Bennet's joy made it anything but subdued. "A wedding, and to such fine gentlemen! Oh, Mr. Bennet, how proud we must be!" she exclaimed, ignoring the mortification in Elizabeth's expression.

Elizabeth could barely suppress her irritation. "Mama," she said through gritted teeth, "this is not the time—"

"Oh, hush, Lizzy!" Mrs. Bennet snapped, her voice shrill. "Would you ruin the happiest day of my life with your nonsense?"

Realizing that anything she said further would only escalate the situation, Elizabeth turned her attention to the food before her. The breakfast table was laden with a variety of delectable dishes, but the even that consolation was marred by Lydia's petulance.

"I cannot believe Wickham ran off with that awful Caroline Bingley," she huffed. "I thought he preferred me!"

"Lydia," Elizabeth snapped, her voice sharper than intended. "Do you realize the danger he posed to us all? I was nearly—" She stopped short and looked to her mother and father. "Papa, please."

"Lizzy is right, Lydia," Mr. Bennet interjected, his tone stern. "You will not speak of that man again, and you will learn to curb your foolish tongue."

"But I didn't do anything!" Lydia wailed, stamping her foot.

"And you will continue to do nothing in your room," Mr. Bennet said firmly. "Go."

Lydia stormed out, her skirts swishing dramatically as she went. Mrs. Bennet shook her head. "That girl will be the death of me."

"Perhaps if you corrected her more often, she might have learned some sense," Mr. Bennet muttered.

Elizabeth glanced at Darcy from the corner of her eye, feeling all the embarrassment of such a scene. The tension only increased when Mrs. Bennet loudly attempted to coax Georgiana to the pianoforte. Mary, who had been playing awkward scales, scowled as Mrs. Bennet bustled her off the bench.

The young woman turned pleading eyes to her brother. "Georgiana is far too shy to play in public," Darcy said swiftly, rising to his sister's defense. Georgiana's cheeks burned crimson, and Elizabeth felt a pang of embarrassment for her mother's behavior.

Charlotte Lucas lingered near Elizabeth, her eyes flickering with barely concealed envy. "Two sisters married on the same day," she murmured. "How remarkable."

Elizabeth hesitated, trying to deflect the comment. "It is a somber day, Charlotte. A man has died—"

Charlotte's tone grew sharper. "And yet, you find yourselves marrying men of wealth and status; the most eligible bachelors in the county, in fact. A tragedy for some is fortune for others, is it not?"

Elizabeth felt her cheeks flush, but she bit back a retort. "I have no interest in such fortune," she said quietly, but Charlotte merely gave her a superior, knowing look and moved away.

The breakfast ended soon after, and Elizabeth retreated to her room to change and collect her valise. She paused at the threshold, her gaze sweeping over the familiar space that had been hers for so many years. The patchwork quilt on the bed, the well-worn books on the shelf, the little vase of flowers she had picked only days ago—all of it felt heartbreakingly small and comforting, filled with memories of laughter, arguments, and quiet solitude.

Her fingers brushed the edge of her writing desk, the place where she had scribbled so many thoughts and letters. It hit her, then, with the force of a wave crashing against the shore.

I will never be here again as Elizabeth Bennet. I am Mrs. Darcy now.

A sob rose unbidden in her throat, and she sank onto the edge of her bed, tears spilling down her cheeks. She pressed her palms to heated cheeks, overwhelmed by the enormity of it all—the loss of her independence, the uncertainty of her future, and the weight of marrying a man she barely understood. Burying her face in her hands, she gave way to her sorrow as sobs wracked her body.

"Elizabeth?"

Her head snapped up, her tear-streaked face meeting Darcy's concerned gaze. He stepped into the room, his brows furrowing as he took in her disheveled appearance. He sat down heavily at her writing desk. "Are you… Is marriage to me truly so terrible?" he asked, looking up with haunted eyes.

Elizabeth didn't know what to make of that look, but she knew that she didn't want to be the reason it was there. She shook her head vehemently, her voice trembling. "No, it isn't—please don't think that. It's just…" She gestured helplessly to the room around her. "This has been my home for so long, and now…"

"I see." He studied her intently, his expression unreadable, but the fear was gone.

Before she could say more, Jane appeared in the doorway. "Lizzy, the carriage is ready."

Elizabeth nodded, gathering her composure. She took one last look around her room, then followed Darcy and Jane downstairs, bracing herself for the journey ahead.

As the carriage rolled toward Netherfield, Elizabeth sat in silence, her heart heavy with the weight of unspoken words.

Dinner at Netherfield was a subdued affair, the lively chatter that usually accompanied such occasions noticeably absent. The massive dining room only magnified the silence, particularly as Mrs. Nicholls had decided that a more intimate setting was appropriate for the light wedding supper, and had instructed the servants to leave the sumptuous spread on the buffet and then vacate entirely. The candles cast long, flickering shadows across faces masked in varying degrees of tension, fatigue, and grief.

Georgiana, sitting to Elizabeth's right, made a valiant effort to maintain the conversation. "The flowers in the church were so lovely." Her voice carried an almost childlike enthusiasm. "I've never seen such a delicate arrangement of garlands."

Elizabeth smiled faintly, though her thoughts were far from the flowers. She nodded absently, her fork tracing the edge of her plate. "It was a beautiful ceremony," she agreed, though her voice lacked its usual spark. Her thoughts wandered to the moments in the church—Darcy's solemn expression, her own faltering hesitation as she said the words that bound them for life.

Jane and Bingley, at the other end of the table, seemed oblivious to the subdued mood. They exchanged quiet smiles and murmured to one another, their happiness forming a bubble that excluded everyone else. Elizabeth's heart warmed to see Jane so content, but the sight also heightened her own sense of unease.

Darcy excused himself to retrieve another helping from the buffet. Mrs. Hurst, on Georgiana's left, had barely touched her food. Her complexion was ashen, and the dark circles under her eyes betrayed a profound weariness. She held her fork limply, pushing a morsel of fish around her plate without ever lifting it to her lips.

Elizabeth hesitated before leaning toward her. "Mrs. Hurst, are you feeling well? Can I do anything for you?"

Mrs. Hurst's head snapped up, her eyes narrowing. "I think you've done quite enough, Miss Bennet," she hissed coldly, her voice trembling with barely restrained anger. "If it weren't for you, my husband would still be alive."

Georgiana gasped, and Elizabeth winced. The accusation struck her like a physical blow. Her breath caught in her throat, and she blinked rapidly to push back the tears that threatened to spill. She forced herself to take a steadying breath; fortunately, Mrs. Hurst had spoken softly enough that only Elizabeth and Georgiana had heard her.

"If I could change what happened, I would," Elizabeth said quietly, her voice steady despite the lump in her throat. "I never meant to intrude. I only wanted to ensure your health doesn't suffer."

Her gaze drifted to Mrs. Hurst's stomach, the faint swell just visible beneath her gown. Mrs. Hurst followed her eyes and stilled. For a moment, the two women simply looked at one another. Then Mrs. Hurst's expression softened, and she sighed.

"I'm sorry," she said, her voice breaking. "It wasn't your fault. It's just... I'm so angry at Caroline, and she isn't here for me to tell her..." Her words trailed away, and she gave a pitiful shrug.

Darcy returned with his plate and Georgiana relaxed, visibly grateful not to be the only person within earshot. Elizabeth nodded, her heart aching with sympathy. "I understand," she said gently. "I know something about younger sisters behaving in less-than-appropriate ways."

Mrs. Hurst let out a shaky laugh, her shoulders relaxing slightly. "It seems we share that burden."

Elizabeth's lips quirked upward. "But while we cannot choose our family, we can choose our friends. And now you have the best sister in the world—Jane. I'm happy to share her, of course, though I might insist on a small leasing fee."

A soft chuckle escaped Mrs. Hurst, the tension between them easing. She picked up her fork again and took a small bite of her food. "You're very... direct, Miss Bennet."

"Incorrigible, I'm told," Elizabeth replied lightly, her tone inviting further laughter.

Mrs. Hurst's lips curved into a faint smile, and she nodded. "Perhaps that's not such a bad thing."

"Perhaps," Elizabeth agreed, a playful twinkle in her eye.

The tension between the two women had vanished, and Mrs. Hurst took another tentative bite of her food. Satisfied, Elizabeth turned her attention back to her own plate, though she could feel Darcy's gaze lingering on her. She resisted the urge to meet his eyes, focusing instead on the intricate pattern of her plate.

When the meal ended, Mrs. Hurst leaned toward Georgiana and whispered something in her ear. The younger woman nodded and rose, her cheeks tinged pink. "I think we shall retire," Georgiana said softly. "It has been such a long day."

Mrs. Hurst followed suit, murmuring her own excuses. The two slipped from the room, their absence scarcely noticed by Bingley and Jane. Elizabeth's brow furrowed as she considered Mrs. Hurst's lingering grief. She hoped the woman would find some peace in Georgiana's gentle company.

Bingley glanced at Jane, his expression tender. "Should we retire as well, my love?"

Jane smiled shyly, her cheeks warming. "If you think it best. I would not like to be a poor hostess to your— our guests."

"We are all family now, so technically you have no guests," Elizabeth teased, attempting to mask her own uncertainty. "Everyone should call me Elizabeth, and we needn't stand on ceremony at all. Go get the *rest* you need; do not delay on our account."

Jane's blush deepened, and Bingley beamed as he escorted her from the room.

Elizabeth watched them go, a pang of envy mingling with her happiness for her sister. The void they left behind in the quiet room made Elizabeth acutely aware of how she was now alone with Darcy.

They were married. The realization struck her like a lightning bolt: she and Darcy were married, and with that came certain... expectations. Her stomach twisted as she remembered her mother's vague and clumsy advice. She had no idea what awaited her in that department; she'd no opportunity to ask her aunt Gardiner, whom she always planned to consult the day before some future wedding.

A wave of nervous energy coursed through her. Her thoughts began to spiral as she considered what the rest of the evening might entail. She had spent so much time focusing on the ceremony, the logistics, the immediate aftermath—she had scarcely allowed herself to think of the wedding night.

Her mother's words echoed in her mind, offering little clarity but ample embarrassment. What would Darcy expect of her? What would he think of her ignorance?

Before she could address the matter with him, he turned to her. "I say goodnight to Andrew every evening," he said, his tone almost hesitant. "Perhaps you would join me tonight. After all, you are his new mother now."

Elizabeth blinked, startled by the unexpected invitation. Relief flooded through her—both for the delay it offered and for the chance to see Andrew. "Of course," she said, rising quickly. "I would like that very much. He is such a joy to be around."

Darcy extended his arm, and she took it, a shiver coursing through her at his touch. Together, they made their way up the stairs without speaking. The nursery was warm and quiet, lit by the soft glow of a single lamp. Andrew was already tucked into bed, his curls falling across his forehead as he clutched a worn stuffed bear. His nurse, Rebecca, stood by his side, her face lighting up when she saw Darcy and Elizabeth.

"Mr. Darcy, Miss— Mrs. Darcy," she said, greeting them with a small curtsy. "He's just nodded off. We weren't sure if you would be up tonight."

Darcy knelt beside the little bed, his voice low and soothing. "Andrew," he murmured, brushing the boy's hair back gently. "We have something to tell you."

Andrew stirred, his eyes fluttering open. "Papa?" He sat up and rubbed his eyes. "Nice lady!"

"Yes, I'm here," Elizabeth said with a small laugh. "Elizabeth, do you remember?"

"Liz'beth," the boy lisped, relaxing against the pillows.

"I have some wonderful news," Darcy said. "Elizabeth is your new mama!"

Elizabeth's heart swelled with the words. Mama.

"New mama?" echoed Andrew.

"Yes, and she's going to stay with us forever."

Andrew's sleepy gaze shifted to Elizabeth, and he smiled faintly. "You stay f'rever?"

"Yes," Elizabeth said, her voice catching. She reached out to take his tiny hand in hers. "Forever."

Andrew's smile widened before his eyes drifted shut again. Elizabeth's thumb gently stroked his palm, her gaze lingering on his peaceful face as he slipped back into slumber. The warmth of the room wrapped around her like a cocoon, but her thoughts swirled in a tempest of emotions.

Mama.

The word felt echoed in her mind. It was foreign and heavy, yet oddly comforting at the same time. Could she truly fill such a role? She had always loved children, and Andrew already held a special place in her heart since the moment she met him—but the reality of her responsibility was daunting. This wasn't merely about reading stories or offering a kind word. She would help shape his life, comfort his fears, guide him through trials. The thought both exhilarated and terrified her.

She glanced at Darcy, who was still kneeling beside his son, his expression soft and unguarded. There was a tenderness in the way he brushed Andrew's curls, a love so evident it made her chest ache. Darcy had entrusted her with not just himself but his family, his world. Could she be enough? Would she fail him or Andrew—or worse, both?

Darcy's voice broke through her thoughts. "Thank you for this," he said quietly.

"For what?" she asked, genuinely surprised.

"For making this transition easier for him. And for me." His voice held an uncharacteristic vulnerability, and she saw the faintest trace of relief in his eyes.

The sincerity in his tone warmed her, even as it added to the storm of emotions within. She managed a faint smile but said nothing more, afraid her voice might betray the nervous energy thrumming through her.

Darcy smoothly rose to his feet and stood beside Elizabeth, his hand brushing hers briefly. The gesture was unintentional, but it sent a jolt through her. She, too, stood up, resisting the urge to begin wringing her hands.

It's time. You can do this, Elizabeth.

Darcy escorted her out of the room and along the corridor to the guest wing. He stopped before a door and opened it, revealing a spacious, tastefully appointed bedroom adorned with soft colors and elegant furnishings. A fire crackled in the hearth, casting flickering shadows on the walls. Near the bed, a maid unpacked her belongings.

"This is your room," he said simply. "I will join you in an hour."

Elizabeth nodded, her throat too tight to form words. He opened a door between her room and, she assumed, his. She watched him go, her heart pounding in her chest. As the door closed softly behind him, she stood frozen in place, the silence of the room pressing in around her.

"If you please, ma'am, I'll just finish putting these last things away, then I can help you into your nightclothes."

"Yes, thank you." Elizabeth's voice was barely higher than a whisper, and the maid gave her an encouraging smile before returning to her task.

Elizabeth wandered to the hearth and forced back a shiver. The warmth of the fire did little to calm the chill that had settled deep within her. Her eyes fell on the bed, its crisp linens and downy pillows an innocent witness to the night ahead. Her heart pounded as the reality of what awaited her came crashing down.

Her mother's clumsy, cryptic remarks about marital duties echoed in her mind, offering no clarity, only discomfort. Elizabeth shook her head, chastising herself for letting such thoughts consume her. She had married Darcy—a man of honor, intelligence, and, as she was slowly realizing, depth of feeling and compassion. Surely, he would not expect more than she could give.

And yet... the question remained: what did he feel for her? Had his offer been born solely of honor and obligation, or was there something more? She had glimpsed moments of tenderness in his gaze, fleeting yet unmistakable, but doubt whispered cruelly in her ear.

He doesn't truly *want you. This is just another duty to him.*

Her thoughts turned to the scene in the nursery, to the way Darcy had spoken about Andrew. It struck her that he wasn't merely inviting her into his life—he was sharing his family, his vulnerabilities, and his trust. The weight of it was staggering, but it also kindled a glimmer of hope.

The maid helped her into a plain nightgown with a hint of lace around the collar and hem. Drawing a deep breath, she dismissed the maid, then approached the small mirror above the dressing table. Her reflection stared back, cheeks flushed, eyes bright.

"You can do this, Elizabeth," she whispered to herself. "You've faced worse and come through stronger."

She had married him. And now, there was no turning back.

Chapter 22

Elizabeth's hands trembled slightly as she stood at the window, looking out into darkness. The room was quiet save for the crackle of the fire, the glow casting soft, flickering shadows on the walls. The small clock above the fire told her there were only two minutes left until the hour Darcy had given her would be over.

The adjoining door opened softly, and Darcy stepped inside. She turned from the window to look at him; he had removed his coat and waistcoat, his cravat slightly loosened. He paused, his gaze sweeping over her with a mixture of warmth and uncertainty. "Elizabeth," he said quietly, his voice low and steady.

She gave him a small, nervous smile, her fingers twisting the sash of her robe. "Mr. Darcy."

He arched a brow at her formality, then stepped closer, his expression softening. "Surely, as my wife, you may call me Fitzwilliam."

"Fitzwilliam," she repeated, the name unfamiliar on her tongue. It felt strange yet oddly intimate, and the sound of it seemed to draw them closer together.

His eyes softened at the hesitation in her voice. "I would never hurt you, Elizabeth," he said, taking a cautious step closer. "You must know that."

"I do," she said quickly. "It's just that… I don't know…. That is, Mama tried to explain…"

She shrugged feebly, abandoning the effort to put words to her anxiety. "She was more confusing than helpful. I'm afraid I—" She hesitated, her cheeks flushing. "I don't know what I should do," she finished miserably, looking down.

Darcy's expression was tender as he reached out to take her hands in his. "Elizabeth, there is no shame in innocence. I will guide you, and if you have any questions, you may ask them. There is nothing we cannot speak of."

She nodded, her throat tight with emotion. "Thank you," she whispered. "That is a comfort."

He led her to the settee near the fire, gently drawing her down to sit next to him, their hands still joined. She closed her eyes and leaned in, pursing her lips expectantly.

"I think we should talk first," he said gently.

Her eyes flew open and she drew back, embarrassed. "Talk?"

"About us. About this marriage."

Elizabeth tilted her head, studying him. "What do you mean?"

"You are not alone in your uncertainty," he said quietly. "I confess, I am just as nervous as you."

Elizabeth blinked, startled. "You? But... surely you've...you were married!" She trailed off, her cheeks burning as the implications of her words struck her.

Darcy's lips twitched into a faint, almost wistful smile. "I am not entirely inexperienced," he said awkwardly. "But, my marriage to Anne was...unconventional."

Elizabeth tilted her head, curiosity mingling with confusion. "I don't understand."

His gaze dropped to their joined hands and to her surprise she detected a faint flush on his cheeks. Was it just the firelight? He stood up and leaned against the mantle, looking into the fire as if for the right words. "Anne was a kind woman. We shared a bond of friendship, affection even," he paused, "but our marriage was not what most would expect."

Elizabeth frowned, her brow furrowing at the implication of his words. "But Andrew..." She stopped, feeling intrusive but unable to stop the question from forming. "You have a son."

Darcy's jaw tightened almost imperceptibly, and he grabbed the poker, jabbing it into the fire. Sparks jumped and he continued. "Yes," he said after a long pause. "But that is a more complicated matter—He is my son now, in every way that matters, but it didn't start that way. Anne, my cousin, needed a father for her child, and I couldn't abandon her."

Waves of relief and unease washed over her in equal measure. "I see," she murmured, not entirely sure that she did. He sat down once more and again took her hand in his. "Then we are both treading on unfamiliar ground."

321

Now it was his turn to flush. "Well, not entirely. My relationship with Anne may have been different than the typical marriage, but my formative years as a youth and young man were not."

"Oh."

He shook his head. "I don't say this to demean you, Elizabeth, but rather to assure you that, as with Anne, I will never demand anything from you that you are not ready to give."

"Then..." she stared at his hands rather than meet his eyes, "what happens tonight?" she asked softly, her voice barely above a whisper.

His thumb moved in slow circles on the back of her hand, sending shivers of electricity up her arm. "That is up to you. I won't lie—consummation is necessary to ensure there is no chance of annulment. But I will not proceed unless you are willing. I would never force you into anything you are not ready for. We can take our time, and I promise to be as gentle as I can."

Her chest tightened at the sincerity in his tone. She could see the tension in his shoulders, the restraint in his posture, and it moved her deeply. "Thank you," she said softly. "But... I think we must. There has been too much risk already, too much gossip. I do not want to leave room for further scandal."

Darcy's eyes searched hers, and he nodded slowly. "Then we will proceed—on your terms, Elizabeth. I will be as slow and patient as you need."

Elizabeth swallowed hard, her pulse racing with an unfamiliar longing. He was asking her. She closed her eyes and leaned forward again, not really certain what to expect, but certain that he was the only man she wanted to share it with. His honesty and tenderness were a balm to her frayed nerves, but the unknown still loomed before her like an insurmountable wall. She met his gaze, her voice trembling as she said, "I'm nervous, Fitzwilliam. But I trust you."

His hand tightened around hers, his eyes filled with a quiet intensity. "I will do everything in my power to make this a night of tenderness and care, Elizabeth. You are my wife now, but more than that, you are my partner. Your comfort is my highest priority."

Her heart swelled at his words, and she managed a small smile. "Then I trust you to guide me."

He leaned down then, capturing her lips in a kiss that was both tentative and full of unspoken promises. It was a kiss that spoke of patience, respect, and a burgeoning affection that neither of them dared name yet. When he pulled back, his eyes searched hers, silently asking for her permission to take the next step.

Elizabeth nodded, her trust in him outweighing her lingering nerves. Darcy rose from the seat, extending a hand to her. She took it, allowing him to pull her to her feet. He led her to the bed, his movements unhurried, his touch light as he helped her settle against the pillows. He leaned down, his lips brushing hers in a gentle, lingering kiss that sent a warmth through her chest.

"You are so beautiful," he murmured, his voice thick with emotion.

Elizabeth's cheeks flushed, but she felt a flicker of courage spark within her. "And you, Fitzwilliam, are very kind."

He smiled faintly, his eyes never leaving hers. Then, with deliberate care, he blew out the candle, plunging the room into soft shadows. Their conversation faded as tenderness took over, the night unfolding not in haste but in mutual trust and quiet discovery. Darcy's voice was the last sound she heard before everything else faded away.

"You are safe with me, Elizabeth. Always."

The room was quiet save for the soft crackle of the fire and the gentle rhythm of Elizabeth's breathing. Darcy lay on his side beside Elizabeth, his head propped up on one hand, his gaze fixed on her as he watched her sleep. The blankets rose and fell with the cadence of her breath, her chestnut curls spilling across the pillow like a halo. She looked serene, the faintest hint of a smile gracing her lips, and he marveled at how truly beautiful she was.

Beautiful. The word barely seemed adequate, but it was far superior to calling her tolerable all those weeks ago. *You were such a fool.*

He had always thought her fine eyes were her most striking feature, but now, with the golden glow of the firelight dancing over her features, he realized there was so much more. The delicate curve of her jaw, the slight upturn of her nose, the way her brows relaxed in sleep—all of it captivated him. He had seen beauty in portraits and admired it in passing acquaintances, but this was something altogether different. This was intimate, vulnerable, and achingly real.

And she was his wife.

The thought sent a rush of emotions through him—wonder, disbelief, and something perilously close to joy. How had they come to this? Only weeks ago, he had resigned himself to a life of solitude, haunted by his past and his duty to Andrew. Yet now, here he was, sharing a bed with the woman who had challenged him, humbled him, and, unwittingly, claimed his heart.

The night had been… beautiful. *For you, that is. But what about for* her? A flicker of doubt crept into his mind. Did she feel the same? She had been surprisingly enthusiastic, once she'd gotten over her nervousness. He had done everything in his power to be gentle, to ensure her comfort, but he couldn't help wondering if she had truly wanted it—or if she had simply felt obligated. The hesitation he had seen in her eyes at the church nagged at his mind, and he felt a pang of guilt.

Is this enough for her? Am I enough for her?

He rolled over onto his back, careful not to disturb her, and studied the canopy. The memory of the evening played over in his mind, vivid and yet intangible, like a dream he wasn't sure he fully understood.

Was she content? Had he done enough to ease her fears? He had seen the courage in her eyes, the determination that had carried her through a day fraught with emotion, but he had also sensed her hesitation, her uncertainty. It had been beautiful—more than he dared hope for—but he couldn't shake the worry that she had accepted him out of duty rather than desire.

What if she regrets this? The question gnawed at him, a dark thread woven into the tapestry of his thoughts. He wanted to believe that the tenderness they had shared had meant something to her, as it had to him, but he feared asking her outright. For now, he could only hope that her gentle smile as she drifted to sleep was a sign of happiness, not resignation.

The fire crackled softly, casting shifting shadows across the room. Darcy's hand lightly brushed against hers where it rested on the blanket. The urge to take it, to hold it in his own, was almost overwhelming. For all the years he had spent keeping others at a distance, there was a closeness here, a warmth he had never felt— not with Anne, and certainly not with the fleeting companionships he'd sought in his youth.

No, this was different. This was *real*.

He debated whether he should return to his own room. It would be the proper thing to do, he reasoned. To give her space, to allow her the privacy she might need after such an intimate evening. Yet the thought of leaving her side filled him with an inexplicable sense of loss. This small, quiet moment—the warmth of her presence, the steady cadence of her breath—was unlike anything he had ever experienced. He wasn't ready to let it go.

Darcy relaxed against the soft mattress. The tension that had gripped him earlier began to ebb away, replaced by a quiet contentment. The room felt warmer now, not just from the fire but from the knowledge that she was here, beside him, bound to him in a way that was both daunting and exhilarating.

The steady rhythm of her breathing soothed him, each exhale a gentle reminder that she was truly in bed, truly his. The worries and uncertainties that had plagued him the last several days began to fade, and his eyes grew heavy.

As his eyes grew heavy, Darcy allowed himself one last glance at Elizabeth. He reached out, his hand brushing hers lightly beneath the covers. Her fingers curled slightly in response, even in sleep, and a small smile touched his lips.

"I'll do my best," he murmured, his voice barely audible in the stillness. "For you."

For the first time in what felt like years, Darcy drifted into sleep with a sense of hope.

The first pale light of dawn seeped softly through the curtains, bathing the room in a gentle glow. Elizabeth stirred, a small smile gracing her lips as she slowly came to consciousness. The warmth of the bed, the faint scent of lavender lingering on the sheets, and the soothing crackle of the dying fire—all combined to make her feel uncharacteristically cozy, reluctant to leave the safety of her blankets.

She shifted slightly, stretching her limbs beneath the covers, when movement beside her caught her attention. Elizabeth turned over, expecting to see one of her younger sisters who might have climbed into her bed for warmth as they often had when they were children. But instead of a familiar girlish figure, her gaze landed on broad shoulders and dark, slightly mussed hair.

Darcy.

She blinked, taking in the sight of him still asleep beside her, his features softened in slumber. His dark hair was slightly tousled, his mouth curled up slightly in his sleep. He lay on his back, one arm resting lightly across his chest, his breathing steady and calm. Elizabeth's heart gave an involuntary flutter, and then... a jolt.

The memories of the previous night crashed into her, vivid and startling. Heat rose to her cheeks as she recalled the way he had looked at her, touched her, and spoken to her; an impossible combination of intensity and tenderness. Her body shifted uncomfortably under the weight of the recollection, a slight soreness reminding her of the undeniable reality of what had transpired.

Oh, my goodness. We... I...

Her face burned scarlet. She clutched the blanket to her chest, her mind racing. They had been... intimate. Not only that, but it had been nothing like the vague warnings and whispered hints she had overheard from married women. It had been... something she had never imagined.

It had been unlike anything she could have ever imagined, filled with a surprising depth of connection. It had felt as though she were cherished, wholly and utterly. His caresses had been gentle, his words considerate. Every moment had seemed crafted to reassure her, to make her feel respected, valued, even loved.

Loved.

The word echoed in her mind, sending a fresh wave of heat to her cheeks. Could it be true? Could he truly feel that way for her? She bit her lip, her thoughts spinning in circles as she tried to make sense of it all. She had felt so safe in his arms, so completely cared for. For a fleeting moment, warmth spread through her chest, and she found herself smiling.

Surely that must mean something—mustn't it?

And yet...

A wave of guilt swept over her. A memory surfaced unbidden; a conversation with her aunt Gardiner. Elizabeth had been but fifteen years of age and was about to make her come out in Meryton. Aunt Gardiner, ever wise and practical, had cautioned her: "Elizabeth, you must be careful in your dealings with members of the other sex. Some men, my dear, will offer a woman tenderness and devotion in the hope of receiving certain favors. And some women, in turn, may offer such favors in the hope of securing affection, believing the emotion must inevitably follow the act. Be wary of confusing one with the other. True affection is proved through time, through actions—not merely through words or fleeting moments."

Elizabeth swallowed hard, the weight of those words settling over her like a cloud. What if last night had been just that—a moment? Had she mistaken kindness for something more? Did last night mean anything beyond the physical act? Had he given her kindness to fulfill a husband's duty, or worse, to take what he desired? What if Darcy's tenderness had been born not of love, but of... of obligation or selfishness?

The idea sent a chill through her, and she drew the blankets closer, as if they could shield her from the weight of her thoughts. The thought that he might not feel as deeply as she did, that this connection might be her end alone...

She shuddered. The thought was a heavy one, and she turned her gaze away, suddenly unsure of how to feel...

Sighing, her gaze fell to her hands. She'd awoken with such joy, such certainty. That was gone now, and all that was left was a terrible loneliness—a sense of being adrift, uncertain of where she truly stood with her husband. Darcy had been everything she could have hoped for last night, but the deeper question of his heart remained unanswered.

And what of my own heart?

She stole another glance at him, her gaze lingering on the relaxed lines of his face. He looked so peaceful, so utterly at ease. It was a far cry from the composed, almost severe man she had first met at the Meryton assembly. And it wasn't just last night. He had shown kindness in so many ways—his care for his sister, his devotion to Andrew, even the small, thoughtful gestures he had extended to her since their betrothal.

Still, she reminded herself firmly, those acts of kindness did not necessarily equate to love. Just as shared intimacy, however meaningful, did not guarantee affection. Her aunt's warning echoed again, tempering the emotions that had risen so strongly within her. She could not afford to confuse the two, no matter how much she might wish otherwise.

Unrequited love is the worst kind of love.

The realization that she cared for him—that she might even love him—had crept upon her gradually, and now it loomed large and undeniable. But how could she give voice to it when she was unsure of his feelings? How could she risk laying herself bare when she didn't know if he would catch her or let her fall?

The thought left her hollow. She pressed her fingers to her temple, willing away the heaviness that had settled there. It was absurd to feel this way—she was married, after all. She had made her choice. Still, she resolved to guard her heart. She could not let herself fall into the trap of equating physical closeness with emotional connection. Not yet. Not until she was certain.

The loneliness deepened, mingling with the memory of his touch, his voice, his warmth. She closed her eyes, willing herself to push aside the confusion, the longing, the ache. For now, she would take one step at a time. She would be kind, be patient, and hope that time would bring clarity.

The faintest sound of Darcy's breathing filled the space between them, steady and reassuring. Elizabeth sighed softly, brushing her hair back from her face. Perhaps, in time, she would learn to reconcile her heart and her mind. For now, she would focus on the present, on the man who had given her more respect and kindness than she could have hoped for.

Darcy stirred then, his lashes fluttering slightly. Elizabeth froze, unsure of what to say, as her own heart betrayed her by skipping a beat.

"Good morning, Mrs. Darcy," he murmured. His voice was low and warm and sent a thrill through her. He opened his eyes and the softness there made her heart ache. It was going to be harder to guard her heart than she'd imagined.

"Good morning," she managed, her voice catching. Her cheeks warmed again, but this time she didn't look away.

Whatever the future held, she would face it with the same courage that had carried her through so many challenges before. And for now, she would take solace in the warmth beside her, even if it was tinged with uncertainty.

Chapter 23

Darcy had never thought himself a man prone to indulging in idle fantasies, yet this morning, as sunlight filtered softly through the curtains, he found himself wishing for nothing more than to remain in bed with Elizabeth. The memory of her warmth, her hesitant but courageous trust, lingered vividly in his mind, making it all the more difficult to face the outside world.

He had sensed she was awake before he opened his eyes. "Good morning, Mrs. Darcy," he said softly, his voice still husky from sleep.

He opened his eyes to take her in. Her hair spilled over her shoulders in loose waves, and her profile, serene and thoughtful, was silhouetted against the light from the window. It was a sight so lovely, so achingly perfect, that he simply lay there, content to watch her for a moment longer.

Elizabeth smiled shyly. "Good morning," she replied, her cheeks tinged faintly pink. "I didn't mean to wake you."

"You didn't," he assured her, sitting up and leaning back against the headboard. "I doubt I could sleep much longer, even if I wanted to." He hesitated, then added, "And, truthfully, I would rather not waste a moment of this morning."

She dropped her eyes and plucked idly at the blanket. "Me either."

He opened his mouth to respond, perhaps to suggest they share a quiet breakfast together, when the distant sound of Andrew's voice carried up the stairs.

"Papa? Papa, where are you?" The boy's enthusiastic calls for his father broke the moment, and Darcy sighed, running a hand through his hair.

Darcy's lips quirked in a smile, though he sighed ruefully. "It seems Andrew is not inclined to waste the morning, either."

Elizabeth looked at him with a teasing smile on her lips. "It seems your presence is in high demand this morning."

"As it should be," Darcy replied, though his tone was warm rather than prideful. He rose from the bed and Elizabeth averted her eyes instinctively. "I will see what Andrew requires," he said, pulling on his dressing gown. "Perhaps you might join us in the nursery afterward?"

Elizabeth nodded in agreement, her expression soft. "I would like that. I'll join you as soon as I'm dressed." He gazed at her bare shoulders appreciatively, and she blushed, spotting her nightdress in a heap on the floor.

A soft knock at the door saved Elizabeth's blushes, but she pulled the blankets up to her chin. "My nightdress!" she hissed. Darcy grinned roguishly and threw it to her before he opened the door. A maid stood in the hall with a neatly folded note. "A message from Mrs. Bingley, madam," the maid said. Darcy accepted the missive, and the maid left with a knowing smile.

"You can dress, now," Darcy said. Elizabeth stared at him with wide eyes, biting her lip in hesitation. Darcy laughed and turned his back, holding the note up.

Elizabeth threw the nightgown over her head and slipped out of bed. "Thank you," she said, taking the note. She scanned the words quickly, her brow furrowing in thought.

"From your sister?" Darcy inquired, turning back to her. "Is everything well?"

"Yes," Elizabeth replied, her gaze lifting from the note to meet his eyes. "She's requested my assistance with meeting the housekeeper this morning. It seems she would like my support managing the household." Her voice held a touch of uncertainty, though it was clear she wished to oblige her sister.

Darcy's lips quirked in a faint smile. "Courage is not something you lack."

Elizabeth's cheeks flushed slightly at the compliment, but she nodded. "It will be good to keep busy. Though…" She hesitated, her fingers toying with the edge of the note. "I wonder if Georgiana might benefit from attending, along with Mrs. Annesley. If Jane has no objection, of course."

Her request startled him, though not unpleasantly. It was an unexpected consideration, one that showed not only her thoughtfulness but her understanding of Georgiana's shyness and need for guidance. He felt a surge of gratitude and something deeper as he regarded her.

"You would include Georgiana?" he asked softly.

Elizabeth's cheeks flushed under his scrutiny, but her voice was steady. "She is my sister now," she said simply. "If Jane has no objection, I believe Georgiana might benefit from learning such matters. And Mrs. Annesley's experience could only be of benefit to us all."

Darcy's heart swelled at her words. That she would so naturally embrace Georgiana and seek to involve her in meaningful ways was more than he could have hoped for. He nodded, his voice warm. "If Mrs. Bingley is agreeable, I think it an excellent idea. And as for Georgiana and Andrew, you may do whatever you feel is best for them, so long as we first discuss any major changes you wish to make. I trust your judgment entirely, Elizabeth."

Her eyes widened, her surprise evident, and for a fleeting moment, Darcy thought he saw something deeper in her expression—something that gave him hope, though he knew it was too soon to dwell on such notions. Still, he couldn't resist the impulse to lean down and press a gentle kiss to her forehead. Her eyes fluttered closed at the contact, and when she looked up at him again, his heart was nearly undone.

"Thank you," she said softly, her voice filled with sincerity.

"It is I who should thank you," he replied, his voice low. "You have already done more for my family than I could have asked."

She smiled, and the sight of it sent his heart into a quiet turmoil. "They are my family now, too," she repeated.

"Shall we meet after our tasks are finished?" he asked softly.

Elizabeth nodded and began to make her way towards her dressing room. Darcy watched her retreating figure, his chest tight with emotions he could scarcely name. Leaving his room in search of Andrew, his young son's face blurred in front of him as thoughts of Elizabeth consumed him. How was he to accomplish anything when her presence lingered so vividly in his mind? He sighed, picking up his pen with a rueful smile.

She had, unknowingly, made a hopeless fool of him already.

The steady jostle of the carriage and the rhythmic clatter of wheels against the road jarred Caroline Bingley into consciousness. Her head throbbed, a dull ache radiating from her temples, and her vision blurred as she blinked, trying to make sense of her surroundings.

The coarse blanket draped over her lap scratched at her skin, its scent of horse and sweat making her stomach churn. The dim light filtering through the small carriage window did little to ease her confusion, though it thankfully did not aggravate the hammer pounding in her skull.

Where am I? What is happening?

She pressed a hand to her forehead, struggling to make sense of her surroundings. The plush cushions of the carriage seat felt unfamiliar, and the coarse wool blanket draped haphazardly across her lap reeked of horses. She blinked, forcing her eyes to adjust, when a figure seated across from her came into focus. Her mind felt sluggish, disoriented, but she clung to the last thing she remembered—the drawing room at Netherfield. Darcy's jacket…

Mr. Darcy!

Panic struck like a lightning bolt. Her head shot up, her eyes darting around the dim interior of the carriage. Across from her sat a man—dark-haired, his mouth twisted in a smug smile.

"Mr. Wickham?" she croaked, her voice raspy and uncertain.

"Ah, you're awake," George Wickham said smoothly, His voice was smooth, as though they were sharing a casual conversation over tea rather than riding in a secluded carriage together.

Her confusion quickly turned to panic as reality came crashing down. She sat up straighter, clutching the scratchy blanket to her chest like armor, as if it could offer protection from the situation in which she found herself.

"What is the meaning of this?" she demanded, her voice rising with every word, her words trembling with both fury and fear. "Why am I here? Where is Mr. Darcy? Why am I not—"

Wickham's mouth curled into a smug grin. "You're here because I saved you from making a dreadful mistake, Miss Bingley. You made a mess of things, and I had to… redirect events. But think of this as just fate, my dear."

"Fate?" she asked in bewilderment.

"Why yes," he drawled, lifting a hand to casually inspect his fingernails. "You're now exactly where you're meant to be…"— his eyes looked up, directly into hers— "…on your way to becoming Mrs. Wickham."

Her mouth dropped open, the words crashing over her like a tidal wave. She clutched at the edge of the carriage seat, her knuckles whitening. "I'm… I'm *what*?"

"I've saved you," he replied nonchalantly, as if the situation were entirely rational.

Her mind raced, fragments of memory surfacing—the tea, the laudanum, her plan to ensnare Darcy. And then nothing. A cold dread settled in her chest. "You... you saved me?" she whispered, disbelief mingling with fury. "No, you *took* me!" she shouted.

He nodded, unrepentant. "Indeed. And we're on our way to Gretna Green. It's all arranged."

Caroline's shock gave way to a tidal wave of rage. She launched herself across the carriage, fists flying as she screamed, "You fool! Do you realize what you've done? You've ruined me, you vile creature! I'll have you arrested—no, hanged—for this!"

Wickham raised his arms to block her blows, but her nails raked across his sleeve. The carriage rocked violently as she lunged at him, her voice a shrill crescendo of anger.

"How dare you! How *dare* you!" she screamed, her fists pounding against his chest. "Do you know who I am? Take me back this instant, or I swear I will have you arrested at the next stop!"

His smile vanished as he endured the onslaught. Finally, he grabbed her wrists, forcing her back into her seat. She struggled, thrashing against his iron grip, but he pinned her arms firmly at her sides.

"Enough!" he barked. His voice was low and cold, each word carrying an edge of steel. Caroline froze, her chest heaving as she glared at him. "Compose yourself, Miss Bingley, or you'll only make this worse."

"Worse?" she hissed. "How could it possibly be worse than this? You've destroyed me—my reputation! My life!"

"Listen to me," he said, his tone cold. "Even if I were to turn this carriage around right now and return you to Netherfield, it would change nothing. You are ruined, Miss Bingley. Everyone saw you leave with me. Your reputation is destroyed, and no one—not even your precious Darcy—will take you now."

His words struck her like a slap, and her breath hitched. Her thoughts raced as she tried to make sense of his accusations. He couldn't be right, could he? Surely, she could explain, insist it was all a misunderstanding. Surely Darcy would—

"Do you think I took you without considering the consequences?" he continued in a growl, his grip firm but no longer painful. "Do you think you can march back into Netherfield after leaving with me, and everything will go back to how it was, Caroline?"

"I did not give you permission to use my given name," she snapped at him, her lip curling in disdain. "This is your doing! I had a plan, and you—"

"You are ruined, *Caroline*. Whether you like it or not, the world will believe the worst. *Darcy* will believe the worst."

Darcy. The thought of him sent a pang of both hope and despair through her. Would he come to her aid? Would he even want to after what she had done? But how would he know it was she who put the laudanum in the tea?

Her throat tightened, a flicker of fear creeping into her fury. "I'll deny it," she said, her voice trembling. "I'll say you abducted me against my will."

"And I'll be hanged for desertion," Wickham said, bitterness lacing every word. "That's what you want, isn't it? My death?"

"Better your death than my disgrace!" she retorted hotly.

Wickham clenched his jaw, his knuckles whitening as he fought to maintain control. Slowly, he leaned back against the carriage wall while still maintaining his grip on her wrists.

"But here's the thing, Miss Bingley," he said, his anger replaced by calculated calm. "Even if I were to turn this carriage around right now and beg forgiveness, your reputation would still be in tatters. You were seen leaving with me. The whispers will have already begun."

Caroline's nails dug into her palms. She hated that he was right. Hated the smug satisfaction in his voice. "No one will know," she tried again. "My plan ensured everyone—"

"You were a fool," he interrupted, his grip loosening even more. "Elizabeth Bennet was still awake when I entered the house. We *had* to run."

"*What?*" Caroline let out a howl of frustration, and his fingers tightened on her arms once again. "I cannot believe this happening to me. My life is over!"

"Not all is lost. You have still have a way— the only way— out of this mess. Marry me, and we salvage what we can. You'll have a husband, and together we can weather the storm. People will forget, eventually."

The words hung in the air, absurd and offensive. For a moment, she could only stare at him, her disbelief giving way to derisive laughter. "Marry you?" she spat, her voice dripping with scorn. "I would sooner rot in a convent than marry the son of a steward."

Wickham's jaw clenched, but he didn't strike back at her insult. Instead, he leaned closer, his eyes dark and glittering. "A steward's son? Is that what you think I am?" He leaned forward, his gaze locking onto hers. "What if I told you I'm more than that?"

"More?" she repeated, her voice dripping with skepticism.

Wickham's lips twitched, his eyes glinting with something dangerous. "I have a secret, Caroline. One that changes everything."

Caroline stiffened, suspicion flickering in her eyes. "What secret?"

Wickham's expression darkened, his voice lowering to a conspiratorial whisper. "I am the illegitimate son of George Darcy, the late master of Pemberley."

Caroline blinked, the words failing to register at first. "You're lying," she said flatly.

"It's true," he retorted, seizing the moment. "My mother, a servant at Pemberley, told me everything. I was meant to inherit."

"You would have claimed your birthright before now," she scoffed.

"There is a unique clause in the will— I must marry before Darcy does," Wickham said, his expression growing serious. "If I wed first, Pemberley becomes mine. The Darcys always honor their promises, even to illegitimate heirs."

Her breath caught, her mind racing to process his words. "Why should I believe you?"

"Why would I lie?" he countered smoothly. "Think about it, Caroline. Have I not always been close to the Darcy family? Do I not resemble George Darcy in certain ways? My mother swore it was true, and I've no reason to doubt her. With you as my wife, we would claim Pemberley together."

She eyed him warily, her sharp mind sifting through his words for any sign of falsehood. *Could it be true?* A flicker of doubt was immediately followed by a surge of hope. "Why haven't you married before now, then? If what you say is true, you could have claimed Pemberley years ago."

Wickham's expression softened, and he released her arms to reach down and take her hand, his touch gentle. "Because I hadn't met anyone worth settling down for. I wanted love, Caroline." His blue eyes met hers, and for the first time, she thought she saw something genuine in his expression. "Pemberley means nothing without someone to share it with, but it needed to be the *right* person."

Her breath caught, and she looked away, trying to suppress the warmth his words stirred in her, her disbelief warring with the heat of his caresses, which were now creeping up past her wrist. "And yet you were willing to help me compromise Darcy. Was that your idea of love?"

His face darkened with what appeared to be genuine emotion. "Because I loved you. I thought you wanted Darcy, and I was willing to step aside if it meant your happiness. But when I saw how he treated you, how he dismissed you as if you were nothing while he sniffed around that annoying Bennet girl… I couldn't let it happen."

Her throat tightened, the raw emotion in his voice unsettling her. For the first time, she hesitated long enough to take him seriously. *Could he be telling the truth?* Heart racing, she was torn between disbelief and something so dangerously close to seduction. His words, his touch—everything about him was so carefully calculated, so perfectly attuned to her vulnerabilities. But she wanted to believe him, desperately.

As she debated within herself, Wickham's hands found her upper arms again, but this time his touch was light instead of bruising, almost soothing. His thumbs traced gentle circles against her skin, his voice dropping to a low murmur. "Caroline, we can still have everything. Pemberley, a future together. Say yes, and I'll take you to Scotland. In just a day's time, we'll be married, and no one will dare question our claim. And when we return, we'll be unstoppable."

She looked up at him, her chest tightening. Could this really be her salvation? Could she still have everything she had ever wanted? His words wove a seductive web around the murky clouds in her mind, still foggy from the laudanum-laced tea she'd imbibed. His fingers brushed against her neck, his thumbs tracing light circles that sent a shiver down her spine.

"How far is it to Gretna Green?" she asked softly, her voice tinged with uncertainty.

"About two more days," he said, his lips curving into a triumphant smile. "By the time we return to Meryton as husband and wife, we'll have only been gone a week. You'll be my bride, and Pemberley will be ours."

He leaned closer, his hand sliding to cup her cheek. "Say yes, Caroline."

Her walls crumbled, the weight of her ruin pressing down on her. She nodded, her voice trembling. "Yes."

Wickham's smile widened as he cupped her face, pressing a soft kiss to her lips. When she didn't pull away, the kiss deepened, his arms wrapping around her in a way that made her forget her anger, her doubts, even her dignity.

For now, all that mattered was the promise of Pemberley. *Perhaps*, she thought hazily as she melted into his embrace, *this is my once chance at happiness. Perhaps ruin can be turned into triumph after all.*

Chapter 24

Elizabeth adjusted her shawl as she walked beside Jane toward the housekeeper's room, her steps echoing softly on the polished wooden floor. Georgiana and Mrs. Annesley followed a few paces behind, their quiet conversation blending harmoniously with the calm atmosphere of Netherfield. Despite the serenity of the house, Elizabeth could feel Jane's nervousness radiating like a faint tremor.

"Jane," Elizabeth said softly, laying a reassuring hand on her sister's arm. "You have nothing to worry about. Mrs. Nicholls is a kind and capable woman. She'll be glad to meet with you."

Jane exhaled shakily, glancing down at the small notebook she carried. "I wrote a few ideas, but I'm afraid they're terribly simple. What if she thinks I'm... inadequate?"

Elizabeth chuckled softly, giving her sister's hand a squeeze. "Mrs. Nicholls is not some ogre— or even Mr. Collins's patroness Lady Catherine de Bourgh! She is practical and fair-minded, and she will appreciate your thoughtfulness. Remember, you are the mistress now—it's your kindness and sense that will guide the household, not an endless list of rules."

Mrs. Nicholls stood as they entered Jane's new office, her calm and competent demeanor immediately setting a tone of professionalism. The room itself was cozy and efficient, with a large desk neatly arranged with ledgers, a small bouquet of winter roses brightening the space. "Good morning, Mrs. Bingley, Mrs. Darcy," she said, curtsying deeply. "And Miss Darcy, Mrs. Annesley, a good morning to you as well."

"Good morning, Mrs. Nicholls," Jane said, her voice soft but warm. "Thank you for meeting with us. I know the shifts must feel sudden."

Mrs. Nicholls smiled kindly. "Not at all, Mrs. Bingley. I've heard much about you from Mrs. Hill, and I assure you, the household is pleased to have you here."

Jane's cheeks pinked with modesty, and she exchanged a glance with Elizabeth. "Thank you, Mrs. Nicholls. That is very kind."

Elizabeth, sensing Jane's hesitation, stepped in smoothly. "Mrs. Nicholls, my sister has a few matters she'd like to discuss, and I know she values your experience and advice. For instance, she was wondering about menu planning."

"Oh yes," Jane said, her voice growing steadier. "I would like to work with you on the menus, though I don't want to disrupt the household routines unnecessarily."

Mrs. Nicholls nodded. "It would be a pleasure, Mrs. Bingley. The Christmas season always brings opportunities to refresh the table. Have you any particular preferences or traditions?"

Jane hesitated, glancing at Elizabeth. "Perhaps something simple but festive? I trust your judgment."

Elizabeth added, "Jane has always been a wonderful hostess, Mrs. Nicholls, but she's not one for excessive opulence. I'm sure your expertise will make the planning smooth."

Mrs. Nicholls smiled again, her shoulders visibly relaxing. "Of course, Mrs. Darcy. We'll ensure everything is balanced and tasteful."

The conversation turned to decorating, and Jane broached the topic tentatively. "I wondered about redoing the mistress's chambers. Would there be any pieces stored in the attic that could be used? I wouldn't want to waste funds unnecessarily."

Mrs. Nicholls's face lit up. "A very sensible idea, Mrs. Bingley. There are several fine pieces stored away—many of them antiques. If you like, I can have the footmen bring them down for your inspection."

Jane nodded gratefully. "Thank you, Mrs. Nicholls. That sounds perfect."

"And the parlor," Elizabeth interjected, her voice steady. "We'd like to see it refreshed, especially considering the events that occurred there."

Mrs. Nicholls's expression turned serious. "A wise choice, Mrs. Darcy. It will help to put certain… unpleasant memories to rest."

Elizabeth glanced at Jane, who looked thoughtful. "Perhaps lighter colors?" Jane suggested. "Something cheerful but not garish. And fresh flowers, if possible."

"An excellent idea," Mrs. Nicholls said approvingly. "We can arrange for new draperies and rugs in softer hues. I'll consult with the upholsterer."

Elizabeth leaned forward slightly. "I also think we should have the locks changed," she said. "On the doors, the tea caddy, everything. Miss Bingley, as mistress, had copies of the keys. I don't want to take any risks."

Mrs. Nicholls gave a sharp nod. "An excellent precaution, Mrs. Darcy. I'll see to it immediately."

Georgiana, who had been listening quietly, spoke up. "Do you think Miss Bingley will return?"

Elizabeth hesitated, her gaze softening as she turned to Darcy's younger sister. "I don't know, Georgiana. But we're staying through Christmas, and we'll remain here until the weather warms enough for Andrew to travel safely to London."

Georgiana nodded, her trust in Elizabeth evident. Mrs. Nicholls glanced at her with a kind smile. "Miss Darcy, if there are any particular arrangements you'd like, please don't hesitate to let me know."

Mrs. Annesley, who had been silent thus far, offered a measured suggestion. "Perhaps some adjustments to the music room, Miss Darcy? It might be a pleasant project for the colder months."

Georgiana brightened at the idea. "Yes, I would like that very much. Thank you."

The discussion moved on to other details—household expenses, holiday preparations, and minor repairs—and by the time the meeting concluded, Jane's confidence seemed to have grown. As Mrs. Nicholls curtsied and left to begin her tasks, Georgiana and Mrs. Annesley excused themselves as well.

Elizabeth turned to Jane with a warm smile. "You were marvelous, Jane. Mrs. Nicholls respects you already."

Jane blushed but looked pleased. "I hope so. She seems so capable—I didn't want to overstep."

"You struck the perfect balance," Elizabeth assured her. "Firm but kind. It's clear you're exactly what Netherfield needs."

Jane hesitated, then said softly, "Thank you, Lizzy. I couldn't have done this without you."

Elizabeth smiled, taking her hand. "Nonsense, Jane. You're a natural at this."

Jane shook her head, her blush deepening. "Perhaps. But I do feel overwhelmed at times. I'm so grateful for Charles and his support. Lizzy, he's..." She paused, a radiant smile spreading across her face. "He's wonderful. I never imagined it could feel like this—to love and be loved so completely."

Elizabeth's chest tightened, a pang of envy slicing through her. She managed a small, forced smile. "I'm glad, Jane. Truly."

Jane studied her for a moment, her expression softening. "And Mr. Darcy? He seems so devoted to you."

Elizabeth looked away, her voice carefully neutral. "He is very kind. He treats me well."

Jane's smile widened. "Isn't it wonderful? To be married to men who love us?"

Elizabeth nodded, the ache in her heart deepening. "Yes. Wonderful."

The conversation turned to lighter topics, but Elizabeth's thoughts lingered on Jane's words. As much as she wanted to share in her sister's joy, she couldn't ignore the aching uncertainty in her own heart. Her marriage was not what Jane believed it to be, and though Darcy's kindness had touched her deeply, she couldn't shake the fear that their bond would never grow into what her sister so clearly had with Bingley.

As Jane spoke, Elizabeth clung to the thought of the Gardiners' impending arrival. Their presence would be a much-needed respite, a reminder of the warmth and love she had always found in their company. For now, she would hold on to that hope and do her best to face the days ahead.

She pushed her own worries aside, focusing instead on the quiet joy radiating from her sister. For Jane's sake, she would pretend—for now—that everything was as perfect as it seemed.

The next few days passed in a similar manner. Mornings, the ladies were often found in company with one another. The afternoon passed pleasantly in the warmth of the nursery for Darcy and Elizabeth, where they would spend time with Andrew. The boy's giggles and wide smiles lightened Elizabeth's heart, and she was grateful for the quiet joy of the moment.

The household gathered together for dinner in the evenings for music and cards. The nights were spent in the quiet intimacy of their bedchambers to discuss the day and their observations on all that had occurred. Elizabeth found comfort in her husband's unwavering kindness, while he cherished her courage and wit.

It was clear that each was still tentative in their new roles as husband and wife. Elizabeth wasn't certain how she felt about the fact that other than their first night married, Darcy would return to his own chambers to sleep after their discourse. Other than on their wedding night, he had not made any overtures to resume physical intimacy.

Perhaps he finds me displeasing?

This insecurity was reinforced one morning when she awoke to realize that Darcy never left her bed after she had fallen asleep mid-conversation. Instead, he had fallen asleep sitting next to her and remained the entire night, just as he had on their wedding night. Her movements had woken him, and he had blushed furiously before hastily retreating through the door that adjoined their rooms.

Now is not the time for such thoughts, she told herself as she stood in her bedroom before her mirror. *Perhaps… perhaps I can discuss it with him tonight.*

The sky was dark as the maid she'd been assigned carefully arranging the final touches to her hair. The dress Elizabeth had chosen was a rich shade of royal blue, simple yet elegant, and the firelight danced on the delicate embroidery along the neckline and sleeves. The maid stepped back, smoothing the folds of the gown before moving to adjust a curl that had strayed.

"You look lovely, madam," the maid said, stepping back to admire her work.

"Thank you, Betsy," Elizabeth replied, her voice soft but sincere. She glanced at her reflection, feeling a flutter of nervousness as she prepared to face another evening in her new role as Mrs. Darcy.

The door opened behind her, and Elizabeth turned to see Darcy entering the room. His eyes immediately sought hers, and for a moment, the world seemed to fall away. His gaze, warm and intent, swept over her before lingering on her face.

"Elizabeth," he murmured, his voice low and filled with quiet admiration.

Betsy curtsied hastily and moved toward the door, hesitating, but Darcy's gentle nod dismissed her entirely. The maid shot Elizabeth a quick smile before disappearing, leaving the newlyweds alone.

Darcy stepped closer, his eyes not straying from Elizabeth's as he reached out to take her hand. "I find myself constantly amazed," he said, his tone soft. "You are even more radiant than I remember from this morning."

Elizabeth's cheeks warmed, but she laughed lightly to deflect her shyness. "You flatter me, Fitzwilliam."

His lips curved into a faint smile. "It is no flattery; merely the truth." He hesitated, then glanced at the door through which the maid had disappeared. "I must arrange for you to have your own lady's maid—someone you are comfortable with and who will attend to your needs exclusively."

Elizabeth tilted her head, a teasing glint in her eye. "Will there be anyone willing to work for me if word spreads that they're dismissed from the room so abruptly?"

Darcy chuckled, the sound low and rich. "They will have to grow accustomed to it. I intend to spend as much time alone with my wife as possible. Let them see it as romantic."

His words sent a flutter through her chest, and she looked down, fiddling with the lace at her sleeve. Darcy stepped closer, bowing his head slightly to lift her hand. He pressed a kiss to the backs of her fingers, his eyes never leaving hers. "How are you feeling?" he asked, his voice tinged with both tenderness and concern.

"I am... well," she replied, her cheeks coloring slightly under his intense scrutiny.

He straightened, hesitating briefly before continuing. "I feel I should apologize for still being here when you awoke this morning."

Elizabeth frowned slightly, confused. "Why would you apologize for that?"

"Most ladies and gentlemen prefer to sleep separately," he explained. "Separate rooms, separate beds. It's not uncommon."

Elizabeth hesitated, gathering her courage before speaking. "I... I never minded my sisters climbing into my bed when we were younger. And I liked that you were there."

Her voice was barely above a whisper, her cheeks flaming as the words tumbled out. Darcy's expression softened into something that left her breathless—a mix of tenderness, gratitude, and wonder.

"You liked it?" he asked, his voice low.

Elizabeth nodded shyly, her heart pounding in her chest. "I.. I did."

The look on his face made her admission feel worthwhile. He hesitated, his hand tightening ever so slightly around hers. "Elizabeth," he began carefully, "may I… may I come to you again tonight?"

Her breath caught. The question hung between them, and she felt her cheeks grow hotter. He hastily added, "You are always free to say no. I will not be hurt or offended."

Elizabeth's pulse quickened, and her gaze dropped to her hands as she nodded. "You may come any time you wish," she said quietly, her voice trembling with vulnerability.

Darcy's hand lifted to tilt her chin gently upward, his eyes searching hers. "Are you certain?" he asked, his tone serious yet tender.

Her lips parted, and after a moment, she nodded again, this time meeting his gaze directly. Warmth radiated from her eyes, filling him with a sudden, undeniable hope.

A slow smile spread across his face, and he leaned down to brush a soft, lingering kiss against her lips. "Thank you," he murmured, his voice barely above a whisper.

His lips captured hers ones again in a kiss that was impossibly soft, filled with an unspoken promise. He lingered, the touch of his lips growing deeper, more insistent. Elizabeth felt herself respond instinctively, her hands brushing against his chest, when a sharp knock on the door shattered the intimate moment.

"Elizabeth?" Georgiana's voice called hesitantly from the other side. "Would you like to walk down to supper together?"

Elizabeth pulled back, her cheeks flushed. She cast Darcy a quick glance before replying, "Yes, of course, Georgiana. I'll join you in a moment."

"Shall I ask William to join us as well?" Georgiana asked, her tone uncertain.

Darcy stepped back and raised his voice slightly. "There's no need, Georgiana. I'll come out with Elizabeth."

The silence on the other side of the door was deafening before Georgiana stammered, "Oh—oh, my apologies! I didn't realize you were... Oh dear, I'll wait at the stairs!"

Elizabeth clapped a hand over her mouth to stifle a giggle, her eyes sparkling with amusement as she looked up at Darcy. "You've scandalized her," she teased.

Darcy smirked faintly, offering her his arm. "She'll recover. Shall we?"

Elizabeth nodded, stepping toward the door. "It's a transition for all of us."

They joined Georgiana in the hallway, who was still pink with embarrassment. Elizabeth looped her arm through the younger woman's, offering a reassuring smile. "You did nothing wrong, Georgiana," she said gently. "We're all making adjustments, but that's part of becoming a family."

Georgiana nodded, though her cheeks remained pink. "It's just... I don't remember my brother ever being in my cousin Anne's room, at least not that I noticed."

Elizabeth hesitated, then said gently, "Different people have different preferences. I cannot speak for the late Mrs. Darcy, but I, for one, enjoy your brother's company."

Georgiana's eyes widened slightly, but she nodded again, her lips curving into a shy smile. Darcy's gaze flickered to Elizabeth with an expression she couldn't quite place.

Together, the three entered the parlor to wait for the dinner announcement. Elizabeth felt a sense of ease settle over her, though her gaze frequently strayed to Darcy, whose presence filled the room with a quiet, commanding warmth. They exchanged light conversation with Georgiana as they awaited Mrs. Hurst, Bingley, and Jane to join them.

Elizabeth took a seat on the settee near the fire, Georgiana settling beside her, while Darcy stood near the mantle, his hands clasped behind his back. The flickering flames cast a soft glow over the room, lending an air of intimacy to the quiet space. The hum of conversation between Elizabeth and Georgiana wove through the air, light and pleasant, though Elizabeth was acutely aware of Darcy's steady gaze lingering on her from across the room.

When Bingley and Jane entered, arm in arm, their smiles brightened the room, and the atmosphere warmed further. Mrs. Hurst—*Louisa now, Lizzy; don't forget*—followed shortly after, her expression subdued but polite as she took her place. Darcy moved to stand beside Elizabeth's chair, his closeness both grounding and invigorating. All was as it had been for the past few evenings, a comfortable rhythm settling over the household.

The door creaked open, and the butler stepped into the room. Elizabeth glanced up, expecting to hear the familiar announcement that dinner was ready. Several guests began to rise, Darcy included, but the butler hesitated, his usually stoic demeanor replaced by an unusual stiffness. His hand fidgeted at his side, and his gaze darted uneasily around the room.

Bingley was threading Jane's arm through his own, oblivious to the tension in the air. Elizabeth and Darcy seemed to be the only ones aware that anything was amiss. He straightened instantly and crossed the room to Elizabeth, reaching for her hand. She felt a prickle of foreboding well up within her.

"Mr. Roberts?" Darcy's brow furrowed as he addressed the man. "Is something amiss?"

Poor man, Elizabeth thought with dread as the butler shifted uncomfortably while clearing his throat, his cheeks faintly flushed. "I… I beg your pardon, sir, but there are… unexpected visitors."

The room grew still, the air taut with curiosity and unease. Elizabeth exchanged a glance with Jane, whose brow knit with concern, while Georgiana's hands clenched the folds of her gown. Darcy's expression hardened. "Who has come?" he asked.

The lump on the butler's throat bobbed as he swallowed nervously. "Mr. and Mrs. Wickham," he announced at last, the words falling like a thunderclap.

The room erupted into gasps and murmurs, the collective shock tangible. Elizabeth felt her stomach lurch as the words registered, her breath catching in her throat. She glanced toward Darcy, whose face had hardened into a mask of cold fury. His dark eyes burned with restrained anger, his hand tightening into a fist at his side.

Beside her, Georgiana emitted a faint, almost imperceptible gasp, her hands trembling as she clutched the folds of her gown. Jane's face mirrored Elizabeth's shock, while Bingley sat frozen in place, his usual genial expression replaced with a blank stare of disbelief. Even Louisa looked startled, her pale complexion growing even whiter.

The butler stepped aside to allow the intruders to enter. Into the room strode none other than George Wickham, his grin as self-assured and insolent as ever, making Elizabeth's skin crawl. His gait had the easy arrogance of a man who knew he had nothing to lose and thrived on chaos.

Beside him was Caroline—no longer Miss Bingley—her hand resting possessively on Wickham's arm, with a sneer of defiance and triumph gracing her lips. Her gaze swept over the room with haughty disdain, as though daring anyone to challenge her presence, her chin raised as she met their eyes with a predatory air.

"Good evening," Wickham drawled, his voice dripping with smug confidence. "I trust we're not interrupting anything too important."

Chapter 25

The silence was deafening. Elizabeth's heart pounded in her chest as she looked around the room, the expressions of shock, anger, and disbelief on every face telling her that no, she had *not* misheard.

Louisa's hand flew to her chest, her eyes wide with horror. Bingley looked utterly flabbergasted, while Jane pressed a hand to her mouth, her serene composure visibly shaken. Darcy's gaze darkened, his lips pressing into a thin line. "Roberts, call for the constable immediately."

He then turned his attention back to his childhood friend. "Wickham," he said, his voice cold as ice. "What is the meaning of this intrusion?"

Wickham's grin widened, his eyes glittering with triumph. "Why, my dear brother, I've simply come to introduce my wife to her new relations. Surely you wouldn't begrudge us the opportunity to share in this... joyous occasion?"

Elizabeth's stomach churned at the venomous mockery in his tone. She looked at Caroline, who stood rigid beside him, her chin tilted upward in defiance. She radiated a cold arrogance, and her eyes swept around the room. When her gaze fell upon Jane and Elizabeth, rage briefly flitted across her face before it smoothed into a smirk.

"Oh my, what have we here?" Caroline said, her tone dripping with false pity. "I suppose I cannot be too surprised to find you two chits here. After all, the Bennet sisters have always been quite... shameless."

Elizabeth stiffened as Caroline's lips curled into a vicious smile. "It seems quite fitting that women of your low breeding and questionable morals should make yourselves so... indispensable to Mr. Darcy and Mr. Bingley. With a mother like yours and those wild younger sisters, it was only a matter of time before you brought disgrace to this household."

Bingley's face flamed crimson with his fury, and he took a step forward, his fists clenched at his sides. "How dare you—" he began, his voice trembling with anger.

Darcy growled low in his throat, a sound so primal and threatening it sent a shiver through the room. His body tensed as though ready to pounce, his gaze fixed on Caroline with a look that promised retribution.

Before either man could act, both Elizabeth and Jane reached out instinctively, their hands finding their husbands' arms. Elizabeth's voice was firm but quiet as she said, "Fitzwilliam, no."

Jane mirrored her sister, gently pulling on Bingley's sleeve. "Please, Charles," she whispered.

The men froze, their anger still crackling in the air, but the steady touch of their wives held them back.

The silence was broken by a trembling but resolute voice that was filled simultaneously with fear and anger. "You are not welcome here."

All eyes turned to Georgiana, who had risen from her seat, her hands tightly clasped in front of her. Her pale cheeks were flushed with anger, and though her voice quivered, her words rang clear. "You… you dare insult my brother in such a way? You have no right to be here."

Wickham's expression turned mockingly wounded. "Ah, my dear Georgiana, such harsh words. Is that any way to greet your new sister?"

Caroline smirked, stepping closer to Georgiana. "You should be grateful to have someone like me in your family. I could teach you so much—how to carry yourself, how to rise above the vulgarity you've been surrounded by.

"Enough," Darcy interrupted, his tone commanding as he stepped forward to block his sister from the couple, his towering presence silencing the room. His gaze bore into that of his childhood friend, the fury in his eyes barely restrained. "You will not speak to her— you speak to me. Explain yourselves. Now."

Wickham's smirk faltered for the briefest moment, but he quickly recovered, his voice dripping with feigned charm. "We've nothing to explain, *Brother*. We are married, and as such, we have every right to be here."

Darcy's voice was low and lethal. "You are no brother of mine, Wickham, and you will find no hospitality here."

"Ah, but that is no longer the truth, is it? You are, indeed, my brother," Wickham drawled, savoring the word. "We are connected, now, are we not? Through this delightful union of mine with dear Caroline," He gestured with exaggerated flourish to the woman beside him, "you and I are both brothers to Bingley."

Caroline tilted her chin with pride, her voice cutting and imperious. "I am Mrs. Wickham now, and I expect to be treated with the respect due to my position."

Elizabeth's anger surged. She rose from her seat, her pulse thrumming in her ears. "Respect?" she said sharply, her voice slicing through the room like a whip. "After everything you've done? The harm you've caused? How dare you—"

Her words broke off suddenly, and suddenly, she began to laugh—a sharp, incredulous sound that filled the room. Everyone gaped at her, their expressions a mix of confusion and disbelief. Caroline's eyes narrowed, suspicion darkening her features. "What is so funny, Miss Eliza?"

Elizabeth turned to her, her expression mocking. "You. You, Caroline Bingley, the ever-so-aspirational, ever-so-superior, ever-so-eager to become Mrs. Darcy… and yet here you stand, married to a servant's son." She laughed again, shaking her head. "The irony is simply too delicious."

Caroline's face flushed deep crimson, her lips tightening into a thin line. "You're mistaken," she said coldly, lifting her chin higher. "My husband is no mere servant's son. He is the rightful heir to Pemberley."

The room fell into stunned silence. Darcy's jaw tightened, his eyes narrowing as his gaze locked onto Wickham. "What nonsense are you spouting now?" he demanded.

Caroline looked directly at Darcy, her tone haughty and triumphant. "George Wickham is the eldest son of George Darcy. And as he is now married while you remain single, he is the new master of Pemberley. The clause in your father's will makes it clear."

Elizabeth blinked, stunned by the audacity of the claim, but then turned to Darcy, who remained stoic. A flicker of confusion crossed his face—the first crack in his otherwise impenetrable demeanor—but it was soon replaced with understanding and tinge of amusement.

"Really, George, is that the best you could do?" Darcy asked, his voice cold and even. He turned to Wickham, his gaze piercing. "Is this truly the lie you wove to ensnare her? I always thought Caroline was more cunning, but it seems she's no better than the milkmaids and shopkeepers' daughters you've duped in the past."

Caroline gasped, her face flushing with indignation. "How dare you!" she snapped. "You know it's true! Why else would he tell me something like that?"

Darcy's lips curled into a grim smile. "Please, produce evidence, then. If such a clause exists, it will be in my father's will, which resides with his solicitors in London. Or perhaps you have a copy of it yourself, in my father's hand?"

Wickham shrugged nonchalantly, though his smirk wavered slightly. "Ah, yes, the tedious matter of wills and legal battles. It could be resolved in the courts sometime in the next several years—but that is no matter, we have plenty of time. And in the meantime," he said smoothly, turning to Bingley, "Caroline's dowry will suffice to sustain us until the matter is resolved."

Bingley, who had been silent until now, took a step forward. His expression was cold, his voice firm. "You will not have it."

Wickham's head snapped toward him, his expression darkening. "By law, her dowry is mine. I am entitled to it as her husband!"

Bingley crossed his arms. "You may be entitled to something, but you'll find the funds less accessible than you'd hoped. The day after you poisoned us with laudanum, I went to London and placed Caroline's dowry in trust."

"What?" Caroline shrieked, her face twisting with fury. "You had no right! That money is mine!"

"Actually, it wasn't. It never was," Bingley replied coolly, his composure remaining intact. "Father's will gave me complete discretion over your dowry. The principal is now in an untouchable trust for your future children. You may enjoy the quarterly interest, but you cannot touch the principal— and *only* Caroline is allowed to withdraw the interest when she presents herself in person at the bank."

Wickham's confidence faltered, and he sputtered, "That's fraud! Illegal!"

"It's entirely legal," Bingley said with infuriating calm. "The changes were made the day after your treacherous plot played out. Gretna Green is a three-day journey, so you couldn't have been married when the trust was established. No fraud was committed."

Wickham's mask of charm slipped, replaced by cold fury. "You'll regret this, Bingley."

"You've already lost," Bingley retorted. "And you have only yourself to blame."

Caroline's gaze darted between the two men, panic rising. "Then we'll live on the interest until the matter of Pemberley is settled," she said desperately, turning to Wickham. "We'll manage. Won't we, my love?"

Darcy let out a humorless laugh. "You're a fool if you believed him, Caroline," he said bitterly. "There is no such clause, no secret inheritance, no path for you to claim what was never yours. Pemberley is mine and will remain so. You've gambled everything on a liar."

"George?" she asked in a small voice, turning towards her husband.

At this, Wickham's smirk turned sour. "Fine!" he spat. "There's no secret clause, and I'm not the illegitimate son of George Darcy. But what does it matter? The lie served its purpose— I've won! It was enough to get what I wanted."

"And what was that?" Darcy demanded, his voice like steel.

Wickham's eyes glittered with malice. "To ruin you. To force you into living a miserable existence. To take your precious name and drag it through the mud. And to use Caroline's dowry to live well while doing it."

Caroline stared at him, horror dawning on her face. "You… you lied to me. You never loved me."

Wickham's sneer deepened. "Love? Don't be ridiculous. You were a means to an end."

Her hand flew out, slapping him hard across the face. Wickham recoiled, his eyes blazing with fury. His response was swift and brutal— without hesitation, he backhanded her as hard as he could, sending her sprawling to the floor with a cry.

"Wickham!" Darcy roared, lunging forward. He grabbed Wickham by the collar, the force of his grip lifting the other man off his feet. "You dare strike a woman in my presence? Your wife, at that?"

The room erupted into chaos as Wickham struggled in Darcy's iron grip, his fingers like a vise against his throat. Elizabeth rushed to Caroline's side as Darcy and Wickham grappled, their movements wild and brutal. "Mr. Roberts!" Bingley shouted, his voice cutting through the commotion. "Fetch some footmen! Now!"

Wickham twisted in Darcy's grip, managing to drive a fist into Darcy's stomach. The force of the blow caused Darcy to grunt and loosen his hold. Wickham stumbled back, shaking his collar free, and smirked again, his confidence returning.

"Ah, Fitzwilliam," Wickham sneered, flexing his hands. "You forget. I was always stronger, always the better fighter."

Darcy straightened, his eyes blazing, and rolled his shoulders as if Wickham's punch had been nothing more than a minor annoyance. "That was true," Darcy said evenly, "when we were boys."

Wickham's smirk widened. "Then let's see if you've learned anything since."

Wickham lunged again, his fist aiming for Darcy's jaw, but Darcy ducked with ease, his movements fluid and practiced. In one swift motion, Darcy retaliated, his fist slamming into Wickham's ribs with a resounding thud. Wickham staggered back, gasping for breath, only to be met with another solid punch to his cheek. Blood spattered from Wickham's split lip as he stumbled further.

Darcy's lips curled into a grim smile. "You'll find I've spent the last decade as my cousin Richard's sparring partner at Gentleman Jack's," he said, his voice calm and lethal. "Do you remember him, Georgie-boy? *Colonel* Fitzwilliam of Her Majesty's Royal Dragoons has taught me far more than you ever could."

Wickham's face paled, but his desperation drove him forward. He lunged again, this time aiming a wild punch below Darcy's belt. Darcy sidestepped effortlessly, his movements sharp and controlled, and delivered a punishing right hook that sent Wickham reeling. Wickham lashed out wildly, his fists swinging erratically, but Darcy evaded each blow with ease, his experience and composure far outmatching Wickham's crude attempts.

Darcy's next punch connected squarely with Wickham's jaw, sending him crashing against a nearby table. Wickham let out a strangled groan, clutching at the edge of the table for support. His eyes were glazed, his breath ragged, but he wasn't finished yet. With a feral snarl, he pushed himself off the table and lunged once more.

Darcy anticipated the move and stepped forward to meet him, delivering a brutal uppercut that snapped Wickham's head back. Wickham crumpled to his knees, blood trickling from his mouth and nose, his once-arrogant smirk now replaced by dazed defeat.

The door burst open, and the footmen surged into the room, followed by Mr. Roberts. The butler's eyes widened at the scene before him—Darcy standing tall and composed, Wickham nearly unconscious on the floor. The footmen hesitated for a moment, awed by Darcy's commanding presence, before moving quickly to subdue Wickham.

Darcy stepped back, breathing heavily but still in control. As the footmen hauled Wickham to his feet and began binding his hands, Wickham let out a string of curses, his struggles half-hearted as his strength ebbed.

"Take him to the cellar," Darcy ordered, his voice cold and unyielding. "And send for Sir William and Colonel Forster."

"Already done so, sir, as soon as they arrived," the butler informed him. "Mr. Bennet and the constable were informed as well. I imagine they're both on their way and will arrive shortly."

"Good man, Mr. Roberts," Darcy said, putting his arm around off Elizabeth, who had rushed to his side to check on him.

The footmen dragged Wickham from the room, his protests and curses fading as they disappeared down the corridor.

"You're fools!" he bellowed faintly from the hallway, his voice growing weaker. "This isn't over!"

Darcy ignored the fading sound of Wickham's threats, his gaze narrowing as he turned back to the room, where the silence was thick and heavy. All eyes were on him, and he let out a slow breath, the fire in his veins finally beginning to cool.

Elizabeth, having reassured herself that her husband was not seriously injured, sent a maid to fetch some ice for his hands. Darcy straightened his coat, then his eyes settled on Caroline, still crumpled on the floor, her hand pressed to her bruised cheek. Elizabeth followed his gaze to glare at the caterwauling woman.

"What are you staring at, Eliza Bennet?" Caroline spat, her voice trembling with rage. She struggled to push herself upright, her disheveled hair falling over her shoulders. Her cheek was red and swelling, her lip split, and her once-polished appearance was now a picture of humiliation.

Elizabeth met Caroline's venomous glare with steady composure. "I am simply marveling," she said coolly, "at the lengths you will go to disgrace yourself and your family."

"Disgrace? Do you know who I am? I am the mistress of this house and—"

"You absolutely are *not!*" Louisa hissed, speaking for the first time. "You are the daughter of a tradesman, the wife of a servant's son, and a *murderer*."

Caroline faltered, her bluster wavering. "Louisa," she began, her tone shifting to pleading, "surely you understand—"

Her voice broke off as the whole of her sister's statement processed in her frantic brain. She turned so white, Elizabeth thought she might genuinely lose consciousness. "What do you mean, a murderer?"

Louisa's lip curled with contempt, her tone laced with icy fury. "I mean exactly what I said. You murdered my husband."

Caroline staggered, her mouth opening and closing soundlessly as she groped for the arm of a nearby chair. "That's absurd," she finally croaked. "I did no such thing."

"My husband *died* when he drank the laudanum you put in his tea," Louisa bellowed, tears streaming down her face. "The combination of the drug with the wine he'd drunk at dinner caused his heart to stop beating, his lungs to stop breathing."

"That's... that's not my fault!" Caroline shrieked. "I didn't know he would... How could I know— it was George's idea to—"

"It is entirely your fault," Louisa snapped, her voice rising. "You *poisoned* him, Caroline. You poisoned us *all* with that cursed tea. If you hadn't been so obsessed with your schemes, he would still be alive."

"But I never had any intention of— I didn't mean to—"

"You didn't *care!*" Louisa shouted, her composure breaking entirely. Tears streamed down her face as she pointed a trembling finger at her sister. "You didn't care who got hurt as long as you got what you wanted. And now your selfish actions mean my child will grow up without a father."

Caroline's jaw dropped, and for a moment, she seemed too stunned to speak. "Your child?" she whispered, her eyes darting to Louisa's midsection. "You're... you're pregnant?"

Louisa drew herself up, her hand resting protectively over her abdomen. "Yes. And because of you, my child will never know its father."

Caroline took a step back, her eyes wide with disbelief. "But it wasn't my fault," she repeatedly weakly, her voice trembling. "I didn't force him to drink. He was a drunkard—a useless, oafish sot! You should be grateful, Louisa, free of the burden of him."

Louisa's hand lashed out with a sharp crack, her palm connecting with Caroline's already bruised cheek. "Grateful?" she hissed, her voice shaking with rage. "You think I should be grateful for losing my husband? For losing the father of my child?"

Caroline reeled from the blow, her hand flying to her injured face. Her eyes welled with tears, but her expression hardened almost instantly. "Fine," she spat. "You want to blame me for everything? Go ahead. But don't pretend that you didn't resent him just as much as I did. He was an embarrassment to this family."

Louisa's face twisted with grief and fury. "You are the embarrassment," she hissed. "You've destroyed everything, Caroline. Our family, our reputation—everything."

Caroline's composure crumbled, and she sank to the floor in a fit of sobs. "It wasn't supposed to happen like this," she wailed, her hands clutching at her hair. "I was supposed to marry Darcy."

"That was never going to happen," Darcy added. "From the very moment I met you, your arrogance, your conceit, your selfish disdain for the feelings of others convinced me that you were the last woman in the world whom I could be prevailed upon to marry."

"No!" Caroline shrieked. "I was supposed to be the mistress of Pemberley!"

"And instead," Louisa wiped away her tears as she straightened her shoulders, "you are the wife of a liar and a criminal. And you will answer for what you've done."

Caroline's sobs turned frantic, her voice rising hysterically and she reached out for her sister. "Louisa, please! You're my sister. You have to help me. You can't let them—"

"I have no sister," Louisa said icily, turning her back on the wailing woman. "My sister died the day you killed my husband."

Caroline stared at her in open-mouthed horror, her face pale and stricken. "Louisa," she whispered, her voice breaking. "You don't mean that."

"I mean every word," Louisa said, refusing to look back. "I never want to see you again."

The footmen moved forward at Darcy's nod, lifting Caroline to her feet as she thrashed and screamed. "No! Get your hands off of me! Louisa— Louisa! You can't send me away! Louisa, please!"

"Mr. Roberts," Darcy said, his voice steady but firm, "Please ask Mrs. Nicholls to see that Mrs. Wickham is sedated if necessary."

As the footmen began dragging Caroline toward the door, her desperation boiled over. "No! You can't do this!" she shrieked, twisting and clawing at their grip. Her wild gaze darted around the room before landing on Darcy. Her voice broke into a pleading wail. "Darcy! Fitzwilliam, darling! Please! Marry me!"

"I regret to inform you, madam, that it would be impossible— bigamy is illegal."

"I'll deny the marriage in Scotland! It can all be undone!"

Elizabeth stepped forward, her voice clear and steady despite the tumultuous emotions swirling in the room. "He would never do that," she declared, her gaze fierce and unwavering. "Because he is already married—to me."

A collective gasp rippled through the room, Caroline's sobs halting abruptly as her head whipped around to face Elizabeth.

"Married?" she whispered, her voice trembling with disbelief. "To you? That's not possible."

Elizabeth took another step forward, her composure unshaken. "It is not only possible, Mrs. Wickham—it is fact." She glanced at Darcy, who stood tall and unyielding beside her, before turning her full attention back to Caroline. "The scandal caused by your drugged tea forced action. Darcy and I were married the same day Jane wed Mr. Bingley—about the same time you would have been getting married in Scotland."

Caroline's face twisted in horror, her voice rising into a hysterical pitch. "No, no, no! It can't be! He would never lower himself to... to you! This can be annulled. Surely, Darcy, you'll see reason! You can't mean to stay tied to her."

Darcy grinned, flashing heretofore unseen dimples that caused even Jane and Louisa to gasp. "I'm afraid, *Mrs. Wickham*, that there is no possibility of an annulment." He turned to give Elizabeth a wicked smirk. "I have made quite sure of that," he finished with a satisfied smile, his eyes never leaving his wife's.

Elizabeth's lips curved into a small, triumphant smile of her own. "And I assure you, I have no intention of letting him go," she said, her tone crisp and resolute. "I really must thank you, Mrs. Wickham, for the part you played in bringing us together. Truly, it has turned out to be the greatest satisfaction of my life to be the wife of Mr. Darcy."

She turned to her sister, sobbing. "Louisa, please! Help me! For the love of a sister—"

Louisa Hurst, her expression cold and resolute, looked down at Caroline with disdain. "I hope they hang you for it," Louisa said coldly, turning her back as the footmen dragged Caroline from the room.

Caroline's wails echoed down the corridor as the footmen carried her away, fading into silence. The room remained still, the weight of the moment pressing heavily on those who remained. Darcy stepped closer to Elizabeth, his hand brushing against hers in a brief, grounding touch.

"She is gone. It's over," he said quietly, his voice steady but laced with exhaustion. "For now."

Elizabeth nodded, drawing a deep breath as she met his gaze. "And we are still here. Together."

Darcy's lips curved into the faintest of smiles, a flicker of warmth breaking through the storm. "Yes, Elizabeth," he said softly. "Together."

Chapter 26

The remainder of the evening was nothing short of exhausting; a grim duty, filled with a whirlwind of interviews, arrangements, and lingering tension. Food was brought into the parlor on a tray—the cold remnants of dinner long forgotten—as Sir William Lucas, Colonel Forster, and Mr. Bennet soon arrived. The air was tense, and the warmth of the fire did little to ease the chill that lingered.

Sir William, always affable but visibly uncomfortable, seated himself with a heavy sigh. "This is a dreadful business," he muttered, his brow furrowed deeply. "I can scarcely believe a lady could behave in such a way, especially one who has been a guest in my home on so many occasions."

Colonel Forster was far less sympathetic. He stood rigidly, his face impassive as he responded. "Wickham will be charged with desertion and theft. During wartime, the penalty for such crimes is death, and there's no question of his guilt. His wife, however, is out of my hands and is left to you, Sir William."

Darcy, standing near the hearth, nodded grimly but said nothing. His eyes were dark with suppressed anger, the tension in his posture still evident despite the calming presence of Elizabeth at his side.

"I could give her mercy," Sir William said, direction his words to Bingley, "out of respect to your family and the friendship we have all enjoyed these last months."

Louisa rose abruptly from her seat, her voice shaking with fury. "I quite disagree. Caroline deserves to hang just as much as her husband, if not more so! She's a murderer, and she deserves to suffer for the pain she caused."

Elizabeth hesitated before speaking, her voice quiet but firm. "Mrs. Hurst, as understandable as your feelings are, you may wish to reconsider."

Louisa turned a scathing look on her, her tone biting. "And what would you suggest, Mrs. Darcy? That we invite her back into our lives with open arms?"

"The scandal of a murderer in the family is worse than any we have so far weathered," Elizabeth said calmly.

"Are you suggesting we let her off?"

"No. But what if she were exiled, instead? Banished to the penal colonies? She would be stripped of her status and face a life of hardship. It would be a punishment fitting her crimes, without bringing more shame upon us. It could be said that she eloped with a foreign minister and has left the country."

Louisa let out a bitter laugh. "You mean, let her live? Give her leniency? That man—" she gestured towards Sir William— "speaks of mercy as though Caroline was some innocent fool. She isn't. She made the choice to add laudanum to the tea. She killed my husband, and she could very well have caused harm to my child."

Elizabeth's composure remained unshaken. "Picture it, Mrs. Hurst. She would be utterly alone, stripped of every comfort and privilege she has ever known. Imagine her boarding a convict ship with no finery, no allies, and no hope of returning to the society she so desperately craves. Life in the colonies is harsh—she would have no servants, no resources, and no means of manipulating her way to safety. She would spend her life laboring under the sun, surrounded by the roughest elements of humanity." She paused for a moment, her voice low. "And she would do so knowing she will never set foot on British soil again. For Caroline Bingley, that is a fate worse than death. That is justice."

Louisa faltered, her expression flickering with uncertainty as Elizabeth continued. "It would spare her life while ensuring she pays the price for her actions. When your anger cools as time passes, you may regret demanding your sister's death."

Caroline's protests, muffled by the walls and distance, could faintly be heard as the footmen dealt with her elsewhere. Louisa's lips pressed into a thin line, her anger battling against the vivid image Elizabeth had painted. "I want her to suffer," she said bitterly. "I want her to feel the same pain I felt when I lost him."

Darcy joined the conversation. "It's a fate few would endure, Mrs. Hurst. And it would bring closure to this ordeal without further bloodshed or scandal, which could ruin us all."

Louisa's lips pressed into a thin line, and she looked away, her arms crossed tightly. "I suppose," she muttered begrudgingly, "it's fitting enough."

Colonel Forster, who had remained silent during the exchange, nodded. "I can arrange for her transportation. With the severity of her crimes, it would not be difficult."

Louisa looked between them, her anger slowly giving way to resignation. "Fine," she said at last, her voice cold. "Send her to the colonies. Let her rot there."

With the arrangements finalized, the officials departed, leaving the household to settle for the night. Mr. Bennet paused to address Elizabeth. He placed a large, comforting hand on her shoulder, he said, "Your aunt and uncle Gardiner will be here in a few days," he reminded her, his expression softening. "I trust their company will bring you some much-needed peace after all this."

Elizabeth smiled faintly, though her fatigue was evident. "Thank you, Papa. I'll be glad to see them."

As the night drew to a close, the household finally began to retire. Darcy made his rounds, first stopping at Georgiana's room. She greeted him with a shy but steady smile, her voice brimming with newfound confidence. "It was difficult," she admitted, "but I'm proud I stood up to him. For the first time, I feel... free."

Darcy smiled warmly, pride evident in his gaze. "You were brave, Georgiana. I couldn't be prouder."

His next stop was the nursery, where Andrew slept soundly, clutching his favorite bear. Darcy stood quietly by the bed, his heart swelling with relief at the boy's slumber, the peaceful sight easing the tension in his chest. He brushed a hand lightly over Andrew's hair before stepping back and softly closing the door.

When he finally entered his own room, he stopped in surprise. Elizabeth was already there, curled up in his bed, her breathing soft and even. The sight of her, so serene amidst the chaos of the day, filled him with a quiet warmth. Moonlight filtered through the curtains, casting her features in a soft glow. The sight stirred something deep within him—a quiet, overwhelming tenderness.

Oh, how I love her.

He hesitated, debating whether to leave her undisturbed and retreat to her room for the night. She looked utterly exhausted, and he finally decided to let her sleep. As he turned, his foot caught the edge of a chair, the noise causing her to stir. She stirred, her eyes fluttering open, and she looked at him sleepily.

"Where are you going?" she murmured, her voice soft and drowsy.

"I didn't want to disturb you," he replied gently.

Her lips curved into a faint smile, her words slurred with drowsiness. "I came here for a reason, Fitzwilliam. If I didn't want to be disturbed, I would have gone to my own room."

Her words sent a warm wave of emotion coursing through him. He crossed the room and slid into bed beside her, careful not to disturb her further. Elizabeth nestled closer, resting her head against his chest and slipping her hand into his.

As he wrapped an arm around her, holding her securely, the tension of the day began to ebb away. Her presence grounded him, her warmth a balm to his weary soul. The soft sound of her slow breathing filled the silence, signaling she had fallen back to sleep, and he closed his eyes, content for the first time in what felt like days.

Darcy pressed a soft kiss to her hair and whispered, "Good night, Elizabeth."

She murmured a sleepy response, her words a soft whisper against his chest. As their breathing fell into a gentle rhythm, the weight of the day's trials ebbed away, leaving only the tranquil warmth of their shared embrace. Together, they surrendered to the serenity of the night, finding solace and strength in each other's presence.

The Gardiners' arrival brought a much-needed sense of normalcy and joy to the Bennet and Bingley households. Their warm presence, coupled with the laughter of their children, infused the often-tense atmosphere with a lightness that Elizabeth desperately needed. Yet, even amidst the cheer, an undercurrent of unease gnawed at her heart.

Elizabeth watched her aunt and uncle warmly engage with Darcy and Bingley in conversation. Mr. Gardiner's easy charm had drawn Darcy into a surprisingly animated discussion about Derbyshire's fishing streams. The sight of Darcy relaxed and smiling caused her heart to twist painfully.

How easily he commands a room, she thought, her gaze lingering on his profile. *How kind and thoughtful he is… how could I not love him?*

The realization that she likely did love him had been creeping upon her for days, each act of quiet gentleness cementing her feelings. It had begun as admiration, then a slow, creeping warmth that had spread through her whenever he was near. Now, she recognized it for what it was: love. Yet the more certain she became of her own heart, the more terrified she was of his.

Does he feel the same? Or am I only fulfilling a role in his life, no different from a piece of his household furniture? He would be kind to anyone in my position.

Elizabeth's smile faltered, though no one seemed to notice. Her mind drifted to moments that had both filled her with hope and stoked her fears: the way his hand lingered at her back when they walked together, the way his gaze softened when he looked at her.

Yet, hadn't she seen that same tenderness in his interactions with Georgiana? Was this simply who he was—a man committed to those in his care, without thought of his own desires? Even his patience with Bingley and Jane as they learned to manage an estate showed him to be a man who shouldered responsibilities with quiet dignity, who treated those around him with unwavering respect.

But kindness isn't love. Not the kind of love I want.

She turned her gaze to her hands, her fingers twisting restlessly in her lap. Every gentle touch, every longing look, every tender word from him had kindled hope in her heart. And yet, how could she ignore the nagging fear that his actions stemmed not from love, but from duty?

The thought struck her like a blow. What if she loved him with all her heart, only to discover he did not—could not—love her in return? It would be unbearable to lay her heart bare, only to find it unreciprocated. She swallowed hard, forcing herself to keep her composure as the room around her buzzed with light conversation.

She feared being in love alone, giving her heart to a man who might never offer his in return. The thought of unrequited love terrified her more than she cared to admit. If he saw her as little more than an obligation, a duty to uphold his reputation or atone for Caroline's actions, how could she bear it?

A soft voice broke through her thoughts. "Lizzy?"

Elizabeth looked up to see her aunt's warm, knowing eyes fixed on her. Mrs. Gardiner leaned forward slightly, her expression both gentle and probing. "How are you, truly?"

Elizabeth blinked, startled by the directness of the question. She looked cautiously around the room, but she found everyone engaged in deep conversation. Jane was leaving to discuss something with the housekeeper, and the gentlemen were in a spirited discussion over the best fishing lures.

She met her aunt's gaze and hesitated, the urge to confide warring with the fear of exposing her vulnerability. But this was her aunt—a woman she trusted implicitly, who had been both friend and mentor. If she couldn't speak to Mrs. Gardiner, who could she confide in?

"I am... well," she said at last, though her voice lacked conviction. "The last few weeks have been trying, but I am managing."

Mrs. Gardiner leaned forward slightly, her expression both kind and knowing. "Managing? That does not sound like the Lizzy I know. Tell me, my dear, what troubles you?"

Elizabeth dropped her gaze to her lap, her hands twisting more tightly together. How could she begin to explain the tumult of emotions roiling within her? Yet her aunt's quiet patience in the heavy silence drew the words from Elizabeth's lips, each one heavy with unspoken fear.

"I…" She swallowed hard, her voice trembling. "I think I love him."

The words hung in the air, the weight of them pressing down on her. Now that it had been spoken aloud, her admission filled the room like a tangible presence. Mrs. Gardiner's brows lifted slightly, but she remained silent, waiting for Elizabeth to continue.

"He is so… good, Aunt. So gentle. He treats me with such respect and kindness, far more than I could have ever expected. But…" She trailed off, her throat tightening as tears pricked at her eyes.

"But you are unsure of his feelings?" her aunt prompted softly.

Elizabeth nodded, her voice barely above a whisper. "I don't know if he loves me, or if he simply sees me as his responsibility. He is a man of honor, Aunt. He would never neglect his duty, and he would always be kind. But… kindness is not love. And I cannot bear the thought of loving him if his heart remains untouched."

The weight of her own words pressed down on her, and she looked away, ashamed of her vulnerability. Mrs. Gardiner's expression softened, and she reached out to place a comforting hand over Elizabeth's. "Oh, my dear Lizzy," she said gently. "Love often begins in kindness. It is not always spoken aloud— especially by men— but is oftentimes shown in actions, in the quiet moments that pass between two people."

"But—"

"Do you share a bed?"

Elizabeth's jaw dropped, and she stared at her aunt, her cheeks flaming a deep crimson. "Aunt Gardiner!" she hissed, her voice a mix of shock and embarrassment.

Mrs. Gardiner merely smiled, her expression knowing but kind. "It's a fair question, Lizzy. You are a married woman now, after all. And a husband's actions in private can often speak volumes about his feelings."

Elizabeth's gaze darted to her hands, which were twisting the fabric of her gown nervously. "Yes," she admitted quietly. "We share a bed. All night."

"And?" Mrs. Gardiner pressed gently, her tone free of judgment, only curiosity and concern.

"And..." Elizabeth hesitated, her voice trembling as she continued. "He is tender, gentle. He ensures my comfort in every way, never demanding anything of me that I am not ready to give. But is that love, Aunt? Or is it just his duty as my husband? How can I tell the difference?"

Mrs. Gardiner regarded her niece with thoughtful eyes, her hand still resting over Elizabeth's. "Lizzy, you say he is tender, that he is careful with your heart. Do you think a man would take such care if he did not hold some affection for the woman in his arms?"

Elizabeth swallowed hard, her emotions swirling. "I don't know," she said honestly. "He treats me with such kindness, but he treats Georgiana the same. And Andrew. And even Jane and Mr.

Bingley. He is a man of great generosity and goodness, Aunt. How do I know that what he feels for me is different?"

Mrs. Gardiner's lips curved into a faint smile. "Ah, my dear, but have you not considered that what makes a man a good father, a good brother, and a good friend could also make him a good husband? Love is not always fiery declarations or grand gestures. Sometimes, it is quiet, steady, and unwavering."

Elizabeth's heart clenched at the truth in her aunt's words. She thought of the way Darcy looked at her, the way he sought her opinion, the way he seemed to light up when Andrew laughed at her teasing. She thought of how he had held her so gently, how he had stayed with her through the night instead of retreating to his own chamber.

"Besides, I have seen the way Mr. Darcy looks at you, my dear. He definitely does not think of you like a sister or a child."

"I am so afraid, Aunt."

Mrs. Gardiner's smile softened, and she squeezed Elizabeth's hands gently. "Lizzy, love is always a risk. But from what you have described, I do not believe you are a duty to him. A man who thinks of his wife as merely a responsibility does not linger in her company, seek her opinions, or hold her at night as you say he does."

Elizabeth's eyes filled with tears, and she blinked them away quickly. "But what if you're wrong?" she asked, her voice cracking with the weight of her fear. "What if I'm wrong?"

"Then you will face it with the courage I know you possess," Mrs. Gardiner said firmly. "You have always been brave, Lizzy, even when the odds seemed insurmountable. And I believe Mr.

Darcy sees that in you. I believe he admires it, and that admiration may already have grown into something deeper."

Elizabeth nodded slowly, though her chest remained tight. "I will try," she said at last, her voice steadier. "I will try to have faith."

Mrs. Gardiner's smile widened, and she leaned forward to kiss Elizabeth's cheek. "That's my brave girl. Love is not always easy, Lizzy— in fact, it is rarely simple— but I have a feeling that you and Mr. Darcy will find your way. I know you; you would not give your heart to a man unworthy of it. Trust in the man you chose to marry, and trust in yourself."

As Elizabeth looked toward Darcy, still deep in conversation with Mr. Gardiner, her heart swelled with a mix of hope and trepidation. She prayed her aunt was right, that love could grow from the quiet, steady care Darcy had shown her. And perhaps, in time, she would find the courage to ask him directly, to lay her heart bare and discover the truth of his.

But for now, she would cherish the moments they shared and hold onto the hope that his kindness might be more than duty. That it might be love.

Mrs. Gardiner gave Elizabeth's hand one final squeeze before releasing it. "Whatever happens, my dear, you are not alone. You have family who loves you, and that will always remain true."

Elizabeth nodded again, her heart heavy with gratitude for her aunt's support, even as her thoughts remained fixed on the man who occupied her heart and mind so completely.

Chapter 27

Elizabeth adjusted the folds of her gown as she stood by the window of the parlor, sunlight casting a soft glow on her features. Across from her, Jane sat near the hearth, her delicate embroidery hoop balanced on her lap, while Georgiana, seated on the chaise, gently plucked at a few notes on her lap harp. The younger girl was content in their company, though her reserved nature kept her quiet as she listened. The atmosphere was tranquil, a rare moment of quiet amid the flurry of Christmas guests and preparations.

The newly-minted Mrs. Darcy's thoughts were miles away, rehearsing what she would say to Darcy that evening. She had spent the past few days wavering between determination and trepidation. The realization that she loved Darcy had taken root in her heart, and she resolved to share her feelings with him, no matter the risk.

Once having finally resolved to speak her heart, to confess her love and face whatever might follow, she knew she needed to do it quickly or become too afraid to do so. She had already decided to wear her wedding dress for the occasion, a symbolic gesture that made her heart race with both nerves and hope. The mere thought sent a thrill of fear and excitement coursing through her.

She turned toward Jane, drawing a steadying breath. "Jane, would you mind terribly if Fitzwilliam and I dined in our rooms tonight?" Elizabeth asked, trying to sound casual. "The guests have been wonderful, of course, but I find myself quite exhausted."

Jane's cheeks flushed, her shy smile brightening the room. "Not at all, Lizzy. I think it's a splendid idea. You ought to have some time alone. I'll have Mrs. Nicholls send up some trays."

Her thoughts were interrupted as the door creaked open. The butler entered, his expression unusually tight. He cleared his throat, drawing the attention of all three women.

"Lady Catherine de Bourgh and Mr. Collins have arrived," he announced.

The air in the room shifted instantly. Georgiana's face turned ghostly pale, her hands clutching the harp with white-knuckled intensity. "I… I cannot stay," she stammered, rising abruptly.

Elizabeth reached out, alarmed by the young woman's reaction. "Georgiana, what is it? What's wrong?"

"My aunt is… terrifying," Georgiana whispered. "I cannot face her." Without another word, she slipped out a side door, her retreat swift and silent.

Elizabeth exchanged a concerned glance with Jane but had no time to pursue the girl as the parlor doors swung open again, this time with dramatic force. An older woman— Lady Catherine de Bourgh, Elizabeth presumed— swept into the room, her imposing figure radiating fury. Mr. Collins trailed behind her, his expression equal parts obsequious and bewildered.

"You!" Lady Catherine barked, her voice echoing through the room. She froze as she saw two women sitting in the room and looked back and forth between the pair of them. "Which one of you is Elizabeth Bennet?"

Jane's face was pale, and she looked to Elizabeth for support, but Elizabeth herself was in too much shock to respond to the imperious woman.

"Well?" Lady Catherine demanded, her lips curled into a sneer. "I asked a question! Where is Elizabeth Bennet?" she repeated, her cane tapping sharply against the floor.

Elizabeth rose to her feet, her chin lifting with calm defiance. "There is no woman by that name here."

Mr. Collins gasped, clutching his hands to his chest. "No, Lady Catherine, forgive her insolence! That is Miss Elizabeth Bennet—she is right there!"

Lady Catherine's eyes narrowed as she turned her piercing gaze on Elizabeth. "You dare to lie to me?"

Elizabeth's composure remained steady. "I did not lie, madam. My name is Elizabeth Darcy."

The air thickened with tension as Lady Catherine's face contorted with rage. "Darcy?" she hissed. "You presume to call yourself Darcy? Do not play games with me, girl!" she thundered.

Elizabeth raised an eyebrow, prompting Lady Catherine's eyes to bulge from her head. "You *are* the upstart Elizabeth Bennet! How dare you presume to enter my family, to take the place that rightfully belongs to my daughter and sister? The mistress of Pemberley! You are nothing but a scheming, impertinent nobody!"

Elizabeth met the onslaught with an unshaken demeanor. "I have taken no one's place, Lady Catherine. I am Fitzwilliam Darcy's wife, his chosen partner. That is the only claim I need."

Lady Catherine's cane slammed against the floor, her grip trembling. "You dare to defy me? To usurp the position once held by my beloved sister and my equally-beloved daughter?" Her voice rose to a near shriek, the unrestrained fury echoing through the room.

"I am very sorry for your loss," Elizabeth replied calmly. "That role did indeed belong to both women, but as they are no longer living, Mr. Darcy was free to choose another wife. And he has chosen *me*."

Lady Catherine's composure cracked further. He slammed her cane against the floor, her voice trembling with rage. "You will seek an annulment at once!" she demanded, her voice trembling with manic intensity.

Elizabeth's eyes flashed, her calm exterior breaking slightly. "I will do no such thing. My husband has done nothing but honor his commitments, love his family, and care for those in his charge. You have no right to demand such a thing."

Lady Catherine's eyes blazed. "Do you have no regard for your husband's status? Have you no shame in dragging him down to the scorn of the world?"

Elizabeth's lips curved in a faint, confident smile. "The world is intelligent enough to see this marriage for what it is— the union of a single gentleman to a single lady. And for those who cannot see that, their opinions hold no weight in my mind."

"You insolent girl!" Lady Catherine snarled. "You think you can speak so lightly of status and decorum? You know nothing of either!"

"And neither, it appears, do you," Elizabeth retorted, her hold on her manners beginning to slip. "I am amazed you would come all this way to berate me when there is nothing you can do about the happy situation of our marriage."

"I am the daughter of an earl; do not dare to speak thusly to me! Bah, happiness— Darcy does not merit such a thing. He deserves to suffer, to live in penance for what he has done. He killed my daughter— his wife— and he should mourn her for the rest of his miserable existence."

Elizabeth's composure broke at last, her voice rising with fiery intensity. "He deserves to be happy! He is an honorable man, a loving father, and a devoted brother. He loves and cares for those in his life with a depth I have rarely seen."

"Positions that he is not capable of filling, as evidenced by his poor choice in a wife. Rest assured, I will be taking my niece and my grandson with me back to Rosings. I demand they be brought to me this instant."

"Absolutely not," stated Elizabeth firmly. "You will not take them from him. I will fight for him, for us, for our family until my dying breath."

Lady Catherine's lips curled into a venomous sneer. "That can be arranged," she snapped, raising her cane and moving toward Elizabeth with a sharp, menacing lunge.

The sudden motion startled Mr. Collins from his shocked silence. "No!" he cried, leaping forward in an attempt to block the blow.

The cane struck him instead, landing heavily on his shoulder. He staggered backward, clutching at the wound before crumpling to the floor with a pained gasp. Lady Catherine recoiled in surprise as Elizabeth charged forward, wrenching the cane from the older woman's grasp.

At that moment, Darcy and Bingley rushed into the room, their faces alight with alarm. Darcy's sharp gaze immediately sought Elizabeth, his eyes raking over her as he rushed to her side. "Elizabeth! Are you hurt?" His voice was tight with concern.

"I'm fine," she assured him, though her voice trembled slightly. "I'm not hurt… but Mr. Collins…"

Bingley moved quickly to help Mr. Collins, who was clutching his side and groaning in pain. "Jane," Bingley called, "he's injured!"

Jane knelt beside Mr. Collins, her soothing presence calming the man as she examined his injury. Bingley then rounded on Lady Catherine. "Who the devil are you?" he demanded, his usually genial demeanor replaced by a rare firmness.

Meanwhile, Darcy's protective hand settled on Elizabeth's arm, his piercing gaze fixed on Lady Catherine. "This is my aunt, who is supposed to be at the Rosings dower hours. Lady Catherine, what is the meaning of this?" he asked, his voice cold and unyielding.

Lady Catherine's eyes blazed with fury, but she said nothing, her chest heaving with anger. Elizabeth, still shaken but resolute, stepped closer to Darcy, her chin held high. "She came here to demand an annulment."

Both gentlemen gaped, and Lady Catherine's fury faltered under the combined scrutiny of the room. But her voice remained sharp as she said, "I was defending the honor of this family!"

Darcy's jaw tightened as he rose to his full height, towering over his aunt. "By assaulting my wife?" he said, his voice deadly calm. "I thought your brother made it quite clear the last time he spoke to you that you were to remain in Kent. How on earth did you even get here without a carriage."

"I am not as friendless as you supposed," she retorted. "I have many people who are willing to help me in my righteous cause."

"It's my doing," Mr. Collins gasped from the floor, attempting to sit up. "She asked if I could convey her to Hertfordshire. A family emergency, she said."

"It *was* an emergency," Lady Catherine hissed. "This… this hussy sought to rise above her station and infiltrate my family!"

Darcy shook his head. "Bingley, I fear my aunt has completely lost her reason, if not her entire hold on reality. If we could have Mrs. Nicholls fetch some laudanum, I shall send an express to my uncle. He should be in London now."

"How *dare* you—"

Raising his voice, Darcy spoke above his aunt's screeching. "Bingley, some footmen, please? And a guest chamber with only one door in or out?"

Lady Catherine spluttered with indignation, her face mottling with red as Darcy's commands were carried out. Bingley stepped to the door and called for Mr. Roberts, instructing him to summon two footmen and prepare a secure room for their unwelcome guest. Lady Catherine's screeches grew louder as she realized she was about to be removed. "I will not be confined like a common criminal! I am Lady Catherine de Bourgh! You cannot treat me this way!"

Elizabeth, still clutching Darcy's arm, glanced at him with a mixture of concern and exhaustion. "She's truly unwell, Fitzwilliam. This anger... this delusion... I don't think she even recognizes the harm she's causing."

Darcy's face softened slightly as he looked at Elizabeth, his voice low enough for her ears alone. "You've handled yourself remarkably, Elizabeth. Better than I expected anyone could. But she cannot be allowed to endanger you—or anyone—again."

Before Elizabeth could respond, the footmen arrived, flanking Lady Catherine on either side. She attempted to push them away, but they remained steadfast.

"This is an outrage!" Lady Catherine cried, her voice reverberating off the walls. "You will regret this, Fitzwilliam. You will rue the day you allowed this... this woman to destroy our family's legacy!"

Darcy turned to her, his expression colder than Elizabeth had ever seen. "You are my mother's sister, Lady Catherine, but you have overstepped every boundary of decency and propriety. This ends now."

"I will not go!" she screamed, her cane now in the hands of one of the footmen. "You will all regret this! Every single one of you!"

Elizabeth stayed rooted in place, her pulse racing. She felt Darcy's hand tighten on her arm, a silent reassurance that steadied her nerves. As Lady Catherine was led from the room, she twisted to glare at Elizabeth, her voice dripping with venom. "You may think you've won, girl, but mark my words—you will never be one of us. Never!"

Elizabeth met her gaze without flinching. "I am not concerned with being 'one of you,' Lady Catherine. My only concern is for my husband, my family, and the happiness we have found together— something you seem incapable of understanding."

Lady Catherine's lips curled into a sneer, but the footmen guided her firmly out the door, cutting off whatever retort she had planned. Mrs. Nicholls appeared at the door with a small vial of laudanum in hand, her expression calm and composed.

Darcy stepped forward, addressing the housekeeper. "Mrs. Nicholls, please see that my aunt is settled in a guest room under watch. Ensure she receives an appropriate dose to calm her, but nothing excessive."

"Of course, Mr. Darcy," Mrs. Nicholls replied with a slight curtsy.

The housekeeper followed behind the footmen, with Lady Catherine's protests grew more faint as they moved down the hall. The tension in the room began to dissipate, though an uncomfortable silence lingered, broken only by Mr. Collins's pained groan as he tried to sit up.

"Stay still, Mr. Collins," Jane urged, her voice soft and calming as she adjusted a pillow behind him. "You've had quite the ordeal."

"I cannot... believe... I intervened against her ladyship," he gasped, his hand trembling as it pressed against his side. "But she was about to strike Mrs. Darcy—such a noble creature deserves no less than my utmost protection!"

Elizabeth blinked in surprise, unsure how to respond to the overblown sentiment. Jane, ever the peacemaker, spoke softly. "Mr. Collins, you should rest before your journey. I'll have Mrs. Hill prepare something to ease your discomfort."

Mr. Collins nodded, his gratitude evident as he allowed himself to be led out by a maid. With him gone, Jane turned to Elizabeth, her expression a mix of admiration and worry. "Lizzy, are you all right?"

"I'm fine," Elizabeth assured her, though her voice trembled slightly. She looked to Darcy, who placed a steadying hand on her back. "But I think I need a moment."

Jane smiled gently. "Of course. Perhaps some tea?"

Elizabeth nodded, and Jane left the room to see to it. The parlor now contained only Darcy, Elizabeth, and Bingley, who seemed to be caught between concern and disbelief.

"Well," Bingley said at last, breaking the silence. "That was... something."

Darcy huffed, running a hand through his hair. "It was madness."

Elizabeth glanced up at him, her brow furrowed. "Fitzwilliam, what will happen now? Will your uncle intervene?"

Darcy sighed, his hand sliding from his hair to rest lightly on her shoulder. "I will write to him immediately. He'll ensure she is removed to a place where she can be cared for. Her state is… beyond anything I anticipated."

Elizabeth nodded, though her heart ached with the weight of it all. "She threatened to take Georgiana and Andrew."

"She won't," Darcy said firmly, his voice steel. "I will not allow it."

She met his gaze, and for a moment, the storm in her chest eased. Darcy's resolve, his quiet strength, steadied her in a way she couldn't yet put into words.

"She's… unrelenting," Elizabeth murmured. "I've never seen such vitriol."

Darcy's hand slid from her arm to her hand, his fingers warm and firm around hers. "You handled her remarkably well. I could not have asked for more composure or strength from anyone, least of all under such an assault."

Elizabeth looked up at him, her heart aching at the tenderness in his gaze. "I only did what I had to do."

"You did far more than that," he said quietly. "You defended not only yourself but also me, Georgiana, and Andrew. You are more than I could have ever hoped for, Elizabeth."

The words, so simple yet filled with such earnestness, struck a chord deep within her. She gave a shaky smile, gripping his hand tighter. "And you are far more patient than I could have imagined, Fitzwilliam."

He smiled faintly, his free hand brushing a stray curl from her face. "Patience is one of my few virtues, I fear. But even patience has its limits, as my aunt has now discovered."

Elizabeth's laughter, soft and unbidden, broke through the lingering tension. Darcy's lips quirked into a rare smile, and for a moment, the weight of the evening lifted.

Georgiana crept cautiously back into the room, Mrs. Annesley following a few steps behind. "Is she… gone?" Georgiana asked hesitantly, her wide eyes scanning the room as if Lady Catherine might materialize from the shadows.

Darcy approached her, his voice gentle. "She's been taken to a room, Georgiana. She won't harm anyone here. Thank you for coming to fetch me."

Relief flooded Georgiana's face, and she sank into a nearby chair. "I never thought I would see her again… not after everything."

Elizabeth moved to Georgiana's side, taking her hand gently. "You were brave, Georgiana. Leaving the room was no small act of courage, especially with such a formidable presence."

Georgiana shook her head. "I wasn't brave at all. I fled."

"But you left to get help," Elizabeth countered. "And then you returned; that is no small thing."

Georgiana glanced up, her cheeks coloring slightly as she gave Elizabeth a tentative smile. Mrs. Annesley patted Georgiana's shoulder, her calm presence grounding the moment.

Jane returned then, her expression serene but firm. "I think we've all had enough for one day," she said gently. "Perhaps it would be best if we *all* took dinner in our rooms tonight, and not just Elizabeth and Darcy. A bit of peace and quiet will do us good."

Elizabeth met Jane's knowing gaze and gave a subtle nod. "I think that's an excellent suggestion."

Her pulse quickened. as a delicate heat rose to her cheeks. Tonight would be the night she shared her heart, her resolve solidifying in the tender weight of his gaze. Whatever fears lingered within her, she knew she could no longer hold back.

As the others began to disperse, Elizabeth turned to Darcy and touched his arm lightly, drawing his attention. "Fitzwilliam," she said softly, her voice barely above a whisper, "will you join me in my room before you take your dinner tray? There is something I'd like to speak to you about."

His brow furrowed slightly, curiosity flickering in his eyes. "Of course, Elizabeth," he replied, his tone gentle. "I'll come to you."

She nodded, her heart thundering in her chest as she watched him leave the room. Left alone, she allowed herself a deep, steadying breath, her hands tightening briefly at her sides. Whatever the outcome, she would tell him the truth.

Tonight, everything would change.

Chapter 28

Elizabeth stood before the mirror in her room, smoothing the delicate folds of her wedding gown. The green of the fabric caused her eyes to shimmer even more brightly in the light of the crackling fire, its understated elegance a reflection of her own quiet resolve. The lace edging at the bodice and sleeves felt like an embrace of strength rather than mere adornment. Her hair, unbound and cascading over her shoulders, added a softness to her appearance that made her feel both vulnerable and bold.

Her reflection stared back at her, her cheeks tinged with nervous color, her heart a tempest of hope and fear. She had spent the past days rehearsing what she might say, but now the words seemed to scatter like leaves on the wind.

Tonight was the night she would lay her heart bare, come what may.

A knock at the door startled her from her thoughts. She turned as Darcy stepped in, his brow furrowed slightly. "Elizabeth," he began, his voice low, "I apologize. I hadn't realized you were not yet ready—"

A faint smile touched her lips. "I am ready," she said softly.

Darcy's gaze shifted, and his eyes softened as they rested on her. For a moment, he seemed at a loss for words, his gaze lingering on her gown before returning to her face. "You look…" He paused, as though searching for the right words. "You look beautiful."

Her heart fluttered at the compliment. Swallowing, she said, "I hope you don't mind, but I asked Jane if we might have trays brought up so we could dine here tonight."

His eyes flickered with a mixture of surprise and curiosity. "Here?" he asked, stepping further into the room. "In your chambers?"

She nodded and gestured toward the sitting room that adjoined their two bedrooms. "I thought we might enjoy a quieter evening… together."

For a moment, he simply looked at her, his expression unreadable. Then, with a slight incline of his head, he said, "As you wish."

They moved to the adjoining sitting room, a cozy space she had come to think of as their own little retreat within the vastness of Netherfield. The fire burned low and steady in the hearth, its warmth filling the room. A thick rug covered the floor, and the comfortable settee by the window beckoned with its familiar cushions. Outside, the world was cloaked in darkness, the faint outline of snow-covered trees barely visible through the frosted glass.

Elizabeth chose the settee, arranging her skirts carefully as she sat. Darcy settled into the armchair nearest her, his posture relaxed but his eyes watchful. The room felt charged, as though the air itself held its breath, waiting for something to break the silence. The quiet between them was not uncomfortable, but Elizabeth's pulse quickened as she tried to summon the courage to say what she had rehearsed so many times in her mind.

A knock at the door broke the silence, heralding the arrival of their meal. Two servants entered with trays, carefully arranging the meal on the low table. The aroma of roasted chicken and warm rolls filled the room, but Elizabeth hardly noticed. She focused instead on keeping her composure as the servants completed their task and exited the room with quiet efficiency.

She sat with her hands folded tightly in her lap, waiting until the servants had left them alone. The room seemed to hum with tension, the quiet crackle of the fire the only sound. Elizabeth's heart pounded in her chest as Darcy turned toward her, his expression open and curious.

The soft click of the door closing seemed to echo, amplifying the sudden stillness. Darcy turned to her, his gaze steady but questioning. "Elizabeth," he began, "you said there was something you wished to speak to me about?"

She had prepared for this moment—rehearsed it in her mind, gone over every possible scenario—but now, under the weight of his steady gaze, her resolve wavered. Her pulse thundered in her ears, and before she could stop herself, the words spilled forth before he had even finished his last word.

"I love you."

The silence that followed was deafening. Darcy froze, his eyes widening and his lips parting slightly as though he struggled to find a response. Elizabeth's cheeks burned with embarrassment. She looked away, the floodgates of her thoughts spilling over in a nervous rush.

"I know I shouldn't have said that," she stammered. "I don't expect you to feel the same. I know I was... forced on you, and you probably see me as nothing more than a duty. I understand that, truly, and I promise I won't bring it up again. I just... I needed to tell you."

Her voice broke, her eyes stinging with unshed tears as she faltered, unable to continue. The silence stretched unbearably, and she felt the urge to flee, to hide from the vulnerability she had exposed. Looking down at her fingers, which were twisting furiously in her lap, she blinked to keep the moisture at bay. She felt foolish, exposed in a way she never had before.

Then, to her surprise, she felt his hand cover hers, halting her spiral. His grip was firm but gentle, his warmth seeping into her cold fingers. Elizabeth's breath hitched as she met his gaze, her heart thundering in her chest. His eyes were soft, filled with an emotion she couldn't quite name, and his touch anchored her in a way that words never could.

"Elizabeth," he said, his voice low and steady.

She held her breath, the air between them crackling with unspoken words, and waited.

Darcy's breath caught. *Did I actually hear that right? Did she just say she... loves me?*

For a moment, he couldn't speak, couldn't even move, as the weight of her words settled over him. He just stared at her, with her cheeks flushed, her eyes cast downward, her hands twisting nervously in her lap. The words replayed in his mind, each syllable reverberating with stunning clarity.

She loves me.

He hadn't expected this—hadn't dared hope for it. Not after the chaos of the afternoon, not after the doubts that had been swirling in his mind ever since.

When Georgiana had burst into Bingley's study earlier, pale and trembling with fear in her voice, to tell them that Lady Catherine had arrived, he had barely paused to gather his wits before rushing out the door. Bingley had followed closely behind, both men propelled by a mix of alarm and anger.

Darcy could still hear the sharp edge of his aunt's voice echoing in his memory as they approached the door. His pace had quickened as he'd approached the parlor, the sound of raised voices growing louder with each step. And then, just as he reached the doorway, he heard Elizabeth's voice—clear, strong, and resolute.

"You will not take them from him. I will fight for him, for us, for our family until my dying breath."

Her voice had rung with such fiery conviction that it had stopped him in his tracks. Those words had pierced through every doubt and fear he'd ever held. He had stood just outside the door, unable to move, awestruck by the strength and love behind her words.

In that moment, any lingering doubts he'd held about her feelings for him began to dissolve.

In that moment, he knew.

Elizabeth was his everything—his partner, his equal, the woman who would stand by him no matter the storm. Even if she never said the words aloud, even if she couldn't bring herself to love him in the way he loved her, she cared deeply enough to fight for their life together.

Then Lady Catherine had raised her cane, and the fragile certainty he had begun to feel was obliterated by a wave of pure terror. All he could think was: What if I lose her?

The image of Elizabeth standing tall, her eyes blazing with determination even in the face of danger, would stay with him forever. He had been terrified—utterly, bone-deep terrified—at the thought of losing her. The fear had been a visceral thing, twisting in his gut, but it had brought with it a clarity he could no longer deny. He loved her. Fiercely, completely, irrevocably.

Even now, as he sat across from her in their private sitting room, the memory of that moment burned brightly in his mind. The firelight flickered softly, casting warm shadows over the intimate space. Elizabeth sat on the settee, her wedding gown flowing around her like a vision. The sight of her took his breath away all over again, just as it had when he first entered her room and saw her dressed so beautifully, her hair unbound and cascading over her shoulders.

But then she had spoken, and the world seemed to tilt on its axis. "I love you," she had said, the words tumbling from her lips with an urgency that stunned him.

Elizabeth's confession reverberated through him, pulling him back to the present with a force that left him reeling. The woman who had fought so fiercely for their family—who had stood unwavering against his formidable aunt—was now looking at him with a mixture of hope and dread, her emotions laid bare.

Darcy's mind raced to catch up. Could it be true? After everything we've been through, could she truly love me?

But before he could respond, Elizabeth began to speak again, her voice trembling with a mixture of nerves and vulnerability. "I know I shouldn't have said that. I don't expect you to feel the same. I know I was… forced on you, and you probably see me as nothing more than a duty. I understand that, truly, and I promise I won't bring it up again. I just… I needed to tell you."

Her words were like a dagger to Darcy's heart. How could she think herself forced upon him? Did she not see how much he admired her, respected her, needed her? As she rambled on, her hands twisting anxiously in her lap, Darcy felt a surge of emotion so powerful it nearly overwhelmed him.

No, Elizabeth. You must know the truth.

He reached out and covered her trembling hands with his own, halting her torrent of words. The touch stilled her, and she looked up at him with wide, tear-filled eyes. For a moment, neither of them spoke, the air between them heavy with unspoken feelings.

Darcy leaned closer, his voice low and steady as he finally found the words he had longed to say. "Elizabeth," he began, his grip tightening on her hands. "Elizabeth," he repeated, savouring the feel of her name on his lips. "I love you, too!"

Her head jerked up, her eyes locking with his in stunned disbelief. His thumb brushed over her knuckles as he continued. "I have loved you for longer than I dared to admit, even to myself. But today, as I heard you stand so fiercely for our family—heard you defend me with such courage and passion—I knew without a shadow of a doubt. You are my lover, my partner, my everything. And if I have not said it before, it is only because I feared I could never deserve you."

Tears spilled down her cheeks, but this time they were accompanied by a shaky smile that lit up her entire face, making his chest ache. "You... you mean it?" she whispered, her voice trembling with hope.

"With all that I am," he said simply, without hesitation.

Darcy raised her hands to his lips. The warmth in her gaze was unlike anything he had ever seen, and he felt his own heart swell with a joy he had never thought possible. Her smile widened, and she let out a soft, almost incredulous laugh. For the first time in what felt like forever, Darcy felt as though the weight of the world had been lifted from his shoulders.

In that moment, the flames seemed to burn brighter, the world outside their cozy retreat fading into insignificance, the very room around them fading away, until only the two of them were left in the flickering firelight. The love that had grown between them—through trials, misunderstandings, and moments of quiet connection—had finally found its voice.

They were no longer bound by duty or circumstance, or even attempted compromises. They were bound by choice, by love, and by the unshakable certainty that they were meant to be.

Four months later

The warm spring sun filtered through the trees, dappling the carriage interior with flickering patterns of light and shadow as it rolled along the well-kept road. Elizabeth leaned back against the padded seat, her hand resting lightly over her middle. It was still too early to feel anything, but the knowledge of the tiny life growing within her filled her with quiet wonder.

She had been ill for weeks, her stomach rebelling against even the simplest of meals, but the discomfort was worth it. She had refused to delay their journey, determined to leave the stifling city behind and see Pemberley for the first time.

Andrew crawled energetically around the carriage floor, his hands patting at the plush cushions as he babbled a string of cheerful nonsense that made both his parents smile.

Georgiana, seated beside her with a book on her lap, leaning forward with wide eyes. "We've reached Pemberley's woods!" She pointed out the window at a large expanse of trees. "Look, Elizabeth—there's the edge of the estate!" Her cheeks flushed with enthusiasm as she took in the familiar landscape.

Elizabeth let out a soft sigh of relief, her gaze following Georgiana's gesture. "At last," she murmured. The journey from London had been arduous, especially with Andrew's restless energy and her own discomfort. But she had refused to remain in the oppressive air of the city any longer. The promise of Pemberley had been her beacon.

"Are you well?" Darcy asked, his deep voice laced with concern. He reached over, his hand brushing hers. The warmth of his touch grounded her, and she nodded with a reassuring smile.

"I am fine, truly," she replied. "Just eager to see your home." She paused, then amended with a playful glance. "Our home."

Darcy's lips quirked into a smile that softened the edges of his otherwise serious expression. Before he could respond, the carriage slowed and came to a stop. He leaned forward, peering out the window. "We've reached the ridge," he said. He tapped on the carriage roof and the carriage came to a stop.

Elizabeth's brow furrowed. "Are we there?"

He chuckled, the sound low and warm. "Patience, my dear. Come and see for yourself."

With a teasing shake of his head, he descended from the carriage and extended his hand to her. She accepted, allowing him to help her down. The air was fresh and clean, carrying the faint, earthy scent of the woods. Elizabeth took a deep breath, her senses instantly invigorated.

"Look," Darcy said, gesturing toward the view.

Elizabeth turned, and the sight stole her breath. Below them, nestled amidst a vast expanse of rolling hills and manicured grounds, lay Pemberley. The stately house was a masterpiece of classical elegance, its stone façade gleaming softly in the sunlight. Wide terraces stretched out before it, leading to lush gardens bursting with spring blooms. Beyond the house, a glittering lake mirrored the azure sky, bordered by weeping willows that swayed gently in the breeze. The entire scene radiated a sense of timeless grandeur, and Elizabeth felt a lump rise in her throat.

"It's…" Her voice trailed off as she searched for the right words. "It's magnificent."

Darcy's gaze remained fixed on her face, not the view. "It will only become more so with you there," he said softly.

Her cheeks warmed, and she glanced away, overwhelmed by both the sight and his words. "Thank you," she murmured.

"You've yet to see the best parts," he teased gently, helping her back into the carriage. As he settled across from her and the journey resumed, Elizabeth leaned her head against the cushioned seat, her heart swelling with gratitude. "Wait until you see more... I'm especially look forward to showing you your new chambers," he whispered in her ear, causing her to shiver with anticipation.

She gave him a cheeky grin, almost overwhelmed by the depth of her love. The past months had been a whirlwind of change and discovery. Their two months in Hertfordshire after Christmas had been filled with family and unexpected moments of joy. Then one warm day in February, they made the journey to Darcy House, where they would spend another two months.

Those two months in London were filled with a whirlwind of activities, including frequently entertaining the Gardiners. Elizabeth had told Darcy one evening that it was Mrs. Gardiner's wisdom and encouragement that had given her the courage to confess her feelings. His gratitude toward her aunt had been profound, and they had made certain to show their appreciation during every visit.

Darcy's family, the Matlocks, proved to be a stark contrast to Elizabeth's family. His titled relations had initially received her with caution, their coolness a palpable reminder of her new station's complications. Yet with time—and her own determination—they had warmed. Lady Matlock had even taken Elizabeth shopping, introducing her to the styles and shops that suited her new station.

Lord Matlock had surprised her by expressing an interest in diversifying his investments. This led to an introduction to Mr. Gardiner, whose business acumen had impressed him greatly. Their warming acceptance had been a small but significant victory.

And then there was Andrew. Darcy's confession about the boy's parentage had shocked her at first. But her surprise was immediately swallowed up in admiration for his integrity. His love and care for Andrew, despite the circumstances, spoke volumes about his character. It had made her love him even more deeply.

If Wickham weren't already dead, I'd kill him myself, she thought.

Now, as the carriage rolled onward, the warmth of Darcy's presence beside her filled her with quiet contentment. He glanced at her, his eyes soft with affection, and reached for her hand. She laced her fingers with his, drawing strength from his steady touch.

Her gaze shifted to Andrew, who had finally tired himself out and was nestled against Georgiana's lap, his small fingers clutching the hem of her gown. The sight filled Elizabeth's heart with hope for the future. This, she thought, was what she had dreamed of—a family built on love, trust, and shared devotion.

As they descended the hill toward Pemberley, Elizabeth allowed herself a moment of reflection. The path to this happiness had not been without its trials. Mistakes had been made, schemes had been thwarted, and hearts had been laid bare. Yet every misstep, every obstacle, had brought them here, to this moment.

She glanced at Darcy, her heart swelling with love, and thought of how close she had come to losing him before she even realized

411

what he meant to her. A faint smile curved her lips, and she gave his hand a gentle squeeze.

The great house loomed closer, its grandeur no longer intimidating but inviting. She rested her hand over her stomach once more, her heart full of quiet joy. Life had not unfolded as she had once imagined, but in many ways, it was far better.

And as the carriage drew near to Pemberley's welcoming gates, Elizabeth thought with a touch of wry humor that she owed her happiness, in part, to the attempted compromises that had failed so spectacularly.

Epilogue

Ten years later…

The sun was warm on Elizabeth's face as she reclined on the picnic blanket, her bonnet set aside to let the gentle breeze toy with her curls. All around her, the sounds of laughter, conversation, and children's squeals filled the air, weaving a tapestry of contentment that had taken years to cultivate. The sprawling lawns of Rosings, now transformed under Darcy's meticulous care, stretched before them, dotted with family and friends enjoying a leisurely afternoon.

Elizabeth's gaze followed Andrew, now twelve, as he raced across the grass with his younger brother, Bennet Darcy—Ben, as he was affectionately called. Andrew's dark hair gleamed in the sunlight, and his posture, so straight and composed, was an echo of Darcy's. She marveled at how much he had grown, his serious demeanor tempered only by the rare but heartwarming smile he gave when he thought no one was looking.

His lungs, once a source of so much worry, had strengthened over the years. The doctor had credited the long walks Elizabeth insisted on in his childhood, especially in Pemberley's warm summer air. Though occasional colds still lingered longer for him than others, Andrew's vigor was a far cry from the fragile boy she had once cradled in her arms.

"Andrew!" Ben's voice called, pulling her from her thoughts. Nine years old and already showing signs of the Darcy gravity, Bennet William Darcy was the perfect match for his older brother's seriousness. Their sibling bond was evident, each complementing the other in quiet understanding.

It was their sister, six-year-old Anne Elizabeth Darcy, who provided the lightness to their dynamic. Annabeth, as she was often called, was the spitting image of her mother, with Elizabeth's chestnut curls and impish grin. Today, she was leading four-year-old Richard Darcy, her giggling accomplice, toward the edge of the blanket where their parents sat, utterly unaware of the handful of grass she held behind her back. Annabeth's mischief and bright spirit mirrored Elizabeth's own childhood, and her antics were a constant source of amusement—and occasional exasperation—for her parents.

"Annabeth!" Darcy's voice carried behind him, a note of amusement mingling with his stern tone. "I see you. Whatever you're planning, think again."

Annabeth froze mid-step, her face a study in dramatic disappointment before she burst into laughter, abandoning her plot to tackle her father in an exuberant hug. Darcy scooped her up easily, his expression one of mock severity as he whispered something in her ear that made her giggle even harder.

"Annabeth, come join us," Jane called from a nearby blanket, where she sat with her brood of children. The four girls, all miniatures of their mother, played with dolls while the youngest—a mischievous toddler with bright red hair—crawled toward a butterfly fluttering just out of reach. Jane's serene smile glowed as she watched her children, her happiness unmistakable.

Mr. Bingley, lounging beside her, caught sight of the toddler's antics and reached out to redirect the boy before he tumbled into the nearby stream. "William!" he called gently, scooping up the boy and earning a peal of laughter in response. "You're as much trouble as your Aunt Lizzy used to be."

"Trouble?" Elizabeth laughed, shifting her gaze to her sister. "I was an angel compared to your little imp."

"Indeed, I seem to recall a certain time when you were climbing trees and breaking your arm," Jane teased back, her eyes sparkling.

The Bingleys had purchased Netherfield years ago but still spent much of their time at Pemberley, where the cousins played together and grew inseparable.

On a blanket not far from Elizabeth, Mr. Collins reclined next to his wife, Mary. Mary's needlework rested in her lap, her hand resting lightly on her rounded belly as her husband rambled on about the virtues of picnics and natural philosophy. Mr. Collins, though still prone to pompous declarations, had softened over the years, his time at Longbourn during his recovery having mellowed his more absurd tendencies. Elizabeth chuckled as he attempted to instruct their four-year-old son, whose attention was far more focused on a butterfly than his father's words.

"Some things never change," Elizabeth murmured with a laugh to Darcy, who sat beside her, watching the scene unfold with a rare, unguarded smile.

Nearby, Mr. Bennet sat with Mrs. Hurst, the pair enjoying a quiet conversation. Though Mrs. Bennet had passed some years ago, Mr. Bennet's friendship with Mrs. Hurst had grown unexpectedly close. Elizabeth had suggested marriage more than once, but her father had waved her off with a twinkle in his eye, insisting he was quite content with their arrangement.

Mrs. Hurst remained with her son at the Hurst estate, which was being managed by a competent steward who showed young Master Hurst all about his duties. , For his part, Mr. Bennet continued to enjoy his solitary life at Longbourn—when he wasn't dropping in unannounced at Pemberley, that is.

"Lizzy," her father called suddenly, his voice gruff with affection. "I'll remind you the Gardiners will be here by tea. You know how they despise being late."

"Of course, Papa," Elizabeth replied with a laugh.

Her gaze then drifted across the lawn to Kitty, who was happily settled with her rector husband at Kympton. She chatted animatedly with Georgiana, whose poise and grace had grown over the years. The former Miss Darcy, now married to a young marquess in Derbyshire, had finally developed the rounded stomach she had been praying for since her marriage.

Lydia, as always, was conspicuously absent, her letters from the Continent growing ever fewer. The Darcys kept informed of her situation through General Fitzwilliam, who remained a steadfast, if weary, guardian of her fate. After Lydia and an officer were discovered in a compromising position in Lydia's room late one night, her brothers-by-marriage combined forces to hasten a wedding and send the eager couple overseas.

Elizabeth sighed contentedly, her hand brushing against Darcy's as he leaned closer. "Look at them," she said softly, nodding toward their children. "All of this... everything we have... I never imagined life would be so full."

Darcy's fingers entwined with hers, his expression tender as he followed her gaze. "Nor did I," he admitted. "But I cannot imagine it any other way."

As Annabeth squealed with delight and the boys raced across the grass, Elizabeth felt a deep, abiding gratitude settle over her. Life had been unexpected, challenging, and more joyful than she could have ever dreamed. She glanced at Darcy, the man who had become her partner in every way, and smiled.

"Strange," she mused, her voice tinged with humor, "to think we owe so much to those attempted compromises."

Darcy chuckled, his eyes warm as they met hers. "Indeed. Fate has a curious way of bringing us exactly where we need to be."

And with that, Elizabeth leaned into his shoulder, her heart full as the sun dipped lower in the sky, casting a golden glow over the family they had built together.

Life had taken unexpected turns, but it had also given her more joy than she had ever dreamed possible. She glanced up at Darcy, who was watching her with an expression of quiet devotion.

She smiled softly, thinking how grateful she was for all the twists of fate, even those attempted compromises that had failed so spectacularly. Without them, she wouldn't have this—a family, a love, and a future filled with hope.

Thank you for reading "Attempted Compromises" by Tiffany Thomas.

If you'd like to read a fun excerpt of how Caroline Bingley adjusted to life in the penal colony of Van Diemen's Land (present-day Australia), please scan the QR code.

Or use the link: https://saving-talents.kit.com/145a7bc611

No spam, ever!

You might also enjoy reading Tiffany's other works:

A Look Behind the Mask

The Sins of Their Fathers

When Summer Never Came

A Most Beloved Sister

Fine Eyes & Beastly Pride

A Dear, Sweet Girl

Pride, Prejudice, & Permutations

ABOUT THE AUTHOR

Tiffany Thomas is a chocoholic former math teacher with Crohn's Disease and homeschooling mom of four kids. She and her husband Phillip (who is an engineer) work together on the blog Saving Talents. They enjoy spending time with their family, geeking out over sci-fi together, and saving money.

Tiffany discovered Pride & Prejudice as a teenager, and even made poor Phillip watch the six-hour version with her on their honeymoon when they got snowed in. After reading fan fiction for over a decade, she finally broke out into writing some herself, with the support of her husband.

www.ingramcontent.com/pod-product-compliance
Lightning Source LLC
Chambersburg PA
CBHW072020020726
47501CB00006B/1877